I0587334

PERCEVAL'S SHADOW

C. C. YAGER

An Original Novel from C. C. Yager

PERCEVAL'S SHADOW

Copyright © 2025 Cinda C. Yager

ISBN ebook (epub): 978-0-9914967-4-7
ISBN paperback: 978-0-9914967-3-0

First E-book and Paperback Editions September 2025

http://ccyager.wordpress.com

Cover Design: S. M. Savoy Cover Designs
Cover Photo: Thank you to Pxhere.com and their library of free photos!
Editor: Kellie M. Hultgren Editing
Digital Design and Paperback Interior produced by BookNook.biz.

C. G. Jung quote from *On the Psychology of Unconsciousness*, 1917

Where love rules, there is no will to power, and where power predominates, love is lacking. The one is but the shadow of the other.

C. G. Jung

BUENOS AIRES

JANUARY 2049

CHAPTER 1

"Che, señores!" Porteños at tables in a sidewalk café lifted their glasses in a toast to them as they ran past. Evan waved. A cheer went up, almost drowning out the café's Latin jazz. The warm night breeze swayed the red, blue, and white lights strung above the sidewalk tables. He smelled the sea. The sky above glowed from the city's lights, and peeking through here and there were twinkling stars. The world war raged, but not here, not in Buenos Aires.

"You've been a people magnet every time we've run together, mate," Brian said, running next to him.

"Don't they do that to all runners on the street?" He knew as soon as the words had left his mouth what the Aussie would say next, and it irritated him.

"You're not just any runner. You're Evan Quinn, the famous American conductor and son of Randall Quinn." Brian grinned. Evan heard pride in the Aussie's voice.

"Naw, it's for the festival." He pointed to the front of his neon-orange T-shirt and the glittery blue letters across his chest: *Festival for the Displaced, Teatro Colón, January 10–24, 2049*. "Can't miss these colors."

The Aussie laughed, shaking his head. Evan couldn't stay irritated with Brian. He liked running with him. They ran in the same rhythm at the same pace. The Aussie had shown him easy and challenging running routes in the city. Evan usually preferred to run alone, but Buenos Aires was a playful, outgoing city that had gotten under his skin and energized the boy in him. Yeah, he was just like any other runner, but running there, late on a summer night, when it was the dead of winter in war-torn Vienna made him feel lucky and safe. No war, no terrorists, no Woody nagging him about Perceval work. No reason to look over his shoulder.

He smiled at the young Aussie. "I'm just like any runner, my friend." Brian had rekindled his frustration with fame, and how people perceived and treated him because of it. Fame veneered his life. He detested its artifice.

The boulevards of Buenos Aires danced into the night around them as the city's residents partied off the remains of the day. Evan knew little of dancing, and nothing of the tango, but he loved running these rhythm-infused night streets with their multicolored neon and sodium lights, their swaying hips and inviting smiles, their joyous laughter and singing, and the smells of the finest steak, the heartiest pasta fagioli, sweet pastries, and strong espresso. Buenos Aires liked to have fun, especially at night. Dress casual. And not a Chinese MAO49 drone in sight.

"You know, I still can't believe the American Arts Council gets away with banning music. You not knowing the Byrnes or the te Kumara before, not being able to conduct Caine. Crikes, you knew Caine, the man himself!"

"Now I know Owen te Kumara himself!" Evan laughed and glanced at Brian. The young Aussie played a rad English horn as principal English horn and oboe with the Buenos Aires Philharmonic Orchestra. He'd soloed in Owen's English Horn Concerto earlier that evening under his baton. He and Brian jogged west on Avenida Independencia toward San Christobal and Brian's neighborhood. The Aussie had agreed at the post-concert reception to join him on a run despite the tropical heat. Again, Evan couldn't believe how safe he felt in this city, safe on the crowded, bustling boulevards lined with full green trees and purple jacarandas. During the last two weeks, he'd not once needed Perceval's paranoia or to do surveillance detection runs.

"What about upcoming gigs? Have you programmed anything they'd banned?"

"Sure. Schönberg's Five Pieces for Orchestra in Toronto next week. Barber's Piano Concerto and Bartók's Concerto for Orchestra in Copenhagen in March."

"You're fearless, mate. I'd want at least a year for score study to fill in the holes before accepting any gigs."

"I study scores all the time—when I'm cooking, eating, even in the bathroom, every spare moment, and when I'm traveling." Evan laughed. "Have you ever met Nigel Fox?"

"Haven't, but I've heard of him. By reputation, he lives up to his name."

Chattering and laughing people streamed out of a movie theater ahead, and they dodged and weaved around them on the sidewalk. The women wore full knee-length skirts that flowed and swished as they swayed around the men.

"Yeah, I'm lucky Nigel believes in me," Evan said. "Never mind my limited repertoire and I'd only conducted one Caine symphony. The first few months last summer were rocky. But I got it. You have to grab the moment, stand out from the crowd."

"Too true. It's brutal for everyone, but conductors can have it the worst. If you don't have your own orchestra, it's travel all the time, yeah? Every gig for guest conductors is an audition. I'm lucky to have gotten my job with the orchestra here. Tough auditions. At least two hundred players competing for one chair."

Evan shook his head. "I can't imagine luck had much to do with it. You probably blew the competition right out of the hall."

The Aussie grinned. "Thanks. I *am* lucky to be here. Especially with the war in Europe and the Pacific."

"The war's ruined my conducting schedule and probably everybody else's too. Forget the Asian orchestras right now."

"¿Cómo anda, señores?"

They smiled and waved to a man who saluted them with his Chinese take-out bag. The man headed for a sleek black car that resembled an emperor penguin parked on its stomach in front of the restaurant, where its red paper lanterns with long silky tassels swayed in the light breeze next to strings of red and white lights around the murmuring veranda. Evan smelled the pungent spices and his mouth watered.

"Was that for you or me, mate?" Brian grinned.

"He said señores. I've enjoyed more anonymity in Buenos Aires than in Europe. I don't want to leave." Evan glanced around the street, feeling a sudden shiver of unease. Nothing unusual about the street's activity that he could see, no one taking unusual interest in them. But he felt unfriendly eyes on him.

Brian was laughing. When he stopped, he said, "It won't

last. Next time you conduct here, it'll be different. It's so bad in Vienna?"

Evan nodded, wiping sweat from his face with one hand. "I cannot go out anywhere without being recognized. Sometimes the people just say hello, good to see you, or something like that. But sometimes they want more—a conversation, an autograph, for me to come to their homes for dinner. One young woman even proposed marriage. It shocked me. Fortunately, an actress friend taught me about disguises. Now, when I want to attend a concert or see a movie, shop, or whatever, I wear a light disguise and no one recognizes me."

"*That's* radical."

"Not for living my life in peace. But I have to admit, with the war, people tend to focus more on other things."

"Survival."

"I checked in with my landlady the other day, and she said the stores had sold out of fresh milk. Only canned and powdered available. She'd lost power for seven hours the day before, after the Chinese bombed. They also hit a couple cell-phone towers and wiped out service for a couple days."

"The Viennese—they've seen their share of war."

"The war's damage extends beyond property or shortages. It's damaged lives," Evan said, thinking of Owen and Lucia and their eighteen-month-old daughter, of Freda, of pregnant Greta, of Sofia. He missed them, not the war. "I thought this war would be over in a month. It's a relief to spend a couple weeks away from it."

"Mate, five months isn't so long. America waged an eight-year war in Iraq and a twenty-year war in Afghanistan at the beginning of this century. The papers here report rumors at the UN in New York City of a cease-fire within months."

"Wait, a war in Iraq and a war in Afghanistan?" This was the first he'd heard about them.

"Yeah, you didn't know? Shit, the New Economic Party censors American history too?"

Evan laughed, a dry, rueful laugh. "Why not? They censor everything else."

Brian grabbed his arm and stopped him at one of the ubiquitous hexagonal information kiosks. A news report on one of the computer monitors showed battles fought in minutes with high-tech weapons that vaporized human flesh.

"Look how efficient those weapons are. America makes them. It's terrifying. They've sold them to the Chinese."

"They don't care, as long as they make a profit." He thought of his experience the summer before at the Four Seasons Pension in Vienna and its low-tech security: old-fashioned metal keys instead of a digital system. People are low-tech. A person could sabotage high-tech weapons or AI or the people using them. Computers were only as good as the low-tech people programming them. No algorithms existed to predict or control another person's behavior. Or a country's. Or his own. He wondered what Brian would think of him if he knew about Perceval; that he, Evan Quinn, had assassinated Chinese vice chairman Jiang Xu last August on orders from the NEP and sparked the global war. "The Chinese don't care either. They've conquered Russia. They're working on Europe and the Pacific nations. If they win the war, no one will be safe, not even America or Buenos Aires."

"They'll never conquer Europe, mate. Or Australia."

They began running again.

"Sorry, Brian. Is your family OK?" He looked around to check their location. Palm trees lined the Avenida, with lavender jacaranda here and there. He felt uneasy again. What was wrong? He saw nothing unusual in the people strolling on either side of the street.

"So far, my family's fine. Thank God. What's the deal with Switzerland refusing refugees?" Brian said.

"I heard this morning on BBC News online that they've taken in more than they can house. Germany and Hungary have been offering transport to northern Africa. I've heard the Austrians have set up a refugee camp, but I'm not sure where it is. A lot of Russians have been arriving from the east. And no one's convinced that the Chinese dropped neutron bombs on Moscow instead of conventional nuclear bombs. Radioactive fallout could also be a refugee from the east."

"To us here, the war's in another galaxy. I hope the money the festival raises for refugees truly helps."

Evan hoped it would help, too. The festival had already helped him, given him a much-needed job and a break from the war. The Festival for the Displaced, in addition to raising money for refugees, protested China's use of nuclear bombs to obliterate Moscow, and the global war whose violence and destruction had not yet touched South America. Last week, Evan had conducted a student orchestra at the Facultad de Derecho in a program of Leoš Janáček's *Sinfonietta* and Pyotr Tchaikovsky's Sixth Symphony, the "Pathetique." He'd attended a concert of Dmitri Shostakovich's string quartets, including the Eighth String Quartet, that had moved him to tears. The next evening, he had heard a magnificent performance of Britten's *War Requiem* in the Teatro Colón.

Brian matched his steady pace. Evan thought about his flawless performance of Owen's concerto. Evan remembered several spots he'd want to discuss with Owen and work on for conducting future performances. The audience had loved their work, however, and the Buenos Aires Philharmonic had played with brilliant precision and depth in Garrett Byrnes's *Solace* and Joseph Caine's Third Symphony, his "We the People" Symphony, composed in protest of the New Economic Party's sweep of the elections in America in 2016. The thunderous applause still echoed in his ears and made him feel invincible. Maybe if he ran fast enough, as he'd tried often as a boy, he could fly.

The sharp crack of gunfire erupted behind them. Evan spun around and crouched, glancing around for cover. His heart pounded. His breathing came in raspy gasps. Where was the shooter? He saw no one with a gun anywhere, only people dancing and strolling along the streets.

"Evan!" Brian's voice pierced the white noise in his ears. "Evan, it's fireworks! Fireworks!"

He looked up at the Aussie, who bent over next to him, his hands on his knees. Fireworks? He surveyed the street again as he rose slowly. Nothing appeared unusual. Brian pointed across the street to a group of laughing teenage boys shoving each other.

"It was them, mate. You're OK. You're safe. It was just fireworks."

Evan reached out and grasped the Aussie's shoulder. "I guess you can tell I've been living in a war zone, huh?"

His voice was grim with the truth of it, but behind it stood another, more painful, truth. He still could be attacked by his own memories, the attempt on his life at the post-defection press conference in Vienna. What was it Leiner had called it? *P*-something. "Let's go."

They jogged for a while in silence, but Evan was aware of the concerned glances Brian shot his way. His heart rate calmed and his breathing returned to its regular rhythm. The street scene and the partying people reverted to their true benign existence, happy in their dancing rhythms and music.

"Che, señores!"

Porteños at four tables in a sidewalk café waved to them with smiles. He waved and glanced around at the street as they jogged past the café. Not as many pedestrians on this block, but he spotted no one showing a special interest in them. Unease again raised the hairs on the back of his neck. Maybe he'd do a surveillance detection after Brian left just to make certain no one shadowed him.

"Well, mate, I turn left at the next intersection. Keep in touch and come back to us soon. You have my number and email."

"Thanks, Brian. Loved working with you. And thanks for the runs the last two weeks."

They shook hands in pace, and Brian peeled off to the left. Evan turned right onto the same narrow street lined with Parisian-style apartment buildings and balconies overflowing with greenery and flowers. Half a block later, a muscle stitch shot pain up his right side. He slowed his pace, breathed into the pain, rubbed his side. The pain cut through his chest.

He stopped and bent over, massaging his muscles. The high summer humidity had given him muscle spasms before during runs here.

"¿Chabón, esta enfermo?"

Evan jerked up his head, startled. A swanky young man in a tailored ivory-colored suit and a woman dressed in a short, lacy black tango dress stopped next to him, their expressions concerned. Evan shook his head, smiled, and waved them on. He had no idea what the man had asked, but he guessed from their faces he'd offered help. The couple walked on, glancing back once. As he straightened, he massaged his right side and looked around the slower-paced street. On the opposite side behind him, a petite woman walked alone, an uncommon sight in Buenos Aires at this time of night. He turned away but continued to observe her in his peripheral vision. She paused, her eyes on him. He bent over again and breathed into the pain, watching a cluster of people split before her and come together again behind her.

Had the woman followed him? He hadn't seen her before Brian left. He couldn't remember if she'd been at that intersection. *Stupid, stupid, stupid*, his father's voice whispered in his inner ear. Yeah, yeah, he knew better. He'd let down his guard. Well, he was about to do a surveillance detection. And this was Buenos Aires, not Vienna.

The woman wore skin-tight white jeans and a soft white halter top accented with gold jewelry that flashed under the streetlight. From what he could see in his peripheral vision, it looked like she wore running shoes. Her black hair fell in thick waves to her shoulders. An attractive woman. He turned and looked directly at her face. She smiled, her full red lips parting to show white teeth. Ah, so, not a surveillance shadow. An attractive woman out for a stroll who'd perhaps recognized him. He hadn't spotted any surveillance in the almost two weeks he'd been in Buenos Aires. Why should there be any now?

He did not return her smile but instead turned away and walked out the muscle spasm, gradually increasing his pace back to an easy jog. Maybe he was crazy to run so late but he could always sleep on the plane to Toronto. His digital watch glowed blue on his wrist: 1:27 a.m. Maybe he needed to just return to the hotel and crash for the night. The next day he'd travel to North America for the first time in seven months. He looked forward to spending the next week in Toronto, working with that city's excellent orchestra, and conducting two concerts. Toronto's program excited him: Arnold Schönberg's Five Pieces for Orchestra, Ralph Vaughn Williams's *The Lark Ascending*, and Jean Sibelius's Second Symphony.

He glanced back. The woman followed about a block behind him. Where was Bernie Brown when he needed him? He missed his protective presence in his life. Brown had always seemed to know where he was, what he was doing, and popped up to let him know he was around. The American had saved his life in Amsterdam. Bernie would have had some snarky but amusing comment, delivered in his South Bronx nasal twang, about the woman. Or maybe he'd suggest they wait for her to catch up and have a threesome. He never knew what the guy would say. He hadn't heard from him in the five months since Brown defected. The Austrians continued to hold the ex-CIA agent in their custody at an unknown location. Evan had done nothing to find out where, and had no plans to investigate. Woody could just wait for him to complete his next assignment. As long as Bernie remained in Austrian custody, he was safe from Perceval.

The toccata from J. S. Bach's Sixth Partita whisper-played in his mind. Vasia Bartyakov played the partita, his curly blond head bent over the keyboard of the black piano near the front windows in his apartment across from the Vienna Hilton. Evan pushed the memory into the darkness at the back of his mind. He focused instead on Greta, Vasia's Somali-Austrian girlfriend, now seven months pregnant with Vasia's child, due to arrive into the world on April eleventh. His anticipation increased with each passing day. He'd told Nigel not to book any gigs that week so that he'd be in Vienna. He'd conduct in Iceland the week before, and in Switzerland the following two weeks. Greta continued to produce her afternoon classical music show on Österreich Eins and planned to work until she went into labor. Although he wasn't sure he believed in reincarnation, he hoped the baby would be a boy exactly like Vasia so they could have the Russian pianist back.

He'd promised Greta to always be there for her and her child and he would. He hadn't told her yet that he'd left his entire estate in trust to the baby. He'd followed Brown's advice about protecting the millions of dollars he'd inherited from his father's trust fund and from Joe Caine's trust fund. Woody had told him the NEP knew he'd claimed both the trust funds. He was rich. If he were in America, he'd now be a member of the 1 percent—the wealthy elite. He'd finally gotten the wily old American to admit they had not trained him to succeed. They'd set him up to fail, for Perceval to be either caught or killed. Woody had claimed that Evan's assignment to kill the Chinese vice chairman had been "on-the-job training."

Now he knew the truth. The NEP had sent him to Europe to claim Caine's trust fund before his assignment. The NEP wanted the Austrians to catch or kill him. Then they would be able to grab his father's money for themselves. They had recovered from their failure, according to Woody, although they hadn't been pleased, and had given him another assignment: kill Bernie Brown. Not going to happen. After Vasia, he'd decided that Perceval had operational guidelines: no women or children, and no friends. Brown was his friend.

When he'd defected, all he wanted was to be free to live his life as a musician and conductor. To be free to choose how he lived. In America, he'd tried to conduct opera and ISS had arrested him. In order to regain his life and career, he'd made a deal with the NEP. That Faustian deal had made it possible for him to defect, to be free. He knew that he needed to find a way to work for the NEP without actually doing any work for them. Not kill Brown, for example.

Evan turned right onto the busier, noisier Avenida Cordoba and back toward his hotel in Microcentro. He ran up fast on a line of five laughing, talking women, their arms hooked together. He slowed in the wake of their floral perfumes, assessing how to skirt them, and smiled at their melodious laughter. He glanced back again. The woman in white had disappeared, or he just couldn't see her amid all the people. At the intersection, the women veered left and he sped up to cross the street and pass a cluster of sidewalk tables. The sight of cascading chestnut-brown hair at one table weakened his knees. Sofia? He tripped over his feet. Sofia? He caught himself before falling.

"Che, señor. ¿Qué pasa?"

Evan shook his head to the waiter who'd reached out a white-gloved hand to steady him. "Gracias. Soy bien," he said, three of the six Spanish words he knew. The waiter nodded, opening his arms to invite him into the café. Evan shook his head and pointed up the street. The waiter pointed to his T-shirt and offered his hand to shake.

"Buenos noches, Maestro."

"Gracias."

The Spanish language swayed and dipped in an arresting rhythm that would always remind him of this city and its people. He jogged on, glancing back. No sign of the attractive black-haired woman on this street with its roiling flow of people. He passed another information kiosk, its computer monitors flashing advertisements, news summaries and idyllic scenes of Argentina.

Sofia Karalis. Her beautiful, long chestnut-brown hair. She was working on location in Italy, a movie whose production had been delayed by the war. Greta had told him that Sofia wore a raven-black wig for her character instead of dying her chestnut-brown hair. He couldn't imagine her with black hair, but she'd probably bought the wig in Vienna, at the costume store where she'd helped him create his disguises. *Stop thinking about her!* He'd failed her and missed his chance.

The driving, defiant rhythms of the scherzo from Caine's Third Symphony pounded into his mind and set his jogging pace. Then the English horn's jazzy theme from Owen's concerto's first movement flowed over the growly bass four-note motif from the Caine symphony's first movement. Evan's torso twisted as he ran, supporting his momentum. He smiled to himself, noticing, as he entered the Plaza Houssay, a group of men dancing in a circle, their arms entwined at shoulder level, in front of pink lapacho and orange blooming tipas. The men sang a lusty song, disrupting the Caine in his mind. He liked the plazas of Buenos Aires, the abundance of green mixed with tall palm trees, the jacaranda and other flowers, so many parks dotting the city. To his right towered the University of Buenos Aires's Facultad de Medicina building on the other side of the open park.

"Che, señor!"

He twisted left to smile and wave at the woman who'd called out to him and felt a fist hit his right shoulder. Something pierced his left side. Then he heard the thunder-cracks of two gunshots. But he couldn't duck or dodge or run because he was flat on his back on the sidewalk, shouting voices all around him. He raised his head. People ran toward him. Blood on the front of his running shorts. Other people pointed toward a building past the plaza. Searing pain radiated out from his left side and his vision blurred. *Breathe, remain conscious.* Spanish voices shouted all around him now, and he felt a hand on his forehead, pain knifing through his shoulder. A man towered over him and spoke into a cell phone. Sirens wailed.

Vasia's face appeared behind his closed eyelids. He remembered Vasia's gigantic, widened blue eyes, the punches from his fists, as Evan held the CZ 9mm muzzle in the Russian's mouth. *Vasia.* Pain stabbed through his chest. Now he knew what his real punishment was for killing the Russian that day only minutes before he shot the Chinese vice chairman.

He'd been shot. Perceval had been shot. He didn't want to die. But he could feel himself sinking, sinking down at an alarming speed. No, he couldn't die. *Vasia, no! I was wrong. You were right. There's always a choice. How could I have been so stupid?* His grip on consciousness slipped away.

CHAPTER 2

The towering man in the dark river-blue uniform of the Viennese police moved his head around in a full circle like Maman's music-box ballerina, his eyes squinting in the sun. "Wo bist du, kleiner Dieb?" the giant policeman said in a teasing voice as several old women bundled in forest-green loden wool brushed past him.

He knew what *Dieb* meant. Thief. He frowned. Thieves took what wasn't theirs and as much as they could for their profit. He took only what he needed to survive.

The Wizard Howl told him no one could see him. He was invisible. He could run like the wind that had blown the night before, a gale-force wind that whipped up dust and debris from the grayish-brown bomb craters and licked up white-capped waves on the slate-gray Danube. He shivered. A cold winter wind. What if it snowed? He must find better shelter for sleeping. Perhaps one of the abandoned houses near home in Grinzing.

The giant policeman's river-blue leather jacket with its fake brown fur collar looked toasty warm. He wanted the jacket to use for his bed. All his clothes were gone, his favorite duvet, all gone with their house in the bombing. But he was strong, fast, and invisible. He was Pierre Levade, the best of friends to Steamboy, the Warrior Ashitaka, and the Wizard Howl. They advised, guided, and protected him.

"Wo bist du?"

Where are you? The giant policeman had no clue how to search. Pierre grinned as he watched the policeman move away, peering into the obvious hiding places behind the stalls, not *under* the display tables and behind the decorative gray canvas skirts. He smiled to himself and looked down at the two potatoes he'd filched from a stall only meters away. Wizard Howl's magic could make people look the other way so they wouldn't see the canvas skirt move when he slipped from his hiding place. He pocketed the potatoes, drew back the canvas, and crawled across the aisle, dodging the hurrying feet of old and young Viennese women doing their shopping. A quick kick to his side lifted him and sent him sprawling against the wood wall of a stall. He jumped to his feet and sprinted toward the butcher stalls.

Naschmarkt, Vienna's sprawling open market south of the First District, had proven to be his best source of food after looters had emptied the bombed shops near their house in Grinzing. Maman had bought their food from those shops, and loved to chat with the shopkeepers, but sometimes had taken him to Naschmarkt to buy Spanish navel oranges in winter or vine-ripened Italian tomatoes in summer. She'd bought other things there, but now he couldn't remember all the delicious fruits and vegetables, cheeses, and meats. The butcher stalls displayed cooked sausages, shaved ham, and sliced deli meats, and they were only meters away from the cheese section. His stomach ached from hunger.

Maman and Papa would return. They must have left on

an errand, just as Maman had sent him on an errand down to the café to pick up the torte she had ordered for the dinner party that evening three months ago. He knew they would return to look for him. Eyeing the deli meats, he stepped closer, eyeing as well the stall owner who spoke with another man.

He strolled down an aisle of the butcher section, one hand skimming the edge of the displays, devouring the sausages with his eyes, keeping his distance from the gruff stall owners. Most of the shoppers had stopped at a stall on the left, four stalls ahead. He increased his pace. The crowd around the stall would hide him while he snatched the meat.

All those Viennese women! They became flustered and fluttery when something extraordinary happened, like meat flying through the air on its own. Imagine! An invisible French boy stealing right in front of their noses. He grinned. Of *course*, flying meat would fluster them. They could not explain how it had happened. The police would come and shake their giant heads at the women with their stories of meat flying through the air on its own.

At the crowded stall, he darted between two rotund women and grabbed a pair of bratwursts with his left hand. One woman cuffed his head and the other reached to grab him, but he ducked and ran.

These two women had tried to stop him. How could they see him?

"Halt!"

They couldn't catch him—he knew it from the top of his head to his toes, as Maman would say in her sweet voice.

The Wizard Howl pointed to a hefty chunk of Emmentaler and Pierre lifted it off the display as he ran past a cheese stall.

"Du, Spitzbube!"

Next, two crunchy, sour dill pickles plucked from an open barrel at the next stall. He really needed a strong cloth bag to carry all his food. He longed for two or three Spanish navel oranges, but the fruit section was on the opposite side of the market. The giant policeman loved Spanish navel oranges, too. Who hated them? No one he knew.

He'd heard from other street kids that the police locked up boys like them and threw away the key. They fed kids dog poop and gruel, and beat the ones who refused to eat. His heart pounded in his ears. If the police caught him, locked him up, how could he find Papa and Maman when they returned? Pierre sprinted down one aisle after another in the market until he came out onto the Linke Wienzeile. No one had followed, but then, he was invisible. Merci, Monsieur Wizard Howl.

He wolfed down bites of Emmentaler and one of the dill pickles as he walked past the white-columned entrance of Theater an der Wien and then the filigree-domed Secession building. The subway, or metro as Maman called it, was faster but not as easy to ride without a ticket. He knew how to buy the tickets for the buses, streetcars, and the metro, but he had no money. So, he would travel as he had traveled for the last three months: ride the "D" streetcar from the Ringstrasse to the outer suburb of Nussdorf near Grinzing.

The sun burst out from behind a cloud. The sunlight felt warm on his face. Warm sunshine existed in the winter. Sometimes the sun melted the snow or icicles dripping from above shop doors. He enjoyed this bright sunshine though he knew the clouds returned always. Not much snow had fallen yet. Only wind-swirled flurries. He felt grateful for that. Papa had said last fall when school began that this winter was supposed to be colder, with more snow. But so far, the cold had gripped the city only in its icy fist and the wind had blown dry. Oui, Maman would like this icy fist image.

An information kiosk loomed to his left on Operngasse. He gravitated to it, hoping to see something helpful on the computer screens. They were his only source of news, especially about the war. He broke off a small chunk of cheese and put the rest of the Emmentaler in his jacket pocket. Last week, he'd watched a report about the neutron nuclear bombs the Chinese had dropped on Moscow. He knew all about nuclear bombs. Papa had told him last summer when the war started. Nuclear bombs vaporized people and everything around them. *Neutron* nuclear bombs destroyed without radioactive fallout so the Chinese could occupy Moscow immediately. But he hadn't yet seen any news reports that the Chinese occupied Moscow, only that the Russians and European Union troops held them off east of the Ural Mountains. He knew where the Ural Mountains were!

But now on the information kiosk's computer screens, he saw only advertisements. Sometimes they were fun to watch, except for the food advertisements that made him hungry. He walked on, comforted by the weight of the potatoes, Emmentaler, and bratwursts in his pockets.

At the streetcar stop across from the Staatsoper on the Ringstrasse, Pierre peeked at the wristwatch of a man with a bulging briefcase. Not even that late in the morning. Perhaps, instead of Nussdorf, he'd ride the "D" to Schottentor and take a Number 38 streetcar to Grinzing. He had not checked the house for two days. Maybe Papa and Maman had left him a note. He'd left a note two days ago. They would be searching for him. If they had returned. And he could check that bakery in Grinzing that sometimes forgot to put away their milk delivery in the back.

That man there by the trees. Pierre had spotted him the day before, noticed him because of his hair. Pierre had never seen that color hair on anyone before, a blond the soft gold color of that cold and crunchy oat cereal from America that Maman bought for him in the summer. Oat blond. Pierre disliked the way the man looked at him. His eyes followed him, too interested. His eyes lacked light.

Disappear, run far away from that man. Suddenly he craved a real caramel. A candy shop near Schottentor sometimes handed out free candy. No, not many people waited at the streetcar stop. The grown-ups—and Oat Blond Man—would see him sneak onto the streetcar and that would not do. No. If a conductor boarded at another stop, the grown-ups would point him out, tell the conductor he didn't have a ticket. The police would come for him.

He left the streetcar stop, and hopped onto the escalator to the Opernpassage that tunneled under the wide Ring Boulevard. Below the street, a uniformed policeman patrolled among the silent crowd. A dirty, bearded man sitting cross-legged on the ground played an accordion, and the song held the policeman's attention for a moment. The song sounded familiar, but Pierre couldn't remember where he'd heard it before. He'd learned that girl police were far more threatening to him than men—girl police always noticed him. Girl police wanted to catch him, take him to jail. He called on the Wizard Howl once again to make him invisible and scurried past the policeman, along the curving line of shops with full display windows of books, pastries, clothes, and cameras, and to the opposite escalator that carried him up to the street near the opera house.

He liked the First District. Innere Stadt. Or "downtown," an American tourist had called it. Few bombs had hit here. People always crowded the streets. Pierre glanced at the Staatsoper, the opera house, as he passed. He'd drawn it for Papa the first time they'd seen it. An example of Neo-Renaissance architecture, Papa had said. He missed his drawing pads, colored pencils, and pens. He missed Papa. Perhaps he was working at his office today.

Pierre pivoted. Oat Blond Man stopped only meters away. Oat Blond Man had followed him.

"Hey, was ist los?" Oat Blond Man said as he approached Pierre.

How could this man speak to him as if they were friends. In a strange accent, also. The skin on his low forehead and around his ice-blue eyes crinkled with his smile. Pierre darted past him back to the Opernpassage escalator. Underground, he weaved through the chaos of people heading in all different directions to the opposite escalator. When he reached the street again, he ran up the Kärntner Ring, turned right onto Dumbastrasse along the side of the Imperial Hotel, sprinted past the Musikverein concert hall, and across the street to the park at Karlsplatz. He loved to play in this park—its duck pond, its sculptures to climb on, its wooded paths all surrounded by city buildings that he'd wished he'd designed. But this morning, he cut through the park and past the Baroque Karlskirche to the other side and then left up to Techniker-strasse, the home address of the French embassy. Looking at this building, Pierre felt at home, felt like he was in Paris with Maman walking along Avenue Victor Hugo. He slipped through the side gate.

Papa's car was not in his parking space. Papa was not at work today. The security guards were at work, however.

"Hinaus! Was machts du? Geh hinaus!"

The security guard, a black-haired man in light blue shirt and navy-blue trousers and no overcoat, was not someone Pierre knew. He shouted again for Pierre to leave. He must have been inside and run out. Sharp eyes, that guard. Pierre decided not to speak with him. The guard might call the police. Pierre obeyed the guard and ran out the way he'd entered.

Bombs had destroyed the Hauptbahnhof and several blocks of buildings north of it on Prinz-Eugen-Strasse, but they had missed the Belvedere Palaces and gardens, another favorite playground when Pierre and Maman were waiting for Papa to finish work. Pierre knew the way to the Belvedere down Prinz-Eugen-Strasse past Schwarzenberg Palace, but now he crossed instead to a streetcar stop. As he waited, he stared at the art nouveau façade of the French embassy.

Maybe his parents' disappearance was a secret. Some-thing for Papa's work. Papa kept many secrets for his work. Papa could not talk about his work with anyone, but Pierre had heard him and Maman talking late into the night some-times. Serious voices. He'd sneak out of bed to press his ear to their bedroom door, catching only meaningless phrases like "travel restrictions" and "access denied" and "diplomatic back channels." He knew what their voices sounded like when they talked about him, their soft, even voices talking about his school work, his piano lessons, his drawings, and his favorite, Christmas presents. The last conversation he'd overheard had been about Christmas—plans to return to Paris to spend the holidays at home. Nothing about presents. He'd desperately wanted his own copy of *Howl's Moving Castle* so he would never have to return it to the library ever again.

Oat Blond Man appeared on Technikerstrasse, walking past the French embassy toward him. Pierre glanced down Prinz-Eugen-Strasse, but no streetcar approached. Oat Blond Man stood out in the open, staring at him from across the street, smiling and waving. He could run south to the Schwarzenberg Garten or north through Schwarzenberg Platz and head into the twisty streets and busy stores of the First District. Oat Blond Man waited for a lull in the traffic to cross the street. Pierre did not wait.

The running warmed him so much that he began to sweat. After going straight through the car park in Schwarzenberg Platz, weaving in and out between the cars, he turned right on the Ring Boulevard. He was proud that he now knew the First District so well. Before the bombing, he'd visited the inner city only with his parents and only specific locations, such as the opera house, the Sacher Hotel for tea, St. Stephen's Cathedral, the Hofburg for a tour, and shopping on Kärntnerstrasse. He loved the First District especially during Christmas, with all the festive lights, the holiday decorations, the vendors roasting chestnuts in big black cauldrons on the street corners and selling them in paper cones. One vendor in the Freyung plaza had given him a cone of chestnuts for free one night. He'd wandered among the stalls of the Christkindlmarkt in front of the Rathaus and remembered ice skating with Papa and Maman.

Johannesgasse brought him to the ice-skating rink on Lothringerstrasse. He'd wanted to go in the other direction. He looked back. No sign of Oat Blond Man. "Don't talk to strangers," Maman said. "Stay in a crowded place and look for police," Papa said. He could feel his heart pounding in his chest. He couldn't look for police. He must find a safe place to hide.

He walked past the Konzerthaus to the giant Beethoven statue in Beethoven Platz. Papa had said that Monsieur Beethoven scowled down at anyone who dared to look up at him. Monsieur Beethoven looked like he'd sat on a pine cone. Pierre checked all around. He didn't see Oat Blond Man any-where. What would Papa do? Papa would take him home. But their house was nothing but a bomb crater now. Pierre sighed. He would not cry. Babies cried. Not Pierre Levade, the best of friends to Steamboy, the Warrior Ashitaka, and the Wizard Howl. He asked Steamboy for help.

And so Steamboy led him back to the Ringstrasse and to the bustling Kärntnerstrasse where Pierre passed the opera house, the Air France office, cafés, aromatic restaurants, a fur store with warm coats in its windows, jewelry shops, music and book shops, the Steffl department store, on the way to Stephansplatz and the towering cathedral, with its mixture of Romanesque, Gothic, and Baroque architecture. Steamboy guided him to the southeastern entrance in the middle under the Gothic spire. He'd been in the cathedral only twice, but he had a feeling that Oat Blond Man would not think to look for him there. Inside, the air smelled of damp marble and cloying sweet incense.

Pierre checked the murmuring voices in the back: two tour groups stood on opposite sides of the main entrance. This wasn't the church he and his parents attended. Nevertheless, he walked to the center aisle, genuflected to the high altar, and took a seat near Pilgram's Pulpit. He liked the pulpit's circular stair and ornate sculpture and Anton Pilgram peeking out of the bas relief window at its base. Each tour group strolled and stopped and strolled again toward the high altar, one on the left and the other on the right. Pierre scrutinized each group. No Oat Blond Man. Two old women in black with black head-scarves kneeled in the front. With the exception of the subdued tour leaders' voices, the church was quiet.

Pierre waited until the tour groups had left and then longer, afraid to leave. He nibbled on another piece of Emmentaler. The air-raid sirens sounded, giving him an excuse to stay. Planes flew over the church, but no MAO49s, which had a buzzing hum like a giant bee. These Chinese planes whined and rumbled, followed by the thudding thunder of bombs. He closed his eyes and listened, placing the sound outside of the inner city but still close. Secretly he hoped a bomb hit Oat Blond Man and he never saw him again.

When the all-clear sirens sounded, he left St. Stephen's and zig-zagged through the First District to the candy shop on the corner of Schottengasse and Freyung. The free candy today was peppermint hard candy. He stuffed his pockets until the pretty young saleslady frowned at him. He smiled and saluted her. She had been nice to him in the past, especially around Christmas. The bell rang as the door opened. Pierre jumped away and hunched down, but it was a businessman, not Oat Blond Man, who entered. He slipped out while the saleslady served the businessman.

Relax, Pierre. Steamboy would get him to the house in Grinzing, and he could check for a note from Papa or Maman.

He smelled smoke and looked to the sky, turning in a circle. The black smoke billowed into the sky to the west, smudging the gathering gray overcast. He knew it could snow. He loved the snow. But his shelter, he had discovered the month before, was not adequate against a snowstorm. No sign of Oat Blond Man. He took a big breath and trotted up the street.

The underground passage at Schottentor had a big hole in the ceiling over the streetcar tracks and the vibrating rumble of the metro below. The aroma of bratwurst made his mouth water. He was relieved to see a lot of people waiting at the stop, and even more people browsing the shops, the wurst stand, the kiosks, talking. The Number 38 streetcar roared down the curved incline to the stop only minutes after he arrived. Several clusters of people surged for the doors, and he joined the one at the middle door. He had learned early that a crowd guaranteed no one would notice him. The adults would think that he was with some adult among them. He glanced quickly to the back: no conductor. He could ride this one all the way to Grinzing.

His window seat gave him a view of the left side. A fat

old woman with shopping bags full of packages sat to his right. He kept his eyes on the window to avoid talking with her. Old Viennese women liked to talk to children. She sighed long and heavy. The streetcar moved forward up the curved incline to the street, its wheels screeching against the steel rails. He unwrapped a peppermint and popped it into his mouth. The route was so familiar to him that he barely noticed the pedestrians, the cars, and tall gray buildings with their ground-floor shops lining Währinger Strasse.

The last time he'd visited the house in Grinzing, on Wolfs-grubergasse, he'd seen that the bomb had damaged most of the houses on the street. He decided to investigate them further this time. Perhaps he could find better shelter than the abandoned house in Nussdorf, and then he'd be easier for Papa and Maman to find. Their garden had suffered a partial uprooting from the explosion, but the rock garden with its cascading fountain in the back had remained intact. He left his notes under the garden troll statue Maman had bought in England. Maman loved that troll. He was certain that they would think to look there, under that singular statue in what was left of their garden, when they returned.

Pierre disembarked the streetcar at the stop before the last one and headed up the gentle slope through residential Grinzing. He saw no one. The air raid must have sent everyone inside for the rest of the day. He climbed through the narrow streets and past the church, avoiding his school. The houses ended, and he continued up the hill, past dead brown vineyards on either side of the road. Halfway up the hill, he turned right onto Wolfsgrubergasse. The sight took his breath away. Someone had cleared away the rubble where their house had stood and flattened the earth. The two houses he passed before he reached their garden stood empty, their windows blown out and walls tipping off their foundations.

Amazingly, the garden troll still stood silent watch over the frosted brown soil and the cascading fountain. Pierre lifted one side. Bare rock. His notes were gone! They must have been here! Papa and Maman. But why hadn't they left him a note with instructions for where to meet them? He searched his pockets for another slip of paper, the stub of pencil he'd stolen from a café. He must leave them another note.

The wind blew the sound of footsteps on the rocks away so that he didn't hear them until they were too close. He whirled around and looked up into Oat Blond Man's face.

"I knew you'd come back here," Oat Blond Man said in German.

His accent was as flat as the Hungarian plain. Pierre turned to run at the same time he felt a prick in his neck like a fingernail pressing into his skin.

"Oh, no, my little rascal. You're coming with me."

Oat Blond Man enfolded him in his arms. Pierre punched and hit and kicked until his vision blurred and he lost the strength to fight. He felt himself lifted up and then felt nothing more in the blackness.

CHAPTER 3

His mother cradled him close, encircled tight in her arms. He could hear her heartbeat, regular and steady, in his ear. He could smell the rose water on her skin, the faint aroma of red wine on her breath. She hummed. The resonant vibrations in her chest passed through his skin like a cat's purring, warm and comforting.

When Evan looked up, he saw a stranger's face, a woman in a light blue uniform. She smiled, said something in Spanish he didn't understand. He remembered, and with the memory came the pain, intense in his abdomen, throbbing in his right shoulder. He turned his head to the right, where more people—men and women in white and blue moved this way and that, and an IV bag hung from its stand, a clear tube snaking down to his arm. There were voices, antiseptic smells. He must be in the hospital. He felt so heavy, so tired, but he wanted to know what they were doing for him.

A black-haired man with a five-o'clock shadow appeared next to him. He wore loose, light blue cotton clothing. He bent down close to Evan's face.

"Maestro, we're waiting for an OR."

At the sound of his American English, Evan's heart rate increased. What was an American doing here? From the embassy? *Not from the embassy, please*, Evan thought. Someone from the embassy might kill him. Brown had said there was an order. The man looked beyond and above Evan. Evan wanted to speak, opened his mouth, but the effort was too much for him.

"It's OK, Maestro. You'll be fine. You were shot twice. Once here," and the dark-haired American pointed to his own abdomen, "from an angle behind, and once in your right shoulder. You are stable. We will operate on your abdomen to remove the bullet." He looked to his left. "Ah, they're ready for us now. Relax. We'll take good care of you. I promise."

Evan felt the bed moving. His sluggish brain thought, *not bed, gurney*. He lost track of the dark-haired American. Who was that guy? An American here? *Please, not from the embassy*. His eyelids were so heavy now he couldn't keep his eyes open. The sounds faded. He felt the gurney stop. He forced his eyes open. Above him hung a giant round light, not on, its glass and metal gleaming. Then his brain switched off into darkness.

His mother wriggled her nose at him. "My boy," she said.

Looking into her face was like looking into a mirror—Spanish black hair and olive skin—except for the craggy nose and high forehead that he'd inherited from his father. Her tea-brown eyes met his, the laugh lines around them crinkling as she smiled. No shadows lived behind those eyes, no lies, only pain. And yet, a warm light shone from them, all for him.

Her eyes drew him into another world, a safe world

where music sounded from the waves of sunlight surrounding them, a sweet chorus of voices, the powerful chords of an orchestra, a penetrating violin singing Bach. The light shimmered and brightened, carried him into the sky, through the clouds, as the orchestra quieted to a perfect *pianissimo* into his heart.

They flew together. He smiled at his mother, and she smiled in return, her thick, black hair riffling back from her face in the wind. She leaned down and kissed him on the forehead. The kiss brushed a velvety rose petal across his skin, warm and soft. His mother had called them "butterfly kisses," but butterflies didn't smell like roses. Butterflies flew around him in a flutter of wings like puffs of breath on his face. Orange and black, neon blue, yellow, purple, striped and polka-dotted, soft butterfly wings caressed his cheeks and forehead.

"Evan."

Vasia, grinning, winked at him, intense blue eyes framed by his mass of golden curls. But no, no. Vasia stood against the wall bookshelves in his apartment, eyes wide, the black muzzle of the 9mm in his mouth, the gun in Evan's hand. Intense pain made Evan moan.

"Evan. Wake up, Evan."

His eyes shot open. Where was he? Was he safe? He struggled to push his body up.

Hands grasped his shoulders, and he looked into the brown eyes of a nurse. "Señor, please calm yourself. Please lie down."

The hospital. He was in the hospital. He closed his eyes. The heartbeat he heard was his own, its sound magnified by the monitor next to his bed. He felt fuzzy, slow. He remembered running with Brian Thaw. People greeting them. Why did he feel so heavy? He'd been shot. A victim. Like Vasia. Was it payback for Vasia? The fuzziness muffled his mind.

"Evan?"

He recognized that voice. Nigel. Nigel would take care of everything.

Evan opened his eyes. A smile softened the sharp, hawk-like features of his artist manager's face. "Nigel, what are you doing here?" He thought his words sounded slurred together.

"You're not happy to see me?" Nigel said, his tone British bone dry humorous.

Nigel had understood his words. He hadn't slurred them together. Evan tried to raise his right arm, but it weighed two tons. "Always happy to see you, Nigel. But not happy for you to see me here."

"Nonsense." Nigel glanced at someone out of Evan's sight. His abundant white hair was combed back from his forehead and skimmed the collar of his ivory silk shirt and light gray suit jacket. "You've no family, so I'm your family, Evan. If you'd let me. Señor Martín at the Buenos Aires Philharmonic has also offered his assistance. Anything we may need."

"Is Brian Thaw OK?"

"Of course. Why wouldn't he be?"

"We were jogging together. No. He left me. To go home. That's right. Now I remember."

"And why were the two of you jogging at one o'clock in the morning?"

Evan smiled, feeling his muscles stiff in his face. "Celebrating. The concert and Owen's brilliant concerto."

"Señor Fox?" A tall porteño with a black pencil mustache and rumpled ivory suit came into Evan's view. "Perhaps five minutes?"

"Yes, yes, Detective." Nigel's mouth stretched into a taut line. "Evan, Detective Ruiz would like to ask you a few questions. Do you feel up to it?"

"I guess so. But my brain's fuzzy."

"Fuzzy?" Detective Ruiz looked to Nigel for help.

Nigel said, "He's on morphine, Detective."

"Ah! I understand."

Nigel stepped back. Behind him, oatmeal-colored floor-length drapes had been pulled halfway across a glass wall, obscuring activity in the hallway outside. Evan looked around. He was the only patient in the room. The detective moved to stand by the bed to Evan's left. Was it the morphine, or were his eyes really that amazing lagoon blue? The morphine blurred his environment, stretched time, offered sensations that Evan disliked. He hated the loss of control.

"We are concerned that you remain safe, Señor Quinn. Hospital security cameras on all entrances and exits and in every hallway. No one enters the hospital without a security screening, and they must also sign in, show identification. You are now in the ICU, the most secure area of the hospital. Police guard the entrance to this area. We want to protect you, and we also need your help. For example, what happened? What did you see?"

The detective in no way resembled Inspector Klaus Leiner, his precise manner, calculating mind and laser-sharp gray eyes. Evan felt a pang in his chest. He missed the Austrian cop, his familiar tenor voice. The porteño detective's black hair was as untidy as his ivory suit.

"I don't know, Detective. That's the problem. One moment I'm running down Avenida Cordoba, the next I'm flat on my back on the sidewalk and people are shouting. I saw nothing threatening, no one threatening. Was it a terrorist? Terrorists tried to kill me in Vienna." *Also in Amsterdam,* he thought, but no one knew about that, and Bernie Brown had been there to protect him.

The detective sighed. "We have not been able to establish who shot you, señor. A terrorist is a possibility. Have you any enemies?"

Enemies? The NEP? He had understood that Washington's life termination order on him had been rescinded. The NEP hadn't been happy he'd claimed his father's and Caine's money from under their noses, but Woody had given him, that is Perceval, another assignment, so no enemies in the New Economic Party. Who else? Had the Chinese found out about Perceval? Or the Russians? *What am I thinking?* He was a musician, an orchestra conductor. That's how the detective saw him. "No, Detective. No enemies that I know of. I didn't know about the terrorists, though, before they tried to kill me."

The detective nodded. "Tell me, señor, describe to me everything that you saw and heard before the shooting."

Evan described his run, Brian's departure, his route back to his hotel, the men dancing in Plaza Houssay, the flowers, turning when a woman called out to him.

"That twist of your body probably saved your life, Evan," Nigel said. "From what Dr. Carreras has told me."

The detective's eyebrows raised. "You knew the woman?"

"No. I heard her voice, but I didn't actually see her. An unfamiliar voice. When I'm running, people often call out to me. Buenos Aires is very friendly. The woman's voice was friendly, like everyone else's."

The detective's hands grasped the silver bed rail. "At that time, anyone else call out to you?"

Evan shook his head, feeling resistance on the right side of his neck where a bandage covered his shoulder. He'd had the nagging feeling that something was wrong earlier in the run when Brian was still with him, but he had no evidence to go with it, no suspicious person, nothing that he'd seen. Only that prickly gut feeling.

The detective lifted his hands palms up as if in supplication and dropped his arms to his side. "I must apologize, Señor Quinn, that this has happened to you. Please do not interpret it to mean Buenos Aires is a dangerous place for you. We will continue to investigate this crime, but I must tell you that we have little evidence—only one bullet removed from you—many witnesses who saw nothing, and no one claiming responsibility, which can perhaps eliminate a terrorist. No one else was targeted. Based on the trajectory of the bullets, we determined in which building the person hid, but a complete search produced no evidence. A *professional*, señor. Someone who had been watching you and who knew what route you run. I will leave my card. If you think of anything else, anything at all, please call me." The detective took a business card from his inner jacket pocket and laid it on the stand next to Evan's bed.

A professional. Someone wanted him dead. But who? The Chinese? The Americans after all? He hadn't done what he was ordered to do, and he wasn't going to do it. He refused to kill Bernie for them.

Nigel shook the detective's hand. "Please keep us informed, Detective."

As the detective left the room, Evan said, "Will I be able to travel to Toronto tomorrow?"

Nigel chuckled. "Tomorrow was two days ago. I notified Toronto before I left London. They had seen it on the news. The attempt on your life has been at the top of the headlines for two days. And, based on Dr. Carreras's orders for you, I've canceled Iceland and Milan, also. All three requested other dates."

He hadn't kept his runs secret. He hadn't thought that it was necessary here. An assassin like Perceval had been watching him, had followed him and shot him. A familiar falling sensation and a knot of frustration in his stomach made him groan. "I don't need this right now."

"I know, Evan. You're lucky to be alive. Your recovery is now the top priority. You can pick up your conducting schedule perhaps in March or April."

"March. Copenhagen. Could you please bring me the scores for the Barber Piano Concerto and Bartók's Concerto for Orchestra from my hotel room? At least I can get some work done for Copenhagen while I'm stuck here. You know what? Bring all my scores. I can work on Glasgow and Lisbon, too."

"Remember what we talked about last fall? Now you have some time to think about what you want, Evan. Where do you see yourself in five years as a conductor? Where do you see yourself as a violinist?"

"I know, I know. I'll think about it. I already know that I want my own orchestra, Nigel. I've told you that already."

Nigel tapped the bed rail. "All conductors want their own instruments to play. Think beyond that. We've gotten a good start the last six months. You've conducted the Vienna Philharmonic and they adore you, the Amsterdam Concertgebouw, the London Symphony, the Berlin Philharmonic, Oslo, Bucharest, Helsinki, and Madrid. You've received invitations for return engagements, but we need to build on that momentum, especially if you want to have any opportunity to conduct opera. Evan?"

His eyelids had closed although he had had no intention of sleeping. He wanted to continue the conversation with Nigel. But his body controlled his life at this time, not his mind, and when his body needed sleep, he slept.

Pain distracted him from the musical notes on the page in front of his eyes. He pushed the knifing sensation away, but it returned, insistent as a manic gangster. *Mack the Knife*. Evan smiled at the memory of that song.

Dr. Carreras had taken him off the morphine yesterday. His mind was clearer, but he still had short-term memory lapses, especially with names. That morning they had moved him out of the ICU and into this private room with a window that looked out on French-inspired apartment buildings and a clear blue sky. The police had removed their guards, but hospital security continued to monitor activity inside and outside the medical complex.

Hunger surfed the wave of pain. He hadn't eaten, he figured, in five days, since before the concert and his run. The emergency abdominal surgery had shut down his gastro-intestinal system. Now Dr. Carreras and the nurses waited for him to pass gas. Wouldn't Paul Caine love that one? He smiled. Paul loved fart jokes. He could hear Paul's wild, high-pitched giggle as if he were in the room with him.

He glanced at the pile of music scores Nigel had brought from his hotel room. Joseph Caine's Third Symphony lay on top. Paul would love that he was conducting his father's music now. At least, that's what he wanted to believe. He had no idea where Paul, or his mother, Brianna, lived. As a kid, Paul had shown zero interest in music, much to his father's sadness. He wanted to be a pilot, an explorer, and a teacher. Paul's natural geekiness and fear of heights, snakes, and spiders made the first two unlikely professions. But Evan could see him as a teacher—definitely not science or math, but maybe history or English, or even a professor of philosophy. He hadn't thought of Paul in years. Memory did weird things after morphine.

A nurse wearing a floral smock over a white blouse and white pants came in. He remembered her as the pleasant but business-like nurse whose daughter played the flute, but he'd forgotten her name.

"Buenas noches, Señor Quinn. How do you feel?"

"Fine except for the pain and hunger. I could use a walk, too, please."

Her full lips twitched into a smile as she checked his blood pressure, his pulse, his oxygen level. "You have not yet passed the gas?"

"You'll be the first to know. My Vicodin?"

She nodded. "You are doing very well, señor. You have hunger, a good sign your system has woken. Perhaps a walk will help move the gas. We can heat broth and make plain toast for you if it moves."

"Oh, yum."

She brought him his evening Vicodin. A male nursing assistant helped him out of bed, maneuvered the IV stand around to his left side for him to use as a support, and walked him out into the broad hospital corridor. Now that he was off the morphine, he'd become more aware of the hospital routine, of answering a hundred questions every day about his body and how he felt, of the faint sharp scent of disinfectant, and of the symphony of Spanish voices, the muffled squeaks of gurney wheels on linoleum, and the occasional cry of pain. The hallway bustled with nurses at alcoves, assistants removing dinner trays from rooms and stacking them in carts, and the occasional doctor or lab technician in a white coat. Evan enjoyed his walks, although on the very first one he'd nearly collapsed from weak legs and dizziness. Now he powered himself easily, stepping carefully on the gleaming floor.

They passed the main nurses' station, where two nurses typed on computer keyboards at the desk. "You walk very well now, señor, very well," the nursing assistant said.

"Thanks. I feel more confident on my feet. I don't remember your name."

"Manuel, señor. You have the morphine now?"

"No morphine. Vicodin."

"The memory returns slow."

"That's what they tell me. I suppose you've seen memory problems in other patients?"

"Surgery patients, sí. You are doing very well."

"Considering I was shot twice?" Evan gave him a rueful smile. "I was lucky that Buenos Aires swings at night, with lots of people around to help me. And the hospital so close."

"The police have found—?"

"Nothing. Although the detective mentioned to us this morning that they found an unidentified woman not far from Plaza Houssay, where I was shot, who had been murdered that same night."

"Terrible! Buenos Aires rarely sees such violent crime, señor."

"When do you think I'll get out of here?"

Manuel grinned. "This is a good sign, this question. After you pass the gas, maybe three or four days. But you know, you must be able to eat well and no complications."

"I don't intend to have complications."

They veered right to stroll down the long hallway that led to a cardiac unit. The unit's family lounge had an aquarium. Evan liked to watch the fish. They reminded him of the simplicity of his former life in America. He'd been a conductor fish in the Arts Council's aquarium, encased by the walls of their bureaucratic rules and threats. He'd shattered the aquarium's walls with his defection but had been flopping around on the ground ever since. Nigel was right. He really needed to decide what he wanted as a conductor and what he wanted as a violinist. He needed to dive into the ocean and out-swim all the other fish to land his own orchestra.

The nature of the uncertainty had changed. Before, it had focused him on figuring out the arbitrary rules and restrictions, established from personal taste by whomever reigned at the Arts Council, but he always knew he had a job with the Minneapolis State Symphony. Now, as a freelance conductor, the uncertainty was about getting gigs, maintaining steady employment. No guarantees. Nigel was trying to scare him, to push him to work more despite his need to fill his repertoire holes. Nigel had not been pleased with his hesitation last summer, a hesitation he'd explained with the need to study scores, but the real reason had been his Perceval assignment, waiting for the Chinese vice chairman to arrive in Vienna for a meeting with Perceval's rifle. The global war, triggered by the assassination, increased the uncertainty. He was ready to work, Nigel was setting up gigs, but would his next gig cancel because of the war? Would he be able to travel to his next gig? Would the Chinese invade Europe now that they occupied most of Russia? Would the Europeans prevail and push them back? When would it end?

The toccata of Bach's Sixth Partita seeped into his mind. He tried to stop it, but the memory followed: Vasia bent over the keyboard in the living room of his apartment on the Landstrasser Hauptstrasse in Vienna, whisper-singing as he played, completely inside the music. Pain stabbed Evan's chest, and he doubled over.

"Señor?"

Evan gasped. "I think it's gas."

"We walk." Manuel helped him out of the chair in front of the aquarium, and they began the return trip to his room.

The pain cut through him, an intimate scalpel. Sometimes he could stop it, sometimes he could block it, but since he'd been in the hospital, it had mounted a frontal assault whenever the memory returned. It felt like he fought Vasia all over again. Vicodin had no effect. The only relief the last five months had been the distractions of work, preparing for a gig, rehearsing with an orchestra, conducting concerts. The two weeks in Buenos Aires making music had been happy. But now all he had was score study and memory.

"The gas has moved, sí?"

Evan shook his head. "It feels stuck."

They made it back to his room. Manuel helped him climb into bed and left him with the light turned down low but not off. He picked up the Barber Piano Concerto score. This music offered challenges for the orchestra—for him— as well as the pianist. It also presented challenges for the listener. He understood immediately why the Arts Council in America had banned it, despite the second movement, the sublime and sweet Canzone. The Arts Council preferred easy listening and crowd-pleasers in order to make the most money possible. If he never again conducted Tchaikovsky's *1812 Overture* or Sousa marches, he'd be quite happy. At least he no longer needed to worry about his programs attracting the ISS to arrest him.

"The bullet nicked the lower part of your liver and then got stuck in your coiled-up small bowel." Dr. Carreras grinned. "I found it easy and fast. It hadn't pierced anything major in terms of blood vessels, which was lucky."

"This chicken isn't going to hurt me, is it?" Evan stared at the piece of baked chicken breast drenched in gravy on his fork. "I'll be able to eat OK now?"

"Yes. Stay on low fiber for a while. I'd say until you're back to work."

"Thanks." Evan popped the piece of chicken into his mouth. He chewed the chicken well. Before the surgery, and then the days-long wait for the gas to pass, he would not have thought he'd savor baked chicken so much. He looked at Dr. Carreras, wearing light blue scrubs and a white coat, lounging in the chair to his left, his hands meshed together on his flat stomach and one foot resting on the bed frame.

"The food's good here," Dr. Carreras said.

Evan nodded, cutting another piece of chicken. It had taken him two meals to get used to operating the automated bed table that folded up under the bed when not in use. "How long have you been in Buenos Aires?"

"What's my story?" Dr. Carreras smiled.

"You're American. How'd you get here?"

"Via the Underground." Dr. Carreras frowned. "I'd developed a new surgical technique in Chicago. I'd been in contact with a Canadian surgeon in Toronto who told me of a surgeon here who wanted me to teach it to him. How he heard about it, who knows? But the medical field still had internet access to other countries, even if it was monitored."

"When was this?" Evan skewered some sliced carrots with his fork.

"Eleven years ago."

"You were lucky."

Carreras ran the fingers of his right hand through his black hair, a gesture of frustration, not vanity. "I arranged to attend a conference in Minneapolis where I was able to connect with the Underground. They arranged transport to

Canada through North Dakota—I have no idea how they managed it, but I'll be forever grateful. It was a wild ride through the war zone, but I made it to Canada. I had fake ID, fake passport. Someone was waiting for me just beyond the border crossing—no name. She drove me to Winnipeg. From there I flew to Toronto and met the Canadian surgeon. Everything was easy after that."

"Family?"

Dr. Carreras sighed, looked out the window. "Only a younger sister left. She lives in Boston. I get news occasionally. She and her husband just had their first, a daughter."

"Congratulations."

"I'd love to get them out." Dr. Carreras leveled his brown eyes on Evan. "I was deeply saddened to hear about your father."

Evan nodded as he finished off the roasted potato. Good boy, he'd cleaned his plate. After he swallowed, he said, "I wasn't surprised. It was only a matter of time before they killed him." He assessed the doctor's expression: sadness, no shock, but also no anger. Evan had learned over the last seven months that his father had had a following of readers outside America who were genuinely sad about his death. They knew little about his Underground leadership, his guerrilla fighting against Washington, or his gross failure as a father and husband.

"Your defection," Dr. Carreras said. "The terrorist at your press conference. Have you experienced any post-traumatic stress symptoms?"

"Post-traumatic stress?" Klaus Leiner had brought that

up to him, and Evan remembered his fear Leiner would send him to a head doctor to be "rehabilitated."

"Yeah. It's common after suffering a traumatic event like a shooting. I wouldn't be surprised if the shooting here will trigger it." He smiled, but Evan had the feeling he wasn't trying to reassure. His tone was too matter-of-fact. "Flashback memories as real and intense as the actual event. Nightmares. Sometimes hallucinations, either visual or auditory. Insomnia. Short temper. Hypervigilance. Depression. Sometimes panic attacks. At the time of the trauma, the mind protects itself from the overwhelming emotions of the event by detaching from the event while storing it and the emotions in memory until they can be processed safely. PTSD symptoms are a sign that the person feels safe and it's time to process the memory and emotions. If you notice any of the symptoms, ask your doctor in Vienna for a referral to a good therapist experienced in PTSD treatment."

"OK." Evan sipped a delicious black tea with chocolate and mint flavors. His memory flashed a snapshot of Lothar Waage at Vasia's housewarming party, sitting next to Sofia. He'd said he was experienced in PTSD treatment. "When can I return to Vienna?" he said.

"Yeah." Dr. Carreras sighed. "You need some PT for your shoulder, and you'll need to continue those exercises in Vienna. You're eating well, walking well, but I want you to heal more and build more strength before I OK travel. Nigel called today and said he'd arranged an apartment through the Buenos Aires Philharmonic. I'll discharge you tomorrow, and you can stay there for the next ten to fourteen days.

We've made great strides in medicine for treating gunshot wounds, but the human body still requires time to heal."

"So that's why I haven't heard from Nigel."

Dr. Carreras chuckled. "He's been busy." In one powerful swing up of his lean, compact body, he stood. "And I need to check on my other patients."

A few minutes after the surgeon left, a young nursing assistant came in to check Evan's vital signs. He was used to this part of hospital routine. He decided to go for a walk, and pulled his IV stand along on his right while another nursing assistant strolled on his left. Outside of his room, he was never alone. He walked to the cardiac unit and back seven times, then settled in bed to study the Barber Essay for Orchestra, Op. 12. After an hour, he felt sleepy and put away the score to watch TV until he fell asleep.

Vasia giggled, his ridiculous high-pitched giggle. "Evan, we play Caine Piano Concerto in MOSCOW!"

Gunshots.

Evan ran across the roof of Vasia's apartment building.

"As long as you work for us, you'll be as free as you want to be."

The old American from Chicago sat across from him in the Chicago Café. Woody Lewis. "You were so smart to make it look like the Russian did it."

No. Evan moaned. *Vasia didn't kill the vice chairman. I killed him. As ordered. Vasia didn't—*

As dreams do, this one ignored Evan's thought and skipped right to the training ground in the northern Minnesota woods where he kneeled, aimed, and fired. The woods morphed into the wooded area of Pötzleinsdorfer Park where he'd practiced with the sniper rifle. Sirens. He ran as fast as he could, gasping, rain pelting his face and wind fingers grabbing at his clothes. The cops were right behind him.

Vasia's face close to his. "You always have choice."

Gunshots woke him. At least, he believed he was awake. The dark room gave him no clues. A faint light came through the door the nurse had left ajar, but not enough to convince him he wasn't still dreaming. He reached for the remote control and pressed the light button. The wall light above the bed came on. He was awake, drenched in sweat and breathing hard.

A nightmare? He thought about it. Most of the dream he had lived. He and Vasia had been scheduled to perform the Caine Piano Concerto together in Moscow. His throat constricted, and he gasped as the tears came, out of his control. Vasia had that uncanny physical resemblance to Joseph Caine—Uncle Joe—and played Caine's music as if channeling the composer. He hadn't thought before about losing their gig in Moscow along with Vasia. He *had lost* the Russian. But he could hear Vasia's voice in his mind, his joy: "Evan, we play Caine Piano Concerto in MOSCOW!"

He would never play Caine's Piano Concerto with Vasia. Because Vasia had chosen to be at home when he was supposed to be rehearsing with a singer.

Evan wiped his wet face with his sheet. Maybe score study would take his mind off the dream. He didn't believe in wallowing in sorrow. The hospital was quiet, even with his door ajar. It must be the middle of the night. He grabbed the Bartók Concerto for Orchestra score to focus his mind on music, not the past.

He lost track of time. Gradually, a sound seeped into his mind that wasn't Bartók's music. Footsteps—the click of high heels on linoleum. He looked up from the score, wishing for Sofia and knowing it was impossible. She was in Italy. He expected a nurse, but in high heels?

A petite woman dressed in jeans and a low-cut white silky blouse pushed open his door and entered the room. She carried a black shoulder bag. A mental tug of familiarity raised his eyebrows even as he reached for the remote to call a nurse.

She smiled. "Señor Quinn, my name is Alicia. We have a mutual friend. Bernie Brown." She stepped closer, glancing back at the door. "He has been concerned for you."

How could she possibly know that? Bernie was in Austrian police custody, being debriefed by every intelligence agency in Europe, inaccessible to anyone else, including him. The woman's black hair waved down to her shoulders similar to another woman's hair he'd seen on his run. His finger found the call button.

"How did you get in here? I have restrictions on visitors."

She pulled a chair up to the bed and sat down. "Bernie sent me a letter, an actual postal letter, in his handwriting. It was postmarked the day he defected. Do you read Spanish?" She opened her shoulder bag and drew out a folded paper.

"Give it here."

He skimmed over the letter. He couldn't read Spanish, but he recognized Bernie's signature. He'd seen it on a note Bernie had written to accompany the government files he'd given him after he'd defected—during their last meeting at the Austrian police safe house out in the country.

"Whenever Bernie wants something only between us, he uses old-fashioned, low-tech methods of communication. He distrusts technology for privacy. Everyone uses technology for surveillance, listening. I also distrust technology."

Her voice was familiar. It had a smooth dark-chocolate quality like a viola, and a Spanish accent. He handed the letter back to her. "I recognize his signature. What did he say?"

"He knows two things for certain: he will be in police custody for some time, and the Americans will try to kill him. What he is uncertain of is if the Americans will now leave you alone. He asked me to keep an eye on you."

He remembered. She was the woman in white he'd seen after Brian Thaw had left him, the woman who'd smiled. He'd decided she wasn't a surveillance shadow. But she had been shadowing him. Was she the woman who called out to him just before he was shot?

"Can't say you've been doing such a great job of it. What was your name again?"

"Alicia. I spotted the shooter too late, that is true. But I called out to you. I know you heard me. You turned. The shooter must not have been experienced. She didn't compensate and she missed the kill shot."

"*She*?"

"Yes. After I saw you would be helped, I searched for her. So inexperienced. She had remained near, watching what happened to you, instead of ditching the gun, leaving fast, and going as far away as possible. Bernie would have laughed."

"How did you know it was her?"

"She carried the gun in a case with her, and she was speaking on a cell phone, describing to someone what she called her 'successful kill.' I allowed her to finish the conversation."

He thought he knew what happened next. "The police found a woman murdered near the Plaza Houssay."

Alicia nodded. "We had only a brief conversation. She made up for her inexperience by refusing to talk. She told me she'd been hired but refused to say by whom. Someone has ordered a contract on your life, Señor Quinn."

"Terrorists?"

Alicia shook her head. "Terrorists want recognition for their violence. No one has claimed responsibility, not in the media, on the internet, or anywhere else. This was professional, but personal. I have been trying to find out who ordered the contract. No one knows anything. Silence everywhere. Whoever ordered the hit either has powerful friends or is deep underground."

"Who was she?"

Alicia crossed her legs and sat back in the chair. "You have good instincts. Bernie said you were smart."

"You don't know who she was."

"She refused to talk. She spoke Spanish with a Chilean accent, and she was young, perhaps twenty-five or twenty-six. She was not afraid to die."

"Someone who chooses assassins with care, even if they are inexperienced."

"No matter what we do in life, señor, we are all inexperienced and young at the beginning. She would have succeeded if I had not called out to you and you had not turned."

He looked out the window at the dark apartment buildings across the street. Hospital security had assured him that his room number was not available to anyone and he need not worry about someone shooting from one of the adjacent buildings. But someone wanted him dead. And Alicia had gotten to him.

"Who are you? How did you get in here?"

"I am a friend. You need to understand that first before anything else. I have worked with Bernie in the past in a mutually productive way."

"You're a spy? CIA?"

She laughed. "I am a loyal citizen of Spain, señor. Bernie tried to recruit me for the CIA, but I refused. He was not happy working for them, either."

"Yeah, that's true." He remembered Bernie's disdain during their last conversation as he described his infiltration of the CIA to avenge his uncle Danny's murder. So, Alicia was a spy for Spain, but a friend. "Bernie must have made an impression on you."

"He is a good person. I was not surprised at his defection, only the timing. I *was* surprised by his interest in you."

Evan smiled, set the Bartók on top of the pile of scores, and picked up his water glass. She had no need to know the whole story of Bernie's uncle Danny, the cultural smuggling, Bernie's crazy desire to protect Evan because of his uncle Danny's love for Caine and classical music. "Let's just say, Bernie and I share a love for freedom."

She nodded. "You are safe as long as you are in hospital. Has your doctor told you when you can leave?"

"You're not going to tell me how you got in here, are you?" Her black eyes met his, but she said nothing. He sighed. "No, you're not. Tomorrow. Or today now, I guess. My manager has arranged with the Philharmonic for me to stay in one of their guest artist apartments until I'm cleared to travel. I want to know who's trying to kill me. Are you going to be my bodyguard?"

She laughed, a low, husky sound. "In a manner of speaking, yes. I will remain invisible unless you want me to be visible. What do you want, señor? You can put me on your visitor list as your cousin from Spain. Your great-grandmother was Spanish, yes?"

He was impressed with her research. "Born in Madrid. OK, I'll put you on my visitor list, cousin Alicia. Then what?"

She pushed back the chair and stood, lifting her bag to her shoulder. "I continue to investigate who ordered the contract. And perhaps I will teach you some survival tricks, yes?"

"Alicia's not your real name, is it? What last name are you using?"

She turned for the door. "If I am your cousin, it would make sense to use your great-grandmother's name, yes? Caliente."

"Alicia Caliente. Since we're cousins, call me Evan."

"Sleep well, Evan."

She left the room on tiptoe.

He pressed the bed control. It hummed as the upper half lowered until he lay flat. He stared at the ceiling. If terrorists had tried to kill him again, bragging about it to the world on the internet, it was the price for being an American in the public eye. The downside of fame. But someone else? And personal? A Chilean assassin? What did Chile have against him? If she'd been Russian or Chinese, it would have made more sense. Then he'd know they were after Perceval because of the Chinese vice chairman's assassination. He hated mysteries.

Bernie Brown was still looking after him. The guy was incredible. He smiled to himself. He would never complete the assignment Woody had given him last September, the order to kill Bernie. Perceval would have some rules of engagement from now on: no friends, women, or children.

The person who'd ordered the contract on him was no friend.

CHAPTER 4

Oat Blond Man scrambled eggs in a black pan on the stove. Pierre sat at the kitchen table and sipped from his glass of milk. He watched Oat Blond Man with his head down, out of the corner of his eye. Who was he? Oat Blond Man had claimed to be German and said his name was Hans, but Pierre didn't believe him. Oat Blond Man spoke simple German with an accent that was not Austrian or German or Swiss, and it also was not French or British. Pierre knew these accents from people at the French embassy he'd met with Papa. So *this* Hans was not German or Austrian or Swiss or French or British. He considered the accent might be Scandinavian—Maman had talked about Scandinavian flat vowels, but he'd decided that this Hans behaved little like a true European. Papa would not like the way this Hans lied.

Maman would be happy that this Hans had given him shelter when the winter had turned so cold in Vienna and also had fed him, but she would say his loud voice was uncultured, his big hands the rough hands of a laborer and sniff at his salty, sweaty smell.

He wanted to check their house, check the garden for notes from Papa and Maman. But this Hans never let him go out by himself. This Hans wanted him to speak, but he had nothing to say to him. He, Pierre Levade, could keep secrets, too. For some reason, he couldn't explain even to himself, he'd decided to keep his name to himself. The Warrior Ashitaka agreed.

Because he didn't believe Oat Blond Man was German or that his name was Hans, Pierre decided to call him *Avoine*, the French word for "oats." Steamboy laughed.

He had grasped the advantage of playing along with Avoine, at least for a while. He was warm, sheltered, and fed. The Wizard Howl had advised it even though Steamboy and Ashitaka had wanted him to run away. Avoine had given him new clothes and his own room in the dingy apartment. They had television and computer games and comic books, but not the Japanese anime he loved. Avoine had given him a new warm jacket and boots, but had not taken him outside. Pierre had not been outside in what seemed like years, but it had probably only been a week, maybe two.

"You'll like these eggs, kid," Avoine said in German. His voice sounded like sandpaper rubbing on wood. "They're my specialty." He shoved the scrambled eggs onto two plates. "How'd you like to go to Naschmarkt with me today?"

Naschmarkt. His favorite place. Pierre nodded without smiling. Lots of police in Naschmarkt. Create a scene in Naschmarkt to get Avoine arrested. Then slip away. But if the police arrested Avoine, he'd lose the warm place to sleep, warm clothes and food. Avoine set a plate in front of him.

"I scramble the eggs with a little milk and then add cheddar cheese and a dash of Tabasco at the end." He sat down opposite Pierre and poured beer from a bottle into a glass. "My mother taught me to scramble eggs. You're going to have to talk sometime, you know. Might as well be today.

Why don't you tell me what you want that I haven't gotten for you?"

He wanted drawing paper, colored pencils, maybe some charcoal. He wanted Papa and Maman. He wanted his Japanese anime and his books. He wanted to go home. He remained silent.

Pierre ate his eggs with a spoon. In all the time he'd been in this apartment, he'd not seen any forks, and Avoine always cut up his meat before giving it to him.

"OK. I know you want something. You look at me as if you want something. What's your name? Give me something, kid."

The eggs tasted delicious. He liked the cheese in them. Avoine had taken him in when he needed help. But Ashitaka was urging him now to leave Avoine, go out on his own again. Something was not right about Avoine.

"We'll go to Naschmarkt this afternoon, and this candy store I know for some treats. Then we'll visit a doctor. I want to make sure you're OK. Healthy."

Pierre was healthy. Maman had taken him to the doctor last August for his usual pre-school check-up. He'd been starving before Avoine had grabbed him, but he wasn't anymore. He finished the eggs and pushed the plate away. He drained his milk.

Avoine stared out the kitchen window. He sat completely still, and Pierre had to squint to see that he was breathing. He'd seen Avoine move his lean, muscular body like a hunting cheetah once, so smooth and silent and concentrated. He'd also seen him talk on the cell phone out of earshot with a serious expression that turned stormy. Avoine didn't leave for work in the morning, didn't have any kind of job. But he had money. Who was he?

Avoine seemed to have some kind of plan, however, that he was following each day. He spent a lot of time on the internet, but wouldn't let Pierre watch. And then there were those phone calls.

As if on cue, Avoine's cell phone began playing music, a song Avoine had told him was "the theme to *Mission: Impossible*." Pierre had never heard of such a song. Avoine pulled the phone out of his shirt pocket and flipped it open.

"Yeah?" he said before his eyes caught Pierre's across the table.

A chill went through Pierre as if those ice-blue eyes had frozen his skin.

"Just a minute," Avoine said in English. Not British English. Pierre knew what that sounded like. He knew that accent. Pierre thought of all the countries he knew where English was the native language.

In German, Avoine said, "Kid, go put your boots and jacket on. We'll be leaving after this call."

Was he Australian? Pierre slid out of his chair and left the kitchen. Was he from New Zealand? South Africa? He listened to Avoine's flat vowels as he went to his bedroom. Canadian? He'd never heard someone from these countries speak. American? Papa had talked to people from all these countries. He would know. Maybe even Maman. All he knew for sure was that Avoine was not British. And he thought maybe people from Australia, New Zealand, and South Africa might sound British, too, because he'd learned in history class they had once been part of Great Britain's empire.

His English teacher spoke it with a British accent and talked about England.

Pierre opened the polished wood door of his bedroom closet, and took out the black leather boots lined with shearling wool and the black Loden jacket. The red knitted scarf had fallen from the jacket's hanger onto the closet floor. He scooped it up and closed the door. Maman would have also bought him a hat. He could hear her sweet voice telling him in rapid French that the human body lost eighty percent of its heat through the head in winter.

"Fertig, Junge?" Avoine's voice came from the open bedroom door. Pierre shook his head as he pulled on his left boot. "Faster, kid." Avoine's retreating footsteps in the hallway sounded like dropped boulders. Why were they going to Naschmarkt? They hadn't gone anywhere before. What if Avoine already knew the police and that's the reason he wasn't afraid to take him to Naschmarkt? Avoine wasn't afraid of the police.

Bundled up and ready to go, Pierre went to the living room and stood behind the old, musty sofa that faced the television. He heard the clacking of dishes in the kitchen. Avoine fussed about cleaning up. Pierre tapped his knuckles on the kitchen door frame.

Avoine, wearing a knee-length brown wool coat and yellow scarf, looked up from the sink where he'd stacked their lunch dishes. "Good. Let's go." He took the ring of keys from on top of the refrigerator and led Pierre out before locking the apartment door.

The brilliant sunshine reflected off a thin layer of new clean snow and hurt his eyes. His breath clouded out from his face. No wind blew. Pierre breathed in the fresh air. It was clear, no scent of smoke from bombings.

"This way."

He followed Avoine to a large black sedan, surprised that they would drive to Naschmarkt. A car. Perhaps Avoine had transported him in that car after he'd caught him in Grinzing. Avoine opened the front passenger door, and Pierre climbed in. While he waited for Avoine to go around to the driver's side, he studied the narrow street lined with gray nineteenth-century apartment buildings. He would see what route they drove to Naschmarkt and figure out the district in which the apartment was located. The Warrior Ashitaka added that he needed to watch for escape opportunities.

Avoine inserted the ignition stick. The dashboard lit up. The computer beeped. The car's engine revved. Avoine liked speed. He drove like an accomplished race-car driver. Papa would like that.

Pierre spotted a blue-and-white street sign on the corner of a gray building after they'd driven through several narrow streets: Alserbachstrasse with a "9" indicating the Ninth District. Across the street was a Baroque palace and park. Avoine turned left. They sped along the wider street, across a river that was too narrow to be the Danube—Pierre guessed it was the Danube canal—past a large park on one side and bombed out train yards on the other. The rubble stretched for blocks. This was not the way to Naschmarkt. They headed east, not south or north. Pierre squirmed in his seat, pulled at the seat belt. Where were they going?

Pierre looked at Avoine, his hands relaxed on the steering wheel, a smirk on his lips. He opened his mouth to tell

Avoine he was stupid, didn't he know this wasn't the way to Naschmarkt? His open mouth said nothing. Avoine looked at him and grinned.

"Surprised? Don't worry, kid. There's something only you can do for me, and you'll do it. Then we'll go to Naschmarkt."

This was new. Avoine had not asked him before to do anything. However, Avoine wasn't asking, he was telling. And what could he do? Refuse? No. Something was wrong. The Wizard Howl's magic couldn't reach him in the car. Ashitaka and Steamboy told him to watch for an opportunity to run.

They crossed another bridge over a wider river, most likely the Danube, and a large undeveloped area like a park. On the left, he recognized UNO City. Papa had pointed it out to him often from a distance. Avoine pressed on the accelerator briefly as they approached yet another bridge. Not far past the bridge Avoine turned left into a street of apartment buildings, then left again, and parked the car in front of a line of row houses painted different candy colors. Avoine, with his usual brusque movements, got out of the car. Pierre didn't move.

He'd seen a streetcar stop back on the street that crossed the river. He glanced back the way they had come. That street was only a block or two away, an easy run for him. He unlocked his seat belt. The passenger door opened, and one of Avoine's big hands grabbed his jacket collar.

"What's your problem, kid?" Avoine said in German, pulling him out of the car. "Stop pouting. This won't take long. Then we'll go to Naschmarkt. You're acting like it's a major disaster or something."

Avoine held his shoulders and walked him to a mint-green row house. A woman opened the door. She wore a gray light wool skirt with matching jacket, a string of pearls around her neck, and shiny black high-heeled shoes, her blond hair pulled into a spiral at the back of her head. She smiled at him.

"How glum you are, little one!" she said to him in German. "I have some milk and cookies for you."

They followed her into a small kitchen with a table alcove under a wide window flanked by frilly yellow curtains. He noticed Avoine hadn't said anything to her. They knew each other. She had expected them. She set a plate of date cookies on the table and gave him a white paper napkin. Avoine disappeared while she poured a glass of cold milk.

"I hear that you don't talk," she said, setting the milk in front of him. She rubbed his upper back gently. "Is it the war? All the bombings? It's terrifying. We are so close here to the freight yards and UNO City, but they haven't yet bombed UNO City. We thought it would be the first to go after the Hilton Hotel in the Third District." She sat down next to him and chose a date cookie. "Try these. They are my favorite. I buy them from a bakery two blocks away."

He picked up a date cookie and took a bite. She smiled. He smiled back.

She dunked her cookie in his milk. "I love to eat cookies this way." She laughed. "My mother would scold me."

He could tell from her German that she was Austrian. She had warm brown eyes and a sweet voice and soft hands, and she was dressed for an office. Did she live here in this house? A fluttering in his stomach made him shift in the chair.

"OK," Avoine said behind him in German, "we're all set."

The woman smiled at him again. "You are such a lucky boy. Hans is going to give you the best present."

A hand holding a white handkerchief appeared from above in front of his face. It smelled sickeningly sweet. He turned away, but the handkerchief covered his face. He twisted and punched, but he couldn't hold his breath forever. His last thought was a plea to Wizard Howl for escape.

He woke in a comfortable bed and in silence. His head hurt behind his left ear, and his left thigh felt sore. He was naked under the comforter. A stomach spasm made him nauseous. He sat up, rubbing his belly and taking deep, slow breaths as Maman had taught him to do when his tummy felt bad. The bedroom contained only the single bed, a stand next to it, and an armoire with a broken leg repaired with white tape near the closed door. Ragged brown carpet covered the floor. He lifted the comforter to check his sore thigh. Under the skin on the outer side, halfway to his knee, he felt a hard square the size of his little finger's nail. No visible cut. He probed the skin behind his left ear and found another tiny, hard square embedded under the skin. What were they? Would they hurt him? He shivered in the cool room.

Shouts erupted in the room below. Two voices. Avoine. Another man. He couldn't hear words, only the sounds of anger, rising and falling. Pierre slipped out of the bed and tiptoed over to the window. Avoine's car remained parked at the curb, the only car on the street. No people walked about. No kids. Pierre tested the window: it opened easily. But when he stuck his head out, he saw an unbroken drop to the ground with nothing to aid a climb. The front porch roof was too far to the right to be of any help. He would have to sneak downstairs and out the door. His stomach seized up again. He took a deep breath. Ashitaka and Steamboy urged him, "Now is your chance to escape. Get dressed."

As quiet as a cat, Pierre opened the armoire. He pulled out his clothes. His black boots stood by the door. He dressed quickly while he listened to Avoine and the other man below. He felt lightheaded when he moved too fast. They must have drugged him in order to put the tiny hard squares under his skin. He'd seen such things on old TV spy shows. Was Avoine a spy? Avoine was a liar, that's all he knew for certain.

He opened the bedroom door and listened. The voices below were loud but no longer arguing. He walked along a narrow, carpeted mezzanine to the top of the stairs. Tiptoe down the stairs, careful! No squeaks. His left thigh hurt. At the bottom of the stairs, Avoine's voice exploded into laughter behind the closed door to the left. Pierre walked straight to the front door two meters away.

The sun hung low in the sky. Pierre sucked in the fresh, cold air and trotted down the street, ignoring the pain in his thigh. The cold air felt good. His stomach calmed. At the intersection, he turned right. Ahead traffic sped over the river, on the street with the streetcar tracks and stops. When he reached it, he turned right toward the river and ran to a group of people waiting at a transit shelter. What luck! So many people waiting for a streetcar. He could slip on board without being noticed. The Wizard Howl must have opened the way for him with his escape magic.

Where was the streetcar? The longer he waited, the more he fidgeted, afraid Avoine would catch him there. His eyes darted back toward the street, but no large black sedan appeared. Finally, the streetcar arrived, a Number 26 that carried him back over the rivers and into the First District, where he got off on the Franz-Josefs-Kai that ran along the Danube canal. Two women dressed in skimpy, clingy dresses and fur jackets strolled up the Kai and veered into a bar with dark windows. A brightly lit ice cream shop caught his eye, the only shop on the street that looked open. He crossed the Kai to Rotenturmstrasse and ran past its busy shops, weaving around shoppers and business people and newspaper vendors hawking *Kurier*. He entered the square around St. Stephen's Cathedral and past a busker playing a cello. Even in winter, music filled the streets of Vienna.

Inside the cathedral, the sight of Pilgram's Pulpit's familiar spiral stair and ornate filigree banister reassured him. He had escaped. But what should he do now? Was he safe? Avoine was out there, he knew it, looking for him. Avoine had a plan. But maybe Avoine would give up looking for him if he could hide for long enough.

It had been days since he'd checked the garden at the house in Grinzing for notes. But, no, Avoine would look for him there. At least he wasn't hungry. He could hide for a day or two before he'd need to find food. He must find the perfect place to hide that was also a warm shelter. Not Grinzing, but maybe Nussdorf was still safe. Avoine had caught him in Grinzing, not at his hideaway in Nussdorf.

He left St. Stephen's by the southeast side entrance. The sunlight had faded into dusk. Shoppers crisscrossed the square, their shoulders hunched against the cold. Pierre looked up at the sky, the bruise of night spreading from the east. He felt safe on the Graben with its brightly lit stores. A steady stream of people entered and came out of upscale Meindl's grocery on Kohlmarkt. He turned up Naglergasse, leaving the pedestrian-only streets behind. The spacious plaza of Am Hof was like an open mouth between the tall buildings. He lingered at a bookstore's windows, eyeing the children's display. Maman had been reading to him *Harry Potter and the Chamber of Secrets* the night before she'd sent him to pick up the torte at the café in Grinzing. He wished now he had the book so he could finish reading it. Harry Potter was a boy, not yet a great wizard like Howl, but Pierre liked him. In Freyung, to his surprise, a roasted chestnut vendor sat near Palais Kinsky, her black cauldron smoking. As he approached, she waved him over and gave him a cone of roasted chestnuts.

"What are you doing out alone at this hour?" she said in German. She pulled her brown wool scarf up over her floating gray hair. The fingers were cut out of her black knitted gloves.

He shrugged. "Thank you for the chestnuts," he replied in German.

"I've seen you before, haven't I?" She squinted at him in the dying light, her thin lips moving as if she chewed something.

"Maybe. I walk home this way often."

She nodded. "Run along home, then." She waved him up Schottengasse.

He ate one chestnut and squeezed the rest into two of his jacket's pockets for later. At Schottentor, rather than join the stream of business people riding the escalator down to the streetcar stop or the subway in the levels below, he walked toward the university and a streetcar stop on the Ringstrasse. He wanted the streetcar to Nussdorf, a "D," and could see a group of thirty or more people waiting at the stop.

A hand grabbed his jacket collar and lifted him off his feet. "So you thought you could get away from me, did you?" Avoine said in German.

Pierre looked up into Avoine's icy blue eyes. His stomach seized into a hard knot. Tears welled in his eyes. But he said nothing.

Avoine carried him to the large black sedan idling at the Ringstrasse's curb near the Schottentor escalators. Where had it come from? Pierre hadn't seen it there, but he hadn't been looking for it. How had Avoine found him so fast? Avoine opened the front passenger door, blocking any escape. Pierre climbed into the seat.

Avoine squatted next to him, pretending to adjust the seat belt. "Did you notice anything different when you woke up this afternoon? Maybe the implants? The one in your leg," Avoine grabbed his left thigh and squeezed. Pierre bit his lower lip to keep from crying out in pain. "That's a GPS transmitter. No matter where you run, I'll always be able to find you." Avoine stood and closed the car door.

Pierre watched him go around the front and check for traffic on the busy boulevard. He wished for a car to hit

Avoine. But no, Avoine safely made it to the driver's door. He was trapped.

"You're a feisty kid, I'll give you that," Avoine said as he maneuvered the car into traffic. Pierre felt his eyes on him but would not look at him. "I need someone with balls to work for me for a while. Once the job's done, we'll remove the implants and you can go do whatever you want. But I'll tell you, kid, from now on you'll do exactly what I tell you to do, and you're going to talk. If you don't, you'll never see your family or friends again."

Pierre looked out the passenger window at the shadows around the gray nineteenth-century buildings of Vienna. Avoine was not lying this time.

CHAPTER 5

Evan finished writing his email to Robert Waldstein, concertmaster of the Vienna Philharmonic, with a viola joke and expressed the hope that he'd see Robert soon, and then he clicked "Send." The computer desk faced the windows, and the morning sun streamed in, warming his face. Nigel's eyebrows had shot up at his demands for a "clean" computer with impenetrable security, but the notebook computer he'd procured gave Evan access to the world again. He deleted advertising, shaking his head that spam still could find him, and came to an email from Sofia Karalis. He stared at the subject line: "Are you ok?"

Voices in the apartment's foyer caught his attention. His room, at Alicia's insistence, was far from the fourth-floor apartment's entrance, down a long hallway and next to the spacious bathroom. It was a small room, but had large windows overlooking the courtyard of the fifteen-floor apartment building not far from the Teatro Colón. He felt safe in this room.

The voices had stopped, replaced by a knock on his door. "Evan?"

"Come in, Nigel. I'm just cleaning out email."

His tall manager entered, dressed in an impeccably tailored

suit as usual. "Alicia tells me that Dr. Carreras has given his approval for travel in a week."

"As long as I continue to eat well and build my strength."

Nigel eyed the rumpled duvet on the unmade bed, eyebrows raised, but sank down on it. He glanced at the closed bedroom door. "Alicia," he said.

"What about her?"

"Who is she?"

Evan pushed the desk chair back and swiveled it around to face Nigel. He looked the manager straight in the eyes and replied, "My cousin."

"From Spain. So you've said before." Nigel shook his head once. "Is she in law enforcement in Spain? She seems to know a great deal about protection protocols and surveillance." His deep-set green eyes held Evan's. "Detective Ruiz told me that she's not with the Buenos Aires police."

"No, she's not." Evan sighed. He understood Nigel's concern. How could he reassure and convince him that Alicia was a friend, that his suspicions were unfounded? He decided that speaking as close to the truth as possible was the best strategy. "Alicia has had considerable security experience in Spain, from what she's told me, and she hasn't told me that much. I believe her. My mother never talked much about our Spanish relatives, but she did tell me their name, where to find them in Spain, and that I do have living relatives there. I was just surprised that they would take an interest in me."

"Why wouldn't they?" Nigel said, his eyes flashing. "Of course they'd be interested in you. You're rich. You're famous. I'm surprised that more alleged relatives haven't shown up before."

So that was Nigel's concern. "I believe her, Nigel." He stared the old Brit down, hoping that his eyes conveyed the sincerity that he felt. "She's not asked me for anything. If she does, I'll consider her request. But I won't be jumping down any rabbit holes for her anytime soon."

Nigel smiled. "That's what I wanted to hear. The old Evan, back again." He nodded. "She's been quite forthright with me, I must say. But I wanted to make certain before I returned to London."

Evan stood and raised his right arm as if he held an overfull glass. He made a slow, small circle with his hand leading, wincing at the stiffness in his shoulder. "She's taking good care of me. I don't think you have anything to worry about. She's agreed to travel with me to Vienna, too, and stay for a week or two to make certain I find a good physical therapist there. I'm kind of glad she's taken an interest in me. Glad to have found one of my Spanish cousins. She's told me there are others."

"Really? Large family is it?"

"I guess. When are you leaving?"

"Before dawn tomorrow morning. I'd stay if you needed me."

"You have other clients, Nigel. Thank you for staying as long as you have." He widened the circle a bit, still moving with slow care. "And thank you for the computer. It's been diverting to catch up on email and the news around the world, especially Vienna and the war."

Nigel stood. "Still not interested in writing a blog? On your own website?"

Evan shook his head. When Nigel had first suggested it,

he couldn't imagine having the time to think of something to write and then to write it. He still couldn't. He widened the circle movement a bit more.

Nigel eyed his circling right arm. "Take good care of that shoulder, Evan. When do you take your walks?"

"We still vary the time and route every day. Detective Ruiz insisted on that. Just in case, he said. Neither of us talks about it to anyone, either. Not that I suspect you of anything."

Nigel laughed. "You can suspect me of being over-protective of my star conductor."

"Your star?" Evan didn't buy it. He knew of two other conductors on Nigel's roster who were the real stars, in his opinion. But he'd decided a couple months earlier that he wouldn't think about the other conductors in the world, his competition, but focus on being the best conductor and musician he could be. Uncle Joe would expect nothing less.

Nigel strolled over to the door. "Shall I return for dinner this evening?"

"Yes. I don't know what Alicia has planned, but so far, she's proven to be a fabulous cook."

Nigel chuckled as he left. Evan listened to his footsteps receding down the hall. Alicia had removed the wide strip of hallway carpet, exposing the polished wood underneath, so that footsteps could be heard. He dropped his right arm and shook it out gently. Her room was on the other side of the bathroom and across the hall from his. The front door, the only way in or out of the apartment, boasted three separate lock systems in addition to the usual deadbolt. There was a panic room. Alicia had drilled him twice on what to do if someone nasty managed to gain entrance into the apartment.

Evan returned to the desk and his email. He scrolled down to see who else had written to him—Greta, Freda, Lucia te Kumara, musicians he'd met in Amsterdam—and cleaned out more advertising before returning to Sofia's note.

Dear Evan—I have only just this morning heard that you were shot in Buenos Aires. I called Greta. She had called your landlady who knew only that you had survived.
Are you ok? Will you be able to conduct? When will you return to Vienna? Sofia

His stomach fluttered with pleasure. She had expressed concern about his conducting. She understood what was important to him. At the same time, he realized that *he* needed to call Freda, his landlady, and Greta. But first, he'd write a note to Sofia. He wasn't surprised that she had heard the news of the shooting so much later than everyone else. She had been filming on location in Italy. He imagined that the director and crew would not want the actors distracted by bad news. He clicked "Reply" and typed *Dear Sofia….*

"More stew, Evan?" Alicia held the full ladle over his bowl.

He groaned, satiated. "No, thanks. It was delicious. Where did you learn to cook like that?" Evan gave her ladle-holding hand a gentle push away. "You continue to surprise me with your amazing culinary skills."

She returned the ladle to the soup tureen with a pleased

smirk. "Bernie taught me this dish. I think it is his mother's recipe, perhaps? He is also an excellent cook."

Evan laughed, his mouth wide and his head back. He could imagine Bernie Brown doing a lot of things, but not cooking.

Alicia frowned at him. Today, she wore jeans in light blue denim and a plain light green T-shirt tucked in at the waist that accentuated her lean, buff body, and running shoes without socks on her feet. She'd pulled her thick black hair back into a single braid down her back. She wore no makeup, not even lip gloss. He'd seen her dress this way before when they went out for his walks around the neighborhood. Before they'd leave today, she'd slip on a shoulder holster and a lightweight leather jacket. She was his bodyguard. He grinned at her, but she continued to frown.

"Alicia. Bernie never cooked for me. Our relationship was a lot different. We couldn't be friends. For a long time, I thought he planned to kill me."

Her smile flashed at him. She sat down opposite at the dining table. The apartment's interior décor possessed a late twentieth-century Hollywood vibe in contrast to the old Parisian exterior of the building. Alicia had explored the kitchen and found everything an adventurous cook might want and a double refrigerator well stocked with produce, beef, chicken, and fish. The plates and other dishes resembled the early twentieth-century British dinnerware he'd seen in movies. The dining table and chairs were sleek polished wood but comfortable. They had spent a lot of time sitting at the table, talking and talking over strong coffee.

"Ask him to cook for you. For certain he will." She tore a piece of brown bread in half and bit off a large chunk.

Evan sipped mineral water from a goblet. "He nagged me all the time about investing in a café with him. I wonder if he was planning to be the cook."

Alicia laughed, a full-throated, almost guttural, sound, jarring to hear coming from her feminine features. "Will you invest with him? I can imagine him managing a café in Vienna. Perfect job for him."

"Well, maybe, if he makes it through everything the Austrians and everyone else are putting him through right now. He's smart. A lot smarter than I am."

Alicia gave him a sweet smile. "Bernie is smarter than most people." She stood and began stacking dishes to carry into the kitchen. "Almost time for your walk. Are you ready?"

"I will be." He'd learned to leave her alone when she shifted into what he thought of as managerial mode. Her voice took on a clipped, business-like tone, and she could not be distracted or teased. Best to follow whatever orders or instructions she gave him. He rose from the table, giving his core muscles time to bring him up to a standing position. The surgery had left him with a scar down the center of his abdomen, and his muscles still hurt at times. The physical therapist had taught him that slow and steady gave his muscles the optimal chance for full recovery. He needed that abdominal strength to stand on the podium for hours of rehearsals and concerts.

Today, Alicia wore a light blue linen blazer to hide the 9mm pistol in its holster. She looked him up and down in the unfurnished foyer, nodding at his choice of jeans, T-shirt, and running shoes.

"Your stomach must feel better if you are wearing jeans."

"Yeah, I decided to try them today. If the zipper chafes against the scar, I'll go back to the lightweight yoga pants you bought for me."

They took the elevator down to the lobby, where they greeted the concierge named Carlos. His boss, Ramón, had visited them the day they moved in to review the building's security and show them photos of all the men and women who worked the concierge desk. Alicia had been impressed with his thoroughness. With Alicia guarding him inside the apartment and Ramón's people securing the building, he felt safe and able to focus on his recovery.

Out on the street, however, he felt exposed, vulnerable. Someone had targeted him. He was prey. *Not an unusual feeling for an American*, he thought. Most people in America were prey: hunted by employers looking for cheap, reliable, and skilled labor; hunted by ISS and their street cleaner vans; or hunted by neighborhood Vigiciv gangs to keep them in line with NEP rules and regulations. His father had taught him how to stay ahead of all of them, so he hadn't felt the intensity of the hunt since Harold and his Vigiciv gang had terrorized his neighborhood when he was a kid. His arrest by ISS in Chicago had been an ambush, although he'd known the risk of conducting an opera not yet approved by the Arts Council. Bernie Brown had hunted him last year, although he understood now that Bernie had been protecting him from other Americans who had wanted him dead. In Buenos Aires, though, someone had found him and shot him. He knew whoever it was would try again. And whoever it was, he realized, they must have some connection to the NEP and the people who'd wanted his father's and Uncle Joe's money in England. Nothing else made sense to him as a reason to hunt him.

They walked side by side, Alicia closest to the car traffic. She matched his pace, mindful that he still could not take his normal long strides. He felt his energy returning—he could feel the difference each day—and his legs felt stronger. He slipped on the vintage Minnesota Twins baseball cap that Brian had given him to shade his eyes. Alicia wore dark sunglasses. Behind the black lenses, her eyes darted everywhere, taking in every person, every movement, every car and bicycle and scooter.

"Che, Maestro!" shouted two young Porteños who passed them on bicycles.

"That was fast," he said to Alicia, glancing at his wristwatch. "Within the first ten minutes. We could start betting on when it hits five minutes."

She gave him a rueful smile. "It does not help that the media covered the shooting as well as they did. Your photo was everywhere."

"It's no different from when I was running in the evenings. People were always shouting greetings at me whether they recognized me or not. I got used to it." Yeah, he'd let down his guard because he wasn't in Vienna and he hadn't believed he was in danger here. Now he understood danger waited around every corner.

They continued west in the blazing afternoon sunshine, passing sidewalk cafés and businesses, weaving around people, always vigilant. Perceval checked store window reflections they passed for anyone showing an interest in him or following them, and surveyed the street almost as much as Alicia. At the same time, they presented the picture of a relaxed couple out for an afternoon stroll. He spotted an ice cream shop and pulled Alicia inside. He bought a chocolate sorbet cone for her and a fresh lemon and ginger gelato for himself.

Back on the street, he decided today was as good a time as any. "So, Alicia," he said between gelato licks. "I think today's the day. Let's walk through Plaza Houssay."

Her head jerked up, but she kept her eyes on the street and her sorbet. "You are ready?"

"Good a time as any."

"Nigel mentioned the other day that flowers still cover the place where you fell, and people have left cards and gifts. Get-well cards, is that the correct name in English?"

He nodded. "He told me, too. He asked if I wanted him to gather it all up and bring it to me, but I told him to leave it. At least until I've had a chance to see it for myself."

She nodded, too. "I remember. You ran east on Avenida Cordoba. You were well into the plaza when you were hit. Are you sure you want to go today?"

"Yeah, let's go."

"It will not be too far for you?" She glanced up at him.

"If I get tired, we can cab it back to the apartment."

She slipped her left arm through his right. "Plaza Houssay is busy with many people. They will recognize you."

He'd thought of that. "No one knows I plan to visit today. If people recognize me and want to talk, we'll take it as it comes. You'd prefer to be able to take a circuitous route to check for anyone following us, right?" He glanced down and saw with satisfaction her slight nod as she checked on the traffic from the right at the upcoming intersection. "A Russian friend in Vienna taught me how to use deserted streets to flush out anyone following me."

"A Russian friend?" She sounded surprised.

"A pianist. The Russians watched him all the time."

"Ah. Bueno. Do you know where we are right now?"

A test. She had insisted that he always know his location, always be aware of his surroundings. He felt his throat constrict. She knew him as a musician, a conductor, not as Perceval. How could she? She didn't know about the extensive arms training at the secluded camp in northern Minnesota, his martial arts training, or his father's lessons in surveillance and shadow busting. Vasia had responded to him in the same way, and the Russian had reveled in teaching him how to spot surveillance and elude it.

"We are now walking west on Lavalle, coming up to the Avenida 9 de Julio."

"Bueno. We continue until we pass the Palacio de Justicia. I think perhaps a different approach to Plaza Houssay than what you took that night, OK? We approach from the south, but we will not stay on Lavalle."

"We could, I think."

"Yes, but I want to avoid a straight line."

"Understood."

They crossed Avenida 9 de Julio just north of the famed Obelisco de Buenos Aires and continued on Lavalle past the Plaza Lavalle, the Palacio de Justicia aka the federal courthouse and detention center, and past two blocks of stores and cafés. Early afternoon crowds had thinned. They turned north on Montevideo. After strolling a block, they turned left onto Tucumán, zig-zagging toward the plaza.

Evan thought about the runs he had done before the shooting. He had not paid close attention to which streets he took, only general directions and one or two specific avenues that would take him back to his hotel. Now he paid attention to their route, to the reflections of people and faces in the store windows, and to the traffic on the street. After three blocks, they turned north again for another block to Viamonte, where they passed an art school on their left and the Paraguay Consulate on their right. A large square building loomed over them on the right on Viamonte, and as they strolled past bookstores, hair salons, and what appeared to be a grocery store, Evan realized that he hadn't really seen much of everyday Buenos Aires. He had seen the streets, and the people on the streets, but hadn't paid attention to the buildings. They turned right up Junín, and a block later, past another museum they emerged at the southeast corner of Plaza Houssay.

Evan surveyed the plaza. Alicia glanced around as she said, "Are you OK?"

"A bit tired, but OK." Few people walked in the plaza. Two skateboarders flipped and arced through the air at the plaza's west side. He hadn't seen skateboarders that night, just the men dancing.

"See?" Alicia said, nodding to the building beyond the skateboarders. "The University Hospital is right there."

He nodded. "Where did the shots come from?"

She nodded to the corner opposite the hospital. Two

high-rise buildings occupied that corner. "Half-way up the second building, not the one exactly on the corner. She must not have been able to gain entrance to the first. She stepped out onto the balcony but then must have knelt out of sight. I saw the rifle, and that is when I shouted to you."

"Come on." He led the way up the street. The shooter had been closer than he'd thought. That night, he had not run as far as the mini market stalls, which were halfway up the block toward the bus stop.

They crossed Avenida Cordoba to the southwest corner of the plaza where he finally saw the cordoned-off space. He had fallen a couple yards before a grassy hillock dotted with trees. Alicia took his hand as they approached. He saw within the cordon bouquets of flowers, candles in colored glass containers, signs that he couldn't read except for *Maestro Quinn*, a pile of cards and a couple stuffed animals—a gray wolf and a white horse. On closer inspection, the horse turned out to be a unicorn with a pink mane and tail.

"That sign there," Alicia said, pointing to a light green sign with black letters, "says 'Dear Maestro Quinn, our hearts have broken for your pain. Please recover and bring music back again to us.'"

"That's nice." He bent like an arthritic man to pick up some of the cards. He opened one and found it had been written in English. He read, "'We love you! We want you to have fast recovery and to return to us soon!'" He counted the signatures. "There's, like, twenty-five signatures on this card."

"Maestro Quinn?"

Alicia snapped to attention facing the bearded man with

owlish glasses who had extended his hand toward Evan. His hand held nothing. She relaxed visibly but scrutinized him. He wore cargo shorts, a loose white cotton tunic, and sandals. In his left hand he carried a tote bag full of books.

"Yes." Evan shook the man's hand. "My first visit since that night."

"Maestro, I am so sorry that you have been so terribly hurt in my city. I attended one of your concerts at Teatro Colón. The Caine symphony moved my soul. You knew him?"

Evan nodded. "He was my father's best friend and my mentor in music until his arrest. He's with me when I conduct his music."

"You are recovering well?" The bearded man frowned. "You will conduct again?"

"I will conduct again, yes."

The man's smile flashed his perfect white teeth. "I hope you will return to Buenos Aires and conduct more of Caine's music, Maestro."

"Thank you." Evan watched the man walk away, noticing other people had stopped and were eyeing him. "Alicia, I need to sit down."

She was at his elbow immediately, guiding him to a round metal table with two matching chairs closer to the grassy area under the trees. He sank onto one chair and set the cards on the table.

"I've been identified," he said. "I'll just sit here for a few minutes in the shade and look at the cards."

"Do you want to talk with anyone else?" Alicia smiled at him as if she'd just said something reassuring or comforting.

"Not really." The bearded man's question about Uncle

Joe had hit his mind like a left hook to the jaw. Uncle Joe had been only four years older than he was now when ISS had arrested him and he'd committed suicide in prison. When he thought of Uncle Joe, though—when he *remembered* him—his memory was from his ten-year-old self looking up to a powerful and playful giant with long blond hair.

The remembered image of Uncle Joe's face melted into Vasia's. The resemblance had been eerie. And listening to the Russian play Caine's music had stunned him. Vasia had *sounded* like Uncle Joe playing the piano.

Evan watched Alicia move away from him, make a tight circle around the cordoned-off area, then pick up more cards for him to read. As she cleared the sidewalk of cards, he saw the dark red splotches. His blood. They had not cleaned away his blood. He checked the cards—they were clean. They'd been left after the blood had dried. He stared for a moment at the bloody sidewalk, trying to recall what it had felt like to lie there, but all he recalled were voices yelling in Spanish and the pain.

Two young women who'd been looking at him exchanged comments, and then strolled up the street. As the foot traffic on the street increased, more people noticed him, but they left him alone. He couldn't tell if it was because of Alicia's protective stance nearby or because he focused his attention on the cards. Those written in English conveyed variations of the message in the first card he'd read. With each card, his shoulder muscles tightened more and more. He began to feel sick to his stomach. None of the well-wishers knew what he'd been forced to do in order to be free to pursue his music. They didn't know about Woody Lewis, the NEP's enforcer, or about Harold Smith. Or the real Randall Quinn. Or what the NEP had required of him for his opportunity to leave America and live and make music in freedom. And Vasia, who, for all his talk about always having a choice, had given him no choice. Vasia, who should have been anywhere but home that day.

He felt a pressure on his right shoulder. "Are you OK?" Alicia said. "You have lost your color."

"Let's find a cab," he said, looking around. A small crowd of Porteños had gathered in the plaza nearby, watching him. He was surprised that no one aimed a camera. On impulse, he waved to them. That simple gesture unleashed smiles and waves and shouts in Spanish and English, but he did not listen. Alicia stood next to him with her cell phone, dialing a number. How did she know what number to call? She took two steps to stand in front of him as the restive, shouting crowd surged forward a yard. Speaking into the phone, her rapid staccato Spanish triggered something in his mind and he felt woozy, like his head was underwater. Then he heard the gunshot.

"Alicia!"

She turned to him as she put away her phone. "What is it?"

"Didn't you hear it?"

"Hear what, Evan?"

She hadn't heard it. None of the people in the crowd had hit the ground or sought cover, either.

"I thought…nothing." He shook his head once as if the motion would clear away the wooziness. "I guess I need to get back to the apartment."

"It's hot in the sun," Alicia said. "We did not bring water."

"Water." The sudden thirst startled him. "I am thirsty."

"There. Our cab." Alicia pointed to a black-and-yellow sedan easing up to the curb. "Do you need help?" She stood next to him, holding his elbow as he stood. The wooziness subsided as Evan took deep breaths. They strolled arm-in-arm to the cab, accompanied by the applause of the small crowd in Plaza Houssay.

"You were right about her cooking." Nigel faced Evan in the apartment's foyer. "But your cousin is an enigma."

"No more than anyone else, Nigel." Evan shook his manager's hand. "Safe trip back to London. I promise to turn on my cell phone tomorrow. It's been nice, though, to have it turned off."

"They can be intrusive. I'll let Copenhagen know that you are recovering well and you expect to be able to honor your commitment to them."

"Wild horses couldn't keep me away." Evan laughed at his manager's puzzled expression. "I'll call Freda and Greta, too. I need to let Freda know when we're returning to Vienna."

"You look tired, Evan. Take care of yourself. Alicia mentioned you'd visited Plaza Houssay this afternoon."

"Yeah, that little excursion tired me more than I expected. A reminder that I'm not one hundred percent yet."

Nigel opened the door. "I think you should call that Viennese police commander, also, Evan. It wouldn't hurt to let him know when you'll be returning."

"Klaus Leiner. I hadn't thought of that. Yeah, I guess so."

The door closed, and Nigel was gone. He felt bereft, fragile. He'd felt that way since returning from Plaza Houssay.

"He's gone," Alicia said behind him.

Evan pivoted. "Yeah. He thinks you're an excellent cook."

She laughed. "Thanks to Bernie." She stepped closer, reached out, and took his hand. "Time for sleep, Gordo. You have had a long day with one long walk. I hope that you are OK tomorrow."

He followed her down the long hallway to his bedroom, where she turned down his bed while he began to undress. His right shoulder had stiffened, and he realized that he'd done the physical therapy exercises only once that day. Too tired now to do them, and he had problems lifting his T-shirt up to slip out of it.

"Sit down," Alicia said. "I'll help you."

She pulled the T-shirt up over his head. He caught her looking at his right shoulder.

"Carreras promised me it will fade."

She traced the healing red exit wound with her index finger. "You were lucky."

"With your help."

She met his gaze with a curt nod. "I am surprised I have not heard from Bernie."

"He may not know, Alicia. It's OK, anyway. It could have been a lot worse, and I'm going to be fine."

"Yes, fine." She leaned down and kissed him on the forehead. "Sleep well, Evan."

She left, closing the bedroom door behind her. Evan

sat for a moment, thinking about her. She had been kind, gentle in her care of him, and protective in the extreme. She still had not said much more about her friendship with Bernie Brown. She did not want to disappoint Bernie. He doubted Bernie would have been surprised about someone trying to kill him. As effective as Alicia was as his bodyguard, he missed Bernie and his South Bronx voice. Bernie would understand feeling like hunted prey. He would appreciate the irony of Perceval now in an assassin's crosshairs. If he knew about Perceval. But he didn't. He closed his eyes and conjured the image of Bernie at the Austrian safe house the last time he'd seen him face to face. He felt again the visceral tingling of the realization that Bernie was his friend, maybe the only friend he had who truly understood what his life had been like. Alicia's face replaced that image. He wondered again just what her connection was to Bernie, what would motivate her to drop everything and travel to Buenos Aires to protect him just because Bernie had asked her to do it. She would probably never tell him, and that's assuming that it was unclassified anyway.

He stood, pushing himself up from the bed with his fists, and headed for the bathroom to brush his teeth.

CHAPTER 6

The airport hadn't been menacing when Evan had arrived in Buenos Aires, but the Aeropuerto Ministro Pistarini, better known as Ezeiza after the area of its location, had transformed into a place of endless opportunities for someone to attack him. The threat was not at the efficient rental-car drop-off, or the clean, well-lit departure terminal itself, but among the hundreds of people inside the terminal, arriving, departing, and working. One person. The most low-tech of weapon delivery systems. He knew in his present condition, despite the strength he'd gained in the last eighteen days at the apartment, it wouldn't take much time or effort for someone to knock him off.

Who wanted him dead? The person on the other end of the cell-phone conversation Alicia had overheard the Chilean assassin having near Plaza Houssay, not long after he was shot. Her handler. Chinese? Russian? American? It could be anyone, and that person could as easily be waiting in the Ezeiza departure terminal as in another country. Their travel plans had been available to the media and anyone else who cared to search for them on the internet. Alicia had made certain of that.

She walked next to him, carrying his garment bag, as the airport security guard maneuvered the wheelchair down the hallway to the VIP lounge. Another guard carried the rest of their luggage. He had wanted to arrive at the airport at the last possible moment before boarding, but Alicia had insisted they arrive early. She had contacted airport security and arranged for their assistance. During the last seven days, he and Alicia had planned this trip almost down to the minute. She'd insisted on arriving early, she'd said, in order to increase the security presence around him in the airport. She would not protect him alone. The travel plans she'd put on the internet were not complete, and they could modify them at any time.

She had reminded him that despite his good progress with recovery, he was still weak and vulnerable. Only twenty-three days since the shooting. Dr. Carreras had wanted him to stay in Buenos Aires for another month and only reluctantly approved his travel to Vienna. Evan knew he could not respond physically the way he could have before the shooting.

At least a surveillance-detection run driving through the streets of Buenos Aires had shown that they hadn't been followed when they left the apartment. Alicia's driving, however, had given him vertigo until he'd told her to slow down. She claimed the hydrocodone caused it. The nausea had embarrassed him. He couldn't even keep it together for a surveillance-detection run. He hated feeling this way, powerless to control his body's responses.

The people in the busy airport hallway regarded him with mild curiosity, their eyes noting the wheelchair and the uniformed security guards. He memorized faces. In the eighteen days since his discharge from the hospital, Alicia had taught him everything he already knew about counter-surveillance procedures. Like memorizing faces. He wanted to learn more from her, determine if any more holes remained in the training that had made Woody believe he wouldn't survive his first assignment as Perceval. She knew, from Bernie, that he had some knowledge of martial arts, and she had grilled him about how much, but it was of only marginal use to him in his present physical condition.

He looked down at his right arm cradled in a gray cotton sling. Dr. Carreras had warned him not to push himself too hard or too fast. Healing required time. If he listened to his body, was conscientious about his physical therapy, and took care of himself, he would regain full range of motion for his right arm and shoulder. He might experience achiness at times, especially in high humidity, and the injury carried the eventual risk of arthritis, but Dr. Carreras had assured him that he had many years of normal movement and conducting before that happened. Dr. Carreras had given him a copy of his medical chart that morning, including X-rays and CT scan, hydrocodone and acetaminophen to last him until he saw his doctor in Vienna, and a detailed list of things he could do for his assured recovery: continuing on the restricted diet for another three to four weeks, walking every day and increasing distance slowly, physical therapy for his right shoulder, and seeing a therapist experienced in treating PTSD. He had to make it home to Vienna first. He glanced around at the hallway security—video cameras, guards at regular intervals.

Alicia's head moved only slightly as her eyes took in the stream of people exiting a gate area. He sensed the security guard behind him; checked on the other carrying their luggage to his right. Were they paying attention or not? The crowd of people ballooned in front of him.

He heard a gunshot. He dove forward, his heart racing, expecting the security guard to push him in a fast zig-zag but nothing happened. They continued at a stroll. The guard to the right looked bored. Alicia continued to scrutinize the people coming toward them.

"Señor, are you ill?"

The guard's hand rested on his upper back. He slowly sat up. "No. I thought I heard a gunshot."

Alicia's black eyes met his. "No gunshot, Evan. No unusual sounds. But we are now passing through a crowd like the crowd in Plaza Houssay, yes?"

Yes, he recognized the similarity. Odd how the mind worked, how memory worked. He hadn't told her about the gunshot he'd heard in Plaza Houssay a week ago. He'd had a similar experience during the security alert one night at the Neusiedl am See safe house in Austria, his sense of power-lessness, helplessness. He'd heard gunshots in the kitchen when there were none, echoes of the gunshots at his press conference in Vienna when the Uighur terrorists had tried to kill him.

"You're right, Alicia." He inhaled a big breath to calm his heart rate. "I'm nervous."

"You are safe, señor. The lounge is there to the left." The guard on his right pointed.

The VIP lounge was like every other airport VIP lounge Evan had seen, with its soft, plump chairs and sofas, walls of windows, and refreshment service with snacks and a bar. The earthy browns, greens, and deep blue of the décor reminded him of photos he'd seen of the Argentine pampas. Ten other people, who gave them only a cursory glance when they entered, occupied the lounge this late afternoon. The security guards left them facing the door and took up positions nearby.

Alicia rubbed his upper back. "Relax, Evan. Relax your muscles. I am confident we are secure here. I am more concerned about Charles de Gaulle Airport."

He surveyed the faces of the other people sipping their drinks, engrossed in their conversations. No one familiar. "I'll relax when I know who wants me dead, Alicia, and they're in prison."

"I know." She settled in the plush chair next to his wheelchair. "But right now, you need to focus on this trip. You know the plan."

"Wouldn't it have been easier to put me in a disguise?"

"It would not help you to disappear."

"I think it would help me a lot."

"Evan. We have already had this conversation, yes? Move on. The flight to Paris is long. You will be able to sleep. Rest is important."

"I'm not worried about de Gaulle."

It amazed him how often she was right. At least she made it palatable by being so matter-of-fact. To simply disappear from Buenos Aires might have alerted his adversary that he had help or expertise an orchestra conductor was unlikely to have. A disguise would reveal his fear, Alicia had explained, while no disguise showed courage and innocence. He had nothing to hide. The media had done an excellent job of portraying him as an innocent victim of a heinous attack, as yet unsolved by the Buenos Aires police, that appeared to be domestic, not international, because no terrorist group had claimed responsibility. The shooter that Alicia had terminated also remained a mystery to them and an unidentified murder victim to the police. Alicia had alerted her contacts in the international spy community, but none had any information. He had no reason to believe that Perceval had been compromised, but he couldn't rule it out. As far as Alicia and the rest of the world were concerned, he was an orchestra conductor, an American, son of a famous writer. A victim.

He wasn't worried about Charles de Gaulle Airport because they would be there only an hour while they changed planes at the same terminal. He was more worried about Air France losing their luggage and arriving in Vienna without his music scores. He'd brought only two to study on the plane, the Barber Piano Concerto and the Bartók Concerto for Orchestra.

His eyes rested on Alicia. She wasn't like Sofia at all, and yet, she was beautiful. Sofia's soft curves contrasted with Alicia's angular lines and hard muscle. For the last two weeks, Alicia had been his constant companion, and he'd found her company soothing and interesting. Her sharp intelligence challenged him in a competitive way he enjoyed. She dressed with simple elegance, whether in jeans and a blouse as today or a flowing feminine dress to show off her angles and curves, with few but quality accessories—diamond stud earrings, for example, or a gold chain necklace—and smelled spicy and musky at the same time. Her black eyes were piercing but expressive. Not more than five feet, four inches tall, she could match someone twice her size in strength and agility. He had no doubt about it.

The most surprising thing about Alicia, however, had been her attentive kindness. They had started as strangers, and she had become his concerned cousin, taking care of all the details a family member would tackle. He had come to rely on her more than he liked. To trust her.

Alicia squeezed his left forearm and stood. She walked over to the check-in counter to confirm their boarding passes and check their luggage. None of the other people in the lounge paid any attention to her. Or him. The security guards strolled at a crab's pace around the room.

He felt sleepy. He glanced at his watch. Their flight to Paris was scheduled to leave in about thirty minutes. They would board soon. He closed his eyes, hummed low to himself the opening theme of Beethoven's Sixth Symphony to breathe with the music and calm his heart. Nigel had called the day before. Helsinki had requested all-symphony programs of his choosing, suggesting Caine (of course) or Bruckner, Beethoven, or Tchaikovsky. He'd decided to create an opportunity for himself and requested a mini-Brahms festival: all four symphonies over two weeks. He knew the First Symphony already, so Helsinki would challenge him to learn the other three before autumn. These programs would also provide a break from conducting Joseph Caine's music. Everyone wanted him to conduct Caine.

"Evan?" Alicia touched his left arm.

He opened his eyes. "Are we checked in?"

She nodded, waved the security guards over. "They want us to board now."

His heart raced as his feet pounded the pavement. The night sky glowed orange from the city's fluorescence. Footsteps ran behind him, but no one was there. He glanced around, expecting a street cleaner van to appear. Empty street. The earth cracked under his feet with a gunshot.

He was awake and asleep at the same time, pain searing through every inch of his body, lying on his back and moving fast into a white and chrome room filled with medical equipment and Spanish voices. He heard himself say, "Speak English." Hands lifted him onto a table. He heard the rip of cloth, smelled the sharp tang of disinfectant. One hand remained on his arm, squeezed it.

"Are you awake?"

He opened his eyes. Sweat skittered down under his arms and wet his face. Alicia peered at him in the semi-darkness of the plane's cabin. Her hand squeezed his left arm.

"You were twitching. Are you in pain?"

Yes, pain. His right shoulder. "Do you have the hydrocodone?" Pain also in his abdomen but not as intense as in the shoulder. He needed to move, to do his physical therapy exercises.

"I will get you water."

Alicia left her seat. He stretched out his legs, listening to the pulse beat in his ear. His heart rate went up when the pain increased, when the hydrocodone wore off. He sat forward, shifted his right arm. Pain. He needed to move it despite the pain. Dr. Carreras had warned him to move it a little every few hours, slow, with care. He slipped the arm out of the sling and straightened it, let it drop down, its weight pulled a little on the shoulder muscles. He looked around.

Sleeping faces in first class. He made a tiny circle with his hanging arm.

Alicia returned with a bottle of water. "We will arrive in Paris in two hours. You slept well?"

Another tiny circle. "The plan for de Gaulle. No security?"

She opened the hydrocodone bottle, shook one of the white pills into her palm. "No security arranged. Guards will be at the gate, of course. I have already reminded the flight attendant that you can walk off the plane but we would like a wheelchair waiting at the gate."

"Good." He took the pill and swallowed it with a gulp of water. He was thirsty. "Would it be possible to get another bottle of water?"

Alicia raised the window shade. Sunlight burst in. "I'll get it. If there is media at de Gaulle?" she said in a low voice, glancing at the other passengers around them.

"You think they'll be there?" he said, matching her volume. Another circle of his hanging arm, a bit larger.

"Possible."

"No time to talk to the media. If they follow, I say I have a tight connection and if they want an interview to contact Nigel."

She frowned. "I need to review the people again. Freda Kirsch is your landlady and she works as a teacher."

"Correct." Evan swigged more water. "Greta Fasching, who is about seven months pregnant, is a good friend. She was Vasia Bartyakov's girlfriend."

"Bartyakov. The Russian pianist everyone thought had

been involved in Jiang Xu's assassination and who was killed also that day."

"Inspector Klaus Leiner of the Viennese police. He told me months ago that they had eliminated Vasia as a suspect. Vasia was a victim like the Chinese vice chairman. The assassin used his apartment. Inspector Leiner still suspects I'm a spy, I think, despite Bernie confirming that I'm not." He swung his hanging arm back and forth about six inches.

"You are not a spy. You are an orchestra conductor. Owen te Kumara? Leader in which orchestra?"

"Composer from New Zealand. I just conducted his English Horn Concerto in Buenos Aires. He's married to Lucia, a pianist. They have an eighteen-month-old daughter, Chiara. Robert Waldstein is the leader in the Vienna Philharmonic and a friend."

She shook her head. "It's easier for me when I see the faces, you know? I remember faces. I'll get you a bottle of orange juice also." She stood. "You need a haircut."

He looked up at her, startled. First time she'd made a comment on his appearance that had nothing to do with his medical condition. "Nigel agrees with you. I like to grow it long."

"But it appears not styled."

"It isn't styled, Alicia. Nigel reminded me that I have the time to get it trimmed now." He sighed. "I'd prefer to be so busy I didn't have the time."

"I am certain you will be so busy again." She moved down the aisle toward the flight attendant's station.

He hadn't told her about Sofia Karalis. Sofia was in Italy, working on a movie, and wasn't expected in Vienna until close to Greta's due date in mid-April. In his mind, he expected Alicia would leave long before then.

And Woody Lewis. He needed to talk to Woody as soon as possible after he arrived back in Vienna. Woody had a network of contacts, too, and maybe he'd heard something about who'd shot him in Buenos Aires. He'd need to talk to Woody alone.

As they emerged from the gangway in the 2D terminal of Charles de Gaulle Airport in the late morning, the last to leave the plane, a blizzard of camera flashes greeted them. The media. Alicia carried their bags as she held his left arm to steady him. No wheelchair waited at the gate.

"Maestro Quinn! Maestro Quinn!"

"How are you feeling, Maestro?"

"Are you staying in Paris for a few days?"

"When will you be able to conduct, Maestro?"

"Do you know who shot you?"

The media pressed in on them as they made their way forward. Alicia waved for help to a security guard standing beyond the check-in counters.

"What have the Buenos Aires police told you?"

"What are your plans, Maestro?"

"What is your prognosis, Maestro?"

The vultures. How had they circumvented security to wait at the gate for him? They surrounded him and Alicia, prevented them from moving. He lifted his left arm. "I have one statement," he shouted above their voices.

The security guard by the counter spoke into his radio.

"Shut up!" a man yelled in French.

The reporters crowded in on him. Sweat beaded on his face, and he began to feel nauseous and lightheaded. He tried to distinguish faces, but saw only flesh-colored blobs. Alicia slipped her arm around his waist. He felt her strength, her steady support against his body. He took a slow deep breath and the nausea subsided. He said to the reporters, "I have just one thing to say. I'm tired but I'm on the mend. I have a tight connection, and I must make my next flight. I don't have time to talk to you now. If you want to request an interview after I'm home and feeling better, please contact my manager, Nigel Fox, in London. Now, please move away so we can leave."

Two grinning male reporters moved backward in front of him as he heard cameras clicking. He blinked at more flashes. Alicia propelled him forward. The security guard waited beyond the media group. He talked on his radio.

The media pressed in too close, too close. Evan looked down at Alicia. Her eyes scrutinized everyone. A hand grabbed his right elbow. Evan turned his head to see a short red-headed man trying to lift his arm out of the sling.

"Alicia."

He didn't wait for her to react. Using Alicia's arm to steady himself, he pivoted on his right foot, swung his bent left leg up and kicked Redhead square in the sternum. When he dropped his left leg, he wobbled and Alicia steadied him. Redhead fell back, accompanied by gasps from the other reporters.

"Do not touch me!"

A silent field of wide, alarmed eyes opened before him.

A woman helped Redhead to his feet. Two security guards joined the one waiting in the hallway, and they began herding the journalists away from Evan and Alicia. Trailed by a security guard, they skirted the herd and headed to the gate for the flight to Vienna.

Evan trembled. "The Uighur terrorists who tried to kill me disguised themselves as Russian reporters."

"Ah. I did not know that." Alicia slipped her arm around his waist again. "Are you OK, Gordo?"

"I bet that'll be in all the media tomorrow. 'Evan Quinn, American conductor, kicks reporter.'"

"Of course. Put your own spin on it, yes? The man had no right to touch your arm, and your kick to his chest showed that you are recovering well." She smiled up at him. "What was this red-haired journalist trying to do?"

"Pull my arm out of the sling. Weird. He didn't say a word."

"It was a good kick."

"Thanks."

No VIP lounge at the gate for the Austrian Airlines flight to Vienna. They checked in. The boarding lounge was not a restricted area. They found two seats together not far from the gangway door. His abdomen screamed in pain. The kick and the walk to the gate had not been good for his healing muscles. He couldn't take another hydrocodone yet.

"Are you memorizing faces?" Alicia said low next to him.

He nodded and surveyed the lounge which was almost full.

"Man standing near the restrooms. He's wearing a brown leather coat and yellow scarf. See him?"

Evan recognized the man. He'd been on their flight from Buenos Aires in the coach section. The man's attention rested on a young family sitting nearby. He was alone. "Yeah. He was on our flight."

"Good. Anyone else?"

"What about Wien-Schwechat?"

"Security expects us."

"The woman by the window. The one who's alone and smoking a cigarette."

"Very good."

A pulsing alarm that sounded like a buzzing fog horn accompanied sirens outside the windows.

"Everyone! Away from the windows!" an Austrian Airlines attendant said in German. Voices rose in volume and intensity as the people moved to collect luggage and children.

"Air raid." Alicia stood.

Evan looked out the windows spanning the wall, the view of their plane at the gate, the baggage handlers abandoning carts of luggage on the tarmac to take cover, the clear blue sky.

"We need to follow their instructions for shelter."

He frowned. "No. We go into the restroom. No windows in there."

They waited until everyone in the lounge headed out, following the instructions of airline personnel, and slipped into the gleaming women's restroom. Leaning against the sage-green tiled wall next to a chair and counter at the end of the line of three sage-green stalls was the man in the brown leather coat and yellow scarf.

"Bonjour," he said with a friendly smile.

"Bonjour," Alicia replied.

"Please allow me to introduce myself," the man said in English. "As long as we have sought same shelter."

Evan's memory flashed on a smiling Vasia, his voice, talking about the Caine Piano Concerto. The man's accent was Russian. He knew to speak English because he knew who Evan was. Evan tensed.

"Alicia."

She had already stepped in front of him, broadening the Russian's grin. Standing hurt his abdominal muscles. He needed to sit down but the Russian had already started forward, extending his right hand.

"My name is Gregori. I work for SVR. We have interest in person who try to kill you in Buenos Aires, Maestro."

The Chinese had nuked Moscow into oblivion last August. The Russian president had survived at his vacation dacha on the Black Sea, but had the Foreign Intelligence Agency survived? He placed his left hand on Alicia's left shoulder and squeezed. He smiled at Gregori.

"The SVR. Why are they interested? You know who it was?"

Neither of them had shaken his hand. Gregori let his hand drop but continued smiling. "We know person who try to kill you was woman from Chile. She may be involved in attack on Russian ambassador in Mumbai last month. We follow her from Mumbai to Caracas to Buenos Aires."

They all turned their heads toward the thud of bombs in the distance. They had returned to the war zone. He'd thought the Chinese had left France alone, that it was a reasonably safe place on a continent fighting for its life, but apparently not.

Evan focused on Gregori. "Is she following me?"

Gregori shrugged the Russian shrug Vasia had used when he knew the answer but wanted no one to know he knew. A definite gesture of interest when taken with Gregori's intense smile and eyes. "We believe that something happen to her in Buenos Aires. Maybe she dead." Gregori's dark brown eyes rested on Alicia.

"This is my cousin, Alicia," Evan said, removing his hand from her shoulder. "I need to sit down."

Bombs thudded closer as he shuffled to the chair near Gregori. The Russian stepped away to the sinks, where he was reflected in the wall mirror above them. Evan observed him in his peripheral vision. The Russian's eyes never left him.

"So, Gregori, have you shared your knowledge with the Buenos Aires police?"

Alicia set their bags next to the chair and took a bottle of water from one of them.

"They not interested because they not believe me. With situation in Russia now...." He shrugged, palms up. "But I work for my country, not Chinese. This woman assassin not terrorist. Who she work for? You see her?"

Evan shook his head and accepted the water from Alicia, who fussed over him, rubbing his shoulders. He had the feeling, an intuitive flutter in his stomach, that Gregori was not who he said he was. Gregori knew more than he was sharing. "I saw nothing. One moment I'm running, the next I'm flat on my back, shot twice. Sorry I can't help you, Gregori. You think she was alone?"

"Like rogue or anarchist? Possible."

A pulsing alarm sounded the all-clear. Alicia sighed. He capped the water bottle after a long drink. "So, are *you* following me, Gregori?"

The Russian grinned. "Good question. You have no security. So." He shrugged. "I travel to Vienna, too. Maybe I can help, if you want."

As the Russian talked, Evan memorized his thin and fine blond hair parted on the left and trimmed above his ears, the high forehead, pointed nose, wide mouth with narrow lips, piercing dark brown eyes, the small chin. He stood about six feet tall. The brown leather coat hid his body, but Evan guessed he was lean and tough. He had broad, rough hands. If Gregori had gone to the Buenos Aires police and Detective Ruiz had not believed him, Evan couldn't believe him, either. Not about the woman assassin, but about his affiliation with the SVR, about him being a friendly, helpful presence.

Evan rose to his feet with Alicia's support on his left. "Thanks, Gregori. Alicia and I feel safe, but it's nice to know you're watching out for us." He looked at Alicia. "We should probably find out when they'll begin boarding. It didn't sound like the bombs fell that close to the airport."

"Good idea." Gregori strode to the restroom door and held it open for them.

As they passed the Russian, Evan said, "How'd you know we'd come in here?"

Gregori shrugged. "I not know. I come in here because it safe. But I am glad we have our talk."

"Good luck to you." Evan nodded to him as Alicia pushed him gently out of the restroom.

They crossed the boarding lounge to seats behind the check-in counter. Austrian Airlines attendants mingled among the passengers returning to the lounge. He heard one say the boarding process would begin in a few minutes.

"What'd you think of Gregori's accent, Alicia?" He spied the Russian standing alone near the gangway entrance.

She shook her head. "Sounded fake to me."

"Is there a later flight we could take?"

She smiled up at him. "You look tired. And in pain. I will consult with the airline."

As she stood, the boarding announcement came over the public address system. An Austrian Airlines clerk began collecting boarding passes at the gangway's entrance. Alicia stopped one of the mingling attendants. Evan watched Gregori surrender his boarding pass and disappear into the gangway. The Russian would arrive in Vienna before them, but would not know when or how they traveled. He knew he needed to trust his gut, and his gut told him that Gregori was trouble. Evan had no desire to learn what kind of trouble.

"Evan, they will move us to a VIP lounge where you can lie down and rest. I will call Vienna." Alicia collected their carry-on luggage, and he followed her to a waiting wheelchair beyond the check-in counter.

Home. On approach to Wien-Schwechat, he could see bomb damage west and south of the city, but the Chinese had spared the airport—perhaps in appreciation for Vienna hosting the Chinese-American talks last year and the Austrians' protection of the Chinese delegation after the vice chairman's assassination. The Austrians had been open with the Chinese during their investigation, even inviting Chinese investigators to join them. On the city's east side, Evan spotted the batteries of anti-aircraft weapons the Austrians had bought from the Americans, who had been a major supplier of weapons to the European Union and Pacific Alliance. The Americans profited in a massive way from this war.

As in Paris, he and Alicia were the last to deplane. To his surprise, a familiar blond man with a dark blond mustache waited with a wheelchair in the gate area. He also recognized the dark-haired cop dressed in jeans and heavy black wool jacket behind him.

"Inspector Leiner. I didn't expect to see you here," he said. "Or Marco. How's Johann?"

The dark-haired cop grinned. "He's fine. He asked me to tell you that if you need anything, to call."

Alicia helped him sit in the wheelchair. He raised his hand to shake Leiner's. "How's your family, Inspector? Laura?"

"All well, Herr Quinn. Laura was quite distressed about the attempt on your life in Buenos Aires. And who is this?" Leiner smiled at Alicia.

"My cousin, Alicia Caliente. Alicia, may I introduce Inspector Klaus Leiner of the Viennese police. And Sergeant Marco."

"A pleasure, Inspector. Sergeant."

He watched them shake hands. Leiner's demeanor was downright courtly, without any hint of his toughness or penetrating intellect. A slight bulge under the left arm of his black wool coat reassured Evan.

Alicia smiled. "I spoke with the chief of airport security. He called you, Inspector?"

"Yes, Herr Reichel called me. I had alerted my contacts that I wanted to be involved with Herr Quinn's security. You have checked luggage?"

Leiner pivoted the wheelchair, and Evan chuckled. "This isn't a Porsche, Inspector."

"I am quite happy to see your sense of humor is intact. How are you feeling?"

"Tired, weak, safer now I'm home." He felt secure with Leiner and Marco. They would ensure that airport security remained alert. He spotted two airport security guards with radios ahead. "I'm glad to see you. Any chance I could interest you in finding out who tried to kill me?"

Marco, walking next to him with their carry-on bags, glanced back at Leiner pushing the wheelchair. Leiner sighed. Evan didn't look back at him.

Alicia said, "Detective Ruiz with the Buenos Aires police told us that he is certain it was not a terrorist. And before we left, he had concluded that it may have been a random crime. But we disagree." She hefted his garment bag up and draped it over one arm.

"I was thinking, Inspector, that you and Dieter could check in with all the sources you used when you were investigating me before and maybe they might have heard something."

The wheelchair stopped. Evan twisted around. Leiner's gray eyes had darkened to slate. The Austrian cop looked straight ahead. Evan glanced up at Marco, who shrugged.

"I doubt, Herr Quinn, that the ministry would approve

an investigation of a crime that occurred outside of our juris-diction. I'm sure the Buenos Aires police performed their investigation with the utmost care and attention. We can recommend security procedures, if you would like. Earlier today, I also sent Johann to secure your apartment and Frau Kirsch's house."

He was surprised. He'd expected Leiner to jump at the opportunity to continue an investigation of him. Bernie had succeeded after all in convincing the Austrian cop that he was only an innocent orchestra conductor. They continued in silence to the baggage claim, where a handful of people from their flight still waited at the revolving carousel. No sign of Gregori. Alicia headed for the luggage-claim office to find their checked luggage, that had arrived on the earlier flight from Paris.

"Inspector, someone has targeted me. Maybe not a ter-rorist, but someone. Detective Ruiz told me it was a *profes-sional* hit. How do I find out who and stop them?"

Leiner squatted next to him and spoke in a matter-of-fact voice. "You may not be able to find out, Herr Quinn. What makes you believe that the attempt in Buenos Aires was not an isolated incident? A random crime, as the Buenos Aires police believe?"

He met Leiner's eyes. "I don't know for certain, Inspector. But the *professional* about it makes me suspicious. The prob-lem was no evidence. Only the bullet they took out of my abdomen, which told them little. Alicia's very concerned. She wants me to hire bodyguards or something. I don't want to live my life like that."

"When can you return to work?"

"Another month, I think. It'll depend on how the physical therapy goes, I guess."

Leiner stood again. "I will ask for an intelligence report on you, Herr Quinn. I think Dieter would agree. We will find out what the electronic chatter is about you."

CHAPTER 7

"Evan, I am so happy and so very relieved to see you."

He embraced Greta Fasching with his left arm, allowing himself to sink into her warmth and her scent of roses, and with this embrace he silently vowed once again to Vasia that he would always be there for this woman and their child. When she stepped back, he caressed her satiny dark cheek, smiled into her ebony eyes, and placed his left hand on her pregnant stomach. "You've grown since I saw you last. Here, come sit down. Tea?"

She smiled as she lowered herself onto the chair he held out for her, next to his own at Freda Kirsch's sitting room table. He, Alicia, and Freda had just finished their midday meal. Greta's statuesque body slumped as she rubbed her stomach.

"No, thank you. I think Lucia will have tea waiting for us."

Freda sat down next to Alicia as she said, "I could wrap some cake to take with you."

Greta gave Freda a grateful smile as she shook her head. "Your home is sehr gemütlich, Freda."

"Greta, I think this is the first time you've met my cousin, Alicia Caliente." Alicia extended a hand to her. "I didn't know I had any family left, so getting shot actually gave me something good." Alicia blushed. He hadn't seen her blush before, and the deepening color of her complexion pleased him.

"A close or distant cousin?" Greta said. "Evan, I had not known you have Spanish blood."

"My great-grandmother on my mother's side was born in Madrid."

"You are from Africa?" Alicia said, smiling at Greta.

"I'm Austrian. My mother was Somali. She emigrated with her parents to Austria when she was a young girl to escape civil war. I'm glad Evan has a cousin. We have been so concerned about him because he has no other family now. Will you stay long with him?"

"I must return to Madrid on Sunday." She squeezed Freda's hand on the table. "I am enjoying so much my visit. It will be hard to leave, but now I see Evan will be in good hands."

"You must return to visit us," Freda said, brushing her feathery blond hair back from her face.

Evan eyed the three smiling women with the odd sensation that they had, in that moment, joined together in a silent conspiracy concerning his care and his life. "Greta, when does Lucia expect us?"

Greta checked her watch. "We should leave now." She rose in one smooth, graceful movement, as if the baby weight she carried was not there. "Oh, Freda. I saw a boy across the street when I parked. He looked like one of those street kids, you know, the orphan kids who have made gangs to roam the streets and steal. Have you seen him?"

"No, this neighborhood hasn't had a problem with them.

They congregate in the First District." Freda stood to escort them out.

Alicia gave him a smile and a nod as she followed them. She had told him the night before, after the arrangements had been made for him to visit the te Kumaras today, that she would use the time to check on a safe house in Vienna used by Spanish spies. (She preferred "operatives" to spies, saying it was a job like any other and should not be sensationalized in any way, but he preferred "spies.") When everyone believed she had left for Madrid, she would in fact have moved to the safe house. She had decided that living away from him, away from the charade of being his relative, would give her more freedom to observe the people around him, identify anything unusual, and find out who wanted him dead. He had disagreed. He wanted her close. She had refused to negotiate. He had the feeling that she might be setting him up as bait in order to catch whoever wanted him dead. That's probably what Perceval would do.

He and Greta left by Freda's stately front door, Greta holding his left arm, his right arm in its gray cotton sling. Freda and Alicia followed them. No young boy stood across the street beyond Freda's tall hedge of winter-bare branches. Evan thought it inevitable that these war orphans should eventually ferret out the wealthier neighborhoods in the city.

"He's not there," Greta said, passing through the black wrought iron gate as tall as Evan.

"I'll watch for him, Greta. What did he look like?" Freda frowned.

Greta unlocked her lime-green Geister, the car that reminded him of a bug-eyed blowfish, with the press of her ignition-stick button. "About ten years old, dirty, shaggy brown hair, blue eyes, ragged clothes, and a black wool jacket. He looked better fed than some I've seen. I worry about these children in the winter weather. The government needs to do more. These children should be in shelters."

After two days of overcast skies and snow showers, the weather had turned clear and cold. About an inch of snow blanketed the neighborhood and towering trees, especially the evergreens. Evan thought about checking the sidewalk for footprints where the boy had been, but it would take time and he needed to conserve his energy. The level of pain during the day had decreased but had not subsided completely. Physical exertion aggravated his abdominal injury.

Greta drove as fast as Alicia. At least she made smooth turns.

"Have you begun the physical therapy sessions, Evan?"

"Yesterday. My first."

"Who is the physical therapist?"

"Otto Glasmann. Please slow down, Greta."

Greta braked with gentle pulses. "Your stomach?"

"Mostly the painkiller I'm on. I need to wean myself off the powerful stuff. But I'm still on it today. Going fast makes me dizzy."

"You have a check-up with your doctor?"

Her tone reminded him of a mother questioning a child. He smiled. She'd be an actual mother soon enough. He could indulge her practice. She made motherhood elegant.

"I'll be very busy the next five weeks, between physical therapy three times a week, doctor appointments, walking every day, eating and sleeping. I don't know when I'll be able to work."

Greta snorted as she executed a gliding right turn. "Your job now is to work on healing."

"Is Owen composing?" he said.

Greta, her eyes straight ahead, shook her head. "The depression has only worsened, Evan. He has taken Vasia's death into his heart, and it is poisoning him. Not even little Chiara cheers him. Lucia has cut back her work schedule to care for him. You know she had been teaching privately until the school reopened last month? They have money saved, of course, but the war has made it difficult for them to earn a living."

The last time he'd seen the Māori composer had been at New Year's. He was still composing, although he'd lost weight and showed no interest in food or his students or even the war. Owen's smile, usually broad and brilliant white in contrast to his walnut skin, had not even turned up the corners of his mouth.

"And then that mad *someone* in Buenos Aires shot you. Lucia tried to shield Owen from the news, but a Vienna Philharmonic musician called and told him. I talked to him the day after. His voice sounded hollow and distant. Lucia said it had taken her hours to convince him that you'd truly survived."

He had not known Owen to be so sensitive, and yet, his music revealed an ocean of emotion the composer did not otherwise express. He had always been affable and energetic with Evan, eager to talk about anything, scrupulously honest, loyal, crazy about his wife and daughter, physically healthy, with an adventurous appetite for food, drink, and the world. He'd considered Owen to be normal, rational, a rock of friendship.

Greta sighed. She turned south onto the wide, traffic-laden Gürtel Boulevard. They passed an area where the rubble of bombed buildings was being collected by huge scoops and dropped into large trucks. "He has not left his bed for a week. He has no appetite, but Lucia has gotten him to eat soup and bread. She said the anxiety attacks are more often."

"Has she called a doctor to examine him?" Anger simmered behind the concern in his voice. What right did Owen have to behave this way about Vasia's death when the rest of them had to go on and couldn't afford the luxury of a withdrawal from life? "I mean, there are drugs that can help, aren't there?"

"I don't know if she's called a doctor or a psychiatrist. Lucia needs our help, Evan, our support. Could you suggest a doctor?"

Why would he know a doctor? Did Greta believe, like Klaus Leiner, that most Americans had psychological problems, so he must also? Dr. Carreras had warned him about post-traumatic stress symptoms, much like the hallucinations and nightmares and depersonalized sensations he had experienced last summer, but he was not crazy. He remembered the business card Leiner had given him last summer and meeting the psychotherapist at Vasia's housewarming party. He felt certain that if Sofia were here, she'd suggest the same thing. "I met a psychologist at Vasia's housewarming, someone Sofia knows."

Greta slapped the steering wheel. "I had forgotten! Yes, Lothar Waage."

"I think Sofia would suggest him."

"I agree. I will look him up on the internet while you talk to Owen."

He had expected to see some life in Owen when he walked into the bedroom in their Lindengasse apartment, not a shadow of the man in the bed. The blue drapes had been drawn across all the casement windows, creating night in the room. Lucia closed the door behind him. He could hear little Chiara's sweet soprano voice in the next room. He yanked open the drapes at one of the windows.

"No. No light," Owen's feeble voice said from the wide bed.

"I want to see you, Owen," Evan said, his voice cold. "I want to see for myself if what Lucia and Greta have told me is true."

One hand shaded Owen's tea-brown eyes as he looked up at Evan. The hand appeared skeletal, the skin a dull brown tinged gray. Owen lay curled on his left side facing the windows, his body a question mark under the light comforter. His emaciation shocked Evan.

"Why aren't you composing, Owen?"

He closed his eyes and turned his face into the pillow.

"What are you doing? Do you think Vasia would be pleased? He commissioned a piano sonata from you. Have you finished it?"

Owen whimpered. He spoke, but the words went into the pillow.

"Talk to *me*, Owen. I'm not leaving until I get some answers from you. The rest of us have to go on with our lives, go on working, go on dealing with the war. Do you think it's easy for us? I'd love to just give up."

"No, you can't." The words were clear though the voice was weak.

"Neither can you."

"What's the point?"

"Who do you think you are, Owen? What makes you so special that you get to give up and not us?"

Owen's voice trembled around the flat vowels of his New Zealand accent. "Someone shot Vasia. He's gone. Forever. I'll never hear him play the piano again, never hear his voice describe his latest wild scheme, never feel that incredibly powerful and warm hug he gave, never hear his laugh. Vasia made me feel alive. I don't know how Greta stands it. Vasia did nothing to deserve to be murdered. He was a pianist and a true friend. Then someone sh-sh-sh-shot *you*, almost killed *you*, and now you have to wear a sling. Will you ever conduct again? What could you possibly have done to deserve to be shot? Nothing. Nothing. It's not safe. Such a terrible world cannot deserve music."

As he listened, Evan heard in his mind the whisper of the toccata of Bach's Sixth Partita, saw Vasia's blond head bent over the keyboard, felt Vasia's punches to his body, heard the silencer *whoof* from the CZ 9mm he'd stuck in Vasia's mouth. He felt sick to his stomach as he pushed a chair over to the bed and sat facing Owen, close enough to touch his shoulder. Owen's face dug into the pillow.

"I'll conduct again. I'm not going to let them win. Are you? Are you going to abandon me?" Evan punched the mattress with his left fist next to Owen's body, making the man jump and look at him. "You have no right. Think about what Vasia would want, Owen. Think. Wouldn't he want you to finish the sonata, put it out there in the world for other pianists to play and for people to hear? Isn't that what Vasia wanted for your music, for all music?"

Tears welled in Owen's eyes. "It's shit, man. No one wants to play my music now."

"Now, *that's* shit. I conducted your English Horn Concerto in Buenos Aires, and the audience went crazy for it. The applause was deafening. And Brian Thaw, the soloist, asked me if you'd written more for his instrument. I'd be happy to conduct your music any time. And I'm expecting you to make sure I have plenty of it to keep me busy. I really thought you were more of a fighter than this."

"It's too hard." The tears dribbled down his face and into the pillow.

Evan stood, yanked the comforter off. Owen, clad in pastel-yellow pajamas, shivered in the open air. "What's too hard? Come on, Owen. You're getting up. If I have to get up every day, so do you."

Owen swatted at his grasping left hand. "Leave me alone. Nothing's safe anymore."

"What was safe before?" Evan's voice caught in his throat. He rested his left hand on his hip, holding his breath against the sudden pain, against the tears. Nothing was safe before, nothing was safe now. Danger permeated the world, the world that had been given to them. Uncle Joe had believed that music could change the world, bring people closer, forge emotional connections and understanding, create peace in the hearts and minds of all people. He had written his music from the depths of that belief. Music had been his weapon and his gift.

"You don't understand, Evan."

The plaintiveness of Owen's voice, the accusation, reignited his anger. "How can you say that to me? How can you lie there in that bed and whine to me about it being hard and unsafe, that"—he parodied the composer's whiny tone—"*no one understands.*" He grabbed Owen by the shoulder, surprised at how light and bony it was, and pulled him upright, resisting the urge to slap the composer across the face. "Remember where I grew up? Remember Joseph Caine? Do you think he sat around whining about how bad it was, how no one understood? *He wrote music.* He spoke and sang and protested and cajoled and poured out his heart and soul in his music because he believed music could change the world. What do you believe, Owen? The world needs your music. The world needs your voice. Lucia needs her husband. Chiara needs her father. *I* need my friend." Evan shook him once. Owen's wide eyes were locked on his. "So, here's the deal. You finish Vasia's piano sonata for us—for Greta, Sofia, Lucia, and me. And then I *dare* you to write music as big as Vasia's personality for the world. Let the world know him in your music. And when you finish it, I'll conduct it."

Owen's hand grasped his on his shoulder, but the composer said nothing, only stared.

"Prima. You don't have to give me an answer today, but I expect an answer from you, and I don't mean lying around in bed, whining and doing nothing." Leiner's voice echoed in his inner ear when he spoke the cop's favorite word, *prima*, the Viennese dialect equivalent of "fine." Leiner had not forced him to talk to Lothar Waage. He wouldn't force Owen, either. "Now, come on. Put a robe on and have some tea with us. Greta is here. When was the last time you saw her? She's grown. The kid's probably going to be built like a wrestler. Like Vasia. Let's hope it's not a girl."

The hint of a smile twitched across Owen's mouth. A beginning.

Evan told himself that the hydrocodone he was taking made him emotional. He'd almost cried seeing Owen like that, and it took almost two days for him to regain his energy. Evan was exhausted. Freda had wanted him to stay with her, in one of her guest rooms next to Alicia, but he'd preferred his own apartment above her garage, where he could be alone in silence, and study scores at his four-foot black Bösendorfer grand piano that Vasia had helped him pick out. He moved between the black leather wing-back chair by the back windows in his living room, where he read through scores on a black music stand, to the piano by the front windows. He had gotten out his violin his first day home, but had only plucked the strings, unable yet to control the bow. Freda had insisted on cooking his main midday meals for a while, and he enjoyed the break from work. He loved her delicious cooking, and she'd been creative with making do with what she could buy because of the shortages. Alicia walked with him after each meal, each day a little farther up Sternwartestrasse and back.

On Sunday, they walked after breakfast in the bracing

cold air. Snow had fallen again the night before, leaving an inch of fluffy white that the wind swirled in funnels up from the ground.

"A beautiful name, Lucia. Was it good news when she called?" Alicia, bundled up in a forest-green loden coat, black knitted scarf, and matching hat, squeezed his left arm against her side, her arm curled around it. The height of the heels on her black leather boots brought the top of her head almost to his shoulder.

"Owen's eating more, but he's weak. She made an appointment for him to see a doctor next week, and another appointment to see a psychologist. The best news was that he'd spent some time at the piano yesterday."

"You are a good friend, Evan."

The approval in her voice made him shiver. Vasia might disagree. He'd wanted to be a good friend but so often fell short of the mark, if not totally obliterating it. He wanted to learn, to be better.

In Evan's peripheral vision, a shadow sprinted around the corner of a snowy hedge on the other side of the street.

"Someone's following," he said in a low voice.

"A young boy. He picked us up as we left Freda's."

"The same boy Greta saw?"

"Possibly. He's harmless. Only curious."

"If we see him in the park, let's try to catch him."

"You think you can make it to the park today?" Her throaty laugh made him blush.

"It's been a month since the surgery. I feel a lot stronger today. I want to make sure the Chinese didn't bomb it into oblivion."

"My cab will arrive in less than half an hour, Evan. There's no time."

He stopped and sighed, looking at her. Dread tightened his throat.

"I know, Gordo," she said, nodding. "You have memorized the safe house address and phone? I am not far. You remember the disguise I will use?"

He cleared his throat, willing the muscles to relax. "The old woman."

"I have seen that your friends are loyal." She turned him around, and they began walking back down Sternwartestrasse's gentle hill. "They will protect you, defend you. Sometimes also the best defense is simply to call the police. Remember that. You are a famous conductor, Evan. This fame is an advantage for you right now."

He laughed, a dry sound in the cold air. "I understand what you're saying, Alicia, but I don't enjoy fame. It can be a disadvantage."

"But it is good that people recognize you. It is a strong defense. Promise me you will not use any of your light disguises?"

"Promise." He laughed again, this time without mirth. "Not sure it was such a good idea showing them to you." But she had insisted on seeing the disguises Sofia had helped him create. He hadn't shown all of them to her. "Still nothing from your contacts?"

"Nothing about the assassin in Buenos Aires. I asked my contacts to find out about our friend Gregori in Paris and the SVR." Her eyes surveyed the street, an approaching steel-gray sedan.

"Let me guess. Despite the loss of Moscow, the SVR is alive and well and Gregori is legitimate."

The sedan passed them with no change in speed. The driver's eyes focused on the snowy street ahead. Evan thought of the white street cleaner vans he had thought he'd seen last summer. They had been hallucinations. The sedan was real.

"The SVR survived, but no one knows anyone who matches Gregori's description." She shrugged. "I doubt he works for the SVR."

"So who was he? What was his interest in me?"

"I think we will meet him again, Evan." She squeezed his arm against her. "When you go out, always be aware of your surroundings, the street activity. Remember what I taught you, yes? I will not be able to always follow you. Better to take cabs or ask Freda to drive you if she can until you are stronger."

A taxi, its roof light glowing, crawled up the street toward Freda's house. Evan spotted it before Alicia. "Your cab is here."

"I have checked your security system and Freda's. They are excellent, both connected to the police. You are fine, safe here."

Although he knew Alicia's departure was only to another residence in Vienna, Freda didn't, and he could see from her clouded expression as she said good-bye at the front gate that she was sad to see his Spanish "cousin" leave. He joined her in her kitchen afterward and managed to chop carrots with more efficiency than he'd expected, considering the limitations of his injured right shoulder.

As they ate together, they listened to classical music on

Österreich Eins. He'd liked Freda from the moment he'd met her, and now he appreciated her companionship, her sensitivity to his moods. She wasn't one of those women uncomfortable with silences between people. He was glad she and Greta had become friends over the previous months. She had met Sofia only once, with Greta, during the Christmas holidays, and had treated Sofia as she treated him and everyone else—simply as people. Fame had no effect on her. And now he didn't want her coddling him and declined her offer to accompany him on his walk after they had finished eating. She tried to insist, but he promised not to go beyond the park, so she made him promise to walk slower than his normal pace. He pocketed his cell phone while she helped him bundle up against the cold.

The sun had burst through the overcast, and a light breeze swept the clouds from the winter-blue sky. Warm in a cobalt blue wool coat, and a black knitted scarf and gloves that Freda had made for him, with his feet toasty in shearling-lined leather boots, he headed up the street, thinking about Owen. If Owen knew that he had killed Vasia, would he understand why? Would he understand that no witnesses could have survived to tell the police that he, Perceval, had assassinated the Chinese vice chairman? Would he understand the deal Evan had made with the New Economic Party so that he could tour Europe, defect, and live free?

Pain like a hand squeezing his chest forced him to pause. The deal he'd made was a shadow dogging him. He glanced around. The street was Sunday afternoon quiet. He could not regret more that deal he'd made with the NEP. According to Woody, their bosses in Washington—people he did not know but he believed were sanctioned by the government, if not part of it—had been quite pleased with how he'd executed his first assignment as Perceval. They had expected him to be caught or killed after the assassination and had been surprised he'd survived and eluded the police. They had wanted him dead.

The NEP always thought in terms of *profit*. And now they had trapped him into working for them. A mental tug at the back of his mind made him shake his head. Were they behind the attempted assassination in Buenos Aires? No, they couldn't be. They'd given him the assignment to kill Bernie Brown. He needed to talk to Woody Lewis.

Vienna hadn't had an air raid in days. He'd seen only one neighbor, two mornings ago, out walking his dog. Some people in the neighborhood had withdrawn because of the war, as a defense against the uncertainty, and even on this pleasant afternoon, they chose to remain inside. He'd been relieved to find the neighborhood still untouched by Chinese bombs. Last fall, bombs had fallen on Grinzing, setting all of northwest Vienna, including his Währing, on edge. People had been killed, beautiful homes destroyed.

Out of the corner of his eye as he turned up Türkenschanzstrasse, he spotted a boy hovering behind an ancient oak tree in the park-like area around the University of Vienna Astronomy Institute. This boy wore a black wool jacket, jeans, and a red knitted scarf, but no hat. His hands burrowed deep in the jacket's pockets. His face was pale and narrow, with delicate features reminding Evan of a gamin. The breeze ruffled the boy's brown hair. Evan filed the boy in his memory as he walked up the street toward Türkenschanz Park only a block away.

Evan loved this neighborhood park and had often walked or jogged through it in the mornings before the day's score study. He was pleased to see people there braving the winter. In one corner, three tables of chess players bundled up against the cold concentrated on their games under bare black maple and beech trees. Not far away, a handful of children shouted and laughed and screamed in delight as they played on the jungle gyms, slides, and swings, in the maze, or in the giant snowy sand pit, watched over by clumps of parents, talking and stamping their feet for warmth, and holding thermos bottles of coffee or some other hot beverage. Evan chose a bench on the other side of the playground near a small, frozen duck pond. He needed to rest before returning home.

The boy had followed him, of course. The way the boy looked at him had cemented the thought that he was the boy's object of interest. He remembered Vasia saying: "Entire workforce of eyes and ears paid to follow objects because of certain subjects." He doubted the boy worked for the police or an intelligence agency. The boy was probably hungry. He wasn't surprised, then, when the boy walked up to him.

"Guten Tag," the boy said with grave courtesy.

The boy's accent was not native Austrian German. Evan couldn't place it. "Guten Tag, meiner junge Herr. Warum spielst du nicht?" A good question: Why wasn't the boy playing with the other children?

The boy continued in German, "I wish to speak with you."

Evan smiled, following his lead. "Really? Why?"

"You are the orchestra conductor. The American. Evan Quinn."

"That's true. You play a musical instrument?"

"I have studied piano before the war."

"Not now?" Evan thought of Lucia te Kumara. She'd welcome another student.

"I do not know where my parents are. They must be looking for me, but I do not know. I cannot go to the police because the police lock up boys from the street. My father talked about you. He loved your concerts. Will you help me?"

The boy's face held no guile, only pain, confusion, and fear. Evan could not believe that the police would not help this boy, but he understood the boy's wariness. He knew what it was like to feel abandoned, to have lost loved ones cruelly, violently at a young age. Uncle Joe. His mother. He had always been wary of the police in America, where they were an extension of Internal Security Services.

"Why do you think the police would put you in jail?"

"I have heard other kids talk about it. They have seen it happen." The boy looked on the verge of tears.

"What's your name?" Evan made his tone as gentle as possible.

"Pierre."

"Are you French?"

"Oui."

That explained the accent. "Well, Pierre, your father would be proud of you, and I am honored that you have asked for my help." Evan stood. "The police are only one possibility. In your case, we can also contact the French embassy. Would you like to come home with me, meet my landlady, and have something hot to eat? I could use a little support walking."

Pierre threw his arms around Evan's waist. Evan smiled. "No, Pierre, take my left arm."

"What happened to you?" Pierre said, grasping Evan's left arm.

"I was shot."

"Mon Dieu." Pierre's blue eyes widened as he looked up at Evan.

In the boy's face, Evan glimpsed his own ten-year-old face, the fear mixed with the excitement. Pierre's parents had probably sheltered him from the dangers of the world, and now he faced them alone. Perhaps, no longer alone. Evan felt certain that Freda would help him with the boy. "I'm healing now, Pierre. I'll be fine."

Maman would be *very* pleased with Madame Kirsch and Monsieur Evan. She would agree with the Wizard Howl, Ashitaka, and Steamboy that Madame and Monsieur were good people. Monsieur Evan towered over everyone, a giant, with such kind eyes! Papa would love to speak with him about music and orchestras. The tallest woman he'd ever seen, Madame Kirsch, stood almost as tall as Monsieur Evan. She reminded him of his English teacher, and she also spoke French! Her hair glowed with a golden light, and her green eyes burned with a beautiful fire. She must be strong because she could help Monsieur Evan to stand. They were his protector giants.

Pierre lay in bed, staring at the ceiling, reviewing the day and his good fortune. He knew what he must do for Avoine, but he wanted to remain in bed under the warm comforter a few minutes longer, basking in the magic of his new protectors. When Monsieur Evan had introduced him to Madame Kirsch, she had given him hot tea and cake. Then a hot bath, and she'd wrapped him in the biggest, softest towel he'd ever seen while she'd washed his clothes. Monsieur Evan had turned on the radio, and they'd listened to Beethoven together, not speaking. Madame Kirsch had made a delicious lentil soup for supper, served with thick slices of bread and real butter, followed by Spanish navel oranges, the exact oranges he loved. He had his own room. An hour ago, Monsieur Evan had read him a German fairy tale and tucked him in for sleep. But Pierre could not sleep.

Avoine had said that Monsieur Evan would feel sorry for him and want to help him, and Monsieur Evan had. And now he was safe in Monsieur Evan's landlady's house, Madame Kirsch's house, snug in a warm bed much more comfortable than the bed he'd had at Avoine's apartment. He wanted desperately to tell Madame and Monsieur about Avoine but he was afraid Avoine would hear. And then something terrible would happen.

Pierre touched the tiny bump under the skin behind his left ear. Avoine had ordered him to stay close to Monsieur Evan so he could hear him through the implant behind his ear. He heard again the voices downstairs. Pierre slipped out of bed, smoothing the flannel nightshirt Madame had given him to wear, and tiptoed to the door.

The voices were louder in the upstairs hallway, drifting up from the sitting room below, but he could not hear what they were saying. Monsieur and Madame. Imagining the Wizard Howl making him invisible, Pierre tiptoed down the stairs until he could hear the words clearly.

"I thought we could begin with the embassy rather than calling the police, Freda," Monsieur Evan said in English. Pierre was glad that he'd worked so hard on his English in school. But there was something else, too. Monsieur's English sounded like Avoine's. Avoine was *American*, not German, not English.

"He told me his name is Pierre Levade. I think he might be the son of that French diplomat and his wife who were killed last fall. Remember? When the bombs hit Grinzing? The police thought the entire family had been in the house when the bomb hit. But what if the boy had been somewhere else? It's too terrible to imagine." Madame's voice sounded full of tears.

No, his parents had not been home when the bomb hit their house! He was sure of it. The Wizard Howl whispered that they would find his parents, and then Papa and Monsieur Evan would rescue him from Avoine.

"Well, if he is a diplomat's son, then the embassy should be happy to take him in, return him to his relatives in France." A long silence. Then, "Freda, he survived. Now we can help him get home. But before we tell him anything, we need to confirm about his parents with the embassy."

"Are you certain about the police?"

"Yeah. I'm not confident they wouldn't put him in an orphanage."

"They would take him to the French embassy. He is a French citizen."

"Why frighten him more? I mean, the poor kid has been through enough with this war, and he's terrified of the police. Let's leave the police out of it for now and deal directly with the French. I think the police have enough to keep them busy without adding a little French boy." A pause in which Pierre thought he heard movement. "I'm tired, Freda. It's been a long day. May I join you and Pierre for breakfast tomorrow?"

Pierre scurried up the stairs as Monsieur and Madame came out of the sitting room. Monsieur stepped to the front door as Madame held open his blue coat for him.

"Of course. You can see he already adores you, Evan."

Pierre crouched behind the banister at the top of the stairs. Monsieur and Madame wanted to help him, wanted to find his family. Avoine hadn't wanted to help him find his parents. The Wizard Howl whispered in his ear not to tell them about Avoine because Avoine would hear and hurt him again.

CHAPTER 8

"Pierre, would you like to spend the morning with me before Freda drives me to my physical therapy session?" Evan said in German. He exchanged a look with Freda. Sasha paced between them at the sitting room table, her feathery tail wagging.

"Ja, bitte," the boy said around the pieces of Emmentaler and bread he'd stuffed into his mouth only seconds before. He reached out his hand to Sasha and she licked it.

"Slow down, Pierre," Freda said, pouring herself more coffee from the infuser pot. "Swallow before you speak."

Pierre swallowed, and a sweet smile took over his face. "The food is so delicious here. And Sasha is so golden and beautiful."

"Vielen Dank." Freda smiled. "And while Evan is at physical therapy, we will shop for new clothes for you."

"Aber nein. I have these clothes."

Evan spread raspberry jam on his toast. "Yes, you have those clothes. You need more clothes, not different."

"But I cannot pay for them."

"I'm buying them for you. A gift, Pierre," Evan said, and took a bite of toast.

"Merci, Monsieur Evan."

The rumble and whine of approaching jets, followed

seconds later by the city's air-raid siren and the booms of anti-aircraft guns, set Sasha barking.

Freda assumed the role of air raid warden. "All right. Gather your food and tea. We'll take it down to the root cellar."

Pierre's eyes had widened into blue pools of terror. He froze in place, his breathing rapid and shallow. Even with Sasha barking next to him, he didn't flinch. Evan had a sinking feeling, a recognition, of that paralyzing fear. He had known that kind of fear as a boy, and as recently as the Neusiedl am See safe house last summer.

"Freda, leave the food and tea. I'll bring Pierre."

"Come, Sasha!" Freda turned for the door.

The dull thudding of bombs began east and south. A buzzing droned overhead. Pierre still did not move. Evan pried his hands from their grip on the table's edge and lifted him with his left arm. He followed Freda through her kitchen and down her cellar stairs as a whistling whine was followed by a close thud that sent vibrations through the house. Pierre was as stiff as steel in his arms.

Freda had transformed her six-foot-by-six-foot concrete food storage room into a bomb shelter. They hurried through the main basement area that Freda had partially renovated into a laundry room and general storage with chests and file cabinets. Off the main basement room, two ropes of garlic hung from the ceiling of the root cellar, a squat barrel of potatoes stood in the corner, and the shelves on one side held canned vegetables and fruit from her garden's harvest last fall. The shelves opposite held store-bought canned goods and boxed food. Under them, twenty two-liter bottles of water had been lined up on the floor, and wool blankets were stacked in the corner with flashlights, batteries, matches, candles, and a portable radio.

As Evan closed the door, the electricity blinked off. The dense darkness enveloped them. His heart raced. The Chinese had left Vienna alone for several weeks but now had returned. The dull thuds of their bombs pounded all around, some far, some close. The house's foundation was solid, the root cellar reinforced enough to withstand a direct hit, but he could imagine how much the bombs shook the structure above and rattled the windows.

Freda turned on a flashlight, its beam wide. She opened a blanket and wrapped Pierre in it, taking him from Evan. Evan arranged more blankets on the floor for them to sit on, their backs against the rear wall. Sasha paced by the door, her head down, alternately growling low and whimpering.

"He feels so cold," Freda said, cuddling Pierre close to her.

In the dusky half-light outside of the flashlight beam's circle, they looked at each other. Freda shook her head, and her face frowned in sorrow. Evan studied Pierre, whose vacant expression showed that whatever lively energy he'd exhibited during breakfast had plunged into hiding. Where had his mind gone to escape the bombs? The boy had been traumatized by the war in general, Evan felt certain, and also by one specific bombing, the one in Grinzing that had killed his parents. The boy's response reminded him of his terror and powerlessness against his father's rampages and violence when he was a boy. To children, adults wielded the same power as the Chinese with their bombs. He needed to be strong for Pierre, to protect him and Freda.

He hadn't checked his watch when they'd headed for the root cellar so Evan had no idea how long the air raid lasted. It felt like hours. By the time the all-clear sounded, Sasha crouched by the door and Freda had reassured Pierre enough so that he'd relaxed, and his breathing had returned to normal. He clung to her, shivering, his eyes locked on Evan. How had he survived alone on the streets? Evan's chest tightened. No way would Pierre have to fend for himself anymore.

"You heard the all-clear, Pierre? It is safe now. We are safe. We can go upstairs now," Freda said in a gentle voice. "Can you walk?"

Pierre scrambled to his feet with an automatic obedience that disturbed Evan for its military snap. Had his parents been strict? Had they insisted on complete obedience? As they climbed the stairs to the kitchen, Sasha trotting ahead of them, he thought about the French musicians he had conducted in Paris, the conversations he'd had with some of them during rehearsal breaks, and he couldn't imagine any of them living their family lives as if in military training. When he thought of French culture, he imagined the pursuit of pleasure, beauty, playfulness, art, intellectual challenge, and peaceful cooperation, although he was well aware, from his conversations with the French musicians, that they were human and quite capable of human weaknesses and secrets. Family life bred secrets.

The Chinese had left France largely alone in this war, prompting much speculation in the media about what kind of a deal the French had made with the Chinese and if it would turn out to be detrimental to the rest of Europe. The French could slide with accomplished stealth through back channels. They knew how deals worked.

Back in the sitting room, Freda paused by the table. "Are you still hungry, Pierre?"

The boy shook his head, and hung his head.

"I need to go for my walk now," Evan said.

Pierre looked up at him. "May I walk with you, Monsieur?" His voice sounded anxious, but his face shone in a waxy immobility.

"Of course, Pierre. You can help me with my errands."

"What errands?" Freda stopped gathering up their breakfast dishes to frown at Evan.

"Nothing far, Freda. The bakery. The Tabak Trafik for a book of streetcar tickets. Shall I bring Sasha with us?"

Pierre scampered out of the sitting room as Freda placed her hand on Evan's left arm. He could see the pain in her eyes.

"I think we need to find a counselor for Pierre, someone experienced with working with children traumatized by violence, by war," she said in a low voice.

"Let's consult with the people at the French embassy, Freda. Are you going to call them this morning?"

She nodded. "Take Sasha."

He and Pierre pulled on their coats and boots and left Freda's house by the back kitchen door with Sasha prancing on her leash around them. As they headed for Türkenschanz Park, Evan paid close attention to the wintry street, which was air-raid still, and the activity around the park, where car traffic dominated the streets. Pierre spoke little but held tight to Evan's left arm with one hand and Sasha's leash with the other. Sasha, seeming to sense Pierre's mood, walked close to him, occasionally butting her head against his side. Their route took them through the deserted park, past the playground that Pierre ignored this morning, to Türkensch-anzplatz, where they stopped at a bakery for Evan to buy Semmel rolls for his breakfasts that week and at the news-agent for his streetcar tickets and a newspaper. He noticed Pierre staring at blank notebooks and told him to pick out what he wanted. Pierre chose two notebooks with unlined pages, and a package of colored pencils and a package of regular pencils. Evan had expected to see Alicia at some point during the outing, whether in disguise or not, but there was no sign of her, even on their amble back to Freda's.

Pierre asked to see Evan's apartment over the garage. Evan released Sasha into the backyard, and Pierre hung her leash by Freda's back door. At the outer door to his apart-ment, Evan pressed his right middle fingertip onto the secur-ity panel pad, and said into the speaker, "Der schattige Affe." Pierre giggled. The door's lock released.

"It recognizes only your voice?" Pierre said rubbing behind his left ear. "If I spoke, would it unlock?"

"Only my voice and Freda's. Freda has her own pass-word. I have a different password for her system. The panel hears my voice, reads my fingerprint."

"But where is the eye scan?"

"No retina scan yet. Freda and I are talking about an upgrade because of what happened in Buenos Aires."

"When you were shot." Pierre rubbed behind his left ear again.

"Yes. Now, Pierre," Evan said, his tone playful, "I need your help with the stairs." He opened the door and gestured to the steep stairs leading up to his apartment. "I need you to walk behind and push me so I won't lose my balance."

Pierre gave him a skeptical frown but planted his small hands firmly on Evan's back at his waist. Halfway up the stairs, Evan swayed, pushed back, and pretended to lose his balance. Pierre exclaimed, "Merde!" and scolded him in French. By the time they reached the top, they were laughing. At the apartment door security panel, Evan repeated his security procedure, to Pierre's giggling delight, and the door swung open. They removed their coats and boots in the foyer.

"Make yourself at home," Evan said.

Evan reset the security system at the panel next to the door as Pierre went over to the four-foot black grand piano by the front windows. Evan padded across his living room's white carpet, tossing the bag of Pierre's blank notebooks and pencils on the black leather lounger facing the electronics wall, and into the kitchen. Pierre played scales on the piano as Evan put away the Semmel rolls, filled the tea kettle with water, and set it on the stove.

The videophone warbled. As Evan walked toward it on the wall to the left of the living room doorway he said, "Hello."

The monitor above the black-and-silver keyboard and fax slot brightened on Nigel Fox sitting at his temporary office desk, a bare beige wall behind him.

"Good morning, Evan. How is your recovery?"

The piano scales stopped in the living room.

"Going well, Nigel, thanks. My physical therapist thinks I'll be fine for Copenhagen."

Pierre entered the kitchen, his eyes searching for the videophone. He took Evan's hand and stood next to him in front of the oak table.

"And who's this?" Nigel said, his green eyes as piercing on the monitor as they were in person.

"Who is he?" Pierre said in German, looking up at Evan.

"Nigel, this is Pierre Levade," Evan said in English. "We met in Türkenschanz Park yesterday, and he asked for my help finding his parents. Freda and I are in the process of contacting the French embassy for their help. Pierre," Evan switched to German, "this is Nigel Fox, my manager. He and I need to talk business for a few minutes."

Nigel said something in French that made Pierre giggle and reply in rapid French. Evan understood not a word. Nigel's broad smile softened his hawk-like nose and the angular lines of his face. He replied in French, Pierre said, "Oui," and trotted back into the living room.

"You have a way with kids, Nigel."

"I told him that I needed his help to keep an eye on you and make certain you keep at your physical therapy exercises. He was quite happy to oblige."

"I'm sure. What's new in my world?" The tea kettle whistled. Evan poured the boiling water into a fat yellow ceramic teapot on the counter.

"Neils Dam in Copenhagen confirmed the program change you requested. The program is set: Barber Essay for Orchestra, Opus 12, Barber Piano Concerto, and Bartók Concerto for Orchestra. He asked about your preference for hotel, especially in light of what happened in Buenos Aires."

"Close to the concert hall, please. I doubt I'll be going on runs there. I'll need to conserve my energy for work. Please email me Neils's contact info."

Nigel nodded and made a note on a tablet computer.

"Helsinki OK with the Brahms?"

"Yes. Quite pleased, actually, despite a hint of disappointment you hadn't suggested Caine. You hadn't suggested an order for the symphonies. They suggested one and three the first week, two and four the second."

Pierre's face peeked around the door frame. Evan winked at him. "That's fine, Nigel. I'll call Doblinger's today and order the scores."

"Iceland rescheduled for the week of April fifth. The Lucerne Symphony has requested the week of April nineteenth, and Zürich the week of April twenty-sixth. I don't think I've seen such schedule scrambling. It's the war, of course. First everyone cancels everything, and then, when they've assessed how the war is going for them, they either call again or not. Budapest has called, the Hungarian National Symphony for the end of May."

"What happened with Canada and Paris?" Evan opened his arms to Pierre. The boy dropped his head shyly and walked over to him, pushing Evan's right arm in its sling against his chest. Pierre stood close to him and rubbed with one finger behind his left ear.

"You will go to Paris?" Pierre whispered to him in German.

"Paris is in a wait-and-see mode," Nigel said. "After Helsinki in September, I may be able to book Canada, but they're anxious about the war."

"Why? It's not like it's on their doorstep." Evan put his arm around Pierre's shoulders.

"The Americans. I haven't worked it out yet. I'll let you know. Iceland wants the same program—what was it?"

Evan let go of Pierre and stepped to the 2049 calendar panel hanging next to the videophone to check what he'd written for the Iceland gig originally scheduled for the first week of February. "OK, it was a Russian first half with Shostakovich's Overture on Russian and Kirghiz Folk Themes, the Rachmaninoff Second Piano Concerto, and then Caine's Third Symphony. What about Lucerne and Zürich? I don't think I'll have much time to prepare."

"They left it up to you. Zürich requested Caine."

"I'll think about it. Maybe Beethoven. I'd love to do an all-Beethoven program, and that'd be review work, not study. Haydn goes well with Caine. I'll let you know in a day or two. Anything else? Your office doesn't look very comfortable."

The artist manager sighed. "Our building in central London won't be rebuilt until the war ends. There's no point. The Chinese continue their bombing campaign with alarming efficiency. Have you noticed how the internet continues to function? If we lose the phones, we could conference via the web. The Chinese seem to know where not to bomb to protect it. Certainly, to protect the money transferred online every day. But if they think anyone will surrender, they're quite wrong. In the meantime, we slog on. My wife wants to decorate these temporary offices, but I'm against it. We're relieved they're heated."

Nigel ended with something in French for Pierre.

The boy nodded with a grin.

"Take care of yourself, Nigel." The videophone monitor clicked to black. "So, Pierre, you're working now for Nigel, are you?" Evan said in German. The boy threw his arms around Evan's waist and hugged, surprising him. He felt pleased the boy liked him. Trusted him. He hadn't expected that so soon.

"You will go to Paris?" Pierre said, looking up at him.

"Yeah, to conduct. They've invited me back. Is that where you lived before coming here?"

"Oui. I was born in Paris. We have a large apartment there."

"You told Freda the address?"

Pierre nodded. "Now what will you do?"

"Work."

Pierre trotted back to the living room. Evan poured them each a mug of tea. When he entered the living room, he found Pierre staring at the electronics wall.

"It does not work," Pierre said in German, glancing at Evan over his shoulder. "Only for your voice?"

Evan smiled. "Exactly."

Pierre nodded, and went to the windows that overlooked the back yard. "But you have few electronics, Monsieur Evan."

Evan set Pierre's tea down on the small table by his black leather recliner. "I have chosen and prefer a low-tech life, Pierre. I have no need for the rabbling world to intrude in my life through high-tech gadgets."

"You have the internet on your phone?" Pierre examined the wall of shelves filled with music scores, books, and piles of digital movies, and the cabinets underneath.

"No internet on my phone." Evan watched Pierre open

the last wall cabinet. He resisted the urge to run over and stop him as the French boy pulled out the first large square cardboard box from the bottom shelf. Behind it rested his sniper rifle in its wood case. "I store empty boxes in that cabinet," he said in as even a voice as he could.

Pierre opened the box and saw it was empty. He closed it, pushed it back into the cabinet, and closed the door.

"This is the living room and my study," Evan said, waving around the room. "Through this door is my kitchen. Off the kitchen in back is my bedroom and the bathroom. Take a look, if you want."

Pierre's blue eyes regarded him as if he'd just told Pierre he must dig holes in the frozen backyard.

"It's OK, Pierre. Or you can sit in my recliner while I work."

"It is very different without technology."

Evan smiled. "I like being the one in control of my space. I really like the silence."

For the rest of the morning, Pierre sat in the recliner as Evan worked at the piano on Barber's Essay for Orchestra for the Copenhagen gig. Pierre drew in one of his new notebooks, first in the black leather recliner, then sprawled on his stomach under the piano, but refused to show Evan his drawings. Freda called when it was time to leave for his physical therapy session. They pulled on their coats and boots and went out to the garage, where the three of them piled into Freda's old maroon Mercedes sedan for the drive to Otto Glasmann's office.

"I will come to your physical therapy," Pierre announced in German in the back seat.

"You and I will shop, Pierre," Freda said.

"No, thank you, Madame. I prefer physical therapy with Monsieur Evan."

Evan chuckled as they passed a freshly bombed area west of the large general hospital. Firemen fought raging flames as smoke rose from other portions of rubble.

"It is not your physical therapy, Pierre, but Evan's."

"I know. I must make certain that Monsieur Evan works hard at his physical therapy."

"Nigel put him up to it," Evan said, glancing sideways at Freda.

"Ah. So Herr Fox has you working for him, Pierre?" Freda smiled.

Evan tried to remember if Freda had ever actually met Nigel in person. They had spoken on the videophone once or twice. But Nigel hadn't attended his last Vienna Philharmonic concerts the previous September. He thought that would have been the only time they could have met. "Freda, the next time Nigel's in Vienna, let's invite him for dinner."

"Monsieur Fox has big white hair," Pierre said, and giggled.

"Splendid idea." Freda checked on Pierre in the rearview mirror. "Fine, Pierre. We will go to physical therapy and shop after lunch."

As Freda parked the Mercedes, Evan surveyed the street of six-story gray-and-white apartment buildings with shops on the ground floor. They weren't far from the Mariahilfer Strasse shopping area in the Sixth District. Alicia knew his physical therapy schedule, but he didn't see her or an old woman who could be her on the street.

Otto Glasmann, dressed in jeans and a red sweater, welcomed Pierre and Freda into his cozy workout room for Evan's session. Freda claimed a chair along the wall to watch. The east-facing windows caught the late-morning sun to her left. The air carried a lavender scent. Pierre stood next to Evan, opposite side Otto. The French boy acted confident, in charge, which reminded Evan of the way he had taken charge as a boy, leading his mother to their hiding place behind the furnace when his father erupted into one of his rages.

Otto, in his smooth baritone voice, said, "Na, ja, Pierre, be positive, say encouraging things, tell him that he's doing well, looking good, and so on."

Pierre's sweet boyish voice accompanied Otto's work on Evan's right shoulder and arm, Evan's work on the equipment, rising as Evan's fingers crawled up the wall, falling as he hung the arm and made ever-larger circles with it. The sound of his voice lifted Evan's mood, moved him as music moved him.

Evan and Otto reviewed the kinds of arm movements Evan used for conducting, and Evan asked Pierre to demonstrate for him. Otto introduced two new exercises to help strengthen the shoulder and back muscles to support the arm better. By the end of the session, Evan felt exhausted. Pierre beamed.

For lunch, they stopped at a family-run bistro two blocks from Otto's office. Evan looked for Alicia, but once again, saw no sign of her or an old woman that could be her in disguise. Where was she? He shook off the sense of dread, telling himself that she had warned him not to expect her following him every second.

As usual after a physical therapy session, Evan's shoulder hurt and he took an extra-strength acetaminophen pill when they sat down at a window table. Evan faced the entrance. He and Freda watched Pierre wolf down his vegetable soup and roast beef with gravy, boiled potatoes, and carrots. He liked to see the boy eat well. He wasn't that hungry himself, earning a frown from Freda when he ordered only a bowl of vegetable soup with bread.

"Freda, what did they say at the embassy?"

Pierre froze in mid-chew, his eyes darting from Evan to Freda.

She smiled. "They want to meet with us, talk with Pierre, of course. They suggested a blood test may be in order. But they were happy to hear he is OK and will help find his family, whatever is necessary."

"When's the meeting?"

"I suggested tomorrow, but they wanted some time to locate a counselor to speak with Pierre."

Evan nodded. "They'll call?"

"Yes." She sighed. "I'm glad to at least get the process started. It could take some time, Pierre. I hope you will be patient."

"I can be patient, Madame."

"Oh, and Greta called. She's having a musical salon at the Landstrasse apartment and wanted my opinion about your condition."

"My condition?" Evan ripped another slice of bread in half and buttered it. Greta could have called him and asked.

The conspiracy truly existed, this conspiracy they had, Greta and Freda, about taking care of him. "What about my condition?" He made a grimacing face at Pierre, who giggled.

"To perform, Evan. I told her I didn't think your arm was up to it yet. What do you think?"

He glanced at the diners at the table to his left and then out the window to the street. "I can't control the violin bow yet, and I wouldn't want to try the piano with both hands. So, I guess you're correct in your assessment." A man with golden oat blond hair and sunglasses hovered across the street from the bistro. He stuffed his hands into the pockets of his brown wool coat. A yellow scarf tucked around his neck reminded Evan of Gregori's brown leather coat and yellow scarf in Paris. Something about the man's dominant demeanor gave Evan an unpleasant mental tug of familiarity. "When's the party?"

"Sunday. I'm sure you'll hear from her. She said Owen and Lucia might be there."

"Really?" He glanced around the rustic bistro at the other diners, suddenly feeling exposed and on edge at a table out in front. When they'd entered the restaurant, he'd been complacent, hadn't been thinking like Perceval. He hadn't chosen their table, although he was facing the entrance. Freda had chosen the table. He hadn't followed counter-surveillance procedures. Alicia would not be pleased. "She say anything else about them?"

"No." But Freda smiled as if she knew a secret.

Pierre was looking out the window, his expression fearful. Evan followed his gaze to the blond-haired man. In an even, quiet voice he said, "Pierre, do you know that man outside?"

Pierre nodded, not taking his eyes off the man on the street.

"How do you know him?"

Freda, her mouth tight in alarm, looked out the window. "What man?"

"In the brown coat." Evan also looked out the window.

The man turned and strolled up the street. Seeing his profile, Evan experienced another mental tug. The man had been too far away to identify and the sunglasses made it hard to really see the face. With a jolt, he imagined the worst. "Pierre, has he hurt you? Who is he?"

Pierre hesitated. His blue eyes were still dark with fear. "He chased me in the First District. Not a nice man."

Pierre had hesitated. Pierre wasn't telling them everything. He wouldn't look at Evan or Freda. Evan said, "You have your cell phone, Freda?" She nodded. "Let's call the police. I don't want some perv—"

"No!" Pierre's hands fisted on the table. "No police. He has left now. This is the first time I have seen him in weeks. Please, no police."

Evan's eyes searched the street. He couldn't remember where he'd seen that hair, that shade of blond, that domineering stance. But the man was gone now. An old woman shuffled into view. She wore a ragged black wool coat over a house dress, and a plaid wool scarf covered her gray head. A pipe stuck out from her mouth. Evan smiled, relieved. Alicia.

CHAPTER 9

A bird warbled as the black furry spider's mouth ballooned into a giant, moist, pink, terrifying mouth open in his father's face, inches away, threatening to swallow him whole. Evan screamed himself awake.

Gasping, his shoulder throbbing in pain, he inhaled the sharp disinfectant smell in the Buenos Aires emergency room, heard the tense Spanish voices clear in his ear, even as he stared at the forty-nine-inch LCD television embedded in his living room wall. Pierre had watched cartoons after breakfast, and now an odd-looking brown bird beep-beeped as it sped ahead of a gray coyote on a desert road. A bird warbled again, his videophone.

He could not talk to anyone right now. His body, heavy as lead, couldn't move. Voice mail would pick up the call.

The cartoon bird beeped as it halted abruptly. The gray coyote whizzed past it and straight over the edge of a cliff. Superimposed over the cartoon in his vision, he saw the operating room lights and then darkness so sudden he felt like he'd fallen into an abyss. Out of the darkness floated the nightmare twitching woman holding the spider.

He hadn't had the spider nightmare for almost two months. He knew it wasn't real, so he didn't bother to search his body for the spider as he had in the past. He wanted to control the nightmare, not allow it to control him. He would not succumb to the fear. But he shivered as shoulder pain pressed into his consciousness.

Spanish voices surrounded him again, the clinking of metal equipment. He closed his eyes. He wanted them to speak English, to tell him if he was going to die. He remembered rolling on a gurney into a white tile and chrome room with medical equipment everywhere. He smelled the metallic scent of blood. His breathing slowed.

Pierre? Where was he? His watch showed him he'd dozed off for an hour. "Pierre?" His voice sounded too loud. He listened but heard no movement behind him in the kitchen. If the boy had been there, his scream when he woke would have frightened him. Evan was glad the boy had returned to Freda's.

"Fernsehen abstellan," he said to his house computer, and the television flicked off. "Radio anstellan." The radio came on, his favorite station, Österreich Eins, where Greta worked, broadcasting a Bach keyboard concerto. He leaned forward in his black leather lounge chair and the back snapped upright. He pushed himself up and out of the chair. Dr. Maas had told him the present shoulder pain wasn't from the injury but the pain of healing. Almost five weeks since he'd been shot, and he was no longer taking hydrocodone during the day—doctor's orders—but he could take the two extra-strength acetaminophen that he hadn't yet taken this morning. The acetaminophen dulled the shoulder pain instead of eliminating it. He hadn't felt pain in his abdomen for a week. He could take one hydrocodone before he went to bed, but he missed it at moments like this. Eventually the hydrocodone would no longer be a part of his pain management regimen, and he'd have to deal with it. Maybe by then, he'd no longer need a pain management regimen.

Their breakfast dishes were piled in the kitchen sink. No sign of Pierre in the kitchen or bedroom. Evan missed his sweet voice, his attentive energy. Pierre's presence comforted him, even as he wanted to protect the boy. How deep was his denial? Evan suspected Pierre's pain was far more than the boy had shared, more than Pierre could accept.

He poured a mug of hot coffee from the wall coffeemaker, took the pain pills, and checked his video voice mail.

"Hello, Evan." Her smoky alto voice, that beloved voice, came from the videophone monitor as her face appeared, her concerned hazel-green eyes framed by her long and wavy chestnut-brown hair. Sofia. He'd missed a call from Sofia. He felt a wail of frustration in his chest blending with the sharp shoulder pain. Sofia continued, looking straight at him from the monitor, "I am sorry I have not called sooner. Greta emailed me news of you every day. Are you all right? I have sent you more email. This movie has had many production problems and too many demands on my time. How are you? Will you be at Greta's music salon on Sunday? I told the producers and director that I must return to Vienna for a few days. I hope I will see you at Greta's. Tschuss, Evan."

"Yes," he said to the videophone as the monitor flicked off, "I'll be there." He thought her face remained on the videophone monitor but then shook his head. The monitor was dark. Ever since the morphine in the hospital, his mind had felt too tricksy in ways that alarmed him. Ever since the morphine, his emotions flowed on the surface of his life. He wanted them hidden, but felt like they controlled him.

He wasn't crazy. He hadn't seen any white street cleaner vans or Harold and his Vigiciv gang for months, but he kept having that spider nightmare, problems with insomnia, moments when he felt someone else occupied his body with him and looked out of his eyes. He'd ask Dr. Maas about it at his appointment next week. He understood that being shot had traumatized him and, of course, there were aftereffects—the too-active mind, the intense emotions. He expected Dr. Maas could provide a prescription to control those effects or productive suggestions for eliminating them.

Wait. Sofia had sent him more emails? He spun away from the videophone and straight for his computer embedded in the electronics wall. "Computer, internet," he ordered. The monitor lit as the internet portal launched and the keyboard silently slid out under it. Using touch commands, he navigated to his inbox. A pop-up notice stated that he'd exceeded capacity. He hadn't checked email since returning home.

Sofia's name in the list of senders jumped out at him. He opened the most recent note.

Dear Evan—How are you? Greta wrote me that you had seen Owen. He has taken Vasia's death the hardest of all of us, nicht? His response is like all our pain expressed by him, all of it in him. Has he listened to you? What is the news of him? I think of you every day and hope your healing progresses well. I think we need to talk. I want to understand what happened that Sunday after the picnic. Sofia.

She wanted to understand something he didn't understand himself. But she wanted to talk to him. That was something good. She had avoided him for months after that picnic. And after Vasia's death.

He'd been so focused on Pierre, work, and physical therapy, he'd forgotten his email. His stomach knotted as he scrolled through the mailbox, seeing notes from musicians, other conductors forwarded by Nigel's office, from the Buenos Aires Philharmonic and staff members from other orchestras, a handful of journalists and... *Bernie Brown*. Evan rubbed his jaw. He opened Brown's note.

Hey, Maestro! Heard about Buenos Aires. Heard you're OK. Hope you got my package from Spain. You won't be able to reply to this—they're letting me send only this one note. Security, you know. I'm fine. Looking forward to working with you on our jazz café. I'll be in touch when I can. Don't believe everything you hear about me, especially in the media. You know how it is. Take care and watch your back. Bernie.

He exhaled a long breath. *Thanks, Bernie, for the package from Spain*. Alicia. He felt deep relief. He wished Bernie were more accessible so they could talk. He moved the note to his Saved folder and returned to Sofia's note to write a reply. He wanted to tell her how often he thought of her, the number of times he'd seen women who resembled her and his heart had raced, and that he wished she were here with him right now. But he wrote: *Sorry I missed your call this morning. I'll be at Greta's on Sunday and I'm glad you'll be there. Haven't had a chance to check email until today. Will write more. Evan.* He touched Send with his fingertip on the monitor, feeling his stomach unknot and his shoulders relax. Now he could work.

"Radio abstellan." Score study must best be done in silence.

He freshened his coffee and carried it to the Bösendorfer. Outside, the morning sunlight sparkled off another six inches of snow that had fallen during the night. He loved the snow, the clean purity of it, the cold. He'd always loved it. Growing up in Minneapolis, he'd especially loved blizzards, the snow mountains he and Paul Caine had built and climbed and sledded down.

He looked through the mountain of music scores on the piano. The program for Iceland, except for the Shostakovich, was review work. The Tonhalle-Orchester Zürich had requested a Caine symphony, and he'd decided on the first, the score he now opened on the piano's music stand. Uncle Joe had composed this neo-romantic symphony four years before Evan had been born, four years before Paul had been born, long before the NEP had been born. He could hear echoes of Samuel Barber's music as he read through the symphony's first movement. Since his defection, he'd had the chance to study more of Barber's music—that is, the works the Arts Council had banned, like the piano concerto, the violin concerto, and more. He was also learning so much more about Uncle Joe's music and the other music influences on him such as Shostakovich and Barber. He thought of Owen, the conversations they'd had about who influenced him. No artist worked in a vacuum, but rather absorbed creative expressions from other artists in all artistic mediums.

He wondered if he read his father's writing he'd see an influence from it on Uncle Joe's music. Not that he wanted to read his father's writing.

His videophone warbled again. Sofia? He lurched up from the piano bench, banging his knee on the piano. The phone rang again. "Coming, coming," Evan said, hurrying into the kitchen.

Inspector Leiner's image appeared on the videophone monitor.

"Good morning, Herr Quinn. How are you?" The Austrian cop sat at his office desk, files piled to his left, a computer behind him. He wore his usual suit, this one navy blue with a red tie.

"Fine, Inspector," Evan said, but winced at the fresh pain in his knee. He massaged his right shoulder. "The usual. How are you? Any interesting chatter about me?"

Leiner nodded and said, "I wanted to discuss that with you in person. I understand that this is perhaps short notice, but would you be able to join me for lunch today? I thought perhaps we might meet at the Café Chicago."

Café Chicago. Woody's café. Evan tried to read between the tones of Leiner's tenor voice, its British-accented English so smooth and friendly. He knew Leiner liked the café's food, but was there another reason he'd suggested it? A test, perhaps? To see how he and Woody reacted to each other? *No. Stop thinking that way.* Leiner no longer investigated him. Bernie had vouched for him. *Relax. It's just lunch.*

"I'd welcome the opportunity to get out of the house," Evan said. "What time?"

Leiner's lunch invitation was indeed on short notice. He

only had time to clean up, change clothes, and call for a cab. He needed to let Alicia know his movements for the next few hours. He'd call her on the way, he thought, slipping his cell phone into his coat pocket. He headed for Freda's to check on her and Pierre before he left.

"But are you certain you feel up to it?" Freda asked him in German so Pierre would understand. "You've only been home for ten days." She placed her hands on hips clothed in brown tweed. The sitting room smelled of chicken roasting in the kitchen, the fifth day that week they'd eaten chicken.

Pierre frowned at him. "I would like to go with you, Monsieur Evan."

"Sorry, Pierre, not this time. I'll be with a police inspector, so I'll be fine. And I know the Café Chicago and that area. It'll be good to visit the First District."

Pierre crossed his arms over his chest and pouted. Evan smiled, remembering his own reaction at Pierre's age when he was told, usually by his father, that he couldn't do something he'd wanted to do.

"If you need me to pick you up after the lunch, call me, Evan. I was able to buy a full tank of petrol yesterday," Freda said and left for the kitchen.

Pierre walked him out to the cab waiting near the driveway on Sternwartestrasse.

"Has Freda told you that we have a meeting at the French embassy tomorrow?" Evan said as he opened the cab's back door. Pierre nodded, hugging himself in the cold air. "Would you like to have lunch at the Café Chicago after the meeting?"

"The same café?"

"The very same. I'll buy you an American cheeseburger."

Pierre shrugged as the whisper of a smile crossed his face. "OK."

Evan slid into the cab and gave the driver the café's address in the First District. As the car pulled away, Evan looked out the rear window and waved to Pierre, who waved with both hands as if signaling a ship. As he faced front again, he flipped open his cell phone and dialed Alicia's safe house number.

"Where are you?" Alicia said.

He hadn't talked with her in four days because his life had stuck to the routine she knew. "In a cab on my way to the First District. Inspector Leiner invited me to lunch at the Café Chicago," he said in English, eyeing the driver, who showed no signs of interest or understanding.

"Where is this café?"

"Judenplatz. Any news?"

"The assassin in Buenos Aires. I am waiting for a contact I have in Santiago to reply. The Americans have been always active in Chile."

"Americans? No, I'm thinking she was working for Gregori or maybe the SVR in Moscow. He knew too much about her. You confirmed she was Chilean?"

"I found the hotel where she had checked in. I sent them a photo, and they confirmed she carried a Chilean passport."

"You had a photo of her?"

He could almost hear the shrug in her voice. "I thought it might prove useful to have a photo."

"Was she alive?"

"Yes. You'll be safe with Inspector Leiner, Evan. Enjoy your lunch."

The cab dropped Evan off in front of the cafe in the intimate Judenplatz. The bell rang as usual above the door when Evan entered. The last time he'd visited the café had been the previous September. Heavy black air-raid curtains still hung at the windows instead of the lush plants that were there before the war, and a dozen lunch customers sat at the tables, including the two old codgers who always sat by a front window, playing chess. The hefty blond waitress greeted him and pointed to a table in the back corner where Leiner, seated with his back to the wall, studied a menu. No sign of Woody. He hoped the spry, white-haired American was working in the kitchen. He needed to talk with him after lunch.

"Hey, Inspector," Evan greeted the Austrian cop in English.

Leiner smiled. He looked rested, his blond hair freshly cut, his mustache trimmed. "I have been looking forward to this lunch, Herr Quinn. I haven't had an American cheeseburger in at least six months."

Evan sat in the chair opposite Leiner, uncomfortable that his back faced the other diners and the doors. His Perceval training dictated that he be able to see but not be easily seen, always facing the doors, back to a wall, no surprises. "Well, this is the place to eat one, Inspector."

The waitress took their orders and bustled off. Evan shifted in his chair, looking at Leiner. "How's your family, Inspector? Laura?"

Leiner smiled again. "All well, thank you. Laura nags me

about you, Herr Quinn. She wants to meet you, and I am certain she will scold me for not including her today. She plays the cello, have I told you? Her teacher would like her to give a solo recital in May, her first one. How are you feeling? You still wear the sling?"

"Yeah, when I'm away from home. It's more comfortable. The physical therapy is going well, very well. I still tire fast, though. I have another check-up with Dr. Maas next week. Let me know when Laura's recital is. If I'm in town, I'd like to go."

"Your conducting?"

"My next job is Copenhagen at the end of March. I'll be ready. I'm working on programs for the Iceland Philharmonic, Lucerne Symphony, Zürich Tonhalle." Evan watched the waitress come toward them with a tray. He waited until after she'd served their drinks and soup before he spoke again. "You wanted to talk to me in person about the electronic intelligence?"

Leiner slurped a spoonful of vegetable soup, nodding. "There is no chatter. At least, not about Buenos Aires. We have examined the usual communication codes, but nothing came up. I called Detective Ruiz in Buenos Aires. He is quite frustrated. They have nothing, except—" Leiner ripped a wheat roll in half—"an unidentified woman who was murdered the same night, not far from where you were shot." Leiner buttered the roll. "Her throat was slit."

Leiner's expression was unreadable, but he knew that didn't mean the cop wasn't thinking. Leiner found the murdered woman interesting. The Chilean woman. Evan blew on a spoonful of his hot Leberknödel soup. He sensed that

Leiner's intuition was telling him the murdered woman wasn't a coincidence. "Detective Ruiz thinks there's a connection?"

"Possibly. He found it fascinating that the tips of the woman's fingers had been treated somehow to remove her fingerprints."

"She didn't want to be identified." He was surprised about the fingerprints. Woody had never suggested that he hide Perceval's identity in that way. He'd worn latex gloves.

"Exactly. Ruiz believes this is another clue that it was a professional hit, a contract killing, not a terrorist. I agree. So the question becomes, who would want you dead, Herr Quinn? And why?" Leiner's clear gray eyes studied him, his soup spoon in midair, his eyebrows raised.

When Leiner asked the question, Evan's mind answered, *The NEP. The Americans.* But Woody had told him they were happy with his Perceval work and had given him another job. The Chinese?

Leiner submerged the spoon in his soup. "Although there was not chatter about Buenos Aires," Leiner continued, frowning, "the Chinese electronic chatter overflowed with your name. The only concrete detail—an expressed concern for your location. The Chinese want to know where you are."

"The Chinese?" Evan felt the tingling in his face as the blood drained from it. "Why?" Although he knew one big reason they'd want to find him. How had they found out?

"Our question, exactly, Herr Quinn. Dieter has asked for electronic monitoring for the next week or so. Will you conduct in China in the future?"

"No." Evan shook his head. "You know, they could call my manager to find out my location. It's not that hard. Nigel hasn't said there's been interest from the Chinese. I'm not sure I'd accept anyway. They started this—this damned war."

Leiner nodded, sipped a spoonful of soup. He gave Evan a thoughtful look. "Dieter wondered if the connection could be someone in your past. Even as far back as university."

Someone from his past? Evan glanced to his left, toward the pastry counter and the magazine rack by the side door. He'd known Chinese music students at Juilliard but he couldn't imagine any of them becoming government officials powerful enough to give any orders about him. Evan thought about his phone conversation with Alicia. Could Gregori actually be working for the Chinese? He claimed to work for Russia, but it wouldn't be the first time someone had lied to him. What if the Chilean assassin worked for Gregori, and *he* worked for the Chinese?

"You know, Inspector, there was a guy at the Paris airport—the reason we took a later flight, actually. He said his name was Gregori and he worked for the SVR. *He* claimed a Chilean woman had tried to kill me in Buenos Aires, a woman the SVR had been following because they thought she'd been involved in the attack on a Russian ambassador in Mumbai. Alicia and I thought the guy was nuts, trying to get attention or close to me or something, and she didn't think he was really Russian from his accent."

Leiner frowned, and a small drip of soup from his mustache hit his soup bowl. "When had this man spoken with you? Why hadn't you notified security?" Leiner removed a four-by-six-inch tablet from his jacket inner pocket and powered it on.

"He wasn't threatening to us, Inspector. A little spooky,

I guess, and annoying but friendly. It was during an air raid at Charles De Gaulle. We went into the restroom, and he was there, too. He introduced himself, only his first name, Gregori. He said he was glad for the opportunity to talk to me, and then his story about the woman."

"Describe him." Leiner tapped on the tablet screen, then held it closer to Evan to record him.

"Sure. He was about six feet tall, fine blond hair, brown eyes, high forehead, pointed nose, small chin, wide mouth. He was wearing a brown leather coat and yellow scarf." As he said the last sentence, his memory flashed on the man outside the bistro after physical therapy three days earlier.

Leiner nodded. "He said he was Russian?"

"Yes. He said he worked for the SVR and that Detective Ruiz hadn't believed his story about the Chilean woman. His accent sounded Russian, but like he'd not lived in Russia for a long time. Alicia thought it was fake."

"Would you be willing to work with a police artist to develop a sketch of this man? I will ask Detective Ruiz about him and pass on your information. I am certain he would want to know about your conversation and the Chilean woman. If you think of anything else, no matter how crazy or small, please call me, Herr Quinn. The investigation is outside my jurisdiction, but I will pass information on to Ruiz."

"Thanks, Inspector. I didn't think to call Detective Ruiz. Let me know if he wants to talk to me." So Leiner wanted to be involved and informed after all.

Their cheeseburgers arrived—real beef burgers and Evan wondered how Woody had managed that with the food rationing—and their conversation shifted to the recent attempts by the United Nations to broker a cease fire with the Chinese. A stalemate in the fighting had been reached in Russia, and before the Chinese had a chance to reconsider using weapons of mass destruction to break it, the European Union and the Pacific Alliance had proposed cease-fire terms at the UN. The Chinese Ambassador had grinned, nodded, and bowed but had not agreed to the negotiations. The Chinese-American talks in Vienna had ended the week after the war had begun last August. The Chinese weren't talking with anyone at the moment. At least not overtly.

The waltz from Tchaikovsky's *Sleeping Beauty* played from Leiner's suit jacket. He took out his cell phone, and glanced at the display. "I'm sorry, Herr Quinn. I must take this call."

Leiner listened to the person speaking to him on the phone. In German, he replied, "I will return to the office." He closed the phone. "Herr Quinn, unfortunately—"

"You have to go. It's OK. Before you leave, is there any news about the investigation into Vasia Bartyakov's murder?"

Leiner's mouth stretched into a tight smile under his dark blond mustache. "No, Herr Quinn. We continue our investigation. It has been six months, however. As they say in old American movies, the trail is cold." Leiner waved to the waitress. "I'll pay for our lunch on my way out. How will you return home? Is there anything—?"

"I'll be fine. I'll take a cab. Thanks for lunch, Inspector." Evan watched him pick up his computer tablet from the table and head for the side door. Woody appeared by the pastry counter and stopped Leiner. They smiled, and shook hands, and Leiner gave him his bankcard to pay.

Evan hadn't seen his handler since last fall, a month after

the war had begun. The day Woody had told him that their bosses in Washington were prepared to expose him to the world as a rogue assassin working for the American West secessionist states—now united and sovereign under the name DWA, Democratic West America—because he'd out-maneuvered them with Brown's help. Woody had given him a choice at that meeting: continue to work for them as the ghost warrior and assassin Perceval or be arrested for the assassination of Jiang Xu and lose his freedom and music. He couldn't bear to lose either.

The white-haired Chicagoan wore his usual white shirt, rumpled dark green pants, and a long apron spattered with ketchup and grease tied around his waist. Woody had still not produced his forger for the alternate ID documents that Evan had requested. At this point, Evan didn't like or trust the guy, but he had little choice. He must deal with him.

After Leiner left, Woody came over to Evan, a cocky lilt in his gait. "Heard about Buenos Aires, Maestro. How are you feeling?" The old American slid into the chair Leiner had left. "You could have called."

"Worried about me?" Evan set his cheeseburger on the plate. "I need to find out who tried to kill me. Have you heard anything?"

Woody nodded. "Not a peep. Glad to see you're doing so well. The question has come up, though, why you haven't done anything about your assignment. It's been five months. Brown is still out there, talking. Our bosses are not pleased."

"I'm just trying to stay alive, Woody. You can tell them that. Between the war and Buenos Aires, and now finding out that the cops in Buenos Aires think it was a professional hit, I'm still in danger. So, I really need for you to do some digging, all right? Put some pressure on your sources and find out what's going on. I can't do anything about the assignment if I'm dead."

Woody giggled. "Such drama. Have you even tried to find out where they're holding Brown?"

Evan picked up his cheeseburger and took a bite. He hadn't expected Woody to bring up the Perceval assignment. He felt a powerful urge to punch him.

"No, you haven't. So, you need to put some pressure on your own sources, Perceval, and find out. Brown should have been terminated months ago."

Evan finished chewing and swallowed. "Excellent cheeseburger, Woody. Where'd you get the real beef?" Evan gave Woody one of his public persona smiles, noting Woody's darkened eyes and scowl. "I'll see what I can find out about Brown, but I won't be acting on it until I'm at one hundred percent physically. What would really speed my recovery is finding out who wants me dead."

"I bet Inspector Leiner would be more than happy to help you with Brown's location. Didn't he set up a meeting between you and Brown just after Brown defected?"

"Brown requested that meeting, not me." Evan took another bite of his burger. He hoped it wasn't too soon after surgery for his gastrointestinal system to be eating this type of food. He met Woody's eyes. "I'll tell you something, Woody. It's different being on the receiving end. Remember that. So, find out who's apparently hired a contract killer—or *killers*—to terminate me, or nothing will happen with Brown."

Woody nodded and got up. "You're welcome here any time, Maestro. How do I contact you?"

"Got a pen? I'll give you my home phone but I don't think it's clean. I'll have to buy another clean cell phone."

Woody's bushy white eyebrows shot up. "You've been without a clean phone for how many months? Don't you know any better, Perceval?"

Evan felt the hot blood of embarrassment rush into his face. "Now that I'm back on my feet, I'll buy one."

"Buy one today. I'm not calling you on anything but a clean phone." Woody sighed. "It's good to see you, Perceval. I'll expect news from you soon about progress on your assignment." Woody sidled away to the pastry counter where he greeted a customer.

Evan returned to his lunch. The nearest telephone store that he could recall was on the Graben. Not too far a walk. And he'd need to find a taxi to go home. Or he could just walk up to Schottentor and take a Number 41 streetcar. He'd see how tired he was after shopping for the cell phone.

He had no intention of doing the Perceval job. The former CIA agent had protected him, kept him alive, and now he intended to protect Brown from Woody and the NEP bosses in Washington. He had no idea where Brown was, anyway. Leiner could probably find out, if he didn't already know, but might be suspicious of such a question from him.

The walk to the Graben in the cold February air and sunshine revived his energy and mood. Several people on the street smiled in recognition but left him alone. He found the telephone store next to the Baroque St. Peter's Church. He and the sales associate, a young man with apple cheeks and blond hair who called him Maestro, perused the different models on display. Evan picked up a sleek black flip phone that looked identical to the one Woody had given him last summer. In a flash, he realized that he probably could have kept that phone and simply brought it to the phone store to set up a new account for it.

"I like this one," he said in German to the sales associate. A flash of yellow outside the store window caught his eye. A yellow scarf. When he turned for a better look, it was gone.

"An excellent choice, Maestro. Would you like to set up also an internet account for it?"

Evan nodded. "Limited internet. No GPS please. Does this model also have the vibrate option as well as a choice of ringtones?"

The sales associate inserted a battery and account card into the back of the phone. "Of course. You have a ringtone in mind, Maestro?"

The choices in ringtones amused him. He considered the opening measures of Beethoven's Fifth Symphony but decided it was too obvious. On the street, on his travels, everywhere, he'd heard all kinds of ringtones, and the two things they had in common were that they were all loud and all music. No one anymore had just a singular tone that repeated. So, he ended up with a plain single-tone ring with the option to change it if it bored him.

After taking care of all the internet set-up, account documentation, and payment, Evan left the store, eyeing the people on the Graben. No yellow scarves. He was feeling tired and vulnerable, and his shoulder ached. He hadn't thought the shopping expedition through. He was not in strong physical

shape. He was alone. No way could he perform a proper surveillance-detection run. He didn't have the energy. No way
could he *run* if it became necessary. He shouldn't have stayed
in the First District alone. He thought of calling Freda, but
decided not to worry her.

Watching the activity on the street, and seeing nothing
unusual, which only made him more nervous—effective surveillance blended into the background—he headed back the
way he'd come. The walk to Schottentor might flush out any
surveillance shadows. He noticed when people recognized
him—their smiles or waves—and was relieved no one stopped
him to chat or ask for an autograph.

He felt certain that Alicia wasn't tailing him now. She
thought he was with Leiner. And, after all, she'd said that
calling the police would be his best defense when she wasn't
following him. He turned left past the Meindl grocery store,
with its forest green and gold façade, onto Naglergasse,
dodging shoppers carrying bags with baguettes and wine
bottles. Halfway to Am Hof, he stopped in a Tabak Trafik to
buy licorice for Pierre. No one followed him into the shop.
Opposite Am Hof, the large plaza where people gathered for
a weekly flea market on Saturdays, he stopped to examine
the window display of a bookstore. The street activity and
people reflected in the window appeared normal. No yellow
scarves.

Then he saw the guy. A lithe Chinese man wearing a
black leather jacket and jeans who stood out on the street
because the Chinese had disappeared from Vienna after the
war began. Evan studied the guy's reflection in the store window. Standing on the opposite side of the street and half a

block toward the Graben, he faced Evan, his eyes hidden by sunglasses. His hands were in the jacket's pockets. His absolute stillness reminded Evan of a panther stalking prey.

Schottentor was almost a ten-minute walk from where he stood, probably longer in his condition. Evan had no choice, however. He took out his old cell phone and turned to face the Chinese guy. Evan stared right at him, lifted the cell phone to his ear. To his surprise, the Chinese guy pivoted and walked away toward the Graben. Evan watched him until he turned the corner.

Taking long strides, Evan headed up Naglergasse, through Freyung, past an old woman, bundled up in black against the cold, and selling roasted chestnuts, and onto narrow Schottengasse. Two blocks later, feeling winded, Evan stopped at the escalators that led to the underground Schottentor passage and the streetcar stop. He remembered the taxi stand by the university and walked toward it. Four yellow taxis waited, the lights on their roofs lit. Evan whistled and waved to the first one in line. Taking a taxi home would be smarter, he decided. No one could follow him inside the car as they could inside a streetcar. He checked around as the cab stopped by him at the curb. The cloud of his cold breath enveloped his head, momentarily blurring his view. The traffic on the Ringstrasse appeared its usual busy normal. Evan slid into the cab's back seat and handed the driver his bankcard.

Now he had two things to watch for when he was out: a yellow scarf and that Chinese guy. Someone watched him here in Vienna. The Chinese? He took out his cell phone and pressed speed dial for Alicia.

CHAPTER 10

"I'll buy you a bratwurst, kid," Avoine said in German.

Pierre eyed Avoine, his brown wool coat and yellow scarf, from his perch on the Türkenschanz Park jungle gym. Another young boy climbed the massive jungle gym at the other end, watched by his mother. A group of children rolled balls of snow to make a snowman. Mothers pushed baby strollers covered with wool blankets. Black tree branches veined through the pale gray overcast morning sky.

Pierre had eaten delicious hot oatmeal for breakfast with a slice of toast slathered with Nutella. He looked forward to the American cheeseburger at the Café Chicago that Monsieur Evan had promised him for lunch today. He wanted no bratwurst from Avoine. He wanted only for Avoine to leave him alone.

Monsieur Evan was an American. Now Pierre knew that Avoine, from his accent like Monsieur Evan's, was also an American. Avoine did not like Monsieur Evan. Avoine was spying on Monsieur Evan.

"I'm not hungry," Pierre replied in German. He climbed away as Avoine walked around the geometric conglomeration of metal pipes to stay close to him. Pierre knew he must do what Avoine demanded. At the same time, he understood that Monsieur Evan (and Madame Kirsch) wanted to help him find his parents and return home. Avoine had never offered to help him, only threatened him, but he had promised to release him once his job for Avoine was done. What could he do? The Wizard Howl had advised he must protect himself, survive.

"You're doing a good job, kid," Avoine said. The American took out of his coat pocket the drawing Pierre had made for him of the layout of Monsieur Evan's apartment. "What about Frau Kirsch's house? Next time, I'd like a drawing of how that's laid out, OK? Including the security system, how it's set up, just like you did with Quinn's apartment. And you need to spend a lot more time with Quinn. The transmitter works fine, but you're not with him enough to get the information I want."

"I cannot glue myself to him," Pierre replied, annoyed. "He works in his apartment, he rests in his apartment, and when he is doing these things, he does not want me there."

Avoine grabbed his ankle and turned it. Pain shot up his leg. "You better find a way to get him to want you there."

"Let go of my leg!" Pierre screamed and kicked out at Avoine, screaming again.

As he hoped, his screams gained the attention of several mothers, bundled up in wool, their breath forming clouds around their heads as they talked, their eyes watching him slap and kick at the tall, muscular man. Pierre did not resemble Avoine as a son would a father. Parental suspicion and alarm electrified the air.

Avoine released Pierre's leg. "Shut up. You scream like that again, you'll wish for a little leg pain instead of what I'll give you. You little shit."

Pierre massaged his ankle. "If you hurt me, Frau Kirsch will see and she will call the police. I will tell them about you."

Avoine stared up at Pierre for a long moment, his expression blank. Then a slow smile spread across his clean-shaven face, crinkling the skin around his ice-blue eyes. "You say one word about me, Pierre, you *will* never see your parents, your family, or your friends ever again. You'll be locked up in a prison with rats that'll chew on your toes and your nose and nobody will know where you are." He cackled, a demented laugh without mirth.

Pierre cringed. He hated rats. Maman hated rats. Vile, dirty creatures with creepy long tails. He'd never told Avoine or anyone else about his hatred and fear of rats. How could Avoine read his mind? And he could never escape from Avoine because of the GPS transmitter embedded in his left thigh. He looked around the park. The other kids and their parents had returned to their own business, their own play, and no longer scrutinized him and Avoine.

"Tell me about Quinn's physical therapy," Avoine said, moving around the jungle gym so that he could see all of the children's play area and the children, the parents guarding them.

Pierre shrugged. "I have told you before. Every day Herr Quinn performs his exercises and becomes stronger."

"Has he showed you the gunshot wounds, the scars? Do you know where they are?"

Pierre shook his head and climbed toward the other end of the jungle gym, taking care to keep several feet between him and Avoine. "I know one in his right shoulder, and also one somewhere in the stomach. The physical therapy is for the shoulder. He takes pain medication. He tires easily." But Monsieur Quinn had not been too tired to listen to him play the piano and give him a little piano lesson. He was never too tired to listen to him talk about his parents, Paris, his favorite books, and even the Wizard Howl, Ashitaka and Steamboy. Monsieur Quinn read to him and had promised they would watch anime this weekend.

"He tires easily." Avoine looked away toward the chess tables where players hunched over their games. "And you're certain Quinn's still going to visit his friend Greta Fasching on Sunday?"

"Yes. Frau Fasching will have a music salon, Herr Quinn said, and everyone there will play music. I wanted to go. But he told me it was for grown-ups."

Avoine nodded. "Stuff like that is boring, kid."

"Not to me."

"Yeah, well, you're weird." Avoine glanced at his watch. "What did you tell them about where you were going this morning?"

"I told them nothing." Pierre stretched one foot down and then the other, climbing toward the ground. "I was afraid Frau Kirsch would not let me come to the park alone."

"OK. Come on." Avoine held out his hand to Pierre, who ignored it. He jumped down to the ground. "You need to be more grateful, kid," Avoine said in his growly voice, the voice that warned of a beating if Pierre didn't obey. "Where'd you be right now without me, huh? You'd be starving and freezing on the streets. Maybe you'd be dead already. And didn't I tell you that Quinn would take care of you? So, come on."

Pierre allowed Avoine to put his arm around his shoulders. He thought of when he'd seen Avoine outside the restaurant, when Monsieur Evan and Madame Kirsch saw him, too. He would call a meeting with the Wizard Howl, Ashitaka and Steamboy. He must find a way to protect Monsieur Evan and Madame Kirsch from Avoine.

"He's been gone for over an hour, Evan. I don't know where he is. He said nothing to me about going anywhere. I thought he was playing with Sasha in the backyard. I think we should call the police." Freda went to her videophone on her kitchen wall.

"Wait, Freda." Evan poured himself another cup of coffee from the silver steel pot on the kitchen table. "He's probably just off exploring the neighborhood and lost track of time. He lived on the streets for four months and survived. I'm sure he's fine."

"What about that man he saw the other day? The one that frightened him so much?" Freda crossed her arms. She had dressed in a loden-green wool suit and pastel-yellow silk blouse for the meeting at the French embassy. "What if that man finds him?"

The man in the brown wool coat and yellow scarf who had seemed familiar even when too far away to identify. Evan sipped the hot coffee. Pierre would run if he saw the Yellow Scarf Man. Evan was sure of it, but he decided that the next time they were alone in his apartment, he'd ask Pierre about the man, find out what the boy knew about him.

"Pierre's a smart kid, Freda. You've seen how smart he is.

I know you're worried. But I think he'll run in here and be upset with himself because he's late. Did the embassy call?" He made small circles with his right arm stretched out to the side. He wasn't wearing his sling today. He'd decided to try going without it but had given it to Freda to put in her purse just in case. For the meeting, he'd chosen to wear a light blue Oxford shirt under a navy-blue crew neck sweater and navy-blue corduroy sport jacket with navy-blue corduroy pants. Business-like but casual and comfortable.

"A Monsieur Cassel. I think he's the case officer investigating Pierre's situation. He said the meeting today was to meet Pierre, talk with him, swab his cheek for DNA."

"What about his parents? I get the feeling there's something they're not telling us."

Freda sat down opposite him at the kitchen table and filled her coffee mug half full. "I think someone will be there today who knows them and Pierre very well and will be able to identify Pierre. I fear the worst about his parents." She looked out the kitchen window.

The front door slammed. Freda flinched at the sound. Evan called out, "Pierre?"

Running footsteps approached the kitchen, and then Pierre burst into the room. His face was flushed and he was breathing hard, but otherwise he looked fine. His sweet voice was higher from the exertion. "I am so sorry. Is it too late? I am so sorry!" he said in German.

"Where have you been?" Freda said in German. "We have been so worried. Please always tell us where you are going."

Pierre gasped a big breath before replying. "I am so sorry,

Madame. I went to Türkenschanz Park to climb on the jungle gym and to watch the chess players. Is it too late? Have we missed the meeting?"

"No, we haven't missed the meeting." Freda emptied her coffee mug into the sink, rinsing it once. "But we will be late if we don't leave now."

Evan winked at Pierre. Pierre winked back with a grin.

The traffic into the First District at mid-morning moved at a steady pace until they ran into a detour from the Gürtel Boulevard near Westbahnhof because of a bomb crater. Evan realized it wasn't far from Owen and Lucia's apartment. Freda turned on Mariahilfer Strasse and drove toward the First District. She turned right onto another street that brought them to Karlsplatz across from the Musikverein. He hadn't seen the concert hall for months. It stood untouched by Chinese bombs. He didn't know yet when he'd conduct there again. Nigel had mentioned a possible date in June 2050. In the meantime, Nigel had booked him to conduct the Vienna Symphony in the Konzerthaus in three months.

At the French embassy's side gate, Freda spoke with a guard, who pointed to a parking space. Evan watched Pierre. The boy looked relaxed, happy. For his sake, Evan hoped that Cassel would tell them that his parents had been sent back to Paris, not killed in the Grinzing bombing. But he couldn't imagine that Pierre's parents would leave Vienna without him.

Inside, after surrendering their coats in reception, they were escorted into a conference room that resembled a living room in a residence more than a meeting room in an office. Two sofas and wing-back chairs stood in front of tall windows framed by deep green drapes. The scent of jasmine hung in the air, but no flowers decorated the room.

Pierre remained close to Freda, who wandered over to the windows as Evan sat down on one of the sofas. After a five-minute wait, the door opened and two men in dark suits entered. The first, a tall middle-aged man with black hair, a matching beard, and piercing blue eyes, smiled at Evan. The second man, a portly blond in his thirties, clapped his hands with a broad grin as he said, "Pierre!"

"Monsieur Boulez!" Pierre said with a delighted laugh.

Evan listened to the torrent of French that flowed among the three. Freda smiled at him. Whatever they were saying, it made Pierre happy. The boy was smiling. Then the tall bearded man turned to him and Freda, addressing them in English.

"I am Paul Cassel." He extended his hand. "My colleague is Jean Boulez. We are quite happy to meet you, Maestro, and you, Madame Kirsch. Thank you for taking care of young Pierre."

As Evan shook his hand he said, "Our pleasure. He's a joy to have around. I hope you can help us reunite him with his family."

"You speak French?" Cassel said. Evan shook his head, feeling painfully inadequate all of a sudden.

"I speak French," Freda said. "I can translate as necessary."

"I'll just listen. Let me know if there's anything...." Evan caught Pierre looking at him with a puzzled expression. He switched to German and said, "Pierre, Freda can handle this."

Pierre nodded and said in a grave voice in German, "May I sit next to you?"

They sat on the sofa facing the Frenchmen on the other sofa. Explaining the process in French, Boulez produced a sterile DNA swab, which he used to collect saliva and cheek cells from Pierre's mouth. A formality to confirm Pierre's identity, he assured them. Although Evan couldn't understand what they were saying, he understood from the warm tone of their voices and their open, friendly body language that both men accepted that Pierre was indeed Pierre Levade, a French citizen, and that Boulez and Pierre knew each other well.

Twenty minutes later, Freda gave him an alarmed look, her eyes pained, after Pierre said something to Boulez. A second of silence stretched into a minute. Pierre shrugged, said something more and waited.

Freda whispered to him in English, "They told him his parents were killed in Grinzing last fall—the bombing, as we suspected. He told them that his parents weren't at home. They'd left on an errand. He asked them where his parents are now."

The muscles in his chest contracted. Denial gripped Pierre in its powerful fists. Evan caught Cassel's eye. He stood and walked over to the windows, followed by Cassel.

"Freda and I think that Pierre needs counseling. He has maintained since we met him that his parents were alive and he needs to find them. Were they buried here? Maybe a visit to their graves with a counselor?" Evan said in English.

Cassel nodded. "We have a counselor waiting to talk with Pierre. From what Madame Kirsch told me on the telephone,

I understood that Pierre is not accepting his parents' deaths. He was living on the streets until he found you, Maestro. He has been traumatized, I think, in more than one way. He seems comfortable with you and Madame Kirsch. He trusts you. Would you be willing to take care of him until we can find his relatives in France?"

"Of course. I'm sure Freda will say the same thing. We'll do whatever is needed to help him."

"Thank you, Maestro. I think now we will have Pierre talk with the counselor."

The counselor turned out to be a clinical psychologist assigned to the embassy after the war began. Her name was Marie Moreau. When she came into the room, Evan was surprised by how young she was. She wore wool pants and a stylish pullover sweater, both in a heather gray. What had he expected? He decided that he'd hoped for someone more like a warm and comforting grandma. He watched Pierre greet her like a proper gentleman and couldn't help but smile. Pierre looked back at him.

"Monsieur Evan," he said, and continued in German. "You agree with Monsieur Cassel? You want me to speak with Dr. Moreau? But I am not certain I have anything to say to her."

Evan nodded, struck by Pierre's seriousness and the oddness of his claim. He said in German, "Freda and I would like you to speak with Dr. Moreau. Why don't you tell her how we met, how your papa told you about me, and what you have been doing since last summer? Find out if she thinks you should return to school. If she says yes, we can find one for you that's open."

Pierre nodded with a frown. He walked over to the door, gesturing for Dr. Moreau to come with him, and she laughed quietly. Pierre was all business. She said something to Cassel and Boulez, and then she and Pierre left. Freda was smiling.

Boulez said in English, "He is so much like his father, Georges. Always the proper gentleman, you see?"

"Could you tell us a little about his parents, his family?" Freda said.

The Frenchmen described Georges and Juliette Levade as cultured people, private people, good parents who encouraged Pierre in his curiosity about the world and completely supportive of his creativity and of his studies in school. Georges was a diplomat. Juliette had been a somewhat rebellious artist from a wealthy Parisian family when she met and married Georges. They had traveled the world together, and after Pierre was born, they simply brought him along with them. She had excelled at the social obligations of a diplomat's wife. The couple was extremely well liked in the French diplomatic service, in Paris, and by the people they'd met in the countries in which they'd lived. Their deaths were a terrible loss. But at least Pierre had survived. His maternal grandparents, who had lived in Paris, were both dead now, but Cassel believed Georges's father and brother lived somewhere in the South of France.

Cassel invited them to wait for Pierre in the conference room where they would serve coffee and pastries, but Evan respectfully declined their offer. He wanted to go for a bit of fresh air in nearby Ressel Park in Karlsplatz. Freda went with him to retrieve their coats in reception.

The sun had finally burst through the overcast, and a brisk

northwest wind had blown away the clouds. They skirted the massive Baroque Karlskirche with its two tower pavilions that reminded Evan of Oriental pagodas, and minaret-like columns the color of sandstone to the frozen pond in front.

"My heart aches for Pierre," Freda said in English.

"I know. I'm not excited about him talking with a psychologist. But friends have told me they're different here. They're not controlled by the government." As he spoke, he was thinking how different it was for Pierre. No one thought he was crazy, only hurt. For Evan, no, no head doctor.

"Or any government," Freda said, glancing up at him. "They are totally independent. Pierre needs to talk about what has happened to him and talk through his feelings. It may take more than one meeting."

He sighed. "Cassel seems happy to provide the service for him. It sounded like Pierre's parents were highly valued and respected."

Freda slipped her arm through his left arm, and they walked around the pond and in among the bare trees in Ressel Park. He thought of Yellow Scarf Man, of the Chinese man he'd spotted watching him the day before, possibly following him, and of the threat against him. That threat put Freda and Pierre in danger, too. He glanced around. In their section of the wintry park they were alone, but up ahead, people scurried for the U-Bahn station entrance. He saw no familiar faces, and no sign of Alicia. No surveillance shadows this morning.

"I've been thinking, Freda," he said, his tone confidential. "After my lunch with Inspector Leiner yesterday, I realized that perhaps whoever tried to kill me in Buenos Aires may still want me dead. Leiner agreed with Detective Ruiz in Buenos Aires—they think it was a professional hit that failed. My good luck. But I'm thinking that we need to increase defenses, to do something to supplement the security at your house and my apartment. Something low-tech that would be unexpected and unfamiliar to an intruder accustomed to high tech. Do you know a security system expert who might be able to set something up for us?"

Freda nodded. "I'm glad you are thinking in this way, Evan. I've been concerned too. What if they tried again? I agree about supplementing the security. I know a man. He was a good friend to my father. I believe he's retired now, but perhaps he could help us."

"Low-tech, Freda. Something not connected to the computers. Something that we could use to communicate between the house and my apartment, just in case."

"I understand. An old-fashioned security system. I don't even know if they make the equipment anymore. I'll call Beni. He will know."

"Ask him about two-way radios too. Then we wouldn't need to involve the phones."

They bought coffee at the Karlsplatz Pavilion Café and sipped it as they walked, talking about his schedule for the next two months, news of Alicia, and everyday matters that during war elevate beyond the mundane, whether they needed to purchase an emergency generator (they had lost power many times during air raids), food shortages, fuel shortages, travel restrictions, and finally which of them would travel with Pierre back to France when the time came. Freda's school would reopen after the repairs to bomb damage were completed in a month. Evan's conducting schedule picked up in April. They decided to discuss the issue further when they knew more about Pierre's situation.

Evan enjoyed talking with Freda. He felt lucky that she was a friend. He wondered why she hadn't remarried, but he hadn't the nerve to ask her. She occasionally mentioned socializing with friends and visiting her father, who lived in a retirement community east of Krems on the Danube River. She loved teaching, loved children—an elegant, attractive woman with a kind and generous heart.

Back in the embassy's conference room, they found Pierre waiting for them with Boulez. Pierre wore his black wool jacket.

"I want to show you something," Pierre said in German. "It is good you wear your coats."

"What have we talked about, Pierre?" Boulez said in English. The Frenchman looked at Evan. "Pierre has been studying English in school, but he is shy about speaking it. I have told him that perhaps you would allow him to practice speaking it with you."

Evan and Freda exchanged surprised glances. Evan said, in English, "I'd be happy to do that. Pierre, why didn't you tell us you could speak English?"

Pierre shrugged, his eyes on the floor. Boulez said something in French. Pierre shrugged again, his hands stuck deep down into his jeans pockets.

"What do you want to show us?" Freda said in German.

Pierre gasped, remembering. "Something Papa showed me!" he said in German. "Monsieur Boulez?"

The Frenchman laughed and gestured for them to follow him. Pierre grabbed Evan's left hand, and pulled him along through a carpeted corridor with Baroque molding and walls hung with portraits, to a kitchen area, then down back stairs into a renovated cellar with storage and a secure, guarded room. Boulez waved to the uniformed guard. They followed Boulez to another door, which he unlocked. When he opened it, Evan felt damp cold air and smelled dank earth and a faint odor of decay.

"Papa showed me this," Pierre said in German. "It is amazing. You will see."

Down the stone stairs they stepped into darkness so dense and complete that Evan thought he could touch it. Boulez turned on a large electric lantern at the bottom of the stairs. The light revealed a tunnel about ten or twelve feet wide and perhaps seven feet high.

"Papa said it is part of a network of tunnels under the streets that have been there for hundreds of years," Pierre said in German, his voice tinged with pride.

Boulez smiled. "Most likely since the Turkish siege, although they could be older. When the Viennese began building their subway years ago, many sections of the tunnel system were destroyed, but some sections still exist."

Boulez walked, holding up the lantern, pointing to painted signs on the walls, openings that led to other tunnels or rooms, the street names with arrows painted in white on the ceiling at a major intersection they came to.

"You see, that says Wohllebengasse," Pierre said, pointing to the sign.

"A friend told me there were tunnels under the streets,"

Evan said in German. "He said they were used extensively during World War Two."

"This is not common knowledge," Freda said, her eyes wide.

"Pierre, you knew about the tunnels," Evan said. "But you didn't use them to hide or as shelter?"

"I only know of this one entrance." Pierre shrugged. "If I knew of others, yes, I would have used the tunnels for shelter."

Boulez spoke to Pierre in French. Freda whispered to Evan, "He's telling Pierre he should have come to the embassy for help and not lived on the streets."

Pierre replied in French, his tone angry. Freda whispered, "Pierre said he needed to stay close to the house because his parents would look for him there."

Boulez talked in a gentle voice to Pierre. Evan looked at Freda's concerned face. He felt certain they were both thinking the same thing: Pierre's logic made perfect sense to him, and he could not see that it made no sense to other people. A child's perception of reality was just as malleable as an adult's. Or was it simply the mind trying to preserve life? Preserve sanity? Pierre needed to box away his parents' deaths in order to survive. Evan knew about boxing up memories and pushing them to the back of the mind's closet.

Pierre stood with his hands on his hips, looking up at Boulez, an angry frown on his face as the Frenchman spoke. Pierre gave no ground. At least not yet.

Evan walked over to the tunnel wall, still within the pool of light from the lantern. It was rough and hard, either stone or hardened dirt, and had been painted black. He could see beams reinforcing the openings into other tunnels. The floor was packed dirt. He wondered how many other entrances there were to the tunnel system and where they were. He wondered how easy it would be to get lost in the tunnels despite the street names painted overhead and the signs on the walls. Without light, a person could wander for hours.

"Freda, how could we find out where all the tunnels and entrances are?" Evan asked her as Boulez and Pierre continued their discussion in French.

Freda shook her head. "I've no idea. I didn't know about them myself until today. Perhaps a city engineer would know. What are you thinking?"

"I don't know." He glanced around. "I guess I'm kind of surprised that terrorists haven't discovered them."

"*That* is probably the reason no one knows of them now. For security reasons. Good luck finding out about where they are."

"Security." Evan nodded. During a war, the security would be even tighter regarding infrastructure.

"No!" Pierre burst into angry, frustrated tears.

Boulez gazed down at him for a moment before looking at Freda and Evan. In English he said, "He is stubborn like his father, too."

CHAPTER 11

"Ladies and Gentlemen!" Greta said clapping her hands. She stepped around a cluster of people seated on the floor of the living room. She wore an elegant champagne-colored cowl neck maternity sweater tunic over black wool pants. Her gold hoop earrings flashed in the candlelight.

Evan watched Greta to avoid looking around the spacious living room, especially at the bookcase by the archway into the dining room where Vasia had died. He'd been in the apartment only once since Vasia's death. Greta seemed to understand. She and Vasia had planned for her to move in with him by Christmas last year, and after his death, she'd stepped in to claim the apartment. The real estate agent had agreed. After all, he'd probably have had a difficult time selling it after what had happened in it, especially when the real estate market had bottomed out because of the war. When Evan had challenged her choice, Greta had explained that first of all, Vasia would have wanted her and their child to live there; and second, living in this apartment that he'd loved so much, she felt close to him. Maybe Vasia haunted the place. Evan shivered.

In German, Greta addressed the crowd packed into the room and overflowing into the adjacent dining room. "This evening, I am especially happy to welcome home my dear friend Evan Quinn." Applause erupted around Evan. He returned their smiles and applauded back. "Death nearly claimed him in Buenos Aires last month. I think I speak for everyone here that we are glad the criminal was such a bad shot!" Laughter and cheers. Evan laughed with them.

"Sofia!" someone shouted near the door.

Evan swiveled in his chair. Sofia stood in the doorway to the front foyer, her smiling face flushed from the cold, removing a purple angora scarf from her neck and shrugging out of a black wool coat. Her hair cascaded over her shoulders and the green cashmere turtleneck she wore. His breath caught in his throat.

Greta clapped again. "Sofia, what took you so long?"

"I have come directly from the airport." Sofia shook her head. "We were supposed to arrive at Schwechat six hours ago. A powerful snowstorm raged over northern Italy. Our pilot decided to detour around the storm instead of over it. She said the clouds were too high." She shrugged and laughed, waved to someone near the piano. "We flew to southern France and then east over Austria. The pilot said at least the Chinese wouldn't be able to bomb northern Italy tonight."

Snickers crackled around the room. Sofia's smoky alto voice reminded Evan again of the viola, a contrast to Pierre's sweet boyish voice. He imagined Sofia would enchant Pierre as much as she enchanted him.

"There's Glühwein in the kitchen," Greta said, and Sofia nodded to her. "And now, more music." Greta motioned for a petite blonde in her mid-twenties to join her at the four-foot black grand piano near the front windows. Evan recognized her as a violinist but couldn't remember her name. Greta continued, "I had hoped that Evan would be able to play his violin for us this evening, but he tells me his shoulder is not yet ready, so we'll expect him to play at a future salon."

"You are planning more, Greta? Schön!" a gray-haired woman said from her seat on the floor about five feet in front of him. Evan was certain he'd seen her at Vasia's housewarming party last summer.

"Vasia dreamed of having a regular music salon for our friends. He loved the idea of the nineteenth-century salons full of music and intellectual discussions. So, I decided to honor his memory in this way. Lisl Schatzmann," Greta put her arm around the young violinist, "and Vasia performed in recital at Palais Schwarzenberg last summer, a beautiful Brahms recital."

Applause peppered the crowd. Now Evan remembered her. He had attended the recital and been quite impressed with her performance. He leaned forward. Her maroon sweater tunic shimmered in the candlelight as she took her violin out of its case on the piano.

"I asked Lisl for something by Bach, and she's also agreed to play something by Mozart later."

Applause welcomed Lisl's tuning, and she smiled. A black velvet headband swept her blond hair back from her face. When she began to play, Evan relaxed into the music. Lisl had chosen J. S. Bach's Partita No. 3 in E Major for solo violin. He dropped his right arm straight by his side, and moved it in small circles as he listened.

A warm hand squeezed his other shoulder, and he looked up. Sofia stood there, sipping deep red Glühwein from a clear glass mug. She dropped down to kneel next to him and she took his left hand. A pleasant electric tingling streamed up his arm and through his body at her hand's touch—skin against skin. She smiled, only at him in that moment. He smiled. She had touched him. What should he say? Something clever, something witty, but he couldn't think of anything. He wanted to say how happy he was to see her and that he wanted her all to himself as soon as possible. But he couldn't think of the right tone, the right words. He was relieved that Lisl was playing so Sofia wouldn't expect him to say anything. He squeezed her hand and smiled when she squeezed back.

Lisl's precise bowing and wrist, her violin singing Bach, slid Evan back in time to her recital, to Vasia's white dinner jacket and scarlet bow tie, Vasia playing Bach at the piano behind Lisl. Greta had left the apartment the way it was when he was alive, with comfortable overstuffed furniture, full bookshelves, and vintage fin de siècle lamps; but then, she had done most of the decorating for him. What Bach had he played? The Sixth Partita, the toccata movement that whisper-played now through his mind in competition with the violin. The shadow memory pushed its way into his consciousness unbidden, an unwelcome reminder of what he was: Perceval. Perceval gave him power, but being Perceval had not protected him in Buenos Aires and wasn't much help now, either. Especially with Sofia.

Lisl played the last notes of the gigue, the final movement, followed by cheers and applause. She pointed her bow at him, but he shook his head to decline the acknowledgment and lifted his hands high to applaud her. He wondered if she knew the Bach Concerto for Two Violins in D Minor or

Samuel Barber's Violin Concerto. He'd talk with her later about them.

Another violinist, a violist, and cellist joined Lisl near the piano and began tuning their instruments. Trays of finger food, fresh fruit, and crackers passed from one group of people to the next around the room. Greta remained on the plush maroon sofa, one hand massaging her pregnant tummy as she talked with a shaggy-haired man next to her.

"Greta has grown, yes?" Sofia said, pulling once on his hand for his attention.

"Yes! I felt the baby move earlier. He's—or she's—a kicker." He looked down at Sofia, into her hazel-green eyes like bottomless pools. "When was the last time you saw her?"

"Two months ago. I feel I have missed so much."

Her English carried a German accent with slight British overtones on vowels. Like Leiner's English teacher, hers had either been British or had learned English from a Brit. It was rare to hear English spoken with an American accent by Europeans. No one wanted an American accent since the NEP took over America in 2016. He was still looking into her eyes and realized she was waiting for him to say something. How could he have let his mind wander away from her?

She said, "Would they miss us if we found a quiet place to talk?"

"The kitchen? I need a refill." He held up his empty glass.

All eyes were on the musicians, who had begun playing a Beethoven string quartet, as Evan and Sofia picked their way around people seated on the floor, to make their way out of the packed living room, through the front foyer, and into the spacious kitchen. A pot of Glühwein warmed on the stove, and the smell of cinnamon and orange filled the air. A buffet decorated the center island: cold meats, cheeses, fruits, raw vegetables, dressings and dips, and olives all nestled in shaved ice, and breads and rolls. Where had Greta bought all of the food for such a party during food rationing? Perhaps some of the guests had made contributions which was more likely. He opened the large stainless-steel refrigerator.

"Greta found grapes!" Sofia said, her tone surprised. "And Spanish navel oranges." She lifted a bunch of red grapes from a bowl.

"Her pregnancy gives her priority status. The city issued her a special food card. Freda has asked for a special card, too, because we have a young orphan living with us now."

"Really? The child of someone Freda knew?" Sofia ladled more of the hot spiced wine into her glass mug.

"No. Actually, I found him." Evan opened a bottle of ginger-flavored mineral water and sipped from it. "Or he found me. He followed me. In Türkenschanz Park he approached me and politely said that he recognized me, that his father had talked about me. His name's Pierre Levade. His father was a French diplomat. We had a meeting at the French embassy on Friday. They're going to find his relatives in France."

"What happened to his parents?" Sofia moved closer to him, offering him the grapes.

"Chinese bomb on their house in Grinzing. He'd been living on the streets since the bombing. He doesn't believe they were killed."

"Gott. This war is terrible." She set her mug down on the counter next to him, plucked a grape, and gave him the bunch. "I hope the Chinese bombers leave Vienna alone now."

He pulled a fat grape and ate it. "How's the movie? I'm sorry I hadn't checked my email. I've been—"

"You've been recuperating. It's fine. I was worried about you even with the news Greta gave me. You look pale. Are you in pain?"

"No, but I probably should sit down. Conserve my energy, you know? I want to stay for the whole party if I can. For Greta."

"Let's go to the guest room. Remember?"

He remembered. At Vasia's housewarming party he'd found her and a small group of people in the guest room when he'd gone in search of a quiet place to eat before performing. He remembered a large, extremely comfortable sectional sofa there. The room was the first door on the right in the hallway that led to the master bedroom. To their surprise, they found that Greta had transformed it into a powder-blue, canary-yellow and tulip-pink nursery with clouds, blue sky, and a sun painted on the ceiling, a birch crib and matching armoire with a birch changing table next to it, and two rocking chairs with blue corduroy cushions. The sectional sofa was gone. Sofia switched on the ceiling light and closed the door, muffling the music in the living room.

He set his mineral water down on the changing table. Now he had her all to himself. He went to her, bent down, and kissed her on the mouth. She responded but placed her hand on his chest, over his heart, and gently pushed him back.

"Evan, we have never talked about what happened at my

flat that Sunday after the picnic." Her cool eyes studied his face.

"I know. You've been gone. I've been gone." He shrugged.

Her voice softened. "Why did you hit me? You shouted 'no' when you hit me, nothing else. What happened to you?"

"I'm sorry, Sofia. I hit—" He remembered punching his father's face, kicking his father's lower back. He looked at her. She would never believe him. How could he have seen his father in her face that day? A wave of hot shame washed over his body.

"Why did you hit me, Evan?"

He shook his head, went over to one of the rocking chairs by the window and sat down in it. She pulled the other rocking chair over next to his.

"Will you talk to me?"

He wanted to talk to no one about it, especially not Sofia. He imagined the shock, disgust, and repulsion of her reaction. Shame burned his face.

"Evan, you need to make the choice."

"Choice." He could not look at her, feared she'd see the shame in his eyes.

She sighed, her eyes looking past him at the dark sky outside the window. "So very easy to become immersed in work, especially when that work is demanding. Actors are in that position all the time. At one point in my life, all I did was work, eat, and sleep. I thought about nothing else. I missed so much…so much of people. My sister, Hilda, and my brother, Anton, with my nieces and nephews, reminded me that I needed a balance in my life among the intellectual, physical, emotional, and spiritual. Not work all the time."

Vasia had talked about balance in life that Sunday in the Vienna Woods before he and Sofia had gone to her apartment. Evan remembered thinking about balancing the sections of the orchestra. Vasia had been prodding him to romance Sofia. He'd wanted no romantic attachments. In America, they put an individual at risk for control and extortion by the NEP. Living in Austria made no difference. Or did it?

"I was an idiot," Sofia continued, laughing low and husky. "For too much time I ignored how unbalanced my life was, how much I needed to balance it."

"I chose life when I defected. Freedom. Music." Evan looked down at his hands resting on his thighs. His hands—tools of communication when he conducted. They also carried things, touched things, fed him, washed him, dressed him. He focused on them so as not to look at her. He felt if she saw his eyes, she'd see it all—his father in his bedroom, everything.

She leaned in closer to him. "Yes. Life. What is the intent of your life?"

"Music," he said without thinking.

"Yes, music." She sighed. "I believe you are a good person, Evan. You come from a violent country, a violent life. You lived with violence and have violence inside of you. But if your *intent* is nonviolent…. For example, my intent is loving kindness, as in Buddhism. Non-judgmental loving kindness. To live my life in this way."

Non-judgmental. He didn't believe anyone could be non-judgmental. He could not tell her about the memory of his father doing to him what she had been doing in her apartment that Sunday afternoon. How could he trust her? She could use it against him. No one must know.

"Evan, what did they do to you in America?" Her tone was sad with an undercurrent of anger. "I know they arrested you."

He noticed her hand on the arm of his rocking chair, her grip tightening until her knuckles blanched.

What hadn't they done to him in America? In a cognitive flash, he realized that whoever was after him must not know about Sofia. He must keep her at a distance for her own protection until he'd figured out who wanted him dead and resolved the problem. He must protect her. And he must protect Greta and her baby.

"The less you know, Sofia, the better it is for you," he said, reaching out and caressing her jawline.

"I disagree. I want to understand. I care about you, Evan. I value our friendship and admire you as a musician. An artist. You showed fearless determination when you defected." She stood up so fast the movement startled him. "You fill your life up with work, and there's no space for anything else. I think you use it as a defensive wall against the world. But now, after being shot, if you need to talk to someone, I can give you Lothar Waage's phone number. Owen is talking to him."

"I'm fine. I'm talking to my doctor about the aftereffects of the shooting. I'm fine." He looked up at her face, expecting anger, but her eyes regarded him with concern. She had said that she cared about him. He couldn't imagine his life without her. But could he trust her to keep his secrets? What would she think of Perceval?

"Please talk with him about what happened in my flat." She turned toward the door. "The music has stopped. Perhaps we should—"

A knock vibrated the door, and it opened. Greta smiled at them as she held the door open. "What do you think of the nursery? Vasia loved staring at the sky, so I painted the sky on the ceiling."

"Lovely, Greta," Sofia said, hugging her. "You created a beautiful world for the baby. Has the music ended?"

"No. We have a surprise for Evan."

He hated surprises. He followed them with wary steps. Back in the living room, Owen and Lucia te Kumara stood by the piano. He smiled at this surprise. Owen's clothes hung as loose on him as on a clothes hanger, and he leaned on the piano, but he was smiling and nibbling on a Semmel sandwich of salami and cheese.

"Owen! The best surprise," Evan said, shaking the composer's hand. He kissed Lucia on the cheek. She went around the piano and sat down on the bench.

Owen raised an arm to quiet the room, and Greta clapped her hands. Evan glanced around. The space appeared even more crowded than when he and Sofia had left. Sofia sat on the floor near an empty chair and pointed to him, indicating the chair was his. Greta, with support from the people on either side of her, descended back onto the sofa, her body no longer as flexible as it was.

Owen cleared his throat as the room quieted. "Not too long ago," he said in German, "I lost my desire to compose music, lost my will to live. I missed Vasia terribly. Then Evan reminded me what Vasia probably would have said to that.

Struth, Vasia would not have been pleased with me at all, but he would have understood. Then he'd tell me to stop being an idiot and finish his piano sonata, which is what Evan said to me."

Giggles bounced around the room. Evan nodded. Lucia smiled at him from her seat at the piano. Sofia had said Owen was talking to the clinical psychologist, the head doctor, Lothar Waage. Owen had transformed from a man wasting away in his bed to a man who was more himself.

"So, I would like this evening," Owen continued, "to introduce you all to Vasia's piano sonata, which he asked me last summer to compose. I'd about finished it when Vasia was killed. The sonata has three movements. The middle movement is a canzone, as Vasia requested. He asked me to make the finale challenging but didn't specify how. My wife, Lucia, will perform it for us." Owen looked around for a place to sit as applause filled the air.

"Here, Owen, sit here," Evan said, moving to the floor next to Sofia.

The Māori composer picked his way between people sitting on the floor to the chair Evan had vacated, resting his hand on the top of Evan's head before he sat down. The two of them had survived. Evan was healing from his physical wounds, Owen from his grief. Evan leaned against the side of the chair to relax his abdominal muscles.

Lucia's shoulder-length dark brown hair fell in front of her face as she sat for a moment gathering her concentration. Evan hadn't heard her play before. In the opening measures of the sonata Evan heard echoes of Franz Schubert's music, which surprised him. He wouldn't have thought Vasia a big fan of Schubert. But then he remembered the Russian pianist had accompanied many vocalists who undoubtedly had sung Schubert Lieder, and Schubert had also composed waltzes, impromptus, fantasies, and sonatas for the piano. The first movement of Owen's sonata followed sonata structure, its long melody lyrical, the development section like a fugue. In the second movement, Lucia played a sweet Russian melody—Evan had heard Vasia sing it but didn't know its name—with variations that contrasted different styles of music: Baroque, Romantic, Classical, minimalist, neo-romantic, atonal, and finally the original song. The finale's angular intervals, sudden fortissimos, and a restless theme played at breakneck speed brought the sonata to a thrilling end. Evan felt excitement buzzing through his body, the tingle in his hands, a pleasant agitation. Vasia would have loved this sonata, he felt certain of it. The loud applause and cheers straightened Owen's posture in the chair and brought back his brilliant smile.

As the applause subsided, Evan struggled to his feet, thinking it'd been a mistake to sit on the floor. He felt the pull on his abdominal muscles, but they didn't hurt. He turned to Owen.

"Owen, thank you. I think Vasia would have loved this music and loved playing it."

"I agree!" Greta said. "And so does Vasia's kid." She pointed to her belly. "He was kicking and moving during the sonata." A roar of laughter filled the room.

"The baby's definitely a boy?" Lucia jumped up from the piano.

Greta's hands flew to cover her face in mock horror, to

more laughter. When the room quieted, she said, "I had not planned to tell you today, but yes, he is a boy. And, Owen, he loves your music."

The loud applause also accompanied people shifting positions as a string quintet took their seats to perform. The music continued—the Shostakovich piano quintet, a Schubert piano sonata, a Mozart violin sonata from Lisl, a string quartet by the Hungarian composer Gerhard Novosti, and the Brahms Piano Trio Op. 8 No. 1. About eleven-thirty, as he'd arranged with Alicia, Evan slipped out to the front foyer and called her on his new, clean cell phone to let her know he'd be leaving in about an hour.

"Are you taking a cab home?" Alicia said in his ear. "Call for one now."

"I'm taking the streetcar to Schottentor. I'll get a cab there."

"Why? Will it be too late for the streetcar? They do not run all night."

"I know, Alicia. It'll be one of the last ones. If I could walk to Schottentor I would for the air and exercise. I'll walk to the Ring instead for the streetcar."

The nervous concern in her voice pleased him. She'd insisted, after he'd told her about the Chinese guy following him after his lunch at Café Chicago, on shadowing him home this evening. He flipped the cell phone closed, thinking about the Chinese guy again. He could have been a surveillance shadow, or he could have been just a guy on the street who happened to be looking in his direction, remembered something, and abruptly turned and left. Evan had no way of knowing for certain which was the case. People often behaved strangely on the street, especially people talking on cell phones.

"Hey, mate," Owen said behind him. "When will you conduct again?"

He turned to see Owen bundled up in wool for the cold outdoors and Lucia holding his arm. "Copenhagen, the Danish National Symphony Orchestra, the week of March twenty-second."

"Am I on the program?" Owen grinned.

Evan laughed. "Not this time. It's Barber and Bartók. I'm thinking of your First Symphony for Zürich. They've asked for Caine, and I'll conduct his First Symphony. I thought it'd be a nice program, you and Caine. I loved Vasia's sonata." He gave Lucia a kiss on the cheek. "I expect you to keep me busy with new music, Owen."

"Caine and me in Zürich. Thank you, Evan." Owen gave him an enigmatic smile. "I'm glad you liked the piano sonata."

"You're leaving?"

"Yes," Lucia said. "He wants to stay, but he's already tired. You can see it in his face."

"I am not so tired," Owen said, his tone peevish. "Come see us soon, Evan."

He saw them out the door before returning to the living room for what turned out to be the final hour of music. A weary Greta shooed everyone out, but Evan was still one of the last to leave. He needed to give Alicia time to take position.

In the front foyer, Greta held his cobalt-blue wool coat for him. "You wear black well, Evan," she said pointing to his black corduroy sport coat and wool pants. "But I love that emerald green sweater on you."

"As do I," Sofia said, coming up behind Greta. "I am so glad to see you are recovering well from your physical wounds, Evan."

"Yes." Greta hugged him. "Thank you for coming."

"Thank you for inviting me. Let me know when you do this again. When do you return to Italy, Sofia?"

"I have an early morning flight."

"When will the filming end?" Greta said.

"Oh, who knows? We are behind schedule. I hope not longer than a month."

Sofia gave him a quick hug and a smile, and he left, thinking how that moment after a hug when the two bodies parted felt like a cold, silent void.

Outside, Evan glanced around. No activity across the street at the construction site where the Hilton Hotel had stood. One car sped past, otherwise no car traffic. A light snow fell. He spotted Alicia in her old woman disguise, wool scarf and coat, half a block away on his side of the wide boulevard. Evan strolled across Landstrasse Hauptstrasse, stretching his legs with his long stride, and headed toward the Ringstrasse. The fresh snow scrunched under his feet. Pierre would want to make a backyard snowman in the morning.

The forest of bare trees at the north edge of Stadtpark formed a spiky wall. Evan passed the entrance. Movement behind him, a sharp intake of breath, made him take a quick step left and turn his body right. He saw the glint of a knife before its wielder ran into him. Evan's Krav Maga training kicked in. His right elbow caught the man's chin and knocked him back.

"Alicia!" Evan faced his attacker. In this part of the street, shadows filled the empty spaces and hid faces. Evan made out a black leather jacket, short stature, and black hair before the man rushed him.

Evan dodged the knife and pivoted. His right foot hit the back of the man's knees, buckling his legs. The man fell on his side but swiveled his body toward Evan. Powerful legs scissored Evan's legs, throwing him off balance. He crashed to the ground and rolled away from his attacker on the snowy sidewalk. His attacker had said nothing. He acted confident and calm, sure of his task and his target. He was a professional. Where was Alicia? Evan rolled onto his back so he could see his attacker's face when the man came at him again.

Where was the guy? Evan sat up. No one in front of him. To his right, he saw Alicia running toward him. Two hands grabbed his shoulders from behind and pulled, dragging him into the park over the bumpy, frozen ground and through brittle bushes. He leaned back into the man's hands and raised one leg but couldn't reach the guy to kick him. He squirmed and felt the sharp pain of the muscle pull in his abdomen. With his left hand, Evan grabbed at his attacker's hand on his right shoulder as his attacker let go and hit the side of Evan's head. He went down. He rolled even as he felt the first kick to his lower back. They were partially hidden now by the trees at the entrance.

Why didn't the man just kill him? Evan curled his body in on itself to protect his abdomen, his right shoulder. Where was the knife? He heard branches snap and a satisfying *whumpf* followed by the *thump* of a body hitting the ground. He rolled up onto his knees, pain shooting through his lower back, right shoulder, and chest.

His attacker sprawled on his back on the snowy ground, Alicia stood above him, holding the man's switchblade on him. "An idiot," she said in English.

Evan crawled over to the man. Alicia shone a pocket flashlight on his face, and Evan's stomach cramped as he recognized him. "The Chinese guy. Following me the other day. But how could he have known where I'd be? Is he dead?"

"No." Alicia prodded the Chinese man's shoulder. She said something in Mandarin. She toed the man's face. His eyes opened, and Alicia aimed the bright flashlight directly into his eyes.

The man's cold expression didn't change. His eyes were like black holes staring at him. Evan thought that those could be his own eyes, Perceval's eyes. "He's ignoring you, Alicia. Maybe he doesn't speak Chinese."

A smirk shifted the man's mouth.

"He understands English," Alicia said.

Evan grabbed his attacker's collar with one hand. "Who sent you? Who wants me dead?"

The man's expression remained unchanged, his mouth shut.

Evan looked up at Alicia. "Some persuasion?"

Alicia moved so fast it was over before Evan could register what she was doing. In one smooth movement, she knifed the man in his abdomen. Evan knew from his own experience that the wound was probably life-threatening. The man gasped in pain and flinched.

Evan shook the guy by the shoulders. "Now *you're* the victim of a mugging. That's what you were doing, right? Making my murder look like a mugging. Tell me. Who sent you? Who wants me dead?" He was aware of Alicia staring at him as if she was seeing him for the first time.

The attacker smiled, a genuine, satisfied smile. He said, his accent American, "You need to take your questions to the library."

"What library?" Evan hadn't been to a library in years. His questions weren't exactly the kind one found the answers to in a library.

"Stop speaking nonsense," Alicia said, pushing Evan away and holding the knife to the man's throat. "Tell us what we want to know."

"It won't help you." The man smiled again. He thought he had the upper hand.

"You see?" Alicia said, nodding to Evan. "Exactly like the one in Buenos Aires. They are not afraid to die. He won't talk to us." She touched her forehead. "You have a cut that's bleeding."

Head wounds bled fast and furious, but in the cold night air, he hadn't felt the blood on his face. He scooped up some snow and held it against his forehead.

"Go home. I will deal with this."

He staggered to his feet, his whole body in pain. A dark stain spread in the snow next to the Chinese man's torso. He probably didn't have much time. Evan looked down into his face. "You're an American. Who hired you? Americans? Chinese? Russians?"

The man laughed. It was the last sound he made.

Alicia wiped the blade on his pants. "Nice blade," she said. "His death will send a message to whoever sent him."

CHAPTER 12

Gunshots jolted Evan as he ran into Plaza Houssay in Buenos Aires. He opened his eyes on his bedroom ceiling but saw operating room lights overhead, heard metal jangle against metal, voices speaking Spanish. The metallic smell of blood, his blood. His heart pounded in his chest. All the sensations, sights, sounds—his mind confronting him with memories.

"Monsieur Evan?"

Pierre's voice bubbled like he was underwater. Evan squinted in the direction of the rocking chair in the corner flanked by windows, all the lines blurred, Pierre's face blurred.

"Monsieur Evan? Are you well? I will call Madame."

"No, no, Pierre." He thought he spoke clearly but heard only a mumble.

Pierre came over to Evan's mattress and box spring stacked on the floor, and squatted down near his head. "You are not eating breakfast today. We came to see you."

"I'm glad to hear you speaking English, Pierre." This time he enunciated clearly. Evan groaned as he rolled onto his left side to face the boy. His right shoulder screamed in pain, and his entire body ached. His mind remembered as well as his body the attack the night before. He remembered that his attacker had known where and when to find him.

How had he known? With the pain, his vision sharpened. "What time is it? Can you tell time in English?"

"Of course. It is eleven-thirty o'clock in the morning." Pierre grinned. He wore jeans and a cherry-red turtleneck sweater and to Evan looked quintessentially French. It must be Pierre's long brown hair, the reckless insouciance of it, the way it hung in his blue eyes.

"What's the plan for the day, Pierre?"

"A Monsieur Beni works in Madame's house. Madame said he will work in your apartment also. I do not know what his work is. What is the cut on your face? Madame thinks you need the doctor for it." Pierre reached out to touch Evan's forehead, the one-inch cut from the Chinese man's knife the night before. Chinese-*American* man.

"It's not deep, Pierre. I'll put a bandage on it or something. Can you get me a glass of water from the kitchen, please?"

The French boy ran out at the speed of eagerness to help. Evan found the hydrocodone bottle on the carpeted floor next to his bed near the white globe lamp. He'd forgotten to take one when he arrived home. He'd been exhausted and collapsed into bed. Pierre returned with a glass half full of cool mineral water that fizzed against Evan's nose when he took a swallow with the hydrocodone.

"You need a haircut, Pierre."

"As do you, Monsieur."

Evan laughed, felt the sharp muscle pull in his abdomen. Pierre's English and manner charmed him. He felt also a fullness, a pressure, in his chest he couldn't recall ever feeling before, and a pinching behind his nose as if he would cry.

"Madame requests you call her when you wake, Monsieur."

Evan lay back down. "My cell is in my jacket. Would you—?"

Pierre dug into the pocket of the black corduroy jacket draped over the rocking chair and produced the slim black phone. "Is it also a videophone?"

"No, a basic phone. I'm not keen on all the bells and whistles for phones. Plus all the bells and whistles are expensive, time-consuming distractions. What idle people do to fill up their lives, to distract them from reality, from themselves."

Pierre handed him the phone. "Bells and whistles?"

Evan dialed Freda's phone number. "Extras. Fancy stuff. Like camera, videophone capability, games, maps, all sorts of software. Internet access also makes it easier to hack into the phone." He heard Freda's greeting in his ear. "Hi, Freda. My new valet, Pierre, told me to call you."

Pierre's eyebrows, barely visible under his hair, rose and he blushed. He ran out of the bedroom, saying, "I will practice the piano."

She chuckled on the phone. "You mind that I left him there? He wanted to stay, and I was concerned. You slept so deeply, it was like you were unconscious. What happened last night? You have a cut on your forehead."

"Some rough-housing, nothing major. I guess I pushed myself too much, though. I'll rest today. Pierre said Beni is here?"

"Yes. He's installing the supplemental security system. We are fortunate. He had saved equipment, thinking he would sell it on the internet eventually."

"Good. Pierre needs a haircut."

"As do you."

Evan sighed. "He can stay until Beni comes over here." He listened to Pierre playing a scale on the piano in his front room. "I don't think Pierre needs to know about the new system until it's up and running. I don't want to frighten him, but he'll need to know how to activate it."

"Agreed. I'll take him for a haircut then."

An hour later, after Evan had done his physical therapy exercises for his right arm and shoulder under Pierre's stern supervision, he washed and shaved and put on the green-and-navy-blue tartan-plaid flannel pajamas he'd bought in Helsinki last November. Freda brought them a three-course lunch in a rectangular picnic basket. Evan returned to bed after lunch. Telling Pierre that Evan needed to sleep, Freda took the boy back to her house.

As he lay in bed, wide awake and not at all sleepy, Evan went over and over in his mind what had happened. The Chilean assassin must have been watching him in Buenos Aires, noting his regular movements, especially his late-night runs. He had not noticed her shadowing him. *Stupid, stupid.* He'd believed he was safe there. The Chinese-American must have been doing the same thing, but he didn't know that in Vienna Evan was more careful. Evan spotted him once. The Russian Gregori at the Paris airport—was he part of this, too? He needed to talk to Woody again. The old American hadn't called him. He needed to talk with Alicia. Were Buenos Aires and the Chinese-American connected? Or were they two separate, unrelated incidents? He couldn't shake the feeling of being a half-dead mouse toyed with by a cat. Who was the cat?

He hadn't yet talked with Nigel today, so he expected to see his manager's familiar hawk-like face and abundant white hair when his videophone warbled. But the face that greeted him on the monitor was Klaus Leiner's.

"Inspector. How are you?" Evan sank onto an oak kitchen chair in front of his videophone and rested his right arm on the oak table.

"I am fine, Herr Quinn. You look tired. Are you all right?" Leiner sat at his usual cluttered desk in his modest office, a line of beige file cabinets behind him. He wore a charcoal-grey suit and yellow tie. His mustache twitched as he frowned. "What happened to your forehead?"

"Yeah, I'm tired. I was at a music salon at Greta Fasching's apartment yesterday. I think I pushed myself too much. The forehead is nothing." He fingered the white gauze bandage that Freda had applied during lunch.

"Frau Fasching. She moved into Herr Bartyakov's apartment, nicht? Near Stadtpark?"

Evan nodded. Why was Leiner calling him today? Was it about Buenos Aires? Or was it about the *Chinese-American* who attacked him last night? But why would Leiner call him about that? Alicia said she would take care of it. He'd assumed she'd hide the body, as Bernie Brown had done with the bodies of Valerie Peters and the Islamic terrorists who'd tried to kidnap him in Amsterdam—hidden them in an abandoned warehouse and staged them like a murder-suicide.

Leiner's frown deepened, pulling down the ends of his

dark blond mustache. "About what time did you leave Frau Fasching's?" Leiner's gray eyes bore into him.

Evan shrugged. "I'm not sure. About twelve-thirty in the morning? I took a cab. Why? What happened?" He stared at Leiner. "Is Greta OK?"

"Ja. Frau Fasching is fine. A man was murdered last night in Stadtpark between one and two o'clock. He carried an American passport."

"Really?" Alicia had left him there. Evan didn't hide his surprise. At the same time, his stomach knotted. Neither he nor Alicia had thought about searching the guy's pockets for identification or anything else. Should he tell Leiner he'd been attacked? No. Leiner would conclude he'd killed the guy. And he couldn't tell him about Alicia's true identity. At least not yet. "Was he really an American? I mean, didn't I hear that the Americans had banned any non-commercial or non-diplomatic foreign travel again because of the war?"

Leiner cocked his head to one side, considering. "An interesting point. I had heard the same thing, although the Americans and their closed borders had not allowed much tourist travel for many years. We will follow up with the American embassy about the passport to confirm identity." Leiner nodded. "Thank you, Herr Quinn. I wonder if you saw anything unusual or anyone suspicious last night when you left Frau Fasching's?"

Evan shook his head. "Was it a mugging? I mean, with the war and the shortages, it's amazing there aren't more robberies."

A smile flew across Leiner's face. "You saw someone suspicious who might have been a mugger?"

"I didn't see anything, Inspector. I mean, I was tired and eager to get home. I wasn't looking around very much." Leiner's expression had closed. Leiner wasn't going to give him any details. The cop had an investigation to conduct. "You're calling me because the victim was an American?"

Leiner's eyes turned steely. "Yes, Herr Quinn. In light of the attempt on your life in Buenos Aires. I wanted to check on you, ensure that you were safe."

"Quite safe, Inspector. In fact, Freda and I decided last week to install supplemental security because of Buenos Aires. A security expert her father knows is here today installing it."

Leiner nodded. "Prima. Connected to the house computers or separate?"

"Separate. Low-tech. I haven't talked to the guy, yet, but I told Freda I wanted an old-fashioned system. I was thinking of The Four Seasons Pension and Frau Herbst's keys."

Leiner chuckled. "I remember, Herr Quinn. Please remind your landlady to notify the police in your district of any codes and if they will be connected to the system. I am very glad to see you thinking in this way."

"Anything new on Buenos Aires?" He rose to his feet, his hand pushing off the kitchen table.

"No. But I have an intuition—a nagging feeling—about that murder in Stadtpark last night. Once I have confirmed the man's identity, I will call you."

Evan, nodding, shuffled over to the videophone monitor. "I seem to remember being told last summer that terrorists of all kinds liked to target Americans, right? Or maybe the guy had an argument with someone and it ended badly. Or perhaps it was a lovers' quarrel."

Leiner chuckled again. "Are you interested in taking on my job, Herr Quinn?"

"Absolutely not." He grinned. "Thank you for your concern, Inspector."

The monitor flicked to black. Evan looked out the kitchen window at the bare maple tree branches gusting back and forth in the wind. The Austrian cop no longer acted as if he was somehow a security threat to Austria or the EU. His probation had ended without incident December 31, and he was now a legal resident immigrant in Austria. However, Leiner was not the type to abandon his suspicions, and Evan assumed Leiner still suspected he was a spy for the Americans. Was Leiner fishing again, suspecting that Evan knew the Chinese-American guy, that they were somehow working together for the Americans, as he had thought last summer that he was working for Bernie Brown? He closed his eyes, recalling the Chinese-American's voice—American English with an American accent. How had he known where Evan would be?

Woody. Where'd he left his clean cell phone? He thought for a moment. He'd left it on the bed, on top of the blanket. He dialed Woody's phone number. The old American answered on the second ring.

"Can you talk?" Evan said.

"Sure. What's going on?"

"You haven't heard? About the American killed in Stadtpark last night?"

"I heard."

"The guy was after me. He knew where I'd be. How? Who's doing this, Woody?"

The giggle in his ear made him wish he could reach through the phone and slap his handler's face hard.

"How do you *know* he was after you, Evan?"

"He jumped me. With a knife. If you know something about this, Woody—"

"Chill, Maestro. You killed him?"

"Self-defense."

"Of course. You going to the cops?"

"I'm thinking about it." Maybe he should have told Leiner everything. Except Alicia had killed the guy. The cops would arrest her.

"Stay cool. I'll see what I can find out."

"It's the second time someone's tried to kill me, Woody. I want to know who's behind it."

"OK! OK! I'll see what I can find out."

"And I'm still waiting to talk to your forger, Woody, about the documents I need. It's been six months." Evan hung up before Woody could provide another lame excuse. Woody failed to support Perceval. Maybe Woody was behind the assassins. Evan shivered at the thought.

He dropped the phone onto the bed. He needed to find a place for it. The previous year, when he'd had two cell phones, he'd left them in the living room bookcase where he could grab them before going out. He couldn't remember where he'd left his other cell phone. He'd check his coat.

As he walked through the kitchen, movement outside caught his eye. Evan stepped closer to the window, gazing out on the snow-covered driveway, the six-foot-tall black iron gate, the stone wall encircling Freda's property. To the right, the front yard was desolate white, the massive oak in the far front corner stark black against the overcast sky. The neighbor across the street emerged from his house and turned up Sternwartestrasse's hill. Evan saw another movement out of the corner of his eye, a fleeting shadow, beyond the stone wall behind the oak, someone lurking there. He shifted position to get a better view. In the winter, with the trees bare, he could see more of the immediate area. He waited. No movement behind the tree. A light blue Citroën truck was parked in front of Freda's gate, alone on their side of the street. People living on this street were at their jobs at this time of the day in spite of the war. Normally, he would be at his job, too.

"One male visitor," his house computer announced in its smooth electronic voice, neither male nor female.

He pressed the video monitor button on the security panel by his front door. On screen, Freda stood at the exterior door with a short, bald man in a black wool jacket over cornflower-blue work overalls. The man carried a worn brown leather satchel and a silver metal case. Evan pressed the entry release button.

Only the man came up the stairs. He introduced himself in German in a friendly tenor voice as Beni Karlinowicz and requested a tour of the apartment. Beni said nothing about Evan's appearance or pajamas, but mentioned that the installation might take an hour or two. Evan showed him the living room, kitchen, bedroom, and bath, and the walk-in closet off the bedroom. Throughout the tour, Beni nodded in silence. In the kitchen, he asked about the videophone and told Evan that he'd install the main panel next to it.

"And how exactly does the system work, Herr Karlinowicz?"

"Oh, that is classified, Herr Quinn." Beni chuckled and winked. "But I can tell you that it will not be connected in any way to your house computer or Freda's. It uses wireless technology like with cell phones. A very popular security system thirty years ago, before the house computers took over the job. You will not be connected to the district police station but to each other so that when Freda triggers the alarm, you will hear it."

"What does it sound like?"

"What would you like it to sound like? I understand that you are a musician."

"Not a musical sound." Evan looked out the kitchen window, thinking about how his videophone warbled like a bird.

"You have three choices, Herr Quinn. A siren, a clanging bell, or a buzzing."

"Make it buzz, Herr Karlinowicz. Now I'll leave you to it. If you need me, I'll be in the bedroom."

Evan retreated to his bed for a snooze while Beni worked, although he couldn't sleep. He felt exhausted. It was a little after two in the afternoon. He could hear Beni working in the kitchen, heard a drill whining, then hammering.

Freda had not done any maintenance in his apartment for months, and no one else had been in his apartment while he was traveling for conducting gigs or at the Fischer School of Martial Arts or on errands or visiting musician friends. His security system would have alerted him to any unauthorized entry. So, he felt confident that other than the Austrian police's bugs, which he'd removed last year, there were no listening devices in his apartment.

Who had known about his plans to attend Greta's salon? Greta, of course. Freda and Pierre. Sofia. Maybe the bugs were in Freda's house? But Woody's bug detector on the back of his wrist-watch hadn't activated when he was inside Freda's house. Freda hadn't told anyone, and who would Pierre tell? Alicia had known, also. Greta had told people, he knew, but he didn't know whom she'd told. Details of his life talked about by others could leak, overheard by anyone in the general public world. He hadn't checked the internet, but the last time he'd searched his name, only his page at Nigel's agency website, concert reviews, and other music-world news came up. He shifted in bed, curled onto his left side to take the weight off his right side and shoulder. He might never know how the Chinese-American guy knew where he'd be.

Evan didn't know how long he'd been asleep when Beni woke him with an apology. "I must show you the system. You want an extension in your bedroom?" Beni said.

The bedroom extension was a two-inch black electronic gadget with buttons to turn the alarm on or off. Beni said that Freda and Pierre each had an extension in their bedrooms. Evan left it by the head of his bed and followed Beni into the kitchen. He listened as the short man explained how to activate the system and deactivate it, then watched him activate the system and test it. The buzzing sound pulsed ugly and loud. Perfect. Evan was pleased by its low-tech simplicity. Any potential intruders would expect the computer security system and deactivate it, but would not expect an old wireless system.

After Karlinowicz departed, carrying his leather tool satchel and metal case, Evan returned to the kitchen to check his videophone voice mail messages. Neils Dam in Copenhagen had called once and Nigel had called twice during the morning while Evan had been asleep. Evan called his manager's London number. The videophone monitor came to life.

"Evan! I was beginning to wonder what had happened to you," Nigel said. His tone was worried, matching the frown lines across his forehead. "You've been injured?"

Evan smiled, putting on what he hoped was a jovial face. "The cut? It's nothing. Some rough-housing yesterday with friends. I attended a music salon at Greta Fasching's."

"I should think rough-housing in your physical condition might be unwise. A music salon? I'd thought music salons had become extinct. Hear anyone interesting?"

"A Swiss violinist. Lisl Schatzmann. She knows the Barber Violin Concerto. Has the Scottish BBC Symphony engaged a violinist yet for the Barber?"

Nigel picked up a pen and pulled a notepad across his desk to write. "I wanted to talk to you about Glasgow. I'll check about the Barber. Is she in Vienna?"

"Yes. Her manager is Wolf in Munich. I've heard her twice now, and I think she'd be fine. What else about Glasgow?"

"Rumor has it they're looking for a music director. No announcement as yet, but I cannot stress enough how important your week there will be, if you'd like to be considered for the job. Have you been thinking about your future, what you want?"

He could count on Nigel to keep pushing him forward. Every gig, as far as he was concerned, was an audition for a music director position. He hadn't really thought specifically about the future since Nigel had brought it up in the Buenos Aires hospital, only that he wanted to survive whoever was trying to kill him. "Not really, Nigel. Is the Scottish BBC a good orchestra?"

"I think it might be a good fit for you, a good place for you to begin your ascent."

"You mean, to get experience as a music director outside America."

"Precisely. They were eager to book you, Evan. They will be watching you closely. They've told me your concerts are already nearly sold out, which gives you a strong position as far as being marketable is concerned. Your name and your connection to Caine are the pluses there. Now you need to back it up."

Evan checked the 2049 calendar panel on the wall between the phone and the window. "I've got Zürich the week before, so arriving early in Glasgow isn't an option, and Lisbon the week after." As he'd noted on the calendar, the program for Glasgow was Dvořák's Serenade for Strings, the Barber Violin Concerto, and Concerto for Orchestra by Seth Landis, a new work. He knew the Dvořák but he needed to get to work on the Barber and Landis. He sighed. "Any other rumors?"

"Despite the lack of radioactive fallout from the nuclear attack on Moscow last August, St. Petersburg has announced that they will not finish their current season. They've had only two or three concerts since the Chinese invaded. They want to begin fresh in autumn."

"I suppose they've had a lot to deal with. They owe me a gig."

"I'll give them a call. Maybe we can arrange something after Helsinki in September. How are you feeling? The physical therapy progressing?"

"Yeah, I'll be ready for Copenhagen. Did you talk to Neils Dam about my security?" Maybe this business of being toyed with by a predatory cat wouldn't be over by the time he arrived in Copenhagen. "I'm actually considering a body-guard."

"Indeed? Hmmm." Nigel made a note. "Shall I call Neils or do you want to handle it?"

"I'll call. He's left me a voice mail today about rehearsal order. Anything else?"

"How is Pierre?"

"We had a meeting at the French embassy last Friday. They recognized him, so confirming his identity is just a formality. They'll find his relatives in France. He refuses to believe that his parents were killed last October by a Chinese bomb. He insists they had left the house on an errand like he had." Evan sighed. "The French have a counselor he's talking to. I don't know." He ran his fingers through his long black hair, combing it back from his face.

"He survived on the streets, Evan. He's a tough little boy. He just needs some time and a safe place to come to terms with what happened. You're giving him the security and sup-port he needs right now. Give him my regards. And when are you going to get your hair cut?"

Evan groaned. "Eventually. I'll call tomorrow afternoon. I have PT in the morning."

"Take care of yourself," Nigel said, and the monitor flicked to black.

Alicia. Before he called Copenhagen, he needed to call her. He got himself a cold bottle of mineral water from the refrigerator. His body felt heavy with exhaustion. He retrieved his black cell phone from the bedroom.

"Alicia?" he said into the phone when she answered. "How are you? I had an interesting call from Inspector Leiner."

"They found the body." Her tone was matter-of-fact. "I left him where he fell."

"Did you check his pockets?"

"No. I checked the woman's in Buenos Aires. She carried nothing in them. I expected—"

"Leiner said he carried an American passport. I suggested it might not be genuine because of the foreign travel restrictions."

The seconds of silence in his ear felt like an eternity. He could see in his mind the Chinese-American's cold black eyes staring at him.

"He spoke American English," Alicia said. "What region?"

"Couldn't tell. Maybe it was fake. You think he was trying to fulfill the same contract as the Chilean in Buenos Aires?"

"There are no coincidences. If there have been two, Evan, there will be more."

"I suppose this is when you tell me to trust no one."

"You must always be careful when you go out. Remember what I taught you about surveillance detection. What is your schedule like this week?"

He exhaled, thinking of his Perceval training. The NEP had put him in this position with their ridiculous Arts Council, their stupidity in arresting him and giving him no choice except Perceval. "I have physical therapy, a doctor appointment, necessary errands. A meeting at the French embassy, but I'll let Freda handle that." He was stiff and sore, and when the hydrocodone wore off, he was sure the pain in his abdomen, lower back, and right shoulder would return. "I've got body bruises, but otherwise no visible sign of the fight except the forehead cut. But I've got pain. It's been six weeks since the surgeries, and I'm concerned about re-injury, especially my shoulder, so I really need to go to the doctor this week." Perceval would need a healed and completely functional body to defend him.

"OK. Will Freda take you to the appointments? You know? I have an idea. They have car services here, I am certain. I will find someone for you, Evan, someone who can protect you and drive you to your appointments."

"I can do that, Alicia. I want you finding out who's behind these attacks. I feel like someone is taking great pleasure in tormenting me. Like a cat playing with a nearly dead mouse or something. Please check your sources. It could be anyone, I think."

"No, Evan. Someone wants you dead *for a reason*."

CHAPTER 13

"You little shit! You speak English!"

Pierre gasped as Avoine grabbed him by the collar. Snow whited out the world around them as he squirmed and punched at Avoine's arms and hands, but the American held him fast in a vise grip. He dragged him to the black sedan parked at the curb of Hasenauerstrasse outside of Türkenschanz Park. The back passenger door stood open. Pierre wedged himself in the door frame so that Avoine would have to let go of his collar to push him into the car. Pierre would have only a second to escape.

His plan failed. Avoine shoulder-punched Pierre's body. Pierre landed on the back seat with another gasp. The door slammed. He reached for the handle, but the handles had been removed. Avoine slid in behind the steering wheel.

"You little shit, Pierre! You better have the information I asked for or you're in big trouble." Avoine inserted the ignition stick into the steering column, and the car roared to life.

Outside the car, giant snowflakes swirled on the wind and created pointillist patterns in the air. Papa would ask him which artist and he would say Monet, but he couldn't remember if Monet had ever painted snow falling. He re-buttoned the top button of his black wool jacket and pulled the red knitted scarf up over his mouth like a bandit. The Wizard

Howl hadn't warned him that Avoine was angry. Neither had Ashitaka or Steamboy. They too had seen a smiling face as Avoine stood on the sidewalk in the falling snow near the entrance to the park. He couldn't trust Avoine's smiling face.

Where were they going? Pierre had lost his bearings, and the curtain of snow obscured much of the landscape outside. If he wasn't back in an hour, Madame Kirsch would worry. She would tell Monsieur Evan. But would they call the police? He had not said anything to them about where he was going, only that he was going outdoors to play in the snow.

What would Avoine do to him now? He shivered in the cold air of the car, remembering the trip across the river, the woozy drug, and waking up naked in a bed, alone, and in pain. Avoine's head smacks were nothing compared to that. And now the American had heard everything at the French embassy meetings because of the listening device embedded behind Pierre's ear. He thought of something.

"Monsieur, parlez vous Francais?"

"What?" Avoine glanced back at him. The American's hands gripped the steering wheel, his knuckles white. "Pull that scarf down off your face."

Pierre rearranged the scarf around his neck as he smiled. "Parlez vous Francais?"

"You little shit. HELL NO." Avoine's voice filled the car, and Pierre's ears, and thundered out into the snow like an avalanche. "But you're going to tell me everything that was said in French at all your meetings at the embassy. And you better not lie to me. I can always tell when you're lying."

He must take the chance that he was a much better liar

than Avoine could detect. The Wizard Howl whispered that Avoine couldn't tell when Pierre lied or when anyone else lied if there existed truth woven in with the lie. "The meetings were about my citizenship. About my family in France. About living with Madame Kirsch and Monsieur Evan."

"Who's Dr. Moreau?" Avoine jerked the steering wheel into a left turn.

Pierre recognized a church in the neighborhood of Avoine's apartment building. Half a block later, they passed an intersection of shops, all closed. "She is someone I must talk to because I lived on the streets for a long time." He noticed Avoine's narrowed eyes in the rearview mirror and shrugged. "Not a medical doctor."

"She's a psychiatrist?" Avoine said, his voice laced with suspicion. "What have you told her about your time on the streets?"

Pierre looked out the door window. He had told Dr. Moreau that Maman had sent him down the hill to the café in Grinzing for the torte, and he had walked back up the hill through the vineyard, the reddish-brown vines empty, the sweet musty aroma of pressed grapes hanging in the air. He had told her about Maman telling him that she also had an errand and Papa would drive the car for her. He had told her about the explosion and fire, about dropping the torte and running. His parents had also left on an errand. Now he must find them. They had gone over this many times during their three meetings at the embassy, and he'd said little about his time on the streets.

"I told her I stole food to eat. She wanted to know how I did this. How the other boys on the street taught me to steal. The police taking some boys off the streets but not me. I always escaped from the police. I told her about always looking for a warm place to sleep at night." He would not tell Avoine about his hiding place in Nussdorf. He might need it someday. He met Avoine's eyes in the rearview mirror. "Why do you want to know these things? You have an apartment. You do not need to live on the streets." The Wizard Howl whispered in his ear that this was good, shift the subject to Avoine.

The American smiled. He was amused. "Yeah, and we'll be there in a minute. But I don't understand why they'd want you to talk to a head doctor. You're a smart little shit. You don't need that. And now you're going to stay with me until you tell me everything I want to know."

Time heals all wounds, his mother used to say. Evan removed the heating pad from his shoulder and turned it off. He circled his right arm, held straight out from his body at shoulder level. He'd feared that the attack in Stadtpark a week ago had damaged his right shoulder and he'd need to begin over with the healing and physical therapy exercises. Or the worst news: he'd not be able to conduct for another month or two. Or maybe ever again. But neither Dr. Maas nor his physical therapist had been concerned about a possible re-injury. Dr. Maas had assured him also that his abdominal wound had healed and he could work now on regaining his strength and stamina, both of concern for him as a conductor.

Glasmann had given him a set of weights to help build up the muscles to support his shoulder joint. He moved over to his bedroom windows and looked out at the snow swirling thick and fast through the air as he lifted the smallest weight up toward his shoulder, bending his elbow, to the slow count of ten. Pierre had loved the weights when first he saw them. Odd that the boy wasn't around to run through his exercises with him. Maybe he was helping Freda in the kitchen. She liked to bake on Sundays, and she'd mentioned she was able to buy butter yesterday so today she might bake a Guglhupf. His mouth watered at the thought of the sweet vanilla cake.

Dr. Maas had warned him in a stern voice to wean himself off the hydrocodone now. He had seven caplets left. He'd save them, take them to Copenhagen. He might need them at night after full days of rehearsals, media publicity for the concerts, and meetings. He looked forward to seeing Copenhagen and meeting the orchestra musicians and socializing with them in the evenings. He missed working with an orchestra, being with musicians. He'd received hundreds of emails from musicians, most forwarded from Nigel's office, and spent an hour or so each day now replying to each of them, answering their questions, reassuring them that he'd be able to conduct again. Musicians, his family.

Conducting required physical stamina and strength in the lower back, abdomen, legs and arms, as well as experience in pacing the physical exertion in order to conserve energy. His conducting professor at Juilliard had hounded him about taking care of his body, exercising, eating well, getting enough sleep. He'd been a runner since junior high school and had developed his own workout routine around daily runs. When he stood on the podium, whether in rehearsal or in concert, he'd felt physically good, strong, coordinated, and confident.

He'd possessed the stamina. Often during concerts, he'd not sit down or rest for over two hours, until the last note had faded in the concert hall. He absorbed energy from the audience, the musicians, his own adrenaline excitement and the music, the sound of emotion surrounding and filling him.

He no longer felt confident of his physical abilities or stamina. Being shot had left him feeling weak, easily fatigued, and often in pain from the bone wound in his shoulder. He wanted to believe that he'd be fine when he traveled to Copenhagen. Would he? Well, Dr. Maas had given his OK for Evan to begin his old workout regimen. He knew it would feel like he'd never worked out before, but he needed it. Even as he continued the PT exercises for his right shoulder and arm.

Evan finished with the weight and set it on the floor by the rocking chair. He looked at the chair, imagining Pierre in it, his hands resting primly in his lap. He imagined Sofia sitting in it, Sofia as she had looked a week ago at Greta's. Greta had said yesterday that Sofia had only the movie's ending to shoot, and she would be home at the end of the month.

He missed her voice, her eyes, her presence, her scent, how she surprised him each time he talked with her. Vasia would be pleased that he was considering breaking his rule of not becoming involved with anyone, not forming a romantic attachment. In America, a girlfriend or lover could be held hostage by the NEP to force obedience. Could he live up to Sofia? Was he good enough for her, would she eventually discover his secrets and abandon him? What would she think of Perceval? Could he trust her? Maybe it was better not to become involved. Romance could be a lot of trouble.

He'd seen it with musicians who had romantic partners or spouses. Romance was a major source of uncertainty and pain. Women left.

He went into the bathroom and ran water in the sink. It flowed at first a pale rust color, then cleared. The war had not been kind to the water-distribution system. He splashed his face, feeling his right shoulder move more easily now, with only a little pain. It felt better immediately after his PT workouts.

Where was Woody? He'd left two voice mails for his handler and had not gotten a response. His silence heightened Evan's suspicion about the old American's loyalties and motives.

The sense of being prey, of someone toying with him, trying to make him suffer before killing him, left Evan restless and frustrated. What could he do? He had no control, no power in this situation. He craved to have the person responsible in his rifle's sights. He scowled at his reflection in the mirror, the almost healed cut on his forehead. His physical condition left him at a disadvantage. But even if he could physically pursue the person who wanted him dead, he couldn't find the person without information, clues to follow, rock solid intelligence.

Leiner hadn't called either. Alicia had uncovered more than anyone else but still not enough. She was as frustrated as he was at the two assassins' defiance and the lack of information. They had agreed, however, that if there had been two assassins, there could be more, and they were organized, professional, highly trained, and loyal to whomever had sent them.

Life goes on, he thought. His mother had told him that often, usually after something bad—his father's rages, the ISS arresting Uncle Joe, Brianna and Paul Caine leaving in the night without a word.

The stack of scores on the piano looked like a striped leaning tower. He righted it and, from the piano bench, picked up the manuscript score he'd received the day before by special courier. The Concerto for Orchestra, composed by a Brit named Seth Landis. But the score was unfinished, the middle movements missing. The music librarian at the Scottish BBC Symphony in Glasgow had told him on the phone that the orchestra had partnered with another BBC orchestra to commission the piece two years ago. The Scottish orchestra had won the right to premiere it and had scheduled it for last fall. The global war had forced the orchestra to shift programs around, and it had landed on the program they had asked him to conduct in May. He was happy and excited to conduct new music, as long as it was ready for rehearsals.

He'd read through the two movements they'd sent as soon as the score had arrived and had spotted issues. He'd emailed the composer in Manchester with his questions and had received the reply, "*Things are hectic right now and I haven't even the time to breathe. Could we talk later?*" Evan had thought, *Yeah, maybe*. Now he fished out the phone number of Leonard Patton in Glasgow, his contact for all things regarding his Scottish BBC gig.

His videophone's monitor came to life on a home scene of children playing in the background of a cozy kitchen and a redheaded woman peering at him. "Hello," Evan said. "Evan Quinn calling Leonard Patton, please."

The woman nodded and disappeared out of frame. Evan watched the two children lobbing dry cereal and chasing each other around the kitchen table. The auburn-haired boy was probably seven years old, the black-haired girl perhaps four or five. A compact man in a blue flannel shirt and jeans appeared, and Evan watched him herd the children out of the kitchen before he turned to the monitor.

"Sorry to make you wait, Maestro Quinn. What can I do for you?" Patton smiled. His smooth baritone voice and Scottish lilt pleased Evan's ear.

"Thank you for taking my call on a Sunday, Leonard," Evan said. "I'm concerned about my program."

"You received the Landis score?" Patton pulled a red vinyl kitchen chair away from the table and sat down in front of the videophone.

"Yesterday. Will it be finished in time? I tried to contact Landis to find out about the two missing movements and when he might send them to me, but he told me he was too busy and wanted to talk later. We *are* at 'later' right now as far as I'm concerned. I am also busy. Considering the concert is two months away and the score is missing two full movements, I'm not comfortable putting the Scottish BBC Symphony in a difficult situation by agreeing to conduct music that's incomplete when the composer has given me no indication that it'll be completed in time. Who is this guy anyway?"

A tense smile passed over Patton's face like a cloud over the sun. "Seth Landis has won numerous honors and awards for his music, which is performed all over the world and has been recorded. He teaches at one of our more prestigious conservatories. His schedule is perhaps too full right now."

"I feel for the guy." Evan failed to keep the sarcasm out of his voice. Joseph Caine would never have left a conductor or anyone else in the lurch like this guy was. He'd known composers all his life, loved working with them for the most part, but was well aware of a tiny percentage whose egos had consumed them. Landis sounded like his ego had consumed him. "I'm really looking forward to my time in Glasgow and working with the Scottish BBC Symphony. I don't think any of us want to mar the experience with Mr. Landis's drama and incomplete score. I suggest you let him off the hook for the concert in May and let him know that he now has more time to complete the score. Schedule the premiere for later. I'd be happy to prepare Sibelius's Second Symphony as a substitute."

This was the first time Evan had done this outside of America—lodged a complaint about a program he'd originally agreed to conduct. He'd protested many programs that the American Arts Council had ordered him to conduct, giving him no choice in the matter. He'd known how to deal with the Arts Council. He wasn't sure about how to deal with a European orchestra, and it was the first time the situation had come up. Nigel had told him to call Patton about anything. Now he waited for Patton's reply. The Scotsman had dropped his head so he couldn't see his face. When he raised it again, deep lines creased his forehead and a lock of his black hair whisked across them.

"It's a delicate matter, Maestro. Because of Mr. Landis's stature, you understand. But I understand exactly your concern. The Sibelius would work fine on that program, and I appreciate you suggesting it. I need to consult with staff and musicians about the change, especially regarding Mr. Landis's commissioned music. Might I give you a call tomorrow?"

"Works for me, Leonard. Has Landis even provided the parts to the orchestra?"

Patton shook his head. "Not that I've heard yet."

"Has he done this before, or is this an aberration for him?"

"Not unusual behavior, unfortunately."

"And no one's called him on it? Or doesn't he care? I was going to conduct the premiere of his major work for orchestra, and he didn't have the time to talk to me."

"I'm terribly sorry about that. As I said, it's not unusual behavior for him, and he's been generous with this behavior with everyone," Leonard said. "Thank you for your call, Maestro. We'll talk again tomorrow."

The videophone monitor darkened. Evan had probably ruined Patton's Sunday afternoon, but he'd learned long ago that it was far better to take care of problems or requests as they arose than to put them off, no matter their size or importance. He returned to the piano in his living room and pulled out the score for the Barber Violin Concerto. This was music he hadn't conducted before—"new music" to him, although it was over one hundred years old—and he loved studying it both as a conductor and violinist.

An hour later his cell phone (not the clean black one) rang from the living room bookshelf.

"Hello."

"Evan, it's Freda. Is Pierre with you?"

"No. Isn't he helping you bake your Guglhupf?"

"He told me he was going out to play in the snow, but he's not in the backyard or in front. I can't find him anywhere."

Evan looked out his living room windows. The snow continued to fall fast and heavy with no signs of letting up. He thought of Uncle Joe and his father teaching him how to track deer in the snow in northern Minnesota. The falling snow would cover any tracks Pierre had left for them to follow. Or it would cover Pierre.

"How long has it been since he left, Freda?"

"Two hours. I'm terribly worried. I think something has happened to him."

"OK. Call the police. I'll check Türkenschanz Park."

"Does Quinn have a bodyguard now?" Avoine said, looking over the pencil drawings Pierre had made of Madame's house.

Pierre drank milk and took a Manner Schnitten hazelnut wafer cookie off the plate on the table in front of him. The kitchen smelled of grease and onions, not like Madame's kitchen. When Avoine had begun asking his questions, the Wizard Howl had warned Pierre to lie, to not tell him everything. He set down the glass and licked his lips. "Thank you for the cold milk and cookies. Monsieur Evan does not have a bodyguard. Why would he need one?" Pierre shrugged.

Avoine studied him with narrowed eyes. "You haven't seen anyone with Quinn when he goes out?"

"I am often with him when he goes out."

"No, not you." Avoine laughed, a creepy, sandpapery sound. "Actually, you'd be the perfect bodyguard for my purposes. You couldn't protect him worth beans." He leaned forward and grabbed Pierre's wrist. "I'm talking about adults. Has he hired anyone to protect him?"

The Wizard Howl whispered in Pierre's ear that he knew how to protect Monsieur Evan. Pierre looked at Avoine's hand holding his wrist. "I do not know. When he leaves, he goes alone in a cab or Madame Kirsch drives him. That is all I know."

Avoine released his wrist. He tapped Pierre's drawings. "You've put the security system panels in the front foyer and kitchen. Are there any other panels?"

"I have seen only those two."

"You know the codes?"

"No." The Wizard Howl whispered again not to tell Avoine about the new security system Monsieur Beni installed last week. Avoine did not need to know about that system. Pierre understood that Avoine hated Monsieur Evan and wanted to hurt him. Pierre also understood that Avoine would hurt *him* if he didn't talk.

"Is the security system connected to the house computer?"

"Yes. Like Monsieur Evan's." Not the new security system, but Avoine need not know that.

"And Kirsch owns a dog, right? A golden retriever."

"Yes. Sasha is very friendly and likes to play." Pierre had also seen her growling, barking, and snapping at strangers who passed on the street. She was a good watchdog.

Avoine smiled. "Your English is good. What's Quinn's

schedule, do you know it? Is he still going to physical therapy?"

"To PT, yes. Three times a week. He prepares for concerts. He has not told me of any other plans."

Avoine nodded and abruptly stood, startling Pierre. "He
eats breakfast and lunch with you and Kirsch. He does his
physical therapy. He prepares for concerts."

Pierre did not like the sarcasm of Avoine's voice or his
eyes of ice. The Wizard Howl whispered it was time to go.

"What time is it?" Pierre said. "If I am gone too long,
they will call the police."

"Will they now?" Avoine laughed.

The thick falling snow obscured the houses and trees along
Hasenauerstrasse and the trees along the perimeter of Türkenschanz Park. The snowstorm reminded him of blizzards
in Minneapolis, when the city shut down. The snow muffled
the sound of his footsteps. Evan knew that it had covered
long ago any tracks Pierre might have left if he'd been in the
park. He spotted the red and blue flashing lights of a Viennese police car as it crept toward him through the plaza.

He tried to remember what Pierre had said at lunch
about his plans for the afternoon. They had encouraged him
to be independent but always tell them what he was going to
do. He had told Freda he was going out to play in the snow.
They had realized, after she'd called the police, that Pierre
hadn't said *where* he was going to play in the snow. Freda had
assumed in the yard.

The park, of course, was empty of children or any other

people. He and two uniformed police officers searched it. A fluffy white geometric sculpture formed from the jungle gym, the seats of the swings carried a foot of snow, and the chess tables had become white mounds. They walked everywhere, checking the snow-covered sand pit, and around the frozen duck pond, kicking the snow accumulating around the trees and bushes in case Pierre lay injured on the ground.

The two cops agreed to cruise the streets around the park, and Evan repeated Pierre's physical description, and described his black wool jacket, red knitted scarf, and the red knitted hat with ear flaps. He could tell from their expressions that they held little hope of finding him.

"With the war, Herr Quinn," one cop said, "children are snatched from the streets all the time and taken out of the country before anyone has missed them."

Evan searched the park again, and then the immediate neighborhood, ignoring the cold and the falling snow. Pierre was smart. He'd know to seek shelter. Maybe he'd gone to one of the neighboring houses and was sipping hot chocolate in front of a fire. At each house he tried, however, the person who answered the door told him that no little French boy had sought shelter with them. His stomach tensed into a hard, painful knot. He returned to Türkenschanz Park and called Freda.

"No sign of him," he reported. "I've checked at neighboring houses on all the streets around here. It's starting to get dark."

"Are the police looking?" He heard the worry in her voice.

"Yeah. I need to warm up. Then I'll walk around the neighborhood again." He flipped his cell phone closed. Out of the corner of his eye, he noticed a black sedan creeping along the street, the only car moving. Who was idiot enough to be driving in this storm? He shook his head and trudged through the snow across Hasenauerstrasse in the direction of home. He opened his cell phone again and dialed Alicia's safe house number. The phone rang and rang. No answer. Not even voice mail so he could leave a message. Where was she? He needed her. She hadn't called. Had she abandoned him? She'd said she'd be there for him, but she wasn't. *Yeah, can't rely on people for the important stuff.* He felt betrayed, left to fend for himself, alone. He closed his phone, dropped it into his coat pocket. He was now covered in snow. He brushed his coat sleeves and shoulders. What else could he do?

"Hey, heretic kid!"

Evan stopped in his tracks and looked around. Harold and his Vigiciv gang swaggered up the street toward him through the swirling snow. They wore their summer uniform, however, of black jeans, red T-shirts, and red-and-black-striped vests. Harold led them, his wheat-blond hair riffled by the wind. Evan hadn't seen this frightening memory vision, this hallucination, since the summer before, the Sunday he'd picnicked in the Vienna Woods with Vasia, Greta, and Sofia. Sofia. She hadn't seen Harold and his gang walking across the Kahlenberg parking lot. He'd realized then that they weren't real. They were a hallucination that he must keep secret. Even as he thought this, Harold and his Vigiciv gang faded away into the whirling snow, leaving Evan feeling worthless. He hadn't found Pierre.

Freda sat at the kitchen table, talking on the phone, when he entered through the back door. She tossed him a whisk broom to brush the snow off. Her side of the phone conversation indicated that she'd called the district police again. She hung up with a sigh.

"There's nothing more they can do. Where could he be?" She got up from the table and filled a tea kettle with water. "Tea or hot chocolate, Evan?"

"Tea." He pulled off his boots and hung up his cobalt-blue wool coat. "I can't believe that he's still out in this storm, Freda. He's a smart kid. He must have found shelter somewhere to wait it out." He knew what they both avoided saying—Pierre might be gone or dead. He felt a pressure in his chest, a weight pressing down on his heart and lungs.

She filled her white ceramic teapot with hot water from the tap. "But where? And why would he leave the neighborhood? In this storm?" She took two mugs from the wood cupboard and set them on the kitchen counter.

"Yeah, that's the mystery." He sat down at the table. He didn't like mysteries. He had a tense, sickening feeling in his gut about this. "Have you called Monsieur Cassel?"

She shook her head. "I feel terrible about it, but I was afraid to call. At least for now. I wanted to give the police a chance to find him."

The front door slammed. They looked at each other. Evan stood, but Freda moved faster. He followed her into the main hallway. She was on her knees, holding a snow-covered Pierre in her arms in the front foyer.

"Where were you, Pierre?" he said. "Are you OK?"

The look in Pierre's blue eyes gave him a chill. Something had happened.

Freda leaned back, brushed snow off him. "Pierre, we are

not angry with you, but we were so worried. Where did you go? Evan and the police looked everywhere."

"You called the police?" Pierre's eyes widened.

The tea kettle whistled in the kitchen. Freda got to her feet. "Of course we called the police. We needed their help to find you. I'll make you a mug of hot chocolate to warm you up." She went into the kitchen, leaving Evan and Pierre facing each other.

Evan helped Pierre pull off his boots and hang up his black wool jacket. Then he squatted and held Pierre's shoulders.

"OK. Tell me."

The boy dropped his head. "I was afraid Maman and Papa had left me a note and the snow can destroy the paper and message. I waited for a streetcar but it did not come. I walked to my house."

"All the way to Grinzing?" Evan thought about his runs to Grinzing. A mile, maybe two, at least to the crater that used to be Pierre's house. "You went to where your house was?"

"I am sorry, Monsieur Evan. I am sorry to worry you and Madame." Pierre dropped his head again, a rivulet of melted snow snaking down his face from his hair.

Evan shook his head. For the first time, he had the feeling Pierre wasn't being completely honest. How could he have walked to Grinzing and back in this snowstorm when he couldn't have been sure of the way? It didn't make sense. Pierre was hiding something. Evan pulled him into his embrace, feeling both relief and dread. "I'm glad you're back and you're OK. But you're grounded for a week."

"Grounded?" Pierre's head shot up. "What does this mean? Grounded?"

"You will not be allowed to go anywhere without an adult, either me or Freda, or someone from the French embassy."

Pierre smiled.

CHAPTER 14

The alarm siren screamed. All the lights came on, and the window shades descended. Evan shot out of bed, hyper-alert, his muscles tense. He felt a slight pull in his abdomen and in his right shoulder. Electric adrenaline tingling spread through his body, preparing him to fight. He ran into the kitchen to the refrigerator, opened the freezer, and pulled out the frozen meals stacked in the front. He grabbed a ball of thick bubble wrap from the back. Not the smartest way to hide his CZ 9mm, but he hadn't thought he'd need it at home. He opened his utensil drawer, pulled out a paring knife, and sliced into the bubble wrap.

His videophone rang, its warble almost obliterated by the siren alarm. But he heard it. Holding the bubble-wrapped gun behind his back, he turned to the videophone and yelled, "Hello!"

The monitor came to life close on the face of a young, bearded man with blond hair. The young man frowned. His mouth moved, but Evan couldn't hear him. Evan put up one hand in a gesture to wait and went into the living room to the security panel by his front door. All the lights were lit up red and flashing. The message on the monitor said in German, "*Unauthorized entry attempted.*" Evan punched in the code to turn off the siren and reset the alarm.

Back in the kitchen, he faced his videophone monitor and said in German, "I couldn't hear you before."

"Are you all right, Herr Quinn? We have an alarm at your residence and at Frau Kirsch's residence."

"I'm fine. Have you called Frau Kirsch?"

The young man looked away for ten seconds to someone out of frame, said something, and turned back to the monitor nodding. "Yes. She is fine. Shall I call the police?"

Evan thought for a few seconds, looking down at his tartan-plaid flannel pajama pants. The security guy had probably seen all manner of dress on clients during emergencies. "Yeah. Please call the police. The message on my security panel said someone tried to enter. I want to make sure that someone is gone and give the police a chance to collect evidence."

The security guy nodded. "The police will contact you on site, Herr Quinn. You have reset the alarm?"

"Yes. Thanks."

The monitor went black. Evan said to the videophone, "Freda Kirsch." Her worried face appeared on the monitor. One of her hands clutched the collar of her pale pink fleece robe.

"The police are on the way. Are you and Pierre OK?" he said in English.

"Yes. Sasha went wild barking immediately before the alarm went off. She woke us. Pierre is fine. Pierre?"

The boy's wide-set blue eyes regarded him with fear under his trimmed brown hair. Something else mixed with the fear—sadness? He wore blue flannel pajamas. Freda held him close.

"You're safe, Pierre," Evan said. "The police are coming and they'll figure out what happened. Sasha's a good watchdog."

Pierre gave him a grave nod. Freda hugged him. "I hear the police siren now," Freda said.

"I'll get dressed."

The siren's alternating musical interval of the fourth approached up Sternwartestrasse. His watch read two-fifteen in the morning. The cops would need time to search the premises, check the buildings. He hid his bubble-wrapped CZ 9mm in the back of the freezer. He must decide if he needed a second CZ or a back-up sniper rifle. After Chinese vice chairman Jiang Xu's assassination last August, he had not replenished his stock of weapons. Now, with his probation for legal residency ended, he could apply for a gun license and buy a handgun for protection. He could join a hunting club or firing range for target practice. He should probably tell Inspector Leiner his intentions up front to allay the cop's suspicions or concerns.

Evan returned to his bedroom and dressed in jeans and a blue turtleneck sweater. Then in the living room, he padded over to open the last wall cabinet under the bookshelves. Empty cardboard boxes hid his Ruger sniper rifle in its wooden case at the back of the bottom shelf. He had felt powerful when he'd target-practiced at night in Pötzleinsdorfer Park, the lives of birds and squirrels in his hands when he aimed the Ruger.

He closed the cabinet door and sat back on his heels. Someone had tried to break in. If they'd tried his place first, why go to Freda's? The alarm would have gone off here.

Wouldn't it be logical to assume that if his place had security, the house would, too? And if they'd tried Freda's first? There must have been more than one: a guy to break into Freda's and a guy for his place. The alarms went off at the same time. What did they want? The only things of value he owned were his violin and the grand piano. He shook his head and sat down on his black leather recliner, facing the electronics wall.

What if two guys who had lost their jobs, needed money or food or something else, had tried to break into their homes to steal what they needed? The blaring alarms had scared them off. OK, that made sense to him.

He had food. Freda had food. Clothing. Fuel in Freda's car. With the increasing shortages due to the war, a sense of desperation had settled on the city. He felt it every time he went out to shop. He never knew if he could buy all the food he wanted, and often he couldn't. Clothing, shoes, fuel, heating oil, soap, laundry detergent, razors, and other goods and services like taxis or buses, things they'd taken for granted, were available sometimes and sometimes not. The power supply had remained reasonably consistent, with only occasional outages after bombing raids. The water supply was the same. Cell phones lost signal often but land lines functioned consistently. The Chinese targeted more or less with precision.

People continued to work at their jobs, those who still had jobs. When Freda's school had been hit by a bomb last fall, she went on involuntary leave until repairs had been completed. Neither she nor any of the other teachers and staff had been paid during the months of repair. He was certain similar things had happened to other people who weren't as fortunate as Freda to have money to fall back on in an emergency. He'd seen a decrease in the monthly royalties paid him by his father's and Uncle Joe's publishers in London as well as cancellations in his conducting schedule. People weren't buying as many books, playing music, or going out to concerts or anything else.

Their neighborhood in Währing offered a tempting target for thieves. The people living here worked hard for their money and all their possessions. The affluent tended not to suffer as much during war. Impoverished in America all his life, he had experienced the deprivations and struggles of people without money and power. Despite his new wealth and position, Evan behaved and thought as he had in America. He knew his American past remained a part of him, reminded him of how money had corrupted America. It seemed that only the poor could comprehend that with clarity. Money blinded the wealthy, made them dumb.

His security system computer announced, "Freda Kirsch and two male visitors."

He went over to the panel, pressed the monitor button. The camera showed two Viennese cops in their dark river-blue uniforms and winter wool jackets with Freda bundled up in her long green loden coat and snow boots. The security spotlights illuminated the entire property. He pressed the speaker button and said in German, "I'll be right down." He went into his foyer to pull on his boots and coat.

The two cops were courteous and mystified. The younger of the two gave their report while his older partner listened. "We have examined the entire property, Herr Quinn, Frau

Kirsch, and have found that the snow has been stirred up near the kitchen windows of the house and around Herr Quinn's front door, the back of the garage, but no clear tracks. The intruders must have walked up your cleared driveway. We walked around the perimeter outside the property and found nothing unusual. There are no signs on or around the doors of anyone trying to break in either here at your apartment or at Frau Kirsch's house. The security company assures us that your systems are functioning properly. We have found no evidence of anyone trying to break into either residence, only trespassers."

Evan nodded as he listened and looked around. His breath formed a thick cloud in the air. The walkways were clear of snow, the edges of the snow piles neat and undisturbed. Same for the driveway where the police car was parked. He could imagine someone walking up the driveway after vaulting over the gate. The front yard snow, smooth and undisturbed, reflected the security spotlights. They hadn't tried to break in. So what were they doing? Or was it a security system malfunction? He met Freda's puzzled gaze and sighed.

"Thank you for your thorough investigation. Perhaps the loud alarms frightened away whoever tried to get in. I hope our neighbors won't be complaining in the morning about the noise and bright lights." He shook the cops' hands.

The tall, older cop chuckled. "That is the problem with these loud systems and false alarms."

The younger cop pulled on his leather gloves. "Perhaps not a false alarm. But only trespassers. We will request a patrol in the neighborhood two or three times each night for a week or so. We have heard of a series of burglaries in Grinzing, yes?" The older cop nodded. "Perhaps they have tried tonight to expand their territory into Währing. Gute Nacht, Herr Quinn, Frau Kirsch."

Evan and Freda stood together, two tall sentinels of about equal height, in the driveway near his front door and watched the cops get into their patrol car and leave. Freda shook her head. "It makes no sense. I will call the security company in the morning and request a complete diagnostic."

"They said the snow was stirred up in places where someone might be if they planned to break in. I think someone was here. They stirred up the snow to hide their tracks. They triggered the alarm. I think the alarm frightened them away. I doubt they'll be back."

"You are usually the paranoid one, Evan." She glanced at him, her mouth a thin line.

He shrugged. "How could we identify who was here and why? You heard the cops. There's no evidence."

"I'll call for a diagnostic anyway. And ask for a price on the motion detection option to add to both our systems. And a connection to the district police. I want to make certain our security systems will function superbly when needed."

Her haughty tone surprised him, but when he looked at her, he saw the fear in her eyes and the set of her mouth. He remembered the fear he'd seen in her face when he'd returned home from Buenos Aires, fear for him, for his safety. "It scared me, too, Freda. With the war and the shortages, it's a good idea to make sure our defenses are in place and in good working order. We don't want any thieves breaking in."

"Oh, this war. When will it end?" She covered her face with her gloved hands.

He put his arms around her shoulders and pulled her into a hug, only the second time they'd hugged. She had hugged him when he'd arrived home from Buenos Aires, a gesture of relief as much as greeting. He wanted to comfort her, but he knew he couldn't give her the relief she needed this time.

She pulled away after a minute, and looked him square in the face. "We will survive this. Will you join Pierre and me for breakfast today?" There was a toughness under her vulnerability.

He nodded. She turned on her heel and went into the house. He checked that the driveway gate had closed and locked before he went inside his apartment, thinking she was right. He was usually the paranoid one. If the intruders hadn't wanted to break in and burglarize their homes, why had they been here? He pulled off his boots in his foyer at the top of the stairs, hung up his coat and scarf in the foyer closet. He was convinced more than one person had set off the alarms. To scare them? Who would want to scare them?

He returned to the leather recliner and said, "Fernseher American Movie Channel." The forty-nine-inch LCD television embedded in the electronics wall came on. He didn't feel sleepy, and he knew from experience it'd be a while before he did. An old black-and-white movie was playing. It looked like the story was set somewhere in post-World War II Europe. He'd watched anime with Pierre but hadn't watched many movies or television shows since his return from Buenos Aires. He'd been too tired, often going to bed quite early in the evenings.

He'd resisted the temptation to watch the digital video downloads of Sofia's movies that he'd collected over the last six months. He had watched only the DVD she'd given him last August, the movie of his father's novel *The Distance Between Two Points*, and had loved her work, loved seeing her, and at the same time felt frustrated and angry that they were so far apart. *Think about something else. Focus on the problem.*

Why would someone want to scare them? In America, it was quite common for the ISS or a Vigiciv gang to carry out a terror campaign against an individual, a family, or a group such as a department in a corporation or the section of an orchestra. If someone had initiated a terror campaign, who was the target? Him? Freda? Pierre? Was it the Americans? Or simply local thugs? No, that didn't make sense at all. They lived in Vienna, Austria, not Minneapolis in America. But what if it were terrorization? Or what if it were connected to the attempts on his life?

He went into the kitchen for a pad of paper and pen. When he was a kid, Uncle Joe had encouraged him to write down his thoughts when he had a problem to solve. Uncle Joe had learned this process from Evan's father, which made sense. Randall Quinn had been a writer and attributed mystical properties to anything on paper whether written by hand or printed by typewriter or computer. Evan had found in the past that the slow process of writing by hand allowed his deep thoughts to emerge, and had a soothing effect. He'd used the technique when he needed to make an important decision.

Sitting at the kitchen table, he wrote, "*Early morning January 24, 2049, in Buenos Aires—shot in abdomen and right shoul-*

der–survived. Assassin expected me to die. That would have been end of story."

But why? Who?

He outlined the series of events and dates—Alicia arriving in his hospital room in Buenos Aires (Was she really a Spanish spy? A friend of Bernie's? A friend and ally of his? Where was she?), Gregori in the women's restroom in Charles de Gaulle Airport in Paris, the Chinese-American guy following him after his lunch at Café Chicago, and then after Greta's music salon, the attempt on his life (How had he known where Evan would be and when?), and finally this night's security scare. He looked at what he'd written. His nagging sense that someone was hunting him was more than a feeling, he saw. Someone *was* hunting him, in the way a boxer dances around his opponent assessing his weaknesses with approaches, retreats, attacks, retreats. Someone with an organization, money, resources.

Terrorists? He'd already been the target of terrorists twice: first by the Right Path Uighur terrorists at his post-defection press conference in Vienna, and then by Islamic terrorists in Amsterdam. His nationality and job made him a high-profile target. Many of the terrorist groups had developed sophisticated organizations and possessed the resources and financial backing necessary to train professional assassins. Their varied purposes boiled down to provoking terror and political chaos. The global war offered an effective and convenient cover to steal across borders with ease and carry out terror operations.

The Americans? His bosses, the NEP. Woody had assured him that they wanted him to continue working for them as

Perceval. They had given him another target: Bernie Brown. Could it be some other American group? Bernie had told him about his CIA boss's order to terminate him. The CIA? But Bernie had deleted the termination order from the CIA database before he defected. Bernie's former CIA boss, Larry Morgan, worked at the American embassy in Beijing. He couldn't rule out the possibility that Morgan had initiated an operation against him to finish old business.

Had the Chinese somehow discovered his responsibility for the assassination of vice chairman Jiang Xu? No, he was certain the NEP would not want the Chinese to know they'd been behind that assassination. He doubted any involvement by the Russians. Since the Chinese nuclear attack on Moscow last August, the Russian government had had more important matters than coming after him for implicating a Russian named Vasia Bartyakov in the assassination, and giving the Chinese a reason to nuke Moscow and invade Russia, starting the global war. Like the Chinese, how could the Russians have found out he'd been the real assassin? But then, there was Gregori, who had claimed to work for the SVR, the Russian foreign intelligence agency. Gregori, who had known about the assassin in Buenos Aires.

What about the Austrians? What if the whole thing was an EU operation initiated by Inspector Leiner's suspicions? Leiner had had no evidence against him, no proof, but he suspected the Austrian cop had figured out what he'd done. No, that didn't make sense. Why would Leiner take an interest in helping him, protecting him? Could he trust what the cop told him?

A thought entered his mind, making him shiver. Whether

thieves or assassins, the security scare could be someone casing the house and garage. Checking the alarm system's effectiveness. He underlined this note twice on the paper.

He left the pad on the kitchen table and returned to his recliner in the living room. On the television, two men argued on what appeared to be a Ferris wheel. He leaned back in the recliner, producing a soft groan from the chair under him. If it were someone casing the property, what could he do? He needed to do something, to act, not to wait for them to return. Waiting made him crazy. Feeling power-less and stupid, as if he should just *know* who was behind it all, he thought of Uncle Joe. He had booby-trapped their house and property to discourage thieves and spies. Uncle Joe hadn't known who *they* were, either, but he knew for whom they worked: the ISS. Evan realized with a start that he and Freda *had* booby-trapped the property with the sec-urity system, and more important, the new low-tech security system. Their defense. Along with Sasha.

A strong defense was essential, of course. He needed to protect himself, Freda, Pierre. He needed to protect his right arm and shoulder, protect his conducting, his career, his cover. He didn't need any more physical fights. Going on the offensive, however, could throw his predators off. They must believe that he was weakened by the shooting in Bue-nos Aires, and further weakened by the attack here. If he lay low, they would continue to think he'd been weakened. He needed to marshal his forces (what forces?) and put them to work for him. More than anything, he needed solid intelli-gence that would tell him who wanted him dead, tell him whom he needed to target. He missed Bernie Brown with an intensity that surprised him. Brown could provide the intelligence he needed. Brown would know what to do next.

The movie had ended, and promotions for upcoming movies on the channel played. When the next movie began, a black-and-white film entitled *Hud*, the American Western drama drew him in. He didn't know when he drifted off to sleep.

His videophone's warble wakened him. The house computer had raised the window shades, and brilliant sunlight reflecting off the snow brightened the living room. "Fernseher abstellan," he said, and as the screen blinked off, he stretched his stiff legs and went to answer the phone. He checked his watch. Freda would expect him for breakfast in a few minutes.

Klaus Leiner, sitting at his office desk, greeted him on the videophone monitor. "Good morning, Herr Quinn. I heard about the security alarm at Frau Kirsch's. How are you?"

"Thanks, Inspector. We're all fine. The police were here, but they found nothing, really. Only evidence of trespassers. But it bothers me."

Leiner's fingers smoothed his dark blond mustache as he nodded. "I don't like that you have been targeted here after what happened in Buenos Aires. In addition, the man who was murdered in Stadtpark. I confirmed his American citizenship with the American embassy, and that he had worked for the Commerce Council. Herr Quinn, what might I do to help?"

Evan started. The embassy had confirmed the Chinese-American guy's citizenship? He had thought they wouldn't. He couldn't tell Leiner what he knew, not yet. But Leiner wanted to help him. "Thieves usually check out a place they plan to rob, right?"

"You agree with the officers, then?"

"Not completely. Someone tried to kill me in Buenos Aires and—" He stopped himself from saying "and here." "I can't help but wonder if our security alarm last night might have been another attempt and the alarm scared them off." He wasn't sure he believed that, but it would put Leiner to work for him. Marshaling his forces.

Leiner wrote something. "So, not thieves checking the property but someone who wanted to finish what was started in Buenos Aires?"

"Exactly. I'm thinking terrorists now. But who? And I'm really concerned about Freda and a young French boy, an orphan, we have staying with us. The police last night said they'd request more frequent patrols of the neighborhood, but now I'm thinking of supplementing that. Any ideas?" A much different experience, working with this cop instead of defending or hiding himself from him.

"Have you talked with Frau Kirsch?"

"Not yet. She said last night she'll have the security company check our systems and maybe add the motion sensor. But will that be enough?"

"I understand your concern, Herr Quinn." Leiner sat back in his chair. He appeared to focus on something beyond his videophone. Thinking. Leiner was thinking.

"I'm not keen on hiring bodyguards, Inspector. Freda has a dog already that did her job last night and woke them with her barking. We also have supplemental security, an old low-tech system we added last week."

Leiner's eyebrows had risen. "Prima. If you suspect terrorists, I can request an electronic intelligence check again." Leiner wrote another note. "Instead of a general request, I'll target the terrorist possibility. It will take a day or two. In the meantime, consider looking at private security firms. They may have other suggestions."

"That'd be great, Inspector. I appreciate your help and concern."

"If you think of anything else, or need anything, please call me, Herr Quinn."

The monitor turned black. Evan rubbed his face and his scalp, ruffling his black hair. He needed a haircut before he traveled to Copenhagen in ten days. He retrieved his black cellphone from the living room bookshelf and dialed Alicia's safe house. Still no answer. He dialed the Café Chicago. A female voice answered.

"Ist Woody da?" Evan said. Maybe she could tell him where Woody Lewis had disappeared to.

"Noch nicht. Er kommt sogleich."

Her response surprised him. Woody wasn't there yet but would arrive soon. "Um wieviel Uhr kommt er an, bitte?"

"Ungefähr halb neun."

This morning about 8:30. He thanked her and flipped the phone closed. He'd visit the Café Chicago this afternoon and then get his hair cut.

Breakfast with Freda, Pierre, and Sasha reassured him that everyone was fine after the scare the night before. Pierre spent the morning with him. First, the boy listened to him practice the violin—his bowing was far from normal but he worked on it each day for thirty minutes. It would take time and work to be able to play the way he had before the shooting. Then Pierre practiced the piano while Evan reviewed the Rachmaninoff Second Piano Concerto score for the Iceland Philharmonic gig two weeks after Copenhagen.

After lunch, without telling either Freda or Pierre, Evan called a cab and went into the First District, asking the driver to drop him off on Wipplingerstrasse near the Altes Rathaus. From there, he walked the snow-covered street for one block to Judenplatz and the Café Chicago. He crossed the plaza to Kurrentgasse, an ancient narrow street where he could flush out a surveillance shadow. After a block, he turned right and waited. No one came out of Kurrentgasse. He peeked around the corner at a deserted street. Satisfied, he returned to Judenplatz.

As he entered the café, the bell over the door rang, drawing the attention of the few diners left from the lunch rush. The two elderly chess players occupied their usual table near the front windows. Evan glanced at all the faces but saw nothing in their expressions or reactions that alerted him to danger. He chose a rear table near the ancient black wall telephone and sat with his back to the wall to observe both the front and side entrances. When the hefty blond waitress stopped at his table, she addressed him as "Maestro." He ordered tea with lemon and asked if he could speak with Woody.

Minutes later, the spry old white-haired American came around the pastry display case, wiping his hands on a long white apron over his rumpled gray pants and white shirt. He smiled, bushy gray eyebrows raised. Evan thought Woody seemed surprised to see him.

"How's business?" Evan said in English.

Woody sank into the chair opposite him. "I bet I know what's on your mind, Perceval."

"Where have you been, Woody? I've called. I've left messages. What's going on?"

"My son got married in Paris. My wife and I made the trip to the wedding. If you'd called the café, Martha would have told you."

"Congratulations. A pleasant trip?" Evan leaned back as the waitress, Martha, served his tea. Steam rose from the glass mug.

"We had one really bad bombing one night, but it didn't affect the wedding, thank God. We like the girl and her family. The ceremony was short and sweet. And I have no news for you about Buenos Aires." Woody cocked his head to one side, his blue eyes regarding Evan steadily.

Evan squeezed the lemon slice over his tea and stirred it. "That Chinese-American guy who jumped me about ten days ago, tried to kill me? Leiner told me the Americans confirmed his identity on the passport and that he worked for the Commerce Council."

"Really?" Woody shifted in his chair, shaking his head. "Why is Inspector Leiner providing you with that kind of information? You reported it to the police?"

"No, I didn't report it. Leiner called because he was concerned about me. What happened in Buenos Aires. All he knew was a guy carrying an American passport had been murdered in Stadtpark. I suggested he confirm the guy's citizenship." Evan leaned forward and lowered his voice. "Who wants me dead, Woody? I don't believe for a minute that

Chinese-American guy worked for the Commerce Council. Is it the CIA? Did Larry Morgan issue another termination order on me?"

The old American shrugged. Not a Russian shrug of knowing nonchalance but more like the Chicago gangster shrug he'd seen in old American movies. The "don't know and don't want to know" shrug used to feign ignorance.

"Woody. What's with your sources? Are you telling me there's nothing?"

"That's what I'm telling you, Perceval. Now, what's with you? There's been nothing on the news about the demise of Bernie Brown. You've got a job to do, Perceval. What's the problem?"

"The problem? Someone's trying to kill me, Woody, and you're not helping me find out who." Evan sipped his tea. He waited for Woody to defend himself, deny Evan's accusation, but the old American said nothing. "So, the assassin in Buenos Aires was a Chilean woman, did you know that? The guy here was Chinese-American. Someone's got an organization, resources, financing. I want to know who and why I'm a target." He'd expected a reaction, but again, nothing.

Woody sighed. "As I told you before, I'll see what I can do. Right now, with the war, lines of communication aren't as good as they are in peace-time."

"I'd expect them to be better. It's easy to use the war as a cover."

Woody shook his head as he got up from the table. "Enjoy your tea, Maestro. How's your arm?"

"I'm fine. I've got a gig in Copenhagen in ten days."

"I'll call you." Woody half-saluted Evan and headed for the kitchen in the back of the café.

Woody had been difficult to work with from the moment he'd met him. Evan had the feeling now that Woody's reluctance was a response to orders not to help him, not that he knew nothing and didn't have the time to help. He couldn't forget how Woody had expected him to be killed or arrested after the Chinese vice chairman job as a result of his incomplete training and lack of support. Evan finished his tea and left, debating with himself whether to go to the hair salon in the Le Meridien near the Staatsoper, that Robert Waldstein, the Vienna Philharmonic's concertmaster, had recommended weeks ago, or walk to Schottentor and catch the Number 41 streetcar to Gersthof and his usual salon. As he approached the Clock Museum at the corner of Kurrentgasse and Steindlgasse, a gust of cold wind buffeted him. His cell phone rang in his coat pocket. He answered it.

"Where are you?" Alicia said in his ear, her Spanish accent softening her tone.

"Where are *you*? I've been calling the safe house and not getting an answer."

"Traveling. I have some information, but it's not wise to talk about it on the phone. I will return to Vienna late Saturday night. Come to the safe house on Sunday."

"OK. Sunday. But where—?" The signal was gone. He slipped the phone back into his coat pocket and pulled up the collar. Ahead on the street, a man wearing sunglasses pulled a black wool watch cap down over his golden oat blond hair and turned his face away. The man wore a brown wool coat with a bright yellow knitted scarf.

Evan recognized the coat and scarf. Another gust of wind stirred up powdery snow around them as they faced each other, less than a block away, frozen in a moment of recognition that each had been seen by the other. Yellow Scarf Man pivoted and headed into a narrow street. Evan broke into a jog, arrived at the street in time to see Yellow Scarf Man running. Evan, forgetting his physical condition, ran after him.

He remembered where he'd seen the man: through the bistro's window when he, Freda, and Pierre had gone out to lunch after his physical therapy session weeks ago. Pierre had been frightened of him. Yellow Scarf Man acted like a surveillance shadow. As he arrived at the intersection with Tuchlauben, Evan, breathing hard, looked up and down the wider street. No sign of Yellow Scarf Man. But as he turned right, he caught a glimpse of a yellow scarf just visible through the display of a store window.

Traffic on the street forced him to wait, his eyes locked on that yellow scarf. It moved away from the window. A car passed and Evan crossed the street safely. He ran to the store, a bookstore, checked the window—no sign of that yellow scarf—and then went inside. He walked all around the store, one eye on the entrance, but found no one wearing a yellow scarf, no man wearing a black watch cap, sunglasses, and a brown wool coat.

Outside again, he stood on the sidewalk's hard-packed and slippery snow and watched the street activity for a minute. He remembered someone else who'd worn a brown coat and yellow scarf, but a leather rather than a wool coat: Gregori at Charles de Gaulle Airport in Paris.

CHAPTER 15

Bombs fell to the west, the concussive thumping and quaking earth hinting at their five-hundred-pound size. Overhead, the drone of bombers, fighters and MAO49s filled the air. They flew unchallenged over Austrian territory. Evan glanced up at them in the clear sky as he walked on Lerchenfelder Strasse behind the Palace of Justice at the edge of the First District. The Chinese had renewed their campaign against Austria in the last four days, targeting the industrial areas around cities they'd bombed before and sparing residential areas and the inner cities—at least for the moment. The war continued in China's and the Asia Pacific Coalition's favor, but the EU, Pacific Alliance and allies were holding the line.

Alicia had given him directions to the safe house that morning when he called her. He had taken a cab to Kahlenberg, the bus to Grinzing, the streetcar to Schottentor, and a cab to the Belvedere Palace, where he'd walked up Rennweg to Schwarzenberg Platz. Through that long, rectangular plaza, he'd observed the street activity with special attention but saw nothing unusual for a sunny Sunday afternoon in mid-March except for the eight-foot piles of snow where plows had cleared the parking area. Vienna would have a late spring this year.

He'd stopped by an octagonal information kiosk on the

Ringstrasse and watched news on the one computer monitor that was working. Icicles dripped from the kiosk's edges. That's when the air-raid sirens had begun to wail. He waited on the street, one eye to the sky and the other on the computer monitor showing video of Chinese troops patrolling the streets of Novosibirsk followed by a report on a UN Security Council meeting in which the members continued to negotiate the terms of a ceasefire. A thick rumble increased in volume under the wailing siren as the Chinese planes approached. They flew over the inner city, heading west.

Evan boarded a "D" streetcar that carried him on the Ringstrasse to the Volksgarten across from the Austrian Parliament. He paused at another information kiosk to observe his surroundings. The air-raid siren had cleared the streets, making it easier for him to spot potential shadows, a good thing for his surveillance-detection run. A uniformed Viennese cop strolled up the street in the direction of the Burgtheater, the only other person he saw. He had jogged across the Ring and up the narrow street next to Parliament and veered left onto Lerchenfelder Strasse. Nineteenth-century four- and five-story apartment buildings in stucco white with shops facing the sidewalks in their ground floors dominated the area. The shops were all closed, except for a Tabak Trafik. A quiet neighborhood enduring an air raid on a Sunday afternoon.

Despite the length of the surveillance detection and all the walking, he wasn't tired. He felt good. One more week and he'd travel to Copenhagen, so he better feel good. Glasmann had commented at his physical therapy session on Friday that he'd made excellent progress in only a month, but he would need to continue with the exercises for another five or six months to ensure maximum recovery and ease of movement. Evan committed to the schedule. He wanted to be able to conduct with ease and without pain, and increase the chances that his shoulder would be fine for many years to come.

At Strozzigasse he turned left into Neubaugasse, a canyon of a street with refurbished dun-colored four-story nineteenth-century buildings on each side and cars parked over the curb, half on the sidewalk, half in the street. Some were mounds of snow in the shape of cars. He found the apartment building and rang the bell marked "Atelier Schweiz." No security cameras over the door, no modern security panel into which he'd insert his identity card. An old-fashioned, low-tech security building similar to the one on the Wollzeile where he'd stayed last summer in the Four Seasons Pension.

The front door buzzed and he pushed open the heavy wood doors, peering through the frosted window in the door. Inside the musty shadowy foyer, his boots scraped the stone floor as he walked to the glass-walled elevator. He opened the exterior door, pulled back the metal cage door as Alicia had instructed, stepped in, and closed both doors. This building was a dinosaur. Before taking off his gloves, he pressed the button for the top floor.

She was waiting for him in the open door to the apartment, three doors down from the elevator. He hadn't seen her without disguise in almost a month. She wore blue jeans and a red cashmere turtleneck sweater, her wavy black hair loose over her shoulders. She smiled, her red lips parting to reveal beautiful white teeth. "Welcome to my home in Vienna, Evan. It is good to see you."

"And you." The hallway smelled of wet dog, and he grimaced.

"Ah, yes. The dog, a large, shaggy dog, loves to play in the snow, and his owner lives at the end of the corridor." Alicia mirrored his grimace.

"A common smell in this city."

"Come in. We have much to discuss." She pulled him by the hand through the doorway.

He'd expected a dump after his experiences with Austrian safe houses, but this Spanish safe apartment was clean, well furnished, bright, cozy, and warm. Alicia offered no details, and he understood not to ask about who maintained it, if someone else normally lived here, if there were other apartments that Spain's spies used as safe houses in Vienna. Alicia hung up his coat. He slipped off his boots and left them on a plastic sheet by the door. He padded in stocking feet over to a window facing west.

"The air raid must have helped your surveillance detection, yes?" Alicia slipped her arm through his, looking up at him, her black eyes wide. "Thoughtful of the Chinese, and also not to bomb the inner city. We will not need to run for the bomb shelter." She tilted her head back. Diamond stud earrings glittered in her ears.

"No one knows I'm here. I told Freda I was going for a walk in the Vienna Woods near Kahlenberg." He squeezed her arm against his side. "Where have you been, cousin?"

She sighed. "First, Madrid. They wanted to know what I was doing."

"What *are* you doing?" She had not been around to protect him. Was she on his side?

She guided him with gentle pressure from her arm into the sitting room, where she'd laid out tea and cookies on the coffee table. A forty-inch LCD television was on but muted in the electronics wall. Evan recognized the war images but not the location. "I told them I had accepted a special independent assignment related to Bernie's defection. Of course, they wanted to know where he is. Do you know?"

He shook his head as he sat down on the overstuffed teal blue leather sofa. Paintings of giant flowers in bright colors decorated the white walls. "You can tell your boss that the last time I heard anything about Bernie, he was still in Austrian custody. That was months ago. The Austrians will know where he is. I received an email from him after Buenos Aires. He wanted to know if I'd gotten the package from Spain."

Alicia laughed, full-throated and loud, her mouth open and head thrown back. She sat down next to him. "You see, Bernie likes you." She poured tea into white mugs for each of them.

"I was actually wondering what he'd sent me when you didn't answer the phone here."

The smiled faded from her face. "I am your friend, Evan. Your ally. I am sorry I was not able to contact you before last week. Madrid was not happy with me, and not pleased that I wanted to travel to Canada."

"Canada?"

"I have a source there. I found out from him that there is a shadow group outside the NEP government, but also within the NEP government, secret, not many members, maybe six or seven, that very, very few know exists."

Evan felt goose bumps rise on the back of his neck. The group he worked for or was there another? What were the chances a second shadow group existed? "What kind of shadow group? And how did he find out about it?"

"You are not surprised?" She handed him his mug of tea and offered the plate of cookies. "My boss was also not surprised."

He chose a raspberry-jam-filled cookie. He needed to hide Perceval, focus on being Evan Quinn, conductor. He wouldn't have known about such a group as a conductor, but as an American, nothing the NEP might do to benefit itself would surprise him. "The NEP will do whatever it needs to do to get what it wants. Power. Money. Secret cabals. That's the American way. Were you surprised?"

She sipped tea and sat in thought for a moment. "Not surprised. Throughout history, governments of many countries have chosen to create deep covert groups or operatives to protect their positions, domestically or internationally, and hide what they are doing. The NEP is not the first or the last. But I could not confirm whether this group is only domestic or also international." She regarded him with an even gaze.

"You think it has something to do with Buenos Aires?"

"Yes. I suspect also that this group operates internationally. But not CIA. Separate from them. Separate from all known American government agencies. There must be no way to trace its activities back to the government, yes? Its operatives are the elite of the elite and the deepest cover. And perhaps specializing only in assassinations rather than wasting energy on other things like counterintelligence. America already has too many counterintelligence agencies that squabble all the time among themselves." Her gaze moved to the TV, then to the mug in her hands.

"Your Canadian source confirmed all this? How'd he ferret them out?"

"No. My source received his intelligence from the American Underground, an organization I believe you are familiar with, yes? Because of your father?" She bit into a hazelnut wafer cookie, and then brushed crumbs from her chest. "They found a secret training facility in northern Minnesota, deep in the woods, not far from the Redfield prison. You know this area?"

He shook his head, as the sinking sensation in his stomach made him nauseous. He knew both the training facility and the prison well. Plus, they were not far from where his family had had their summer cabin years ago. The Underground had found the training facility. He'd bet they were keeping that information on a need-to-know basis. Alicia was talking about the shadow group he worked for. He was certain now. She couldn't know that he knew more than anyone could guess he knew, or about Perceval.

He thought of Woody's stonewalling. If his bosses wanted him dead, Woody would not tell him. Woody would not help him. He breathed slow and deep.

"You are quite pale, Evan. Are you ill?" She reached up and felt his forehead, her hand warm and dry against his skin. She smoothed his straight black hair from his face. "Finally you have cut your hair." She smiled.

"Pierre was angry with me because it's longer than his."

"Pierre?" Alicia set her tea mug on the coffee table.

"A French orphan who found me in Türkenschanz Park about three weeks ago. His parents were killed in a bombing last fall. He was terrified of the police and had been living on the streets. He recognized me. He said his father had told him about me. Freda and I have been taking care of him while the French embassy searches for his relatives in France."

Alicia's eyes had studied him as he spoke. "You are a good person, Evan. You have a good heart. You and Freda. I am glad to know you. How is Freda?"

Evan sipped more tea, feeling his stomach quiet. "Fine. Frustrated by the war, like the rest of us. Her school re-opens in a couple weeks, so she'll be going back to work. She's been teaching Pierre, helping him with his English. You know, watching her with him the last few weeks, I've been wondering why she hasn't remarried. She's great with kids."

Alicia shrugged. "Have you asked her?"

"No." He couldn't imagine asking Freda that personal a question. She was his landlady—a friend, but still his landlady. "So, your Canadian source confirmed a super-secret group believed to be sanctioned by the NEP government that you think may be behind Buenos Aires. I found out the American embassy confirmed the American citizenship of the assassin in Stadtpark and claimed he worked for the Commerce Council."

"I do not believe he worked for the Commerce Council. Perhaps for this shadow group." She sipped more tea from her mug, her eyes on the war images on the TV.

"Maybe. I had another thought. Larry Morgan. When he was Bernie's boss here, he ordered Bernie to kill me. Morgan's at the embassy in Beijing right now, I think. He could have ordered an operation against me through the CIA after Bernie defected."

Alicia frowned. "A possibility. I will check with my CIA sources again. As I recall, Bernie detested Morgan."

"We had a security scare in the middle of the night last week. The alarm went off in the house and my place. The cops found only indications of a trespasser. Leiner called me and I told him that I suspected terrorists. He's checking on that angle."

"Good." She glanced out the window. "How are you physically, Gordo? Your shoulder?"

"My strength and stamina have increased. My shoulder is OK. I'm ready to conduct again. Carefully." He said with a nervous titter.

"Why are you a conductor?" she said. "Tell me what a conductor's life is like when you are working."

He smiled. "I'd wanted to be a conductor since I was six or seven years old. My father's best friend, Joseph Caine, was my mentor. He began teaching me music when I was about four years old. He taught me discipline. Dedication. So now, as a conductor, I study scores for each concert and prepare thoroughly before I arrive to rehearse the orchestra for the concerts. I am at home on the podium. But it's a solitary life, really, and a lot of hotel rooms. I don't eat well on the road. It's a lot of travel, Alicia. Like your life, huh?"

She smiled, sighed. "But you meet many people, many musicians. You can have friends, a family. I must not."

"I'll always be your friend. Bernie's your friend." He sipped tea, thinking about Uncle Joe and his warnings about music being a "demanding mistress." "If you'd known what the life would be like before you got into it, would you have become a spy?"

"Would you have become a conductor?" She bit into a raspberry-jam-filled cookie.

"I can't imagine doing anything else." But he could. Perceval. "Yeah, I meet a lot of people, but it's rare to make deep connections. I consider musicians to be my family, though. Musicians stick together, try to help and support each other."

"Girlfriend?"

Sofia's hazel-green eyes appeared in his mind, her smile, her long chestnut-brown hair. "Not really," he said. He hadn't had a girlfriend since high school. Even though he was no longer in America, he knew attachments could still be dangerous for him…and for them.

She nodded slowly. "A lonely life. I understand your self-containment. And you are famous. You must be careful who you allow close into your life. But what did they do to you in America? Why are you so sad? You are a lovely man. You deserve to have joy and love in your life."

His stomach muscles tensed. Music had provided him with all the emotional connections he'd ever needed, the spiritual connection. He had been fine without the complications of people. Vasia had changed that, he realized. Pierre. Sofia. Freda. Greta. But love? His father's baritone whispered out from memory, "I love you, Evan. You always know how to please me." He shook his head to clear the voice from his mind. Love was humiliation and degradation, as his father had taught him well.

"The NEP did their best to dictate what I could do, where

I could go, who I could know, treated me like a farm animal, arrested me, put me in prison. I couldn't wait to leave."

"But your father was famous. Although, I confess, I have not read any of his books."

"I haven't read them either." Evan laughed. "Fame protected him until the ISS figured out a way to arrest him and not look like thugs." He had helped them, fed them information about his father's Underground activities and where he kept incriminating documents. "They wanted his money— the money in London from sales of his books that he'd smuggled out. I think they believe if they kill me, his heir, then they can grab all his money."

"Is it that much?" she said, standing and facing the electronics wall. She addressed it in Spanish, and the volume snapped on. "I wanted to check BBC News," she said, glancing back at him. "They have the best coverage of the war on Sundays."

"I don't know the exact amount—millions."

"Millions." She breathed the word, looking at him with wide-eyed surprise.

"A special report out of Glasgow," the BBC announcer said in his crisp voice.

Evan focused on the television as Alicia returned to her seat on the sofa next to him.

The screen showed a wan Bernie Brown, his mud-brown hair wind-tousled, his swaggering gait recognizable, being escorted by police through a crowd of photographers and reporters and pushed into a shiny black sedan.

"This morning, during a transfer from London to Glasgow," the BBC announcer's voice said, "Bernard Brown, the high-level American CIA official who defected in Vienna last summer, was shot."

"No!" Alicia shouted.

"Why did they allow all the media access?" Evan said, his fists hitting his thighs.

The announcer continued, "Glasgow had been chosen by government officials to ensure Brown's safety from the continued Chinese bombing of London." Video of Bernie with a group of suited men and women came on screen. Bernie was smiling. Alicia groaned. "Mr. Brown had agreed to meet with government officials to discuss American CIA activity in Britain over the last decade, as he has met with officials from other European governments since his defection last August. It is uncertain at this juncture how Mr. Brown's travel details became known to the person or persons who assassinated him as he and his security escort were leaving Glasgow airport. What is known is that two gunshots were fired at Mr. Brown from a distance."

"They killed him!" Alicia shouted at the TV, pointing her finger as if pointing a gun. "The CIA. *They* killed him!"

Evan couldn't move. His face felt as cold as the stone in his stomach. He stared at the TV screen. *It can't be true*, he thought. Perceval was supposed to kill Bernie Brown. He'd decided not to complete that assignment. He had believed that by not doing the job, as Bernie had refused the order to kill him, he'd save Bernie's life. He'd been an idiot. What the NEP wanted, the NEP got.

"Alicia," he said.

Alicia gave him a look of torment, rage, and pain. "The Americans did this. I hate them. Those CIA bastards!"

While the announcer's voice moved on to the latest news of the war, Alicia sobbed as she spoke. "He wrote it in his letter to me, Evan. The CIA would come after him. He knew so much about their activities in Europe, and they would want to silence him."

"But why now? He's been talking to European governments for over six months. If they'd wanted to shut him up, they should have gotten him months ago." As Woody had told him to do. Were his bosses after him for not killing Bernie? But what would they care if they could send someone else after Bernie? They'd gotten him. Bernie was dead. Gone. He'd never see him again. Deep in his belly, the cold stone flashed into a white-hot pain and the urge to hit something. His eyes met Alicia's. She had stopped crying.

"Whoever is after you, Evan, they will not succeed. I will protect you. It was the last thing Bernie ever asked me to do."

He put his arm around her shoulders, and she crumpled into him. In his mind, he saw Bernie squatting next to Valerie Peters's body in Amsterdam and grinning up at him. Bernie had taken care of him, had protected him, always had his back. His friend. He could hear his South Bronx voice: "Hey, Maestro! I found a great café in the Third District. Wanna invest in it with me?"

"I wonder what Bernie would do?" Evan said.

Alicia looked up at him. "I have an idea." Alicia pressed her palms together in front of her face. "I will contact my source in the SVR again to see if we can find Gregori. Perhaps he can help."

"But they didn't confirm he was SVR, did they?"

"If I give them a reason to move against the CIA, and

the means, they will help. They may not have wanted to reveal his status before." She thought, tapping her fingertips against her lips. "And we need to plan Copenhagen. I will go with you."

They planned Copenhagen. After, neither of them talked much while they ate the chicken and rice dinner Alicia had made. Nothing tasted good to him. He studied Alicia sitting at the other side of the kitchen table, slicing up chicken on her plate. Her mood had changed. She looked angry, seriously angry. He had no doubt that she'd find Gregori as well as whoever had killed Bernie. He toyed with the idea of telling her that he believed Woody Lewis had something to do with it but decided to wait. Woody might still be useful.

Later, as he walked back to the First District on Lerchenfelder Strasse in early evening shadows, he pulled out his black cell phone and dialed Woody's personal number. He glanced around to make certain no one was close enough to overhear, and no one else on the street looked like they might be eavesdropping electronically. Cars sped toward the Ringstrasse. The air raid had ended hours ago, and Vienna's normal Sunday evening activity had resumed.

"I heard, Perceval," the old American said in greeting. "Are you in Glasgow?"

"No. It wasn't me. Who was it?"

"Oh." Woody grunted. After a pause he said, "Probably the CIA."

"Is the CIA after me, too?"

"No, why would they be after you?" Woody's dry chuckle filled his ear. "Your paranoia never ceases to amaze."

"Paranoia is self-preservation, Woody. Larry Morgan's in Beijing. He wanted me dead."

"Larry Morgan's got other things on his mind, beginning with the war."

"Selling American weapons to China?"

"That, too. I'll let you know when our bosses have another job for you. Safe trip to Copenhagen."

Dead air in his ear. The American had hung up. Evan flipped his phone closed. He'd reached the bend in the street behind Parliament and veered right. The closest taxi stand was near the University of Vienna at Schottentor. At the Ringstrasse, he trotted across the wide boulevard, dodging light evening traffic, and walked along the Ring past the Volksgarten, a snowy wonderland, and the Burgtheater. Only one woman nodded to him and said, "Guten Abend, Maestro," as he passed. The other dozen or so people were focused on their own thoughts and business and took little notice of him.

At Schottentor, he engaged a taxi. He asked the driver to drop him off on Gersthofer Strasse, and he walked home from there. He heard Pierre before he saw him.

"Sasha! Sasha! Komm hier!" Pierre shouted from the backyard lit up by the security lights.

Evan stopped at the driveway gate, pressed his right middle finger into the security pad, and bent down to the speaker, "Der schattige Affe." The gate hummed as it swung open.

"Monsieur Evan!" Pierre turned, a snowball held high in one hand while Sasha jumped to grab it with her mouth.

"Hello, Pierre. Are you training Sasha to fetch snowballs?" He smiled at the boy as he walked up the driveway.

Pierre threw the snowball at him, hitting him in the

chest. Sasha followed and leaped up onto him, nearly knocking him to the ground. "Pierre!"

The French boy kicked snow at him as he approached, his head down but his eyes looking up at him. Angry eyes. "You have been to Kahlenberg all this time? Madame wanted to call the police, and I told her to wait, but she was so concerned that she called the police and they are right now searching the Vienna Woods for you. Where were you, Monsieur Evan?"

He looked at Freda's house. The lights were on upstairs and in the front sitting room. If she was so worried, why hadn't Freda come out when Pierre had called his name? His eyes met Pierre's and he understood.

"You rascal!" he shouted and grabbed the boy by the waist, lifting him off the ground and spinning him around as Pierre screamed in glee.

"You believed me, yes? You believed me," Pierre said when he was standing again in front of Evan, holding Evan's hand in his, his grin brighter than the security lights.

"Yeah, you got me. Let's go see if Freda has any hot chocolate in the kitchen."

Sasha pranced around them as they headed for the back door. Evan had to figure out a cover story fast about where he'd been all afternoon and into the evening. Freda would be a tougher sell. But she'd believe that he'd stopped in a café in Grinzing and lost track of time. That's probably what Bernie would suggest.

The white-hot pain returned to his gut. He'd find a way to punch back hard at the Americans for killing Bernie.

CHAPTER 16

"Monsieur Evan, how do you study the score?"

Evan turned away from his videophone to Pierre's voice, his mind mulling over the phone call. Neils Dam in Copenhagen had delivered bad news about the Barber Piano Concerto at the Danish National Symphony next week. The piano soloist had become a casualty of the war bombings while in Berlin to perform a recital earlier this week. Confined to a hospital bed for at least ten days after surgery, she would not be able to perform. Evan knew the frustration and physical pain she must be feeling from his own hospital stay in Buenos Aires. He'd asked Neils the best way to contact her and Neils had given him both a phone number and email address. He'd not met the pianist before, but the least he could do was to call, wish her a speedy and safe recovery, and assure her that he looked forward to working with her another time.

Neils had found a Norwegian pianist named Lars Sven Larson who was available and could play the Barber, but wanted to obtain Evan's approval before booking him. No Arts Council here to dictate a soloist to him and the orchestra. Since his defection, when he didn't know and hadn't worked with a soloist before, Evan had learned to rely on an orchestra's staff to advise him. Neils had worked with Larson and described him as a brilliant technician with a powerful musical imagination who had an affinity for Samuel Barber's music. Evan had approved the pianist. Neils had confirmed again Evan's flights and hotel, and that he'd meet Evan at the airport with two security guards. Evan couldn't wait to return to work.

"Monsieur Evan?" Pierre leaned against one side of the kitchen door frame, rubbing his nose. His trimmed brown hair refused to stay in place and now flopped over his forehead. They had spent much of the last two days together in quiet routine, waiting for news of Pierre's relatives in France. Evan hoped they'd know before he left for Denmark.

The quiet routine had helped him not only in his score study, but also in his black grief over Bernie Brown's death. Freda had given Pierre lessons in the morning at her house, and after their midday meal together, he returned with Evan to his apartment. In the afternoon, Evan did his physical therapy exercises and studied a score, and Pierre drew until the hour before supper, when Evan gave Pierre a piano lesson. Over the last two weeks, Pierre's drawings had begun to cover the walls of Freda's kitchen and Evan's living room like colorful ivy. The boy had a sharp eye for perspective and the play of light and shadow to add depth. Although he'd drawn good portraits of both of them in colored pencil, Pierre excelled at drawing buildings.

"How do I what?" Evan combed his straight black hair back from his face with his fingers.

"You told the man on the videophone you study scores for other gigs," Pierre said, pronouncing the last word as "geeks." Pierre grabbed his hand. "You never have shown me how to do this. I want to show Papa. He will be so excited I learn this from you." He pulled Evan into the living room and the piano near the front windows.

Pierre talking about his father in this way startled Evan. Dr. Moreau had told him and Freda that she believed Pierre had seen the bomb hit his house and was so traumatized by it that his mind could not accept what had happened. In order to cope and maintain his connection with reality, he had decided that his parents had not been at home at the moment the bomb hit and so he must find them. Dr. Moreau had advised them to play along for now. Pierre would face what really happened in his own time as the evidence of his parents' deaths was given to him.

"OK, Pierre," he said, sitting down on the piano bench and opening the score on the stand above the keyboard. "Let's work on a symphony by the composer of silences."

"The composer of silences?" Pierre's skeptical tone made Evan smile. "But music is not silent."

"No, you're right. But this composer, Jean Sibelius, composed both sounds and silence in his symphonies. Look." He flipped the pages to the second movement. Hearing Sibelius on the radio while in Helsinki last fall had been a revelation. The Arts Council in America had banned his music, and even considering the Council's notorious arbitrariness concerning repertoire, Evan could not fathom why. Unless it was because of the silences. They were provocative. Nigel had suggested that he begin learning Sibelius's music with this symphony, his second. Of course, every musician in the Helsinki Philharmonic had his or her own suggestion for how to begin studying Sibelius, but they had all agreed that the

Second Symphony was much loved by audiences and a fine introduction to this composer, along with his First Symphony, *Finlandia*, and a tone poem called "The Swan of Tuonela."

"I see this line of music," Pierre said, pointing to the score. "Only one instrument plays."

"Well, that line is for the entire bass section, not just one of them. Have you ever seen an orchestra score before?"

The boy shook his head, his lower lip sticking out.

Evan grinned. He envied the boy his first time. For himself, it had been like actually seeing and hearing an orchestra for the first time—a bazaar of sound and motion, colors, and the flash of brass. He pointed to the first bar of the symphony. "See how the music begins? With timpani rumbling. Then pizzicato in the basses." His finger followed the music and he sang the pizzicato line. "More timpani, like thunder in the distance. The cellos—see—pick up the pizzicato now." As naturally as breathing, he began to move his right hand to beat out the music he was hearing in his mind.

Pierre concentrated with a laser-like intensity as Evan sang and talked him through the second movement, describing how he wanted to work on articulation of the sound, attention to tempo and dynamics, the trouble spots he'd work on in rehearsal, and then the moments of silence that reminded him of seeing the Bay of Finland reflecting the sky and how, as a result, the horizon had disappeared into the water.

Evan talked about the importance of knowing who Sibelius was, the world Sibelius lived in during the first half of the twentieth century, and how his nationality influenced his music at that time. He talked about how the composer

Joseph Caine, his father's best friend, had taught him about composers and how they work. He wanted to open in Pierre the same love for music, the love for reading and experiencing music, that Uncle Joe had opened in him when he was a boy. Joseph Caine had begun much earlier with him. Evan had been seven years old and had already been playing the piano and violin for two years, had already seen an orchestral score, had already attended several orchestra concerts with his parents. Uncle Joe had encouraged him to use his imagination as well as the violin and piano to hear the music on the page. Pierre had been playing the piano, he said, for only a year and showed average talent. But the boy clearly loved music.

For the next five hours Evan worked on the symphony at the piano, Pierre sometimes sitting next to him, sometimes standing next to him and playing the chords with him. He felt the boy's energy, his warmth, and smelled the faint lavender scent on his hair from the shampoo Freda gave him to use. Was this how Uncle Joe had experienced him when they had studied scores together? Evan had not thought of it before, only how he had experienced Uncle Joe: the scent of oranges, the rough denim of his jeans, his smooth hands with their long fingers, his soft baritone voice that could persuade a dog to sing, his shoulder-length blond hair falling forward over his face. He'd felt safe, protected in Uncle Joe's presence and in his house. Now, when he tried to imagine himself there with Uncle Joe, it was as if only a shadow of him as a boy remained there, blurred, a smudge on the memory.

"Beethoven also played the piano?" Pierre said, in his sweet child soprano.

"Yes, quite well. He gave piano lessons to the children of the aristocracy of Vienna."

"Children like me?"

"All ages, Pierre. Have you practiced the Beethoven sonata?"

"Only a little. It is hard."

Evan slid off the bench. "Go ahead and practice it now. Slow down and take it one bar at a time until you know the notes." He placed the Sibelius score on top of the pile on the piano and picked up the three scores he'd take with him to Copenhagen. While Pierre practiced, he sat in his black leather recliner and reviewed them, especially the Barber Piano Concerto.

Freda called an hour later, and they bundled up in their boots and coats for the short walk over to her house for tea and lentil soup. Instead of eating in the kitchen or dining room, Freda set up old standing trays in front of their chairs in the living room so they could watch the *BBC World News* on television while they ate, followed by the local newscast. Pierre sat bolt upright, holding his soup spoon like the news anchor held his pen.

The global war dominated the news. With fighting in Asia and Europe, the war had coalesced into two fronts: in Russia along the Ural Mountains and in the Pacific where, in Indonesia, the Chinese seemed to be doing their best to annihilate the Muslim population. The Islamist Coalition had complained bitterly in the UN but had not moved to intervene. The Western allies had re-taken western Australia from the Eastern Coalition (China and APCO), which was good news.

Evan paid particular attention to European news likely to affect his travel to Denmark. So far, nothing different— the Eastern Coalition forces were being held at the Ural Mountains while the Chinese continued to send MAO49s and bombers to destroy supply lines and supply sources in Europe. In Vienna, there was news of a shortage of fruit from Spain but predictions of shipments of produce from South America. Hauptbahnhof, the train station serving south European routes, had been repaired enough to reopen at the end of the week. Petrol rationing would continue until summer, and the heating oil supply was running low so Viennese residents were urged to conserve.

"How are we set for heating oil, Freda?" Evan asked as he gathered up their dishes to carry into the kitchen.

"I think we have enough, but it would not hurt to conserve." She ruffled Pierre's hair, and he squirmed in the chair next to hers. "We can take fewer baths."

"Good idea," Pierre said with a grin.

Evan smiled at the two of them: the sweet French boy with the huge blue eyes and reckless hair next to the Viennese woman who stood almost as tall as Evan, whose earthy blonde beauty, air of experience and wisdom, and sad green eyes had become so much a part of his life. "My turn to wash dishes," he said.

"Evan, I forgot to tell you. Greta called this morning. She's fine. Ready for the baby to come. She mentioned Sofia is returning next week."

"Oh, OK. While I'm in Denmark. OK."

He went into the kitchen, stacked the dishes next to the sink, and turned on the hot water. He felt good, almost without any physical pain. They had a nice, comfortable life together at the moment, despite the war and the shortages. He glimpsed the importance of having a stable and secure base in his life, a home, from which to work. Freda had created a safe, warm, comfortable, and accepting environment for him. Freda understood what he needed in order to work.

And now Sofia was coming back to Vienna. He looked up and out the kitchen window into the backyard, where Sasha explored the perimeter trees in the snow. Sofia was coming home. His breathing increased in tempo, but what he felt in the pit of his stomach was fear, not excitement. What was the choice she wanted him to make? He chose her. He closed his eyes and remembered the first time he had met her, after Lisl Schatzmann's violin recital the previous summer. He had felt drawn to her, every cell of his body resonating to the energy of her presence, the same way he felt when he connected with music. He didn't want to lose that, but what could he do to keep it? He didn't understand what she wanted from him. He filled the sink with soapy water and sank a stack of dishes into it.

"Pierre! Press the alarm! Press the alarm!"

Madame's voice screamed at him in French and jolted him out of a dream about his maman cooking cassoulet for Christmas Eve. His heart pounding, he grabbed from the nightstand the small black cube that she had given him after Monsieur Beni had finished his work in the house. He pressed down hard on the red button with both thumbs. Now Monsieur Evan would hear an alarm in his apartment.

"Pierre, run! Run! Out of the house!" Madame shouted in French.

What was happening? Where was Madame? What was happening? He felt a tense sickening in his stomach. In the faint glow through the windows from the streetlights, he looked around the bedroom, his eyes stopping on the door. Would Madame come for him? He heard a loud thumping out in the upstairs hall. Madame screamed, a frightening sound that propelled him out of bed. He opened his bedroom door a crack.

To the left, in the light from her open bedroom door, Madame in her white flannel pajamas struggled against a tall man with blond hair. The man wore a brown leather jacket and yellow scarf. Avoine? Pierre slipped out of his room, staring. The man pushed Madame to the floor. She crawled, and the man followed her. He bent and grabbed Madame's short blond hair and pulled back her head.

"Run, Pierre! Get out!" Madame screamed in French, her green eyes dark with fear.

He ran for the stairs. He must warn Monsieur Evan, must tell him to run, to get away from Avoine. Behind him he heard an odd, wet swish like a shoe squashing rotten fruit that made his skin crawl. Without looking back, his heart racing with his feet, he rocketed down the stairs in darkness and into the hallway, calling for Monsieur Evan without hearing his own voice.

He must protect Monsieur Evan. Footsteps thumped down the stairs. Protect Monsieur Evan.

He reached the kitchen and the back door, breathing hard,

glancing at the security panel which was dark. He'd never seen the panel dark before. Something was wrong with it.

He must warn Monsieur Evan, must protect Monsieur. The footsteps paused in the front foyer. Monsieur Evan.

Fumbling with the chain and the bolts, he unlocked the back door, flung it open, and flew out into the frigid March night.

He ran as fast as he could into the darkness off the back porch. No security lights illuminated the snow-covered yard and driveway. Where was Sasha? Why wasn't she barking?

Monsieur Evan. He must warn Monsieur Evan.

The heavy footsteps hit the small back porch behind him. Avoine had turned on the kitchen light. But it wasn't Avoine wearing the brown leather coat and yellow scarf and standing on the porch in the light when he looked back. He didn't know this man's face.

He raced for the garage and Monsieur's apartment as he heard a soft hissing *thump*, followed by two more. He was almost to Monsieur's exterior door. He heard the man coming after him.

He must reach Monsieur, warn him, protect him, tell him to run.

He heard another hissing *thump* behind him, a snap in the wood of the garage, and then a sharp loud intake of breath, followed by a heavy muffled *thud*. He hit Monsieur's doorbell on the dark security panel over and over and over.

A sharp crack cut through the air like when his Papa had broken a large stone with a hammer. He looked back.

Monsieur Evan straightened to his feet over a prone figure in the snow.

Pierre ran to him, yelling, "Monsieur, run! We must run!" He grabbed Monsieur's arm. Monsieur Evan swung him up into his strong arms and embraced him. Pierre gasped for breath. "We must run, Monsieur. Run away!"

"It's OK, Pierre. You're safe. It's OK," Monsieur Evan said, his mouth close to his ear. "Was there only one man?"

Pierre held tight to Monsieur. "I saw only one."

"OK."

Monsieur Evan's voice sounded so calm, so strong. Pierre heard the musical tones of a cell phone being dialed, heard Monsieur Evan talking to the police. The police would come right away. They were not far away; the station was near. And the security company would come because the security system was not functioning. Pierre couldn't catch his breath, he felt like he was suffocating.

"You're safe now, Pierre," Monsieur Evan's voice said in his ear. "We have to wait for the police and the security company before we can go inside my apartment. OK?"

"I pressed the alarm. You heard it? Madame shouted to press the alarm."

"I heard it, Pierre. You're safe now. The man can't hurt you now. No one can hurt you now."

Flashing red and blue lights approached on the street but no siren. Pierre gasped when Monsieur set him down and his bare feet touched the icy cold snow. He wore only his flannel pajamas, nothing else. Monsieur Evan wore jeans, a sweater, boots, his wool coat. Pierre began to shiver. Monsieur took off his coat and put it around him. He could smell Monsieur's sweat on the coat.

"Wait here. I'll be right back."

He watched Monsieur Evan trot to the driveway gate. The flashing lights stopped on the street outside it. Monsieur Evan was alive. Where was Madame? Sasha?

"Pierre is in my apartment, Inspector. There's a cop sitting with him." Evan stood over the man he'd killed lying in the snow, the man who had been turned over carefully by the police to reveal in the light of their flashlights the face of Gregori. "When I came out, I heard Pierre inside Freda's, screaming my name. He came out the back door. That guy," Evan pointed down at Gregori, "chased him, shooting a gun with a silencer at him. I was hiding over there by those ever-green bushes between the back porch and the front of the house. I jumped the guy. I can't believe I actually killed him." Perceval was feeling exhilarated and powerful and confident in his ability to kill. He'd forgotten about the power rush killing produced. Bernie would tell him to party, to do something to use up the energy. He met Leiner's steady gray eyes, relieved that Leiner was here and not a detective he didn't know.

"Your lessons at the Fischer School of Martial Arts have paid off," the Austrian cop said in a subdued voice. "Was the boy hurt? Are you all right?"

Evan rubbed his right shoulder. "He's OK. I may be sore tomorrow, but I'm OK."

"You recognize this man, Herr Quinn?"

Evan nodded. "It's Gregori, the Russian who claimed to work for the SVR that Alicia and I met in Charles de Gaulle Airport on the way home from Buenos Aires. He claimed to have been following a Chilean woman he believed had tried to kill me in Buenos Aires. The police there didn't believe him. We didn't believe him. I told you about him at lunch three weeks ago." Alicia was looking for Gregori. She'd be surprised he was here. Or maybe not.

"Ah, I remember." Leiner's eyes widened. "I spoke with Detective Ruiz in Buenos Aires about him. Ruiz thought he was a Verrückte."

A forensic team came out of Freda's back door carrying bags of evidence. Leiner squatted and searched Gregori's pockets, careful not to disturb the body, although the photographer had already documented it before the coroner had examined him and after they had turned him over. Cause of death: broken neck. From the brown leather jacket's breast pocket Leiner slipped out a wallet that contained no credit cards or identification, only a mixture of euros, Canadian dollars, and Kenyan shillings. "No Russian currency," Leiner said, glancing up at Evan. "No Russian identification. No coins that would make noise when he walked. No receipts or notes. No passport. We'll need to fingerprint him and check his DNA for identification."

"You think the Russian embassy will know who he is?" Evan said, glancing at the security company technician leaving his apartment. She had told the police that someone had hacked into the house's and his security system computers, and shut down the system. She would need to reboot and reset both systems. She had estimated it would take one to two hours.

"We will ask them." Leiner sat back on his heels. "Why Frau Kirsch?" He looked up at Evan. "Why the boy?" He shook his head. "Frau Kirsch worked for me. Had you known that, Herr Quinn?"

Freda a cop? Evan felt his mouth drop open. No, Freda was a teacher. "What do you mean? How did she work for you?"

Leiner stood, pulled out a small plastic bag, and dropped Gregori's wallet into it, then sealed the bag. "She watched you for me, reported anything unusual."

"Surveillance?"

"Yes."

Freda had had him under surveillance, and he'd never suspected a thing. He hadn't thought he might need to be especially careful around her. She was his landlady, a friend. "Was she reporting to you all the time I've been living here?"

"Initially, when you first moved here, she reported daily. Over time, it became clear that a weekly or monthly report would suffice. Do you want me to assign someone to live in Frau Kirsch's house to guard you, Herr Quinn?" Leiner's gray eyes remained steady on him. "Gregori's attack cannot be a coincidence."

Not a coincidence. He thought of telling Leiner that the Chinese-American the police had found murdered in Stadtpark had tried to kill him, but he needed to talk to Alicia first. "I don't know, Inspector. Let me think about it." Maybe he could persuade Alicia to move in. "If Gregori was after me, why target them?" He could feel the burning heat of anger building out from his gut and up his body as he watched a woman wearing protective clothing approach them. Leiner turned to her.

She addressed them in German. "Inspector, we are ready now for the official identification before we move her."

Leiner nodded, reached out and grasped Evan's arm. He said in English, the British inflections making Evan think of a judge, "You feel up to making the official ID, Herr Quinn?"

"Yes." He hadn't seen Freda yet. He knew she was dead and that she'd been stabbed. He braced himself for a lot of blood.

Two klieg lights illuminated the upstairs hall, the forensic technicians, and the shiny yellow plastic tape marking the perimeter of the murder scene outside Freda's bedroom. Evan smelled the sharp metallic scent of the blood before he saw the immense darkening pool soaking the beige carpet around Freda and staining her white flannel pajamas. His breath caught in his throat, and his chest muscles tightened. Freda was dead because of him, because someone wanted him dead, he was certain of it.

"Herr Quinn?" Leiner's voice came from his right.

Her eyes were closed. Her skin was almost as white as her pajamas. Her feathery golden-blond hair was matted with blood on one side of her face. He saw that her throat had been slashed.

"I thought she was stabbed, Inspector?"

Leiner exhaled. "She was stabbed in the heart, and then her throat was cut."

The preferred method. Tears welled in his eyes. That was the way to kill with a knife taught at the training facility where he'd become Perceval. Gregori was one of the "elite" assassins from the shadow group? Like him? He fisted his hands and inhaled. He said in German, "I know this woman to be my landlady, Freda Kirsch."

The woman wearing protective clothing said in German, "Thank you, Herr Quinn." She nodded to two men, who unfolded a metal stretcher.

"Come, Herr Quinn."

He followed Leiner back out to the snowy driveway. In their absence, someone had collected Gregori's body. Uniformed police guarded the perimeter of Freda's property and the investigative activity occurring inside the house as well as outside. Evan knew little about what they were doing, but he knew they were collecting evidence. He thought of something.

"Freda owned a golden retriever, Inspector." He glanced around the yard, looking for any sign of Sasha.

"We found her dog by those trees over there," Leiner said, pointing to the tall, dense evergreens in the back corner. "He killed the dog first. Then I believe he disabled the security system—the company's technician will provide us with a report on his exact method—before he broke quite expertly a rear window to the cellar of the house."

"He knew what he was doing, obviously. I wonder if he was the one who set off the alarm a week ago. We thought it was a couple of burglars, but maybe he did it to find out about the system and the house."

Leiner nodded. "A possibility. I'm glad I'm not sending you to the morgue tonight."

Evan laughed, a rueful sound in the cold air. His breath clouded around his face. "You and me both, Inspector. The low-tech alarm saved me and Pierre. He's going to be really upset about Sasha and Freda."

"Tell him now, Herr Quinn. Gently but clearly, matter-of-factly. He deserves to know the truth. Would you like me to call a police counselor to be there with you?"

Evan shook his head. "He's already talking to a counselor at the French embassy." He sighed. He must call Dr. Moreau first thing in the morning, and also talk to Monsieur Cassel. He needed to find someplace safe for Pierre to stay while he was in Copenhagen.

"Do you know Frau Kirsch's family, Herr Quinn?"

He suddenly thought of his mother, when she had committed suicide, the police questioning his father about relatives and his father's surliness. He was not his father. "No. I know her father lives in an assisted living facility out in the country, but I'm not sure where. He has Alzheimer's. No siblings or other family that I know of. When the war started, she spoke with a lawyer about the house. She told me where she kept the papers regarding it."

"We will need that information, Herr Quinn."

For half an hour, he and Leiner glanced through the legal papers that Freda had kept in a safe hidden in the pantry. The cop assured him that he would contact Freda's lawyer, who was named executor of her will, and would also arrange for a professional clean-up crew to remove the carpet in the upstairs hall and scrub the floor beneath it once the crime scene had been processed and released. Evan filled two cloth shopping bags with clothes for Pierre, his drawing paper and pens, and some of his books. The boy would stay with him until the house no longer smelled of blood.

The security company technician found him in Freda's kitchen checking their food supply for the next few days with Leiner. "Herr Quinn? I have tested both systems, and they are functioning fully now," she said in German. "Would you like to check your access, please?"

"I will check in with you tomorrow, Herr Quinn," Leiner said as he left.

Evan couldn't lock up Freda's house yet. The police were still processing the scene. Carrying the cloth shopping bags, he walked with the security company technician to the rear garage door, his apartment's exterior door. Pressing his middle right fingertip into the security pad, he leaned down to the panel's speaker and said, "Der schattige Affe." The lock released. He set the bags on the steps inside the door.

He shook the technician's hand and said in German, "You know how he disabled it?"

The technician nodded. "We will use this knowledge to improve the system. And it will be in our report to the police."

"Thank you for coming out in the middle of the night and helping us."

"If you have any further problems, Herr Quinn, please call us."

Before he climbed the stairs to his apartment, the anger that he'd been pushing down punched out, his gloved fist pummeling the wall next to the door. His eyes focused on the black knitted glove on his fist. Freda had given it to him. He pulled out his black cell phone and dialed Alicia's safe house. She answered on the first ring.

"Where are you?" she said instead of hello, her voice alert.

"At home. I found Gregori. He was here tonight. He

attacked Freda and killed her, tried to kill Pierre." He spoke low. He could hear movement above inside his apartment.

"Is he alive?"

"No. I had to kill him to stop him from killing Pierre."

"Damn."

"Inspector Leiner's on the case. We need to talk about how much to tell him and about Copenhagen."

"You want me to go to Copenhagen today?"

"No. I want you to travel with me. Until I leave on Sunday, I'll have police protection. I don't think they'll try again here anyway."

"I agree."

"I have to talk to Pierre, take care of him."

"Call me tomorrow, Gordo."

He carried the bags up the stairs. Inside his foyer, he set them down, hung up his coat, and slipped off his boots. When he opened the door to the living room, Pierre slid out of the black leather recliner where he'd been watching television and ran to him, holding Evan tight as if keeping him from lifting off the ground and flying away. The TV screen showed an undersea nature program. The uniformed cop, a woman, was in the kitchen, reading something at the table.

"Pierre, I have to talk to you, OK? It's bad news. Let's both sit in the recliner."

The cop came out of the kitchen, putting on her cap and zipping up her winter jacket. "Herr Quinn, do you want me to stay?" she said in German.

"No. Thank you for taking care of him for me."

She nodded and slipped out quietly. Evan reset the security system. Pierre waited for him in the recliner.

"Fernseher abstellan," Evan said, and the television flicked off. The silence in the apartment felt like an ocean of water pressing down on him.

"Sasha was not outdoors," Pierre said. "Did the man hurt her?"

Evan pulled Pierre close to him in the recliner. "Yes. The man killed her, Pierre."

Evan watched Pierre's face. The boy's blue eyes widened a little, but otherwise his expression remained serious.

"Sasha was a good dog. Maybe she bit the man. I hope she bit the man and hurt him, too."

Evan took a deep breath. "I hope she bit him, too. You understand, Pierre, that the man is dead?" The boy nodded. "You understand that I killed him?"

"Good." Pierre nodded. "He wanted to hurt all of us. We must have a special burial service for Sasha."

Evan thought for a moment, brushing Pierre's hair back from his face. He could not remember how his father had told him about his mother's death. He remembered coming home from school that day, finding the police talking to his father in the living room. His father had told him to wait in his bedroom, so he'd gone there and waited, listening to the furtive sounds coming from the front of the house and from his parents' bedroom. Then he remembered. He'd slipped out and down the hall to his parents' bedroom, but a man with a black leather bag had stopped him. His father hadn't told him about his mother's death, the coroner had.

"Pierre, did you see Freda?"

The boy nodded his head. "She fought with the man outside her bedroom. She shouted for me to run. I ran to warn you." Pierre looked up into Evan's face.

"Freda loved you very much, Pierre. She fought hard to protect you, to give you time to escape. You saw what the man did to her?"

Pierre tilted his head to the side, the sign that he was thinking. He frowned. "No. What did he do? The police have taken her to hospital?"

"No, Pierre. The man killed Freda. She's dead." He watched the boy's face, saw the smooth skin pale and fear flicker across his eyes. "Do you understand?" he said as softly as he could.

"Madame… he killed her, truly?" Pierre sniffed and tears filled his eyes. "But you are here, you are alive, I protected you."

Evan hugged Pierre close as the boy cried into his chest. No one had held him when his mother died. No one had comforted him. "Big boys don't cry," his father had growled at him. Anger blocked his own sorrow, but he still felt, as he held Pierre and tried to soothe his pain, that somehow, maybe, he was reaching back into the past and doing the same for the boy who had lost first his uncle Joe and then his mother.

CHAPTER 17

"Thank you, Herr Cassel. I'll bring Pierre to the embassy this afternoon to meet with Dr. Moreau." Evan faced his videophone, hands on his hips. The bearded embassy official on the monitor was frowning, deep lines radiating from the corners of his blue eyes.

"We believed Pierre's relatives lived in Paris. We have learned only Pierre and his parents, and his father's parents, who are both dead, lived there. We have found his mother's sister and her husband in the South of France in Narbonne. They are making arrangements to come here, but with the war, travel is difficult. As you must know." The Frenchman sighed. "You understand, Monsieur Quinn, we cannot keep him here at the embassy. If you would like, I will inquire among the staff for someone to care for him while you are in Copenhagen."

Evan heard Pierre's bare feet padding toward him from the bedroom. "That's great news about his aunt and uncle. As I said, Herr Cassel, I'm very concerned for Pierre's safety. If he can't stay in the embassy, I'd like to find a secure place with someone to care for him myself while I'm in Copenhagen." He didn't want to offend the official, but he'd feel better finding someone himself. At the moment, he hadn't any idea who, but he would figure it out.

He felt Pierre's small warm hand slip into his and looked down. Pierre's eyes were puffy from crying, his brown hair tousled from sleep, but otherwise he looked fine. "Good morning, Pierre," he said, glancing at the Frenchman on the monitor.

"Ah, Pierre!" Cassel launched into French.

Evan watched Pierre, who started after a moment, his mouth open. He replied in French. Evan wished Freda were here to translate for him as she had done during their meetings with the French. Freda.

Pierre tugged his hand and said in English, "They have found Aunt Dominique and Uncle Julien. They will come for me and take me back to France. But I do not know when."

"Do you know them, Pierre?" Evan said, not wanting to turn the boy over to relatives who might be complete strangers.

"Yes, of course," Pierre said, his tone subdued. He spoke to Cassel again in French.

Cassel smiled and said in English, "That is your choice, Pierre." Cassel's eyes moved back to Evan. "Please inform us, Monsieur Quinn, where Pierre will be staying while you are in Copenhagen. And again, I am so very, very sorry about Madame Kirsch." The monitor flicked to black.

Evan turned to Pierre. "Your choice about what, Pierre?"

"When I return to France and if I want you to know where I am living in France." Pierre looked up at him, still holding his hand. The boy's blue eyes began to fill again, the tears from an ocean swell of sorrow. His thin shoulders sagged.

Evan squatted, and grasped his arms. "I want to hear

from you. OK? No matter where I am in the world, OK? And remember, when I conduct in Paris, I'll see you then, OK?"

A fat tear trickled down Pierre's cheek. Without a word, he went into the living room. The videophone warbled. Evan pivoted to answer it, massaging his right shoulder.

Greta's worried face appeared close up on the monitor. "Evan? Are you all right? I heard what happened last night on the news this morning. My God, I am so sorry about Freda."

"We're OK, Greta. Sad and sore but OK. It was on the news? I didn't see any media here." He glanced into the living room. Pierre was collecting his drawing pad and pencils.

"The police perhaps herded them to a spot away from the house. They are saying it is related to the attempt on your life in Buenos Aires, that you were the actual target. What about your security, Evan? You must have more security, hire bodyguards, something." Her black eyes flashed, the eyes of fierce protectiveness.

Pierre returned to the kitchen and sat at the table, opening his box of colored pencils and drawing pad. Evan watched him for a moment, and then said to Greta, "Security's not something I want to discuss on the phone, Greta. How are you? How's the baby? Are you at work?"

She nodded. "The baby kicks a lot today. I cannot wait for him to be born. He has gotten to be quite heavy to carry around inside." She smiled. "I think he is eager to join us in this world."

"We're eager to see him." Evan chuckled. "You're not going to have him while I'm in Copenhagen, are you?"

He considered asking Greta to care for Pierre but decided against it. He needed to protect Greta and the baby, which meant keeping them at a distance from any possible threat. If someone came after Pierre in his absence, Greta might be hurt, and Pierre…as Freda was. Perceval stirred within him. Perceval's thinking had its place.

Pierre slipped a piece of paper into his hand. He looked at it. In red pencil Pierre had written, *He listens.* Crying silent tears, Pierre looked up at him and stood with his back to Greta.

She was laughing, a low throaty sound. "No, we will wait for you, Evan. Is there anything I can do to help? Do you have enough food?"

"We're fine, but thanks. Could you call Owen and Lucia? Tell them we're OK? I'll send an email to Sofia. I bet she's already sent me one. I'll call you before I leave on Sunday. I need to make some breakfast now for Pierre."

Greta nodded and waved as the monitor flicked off. Evan, holding up the slip of paper, turned to Pierre and opened his mouth to speak, but Pierre raised his index finger to his lips, signaling him not to speak. He took Evan's hand and brought it up to a spot behind his left ear. Evan felt a tiny bump under the skin there. His stomach muscles contracted. What was it? Was it a tracking device like the one he'd had removed from behind his ear not long after his defection? He bent down to take a closer look. Directly behind Pierre's left ear, a tiny square had been embedded under his skin. Evan went over to the drawing pad on the table as he said, "I need to find a safe place for you to stay while I'm conducting in Copenhagen, Pierre."

"I will come with you."

Of course, that would be the boy's logical solution to the problem. Evan wrote on the drawing pad, *Austrian?* The boy, still crying and looking miserable, wrote under it, *American*, as Evan said, "I'm sorry, Pierre. You can't come with me. I need for you to be in a safe place, OK?" He read Pierre's reply, feeling his stomach muscles harden with anger. He wrote, *Name?* as he said, "I have to think about what's best. I thought the embassy would be the safest place, but Herr Cassel said they cannot have you stay there. Do you want to stay with someone on the embassy staff? Or I could find someone."

"I want to come with you to Copenhagen." Pierre drew on a clean sheet.

Evan watched him work and realized that he was drawing a portrait. He drew fast. "I know you want to come with me, Pierre, but I'll be in rehearsals most of the time, doing media interviews, and then the concerts. We won't be able to spend much time together. I also want to know that you are in a safe place while I'm working." The boy drew the nose, eyes, and mouth. Evan stepped closer and stood behind him. The face the boy drew looked familiar, and as Pierre filled in more detail and color, Evan felt a searing blush of recognition. The drawing was a portrait of Harold Smith, unmistakably the same eyes, nose, the smirk on his lips, his blond hair, now more golden than the wheat color he remembered from last August in Vienna.

"I am safe in the hotel room in Copenhagen. I want to see you conduct." Pierre spoke matter-of-factly, no longer crying, putting finishing touches on the portrait.

Harold and his Vigiciv gang. They had terrorized him and Paul Caine and his neighborhood when he was a kid. After Evan graduated from high school and moved to New York City to attend Juilliard, he'd believed he'd escaped Harold forever and hadn't thought about him again until his defection, when the hallucinations of Harold and his Vigiciv gang began to haunt him. He hadn't told anyone about those hallucinations. They'd think he was crazy. And then Harold had showed up—Harold in the flesh—in Vienna and had told him "I'm your shadow," in his sandpaper voice. Evan picked up a pencil and wrote at the bottom of the drawing, *Where is he?*

Pierre's response was an I-don't-know shrug. His eyes welled up, but no tears spilled onto his cheeks this time. Evan bent over and hugged him from behind.

"I have an idea," he said in a low voice. He wrote on another sheet of paper, *Any other listening devices?* as he thought of Woody's bug detector on the back of his watch. It hadn't alerted him to the listening device embedded behind Pierre's ear. The detector couldn't pick up all bugs. It wasn't as reliable as Woody had claimed. The bug behind Pierre's ear must be sophisticated, a new generation, and powerful.

Had Woody known about Harold? Woody hadn't called him to check on him after last night. Perceval stirred again. The nagging suspicion he'd had about the old American flared in a burst of anger. He couldn't let Pierre see his anger.

Pierre shook his head and wrote *GPS* next to Evan's question. He pointed to his left thigh.

So, Harold had wanted not only to hear everything that Pierre heard, but also to know where Pierre was at all times.

He looked out the kitchen window at the naked maple tree branches as the realization hit him: that's how the Chinese-American guy had known where Evan would be the night he tried to kill him. He and Pierre had talked about Greta's party, where it was, why Pierre couldn't come with him. The Chinese-American guy had worked for Harold. He'd also bet Harold gave the orders to the Chilean assassin in Buenos Aires, and Gregori last night—Harold had created another Vigiciv gang, one of assassins, to come after him. Why?

A memory flashed behind his eyes: Harold's face close to his, Harold's lips puckered up into a kiss. At the same time, he could feel Harold's hand rubbing his crotch. He cringed, nausea rising into his throat. He swallowed and wrote, *Did he hurt you?*

Pierre said in a loud, whiny voice, "But I want to go with you to Copenhagen." The expression on his face was pure fear. Pierre nodded. Yes, Harold had hurt him.

He could hide his anger no longer. On the paper he wrote, *I'm angry at him, not you*, followed by, *Can the chips be turned on to hurt you?* Evan's mind raced into Perceval's mind. If the chips could hurt Pierre or even kill him, he'd need to take him to Dr. Maas as soon as possible to have them removed. But if they were removed, Harold would know that he knew about the chips. Keeping Harold in the dark a while longer might be to his advantage right now.

Next to his first statement, Pierre wrote, *I know*. Next to the question, he wrote, *No*.

Evan sighed with relief. "How about some scrambled eggs, toast, and sausage for breakfast? And you need to wash and get dressed. Think about what you want to wear to the embassy this afternoon. Herr Cassel asked me to bring you there to meet with Dr. Moreau."

Anger energized him, made him forget his physical soreness, as he began breakfast for the two of them. Underneath the anger, pain and guilt simmered. Perceval. Freda was dead because of him; he was certain of it now. Perceval existed because of the Americans. He'd made the deal with the NEP in order to escape them and live free, but right now he couldn't feel more trapped. They had ensnared him. Again. He'd performed beyond their expectations in completing his first assignment. But because of them, because of Perceval, Vasia was dead. He stopped chopping green pepper and listened to the shower running in the bathroom. Vasia would have loved Pierre, but because of Perceval, the French boy would never know the Russian pianist. Perceval could protect Pierre, but the boy must never see Perceval, especially the way Vasia had seen him.

He finished chopping the green pepper, scooped it up, and added it to the chopped onion in the pan on the stove. He broke eggs into a bowl. Vasia was dead because of him. Freda was dead because of him. And now the rest of his friends were probably in danger because of the NEP. He wanted nothing to happen to his friends or to Pierre. He needed to figure out a way to terminate Perceval and his relationship with the Americans to ensure their safety. He'd been stupid not to think of it last September, after Woody gave him his second Perceval assignment and explained how the Americans had sprung their trap on him so that he would have to work for them if he wanted to continue his music career…and his life. Woody.

The videophone warbled again and he felt a flash of annoyance at the interruption.

Inspector Leiner's face appeared on the monitor in response to Evan's "Yeah."

"Good morning, Herr Quinn. How are you and Pierre?" Leiner closed a file in front of him on his desk. He spoke English.

"Coping, I guess, Inspector. Any news?" He wiped his hands on a kitchen towel.

"I have spoken to Frau Kirsch's lawyer. He will visit you later this morning regarding Frau Kirsch's will and the house. We have not yet confirmed the identity of the man you called Gregori, but we continue to work on it. I am sending a clean-up team to the house. They are professionals we use regularly for crime scenes. They will have police identification."

As Evan listened, an image popped into his mind of the Austrian cop standing in his driveway on Chimanistrasse with his two daughters. What safer place for Pierre than with a Viennese policeman? "Thanks, Inspector. I will ask for the IDs. I have a favor to ask."

The Austrian smoothed his mustache and nodded. "You want referrals for additional security?"

"No." He felt suddenly shy. He'd not asked Leiner for a favor before, and he couldn't remember the last time he'd asked anyone for a favor. His mouth felt dry. What if Leiner refused? "I need your help, Inspector. I can't take Pierre with me to Copenhagen, much as I'd prefer to take him with me, and after last night, I want to find a highly secure place for him to stay for the week I'll be gone. Would it be too much to ask of you and your wife if he could stay with you?"

Leiner's face split into a broad smile. "I would be happy to take care of him, Herr Quinn, and I am certain Eva would, also. You've inquired at the French embassy? They know what you are doing?"

"Yeah. Pierre can't stay in the embassy and Paul Cassel, his case officer, told me this morning that he'd ask around with the staff to see if anyone would take him, but I told him I'd find a safe place myself. Anyway, I'd feel a lot better if he were staying with you."

As if on cue, Pierre walked into the kitchen from Evan's bedroom, his wet hair combed back and wearing jeans and his red sweater. He went to the refrigerator and lifted out a liter bottle of apricot juice.

"I understand, Herr Quinn. You mentioned last night that the embassy was in the process of finding his relatives. Any progress?"

"They've found Pierre's aunt and uncle in the South of France. They're making arrangements to travel here to get him."

"But I will not return to France before Monsieur Evan returns from Copenhagen," Pierre said in English in a firm, confident voice from the kitchen table. He had poured two glasses of apricot juice for their breakfast.

"Inspector, may I introduce Pierre Levade. Pierre, this is Inspector Klaus Leiner with the Vienna police. You'll be staying with him and his family while I'm in Copenhagen."

Pierre approached the videophone, his eyes narrowed. "You are a policeman? You cannot arrest me now, yes?"

Leiner laughed, a deep rumbling sound Evan couldn't remember hearing before. "Why would I want to arrest you, Pierre? Have you committed a crime?"

Pierre turned to Evan and buried his face in Evan's stomach, throwing his arms around his waist. Evan hugged him.

The smile faded from Leiner's face. "Pierre, I am sorry if I've upset you. Of course you have not committed a crime. I have no reason to arrest you." Leiner gave Evan a questioning look, and shook his head.

"Pierre lived on the streets for a while. Some street kids told him that if the police caught him, he'd disappear and never be seen again. Was that it, Pierre?"

"The police throw little boys in jail," Pierre said, his voice muffled by Evan's jeans.

Evan rubbed Pierre's back. "It's been a rough twelve hours, Inspector."

"Of course. When do you leave for Copenhagen?"

"Sunday."

"I am certain we will talk before then."

"Thank you, Inspector. I will feel a lot better knowing he's with you."

Leiner nodded as the monitor flicked off. Evan patted Pierre on the back. "Now the police will protect you for me, OK? Inspector Leiner is a friend. He's a Mensch, OK? You want to help me with the toast?"

Pierre stuck close to him for the rest of the morning, as if fearful that if he let Evan out of his sight, Evan might disappear forever. For his part, Evan was glad the boy followed him around, although he doubted Harold would try anything the day after Gregori's attack. The police were still working in Freda's house during the morning. Freda's lawyer, Herr Bothmann, arrived late that morning, and Evan talked with him over coffee in his kitchen at the table while Pierre practiced the piano in the front room.

"Freda rewrote her will, Herr Quinn," Herr Bothmann said, his growling bass and thick accented English reminding Evan of the opening of Jean Sibelius's Fourth Symphony. The lawyer wore brown tweed and flannel slacks. Evan wondered where his pipe was. Herr Bothmann handed him a document. "She possessed a concern about the war, naturally, and the bombings and her safety. She wanted to ensure her father would be able to continue to live in his facility if, as she said it, she became a statistic of the war."

Evan skimmed the will as Herr Bothmann spoke. "She's left me the house," he said, his voice rising in astonishment.

"Yes. She asked me to administer the trust set up for her father to pay for his living expenses. She wanted you to have everything else, including the house."

He sat back in the kitchen chair, his hands cupping his coffee mug, and stared at the lawyer. Freda had said nothing to him about it. Why? Maybe atonement for her surveillance of him? They had become friends. What was he going to do with the house? Evan didn't want to own a house.

"I understand, Herr Quinn, that you will leave for Copenhagen in several days. I need only for you now to sign these papers so that I can begin the probate."

Evan signed.

"Freda wanted to be cremated, Herr Quinn. Would you like to organize a memorial or would you like me to organize it?"

He hadn't even thought about a funeral. Pierre wanted a special burial for Sasha, and he wasn't certain that would be possible. The police had taken Sasha's body last night along with Freda's. But Freda would be cremated. "She wanted a memorial and no funeral?" The lawyer nodded. "I don't know the first thing about organizing a memorial, Herr Bothmann. I would really appreciate it if you'd do it. The police told me last night that they'd release her in a few days." Evan sighed, trying to ease the tightness in his chest. "Could you take care of the cremation, also? And please schedule the memorial for…well…." He looked at his conducting calendar on the kitchen wall. "Maybe the week of April twelfth?"

The lawyer nodded again. "Excellent, Herr Quinn. These things take time."

After Herr Bothmann had left, as he made grilled Swiss-cheese-and-ham sandwiches for their lunch, Evan felt anger toward Freda, something he'd not felt before. First of all, she'd died and left him, abandoned him, but that wasn't her fault, it was the Americans' and Harold's. Second, she'd left him nearly everything, and he didn't want it. The money and property felt like a burden. And he felt guilty because when he'd written his own will the previous fall, to protect the money he'd inherited from his father and Joseph Caine from the NEP in America, he hadn't thought about Freda as an heir. He'd left everything to Vasia's baby in a trust. Perhaps he could set up a trust for Pierre using Freda's money. The boy had lost his parents, and Evan knew nothing about this aunt and uncle who were coming for him. *Freda would be happy for Pierre to have it*, he thought.

Behind his thoughts lurked the image of Woody Lewis,

his white hair like a dandelion gone to seed around his head, his glacier-blue eyes under his bushy white eyebrows, the lines in his forehead and cheeks, his Chicago twang when he spoke. Woody hadn't called. Maybe he'd heard the news that Evan had survived the attack the night before, but Evan was still surprised his handler hadn't called to check on him. Had Woody known the attack was going to happen? Did he know Harold and his assassin gang? He needed to talk to Alicia about this, but he hadn't yet figured out how to do it without telling her about his job as Perceval.

Early that afternoon at the French embassy, Evan watched Pierre run to the slim and stylish Dr. Moreau and felt a sharp pain in his chest. The boy ran to her as he had run to Freda, as Evan had run to his mother at that age.

"Monsieur Quinn, will you wait here or...?" Dr. Moreau smiled and gestured to the sofa in the room where he and Freda and Pierre had waited on their first visit.

"I need to visit someone." He looked at Pierre, who frowned at him. "It could take longer than an hour. Will Pierre be OK here until I return?"

Dr. Moreau nodded, her hair swishing over her shoulders. "Of course. We will have our talk, and then perhaps Monsieur Boulez would also like to speak with Pierre, eh?"

Pierre's face brightened. He insisted on walking Evan out to the reception area, where he hugged Evan goodbye. Evan felt a twinge of guilt. He'd not told the boy about his Spanish "cousin," Alicia. But Pierre didn't need to know.

Outside in the bright early spring sunshine, Evan stepped

over a puddle, the product of slow-melting snow on the sidewalk, as he headed for Karlsplatz. He flipped open his slender black cell phone and pressed the speed dial for Woody's number. The old American's voice mail message answered. Evan left a message for Woody to call him. He also called the Café Chicago. The woman who answered told him that Woody would not be at the café until the next Monday, which was after Evan's departure for Copenhagen. Where was he? The woman said only that he was out of town on family business. Only weeks ago, Woody's son had gotten married in Paris. Evan wondered how many children the guy had.

Alicia's safe house on Neubaugasse was too far to walk in the time he had, so he took the subway from the Karlsplatz station to Stephansplatz where he planned to switch to the U3 line. In the crowd that disembarked with him from the subway car he spotted a man with golden oat blond hair who wore a brown coat and yellow scarf, but his face was hidden by people's heads in front of him. Evan let the crowd carry him along, past Yellow Scarf, their jostling an excuse to turn and glance behind him. Yellow Scarf walked in the crowd, his head down as if concentrated on keeping his feet from stumbling. Evan stepped onto the ascending escalator, hemmed in by two young couples bundled up in loden wool and bright knitted hats and scarves against the cold, one in front of him, one behind. He listened to their discussion in German about where to buy tickets for the opera that evening and whether Wagner's *Parsifal* was the same story as Chrétien's *Perceval*. Hearing that name gave him a jolt, and he glanced back down the escalator. Yellow Scarf was there, his back to him.

In the bracing air and bright light above ground in Stephansplatz, Evan started to walk toward the towering cathedral. If he could lure Yellow Scarf inside, he'd confront him. But then what? He wanted to beat the guy to a pulp. He glanced over his shoulder. Yellow Scarf stood behind him about thirty feet away. Evan saw Harold Smith's face, the smirk caught in the cold granite of his expression. Their eyes met, and recognition flashed between them. Harold pivoted and jogged away, turning the corner into the Graben. Evan followed, dodging shoppers crossing the square. Now was his chance to end the hunt, to stop Harold once and for all. Anger burned through his mind, and Perceval used his anger for energy.

On the Graben, Evan spotted Harold almost a block away on his right, already crossing Trattnerhof. The next block was a long one, full of luxury shops. Now it seemed hundreds of shoppers had emptied out of the shops and hurried on the pedestrian street, creating an impenetrable crowd. Evan half-walked, half-jogged after Harold, keeping his eyes on the yellow scarf, trying to avoid collisions with the shoppers without much success. The image of Joe Caine skinning a rabbit for campfire stew popped into his mind. Hunting. He was hunting Harold now much as he, Uncle Joe, and his father had hunted rabbit and deer in northern Minnesota. Perceval hunted. Perceval wanted to catch Harold, interrogate him, and end him. Harold passed a bookstore and glanced back at him.

Evan increased his pace to a full jog, weaving around the pedestrians on the sidewalk, bumping into some of them. At Jungferngasse, Harold turned right. By the time Evan arrived at that corner, Harold was entering Peters Kirche, an ivory and gold Baroque church with a green dome. Evan stopped. Harold wanted to lure him into the church, but he knew Harold wouldn't be there. He'd have already exited by a side door. But which one? Evan bumped into a red-haired woman in white fur, her floral perfume wafting around him. He mumbled "Excuse me" in German and jogged toward the side of the church. He didn't stop at the side door, however, but continued around to the back, where he spotted Harold ducking into Milchgasse.

By the time Evan had followed Milchgasse to the broader Tuchlauben, Harold had disappeared. Evan surveyed the street, the traffic, the people on the sidewalks, people coming out of shops as he caught his breath, his hands on his hips. Harold couldn't be far, unless he had a car waiting somewhere. He pivoted, getting a full-circle view of the activity around him. If Harold had sent assassins to kill him, why run from him now? Or maybe Harold wasn't running so much as leading him. In that case, where was he?

Almost the instant the thought entered his mind, Evan spotted the yellow scarf and blond hair a block away, emerging from a side street. He broke into a run up Tuchlauben. Harold sprinted across the street, dodging cars, and ran up Tuchlauben on the opposite side from Evan. Harold waved to him just before turning into a side street. Traffic on the street forced Evan to wait for a lull, dancing from one foot to the other. He wondered if Harold would wait for him. The wave and cocky grin seemed to indicate that he believed he was in control of this chase, The same self-assurance Evan remembered in Harold as a teen leading his Vigiciv gang. A break finally came in the traffic flow, and Evan jogged across the street.

The unfamiliar side street was narrow and empty of pedestrians. Old Baroque buildings rose up on either side. Evan walked, alert to the silence of the street, the sound of car traffic behind him, his boots squishing the slush on the sidewalk. Ahead he saw a cross street and slowed. Harold might be waiting just around the corner to jump him. He glanced at his watch. He'd be very late for his meeting with Alicia.

He approached the corner on tiptoe. He breathed slowly. He listened. Only the sound of car traffic coming from Tuchlauben behind him. Backtracking about five feet, he stepped out into the middle of the street. In a burst of energy, he ran past the corner and into the cross street, which turned out to also be deserted. He turned in a complete circle. No Harold in any direction.

Disappointed, Evan walked a short distance to another street and recognized where he was. Judenplatz. The Café Chicago. Maybe Harold had gone there. Evan used the café's side entrance to avoid the bell ringing when he entered. But there was no need for such caution. Inside the café only two patrons sat at a front table, the two elderly gentlemen Evan had seen before. They glanced up from their chess game. Harold wasn't there. He'd vanished.

The hefty blond waitress came out of the back kitchen. "Guten Tag. Was möchten Sie heute?"

He bought a small Linzertorte for Pierre and left. The fastest way to Alicia's, he decided, was to backtrack to Stephansplatz and take the subway. As he walked at a brisk pace, he noted the people around him, what they were doing, if anyone took special notice of him. He saw no yellow scarves. Just like Harold to have a uniform for his gang—brown coat, yellow scarf—just like his Vigiciv gang wearing black jeans, red vests, and white T-shirts. Now that he knew about it, though, Harold would switch it up, use it on innocents to deceive and deflect him. If Harold wore a yellow scarf after today, he'd be surprised.

As he rode the escalator down to the subway, he noticed only one person stared at him, a young woman who carried a violin case. He smiled. She blushed but smiled back. The subway ride out to Neubaugasse was uneventful. But when he emerged from the station, he discovered that he wasn't where he'd expected to be. Mariahilfer Strasse was on his left, not Lerchenfelder Strasse.

The walk north on Neubaugasse took longer and made him later. The street was quiet, although he passed open shops, a post office, and the Rembrandt Theater. No one marked him. No one followed him. Perhaps Harold hadn't been following him on the subway from Karlsplatz. Evan had just left Pierre and his GPS tracking chip. From the audio transmitter chip embedded behind Pierre's ear, Harold would have known that Evan was leaving the French embassy.

Five blocks later, he stood at the front door of Alicia's dun-colored nineteenth-century apartment building. He rang the bell marked "Atelier Schweiz." The heavy wood door buzzed, and he pushed it open.

She was waiting for him in the open door to her apartment as he stepped off the old glass-walled elevator and closed the metal cage door. She wore jeans and a black cashmere V-neck sweater. Worry lines creased her forehead, and her red lips were a thin line.

"Where have you been, Evan? What has happened?" She grabbed his arm and pulled him into the apartment.

"Alicia, I know who's trying to kill me."

CHAPTER 18

Tierartz. Monsieur Evan had called Herr Doktor Schneeberger, "der Tierartz." In English, Monsieur Evan had said, the word was *veterinarian.* Pierre had stumbled over the English pronunciation but had no problem with the German word, which meant "animal doctor."

Pierre walked toward the jungle gym in Türkenschanz Park, kicking up the sparkling snow in the early morning sunshine. Monsieur Evan had been in the shower when he had left the apartment. He did not know when or where Monsieur Evan slept. The Wizard Howl had told him not to worry so much about him. Steamboy had whispered that now Monsieur Evan could protect him for a change. Ashitaka had remained silent on the matter. They had all agreed Pierre would be safe staying with Monsieur Evan's police detective friend while Monsieur Evan was in Copenhagen.

Pierre reached up to the frosty piping of the jungle gym. Where was Avoine? He shivered. He did not want to see this man anymore, but if he did not meet with him, he feared what might happen. Monsieur Evan had understood not to speak when he had showed him the tiny lump behind his ear. Pierre felt confident that Avoine did not know he had betrayed him.

Monsieur Evan's face had paled when Pierre had drawn the portrait of Avoine. Monsieur Evan recognized Avoine. Well, they were both American. But as far as Americans went, Pierre preferred Monsieur Evan. He climbed higher on the jungle gym for a better view of the park and all the approaches to the children's playground.

Der Tierartz. At the top of the jungle gym, Pierre hooked his feet around the piping to steady himself. He took out the photograph Monsieur Evan had given him of Madame Kirsch and Sasha. A beautiful photo. Madame sat on the grass in her backyard, the summer sun shining on her feathery short blond hair, her head tilted back slightly. She laughed, her mouth the way he often had seen it: open, but *smiling* open not laughing open, her straight white teeth inviting him to smile too. Behind her in the photo, her flower garden provided a colorful backdrop with the gazebo and swing behind the flowers. His black gloved index finger traced her form in the photo, including Sasha sitting next to her, the golden retriever appearing also to smile.

Pierre! Press the alarm! Press the alarm! Madame screamed in French in his memory, but he heard it as if Madame was only a few feet away, as she had been that night. *Run, Pierre! Get out!* He closed his eyes and concentrated until the memory of her shouting voice changed to her regular speaking voice, asking him what he wanted for breakfast, her voice as she read to him a bedtime story.

Dr. Moreau had told him that he would hear Madame's screams for a long time and it was OK, it was nothing to fear. They had talked about why she had screamed at him. She had wanted him to escape so he would not be hurt. They had talked about his fear, about not knowing what was happening at the time. Dr. Moreau had taught him how to overwrite the memory of Madame's scary screams in his mind to her regular voice, to concentrate, to imagine Madame in the kitchen, and then the other memories would come. The good memories with her and Monsieur Evan.

Der Tierartz. He hoped Madame would have liked the service they had held for Sasha. He had heard Monsieur Evan speaking with Herr Doktor Schneeberger on the phone about it, asking the doctor if they could "view the body." Monsieur Evan had asked him to prepare something to read for Sasha, and he had written a short poem in French for her, a poem about running with her on the street toward the park, her soft fur, her warm tongue kissing his hand, her adoring brown eyes. They had had to wait in the doctor's waiting room that smelled of wet fur and had been empty except for the receptionist. Pierre did not know how Sasha had been treated by the police or how the doctor had received her from them. He had wanted to bury Sasha in Madame's backyard, but Monsieur Evan had said the ground was still frozen.

Where was Avoine? Pierre squinted in the sunshine. Two women with strollers walked over by the chess tables, but otherwise the park was a deserted expanse of white snow. Avoine should have come by now. Would he not come to the meeting today? But Avoine could not know that Pierre had betrayed him, and anyway, if he had known, Avoine would want to come to the meeting to yell at Pierre and hurt him in punishment for the betrayal. Avoine's absence only confirmed he did not know.

As the two women approached the playground, Pierre

called out to them in German, "Excuse me, please. What time is it?"

"Almost eight o'clock," said the tall one with the red hat.

Pierre had been in the park half an hour. Avoine was not coming. He felt relief but also a terrible black dread. Perhaps it could not be a good thing for Monsieur Evan that Avoine had not come to this meeting that he had insisted on the last time they had met. It could not be a good thing that Avoine had wanted to know everything about Monsieur Evan before. He tucked the photo back into his jacket pocket and climbed down from the jungle gym. He headed for the park's south entrance, which was closer to Sternwartestrasse and Madame's house. Monsieur Evan would be out of the shower by now and looking for him.

Sasha had appeared to be sleeping. She lay on a stain-less-steel examination table, her golden fur silky and shiny and smelling of soap. He knew she wasn't sleeping because when he stroked her head, she had not woken up. She wasn't breathing. Monsieur Evan told him that the Tierartz would cremate her just as Madame would be cremated. Sasha and Madame would be together in Heaven. Pierre read his poem to Sasha, glad that Monsieur held his shoulders. He had also been glad that he had not cried in front of der Tierartz.

The following day, the animal doctor had given them Sasha's ashes. Monsieur Evan promised to bury her in Madame's backyard in the spring, after the ground had thawed. Monsieur Evan had let him keep Sasha's urn by him when he slept in Monsieur's bed. But where did Monsieur sleep? Perhaps he had not slept at all since that night. Perhaps he had watched the American movies that he loved on the television all night, although Pierre had heard nothing. The only time they had not been together was the afternoon Monsieur had left him at the embassy. But Monsieur had brought him a Linzertorte when he returned to pick him up. This afternoon, Monsieur would fly to Copenhagen. Pierre did not want to think of Monsieur leaving.

I will return to Vienna while you are in Copenhagen. Evan, I am thinking of you.

Evan read the last line of Sofia's email again. She had written to him twice a day after the news hit the international media about the attack and Freda's death. He had wanted to hear her voice, but he hadn't thought it a good idea to call her. She had not called him.

He tapped the Reply button and glanced past his piano and out his living room windows. Pierre had not been in the apartment when he'd finished his shower. The boy had not left him a note, either. He had gone over to Freda's house, but the boy didn't know the security code to gain entrance so he hadn't expected to find him there. He'd gone to Freda's because action had been required. Now, he was trying not to worry. Pierre had always shown up again, safe and sound, in the past. He glanced at his watch: 8:15 a.m. Where was he?

Returning to the email, he finished the note to Sofia, *I am thinking of you, too. I'm looking forward to seeing you when I get back.* Was it too formal? What he wanted to say was how much he missed her, that the missing was like an ache in his chest and skull and he couldn't wait to see her. He wished she would be in Copenhagen, but then he thought of Harold. No, better that Harold not know about Sofia Karalis and that Sofia remained distant from him until he and Alicia had found Harold and taken care of him. He clicked Send, closed out the program, and slid the keyboard back into the wall under the monitor. The rest of the inbox could wait until he returned.

The security system computer announced, "One male visitor."

On the security panel's monitor, Pierre hopped from one foot to the other at his exterior door. Evan pressed the access button and seconds later heard Pierre's footsteps on his stairs. *Be cool,* he warned himself. *Pierre has been through a lot the last few days on top of what he's been through the last six months.* Evan's protectiveness stirred Perceval. The image of Harold on the street, that smirk, those same icy eyes—Harold would pay for what he'd done. Pierre opened the door.

"Pierre—"

"I forgot to write to you a note, Monsieur. I am sorry. I went to Türkenschanz Park."

He watched the boy take off his black wool jacket and return to the foyer closet to hang it up. His parents had taught him well. "You and Freda and Sasha used to walk up to the park." He was afraid to make it a question. A statement of fact, said in an even voice, seemed less uncertain, less challenging, less painful somehow.

Pierre's blue eyes regarded him with a steady gaze. "You told me Madame's memorial service will be in a month. I will be in France. So"—his thin shoulders shrugged in the sky-blue sweater Freda had bought for him—"I make my own memorial service in the park."

Evan nodded. "Are you hungry?"

The grin lit up Pierre's face. "I can help you, yes?"

He felt that sharp momentary pain in his chest again that the boy provoked at times. "Sure. You know more about cooking now than I ever did as a kid."

But today, Pierre wanted only a hard-boiled egg with cheese, slices of cold ham, and toast for breakfast. Evan made himself a cheese omelet, finishing off the eggs in the fridge. They'd run out of orange marmalade but still had some honey, and they ate the last of the bread. There was no sugar for his coffee, so he poured a little milk into it. Evan told himself the food situation was OK; he'd not be home for a week, and Pierre would be eating at Inspector Leiner's house.

"You are ready for Copenhagen?" Pierre said, stacking a slice of egg on top of cheese and ham on a triangle of toast. "No more calls from Monsieur Fox or Monsieur Dam? Tell me again about this police inspector."

Evan smiled. He'd already told Pierre three times about Leiner and his family. "I still have a little packing to do, which I'll do after I take you over to the Leiners'. No more calls from Nigel or Neils, at least not until tomorrow in Copenhagen, where I expect I'll see Neils first thing. I've known Inspector Leiner since my defection. I haven't met his family, but I know he has a wife named Eva and two daughters, Laura and Anna, both older than you."

Right on cue, Pierre screwed up his face as if he'd eaten something sour. "Girls," he said.

"I think Inspector Leiner will be happy to have another guy in the house."

Pierre's head tilted to the right as he considered this. He

took a bite of his honey toast. "You meet them today also for the first time?"

"Oui," Evan said.

"And you are nervous, yes?"

"Yeah. It's OK. They're good people, Pierre. Be sure to ask permission to use their computer to send emails to your aunt and uncle."

"And you? I can send emails to you in Copenhagen?"

"I'll call, Pierre. I'd rather hear your voice. Then I can really tell what's going on."

Pierre gave him a sly, sidelong smile.

After breakfast and Evan's physical therapy exercises for his right shoulder, they trudged over to Freda's house, entering by the back door, and leaving their boots and jackets in the back foyer off the kitchen. Pierre had not been in the house since the night of the attack. Evan watched him. Pierre sniffed at the strong disinfectant smell that permeated the house. The police's clean-up crew had done a superb job upstairs, and had also cleaned up the kitchen. The disinfectant had a sharp chemical smell, not hidden by citrus or floral. Evan thought the house would need a good airing out once the weather warmed enough.

He followed Pierre up the stairs, and down the hall to his bedroom, where he stopped outside the door. Pierre stared at the floor near Freda's door. The clean-up crew had removed the hall carpet and scrubbed the wood floor.

"I need to get a suitcase out of Freda's room. You want to come with me or start collecting your things?"

Pierre's eyes darted up to his. "I will come with you."

Evan knew Freda's bedroom door had been processed for

fingerprints and was now clean. He knew the police had put the nightstand lamp upright again, and returned everything to its place on the stand after they'd processed it for evidence. Pierre went over to her double bed, where the blue comforter and pastel-yellow sheets were still twisted. Her slippers had been kicked away. Her robe lay at the foot of the bed.

"He must have surprised her, yes?" Pierre nodded to himself. He picked up the square black security alarm activator from the stand next to her bed. "She did not have time to press the alarm."

"She did, Pierre. The alarm went off twice in my apartment, minutes apart."

The boy looked surprised. Evan wouldn't tell him that she had still clutched the alarm activator in her hand when the coroner's team had lifted her onto the gurney that night. They had to pry it out of her fingers. He went over to Freda's walk-in closet, not looking around at the photographs on the walls, the full bookcase, the armoire in the corner, the door to her dressing room. He thought she'd said she stored a large suitcase in the closet, one she rarely used anymore. Her clothes hung neatly. Shoes lined up in rows on the floor beneath them. Evan found the old brown leather suitcase on the upper shelf.

"It is so big," Pierre said with approval. He stood now with his small hands on his hips.

His stance reminded Evan of himself. Was the boy imitating him? Evan smiled. "You have a lot more stuff now than you did when you first arrived, am I right?"

"You are right." Pierre looked at Freda's bed, his lower lip quivering.

"When I get back from Copenhagen, Pierre, I'll take care of the house, fix up this room. I just don't have the time now."

"It is better to leave it this way, the way she left it, yes?" Pierre pivoted and left the room.

Evan studied Freda's bed. He set down the suitcase and went over to it. With a quick glance at the door to make sure Pierre was not there to see him, Evan bent and buried his face in the pillow, breathing in Freda's scent of light lavender. Vasia's voice came out of his memory pure and clear: "You kill someone and you kill your soul, your music." He stood up abruptly. Perceval inside him disagreed, as he had disagreed when Vasia had said it to him last August. There are times when killing can be necessary, that's what Perceval believed, when killing meant power preserved. But Evan wasn't sure he agreed anymore. He'd now experienced both sides: the hunter Perceval and the hunted Evan. He'd experienced the consequences of the killing, also. He missed Vasia beyond words. Bernie Brown. And now Freda. When Perceval found Harold, that would be no loss.

"Monsieur?"

"Sorry, Pierre." Evan picked up the suitcase and followed Pierre to his bedroom.

While the boy gathered his books, DVDs, toys, and clothing and stacked them in the suitcase open on the floor, Evan made the bed and tidied up the room. He thought of something.

"Pierre, I need to go downstairs to check the furnace and turn down the heat, OK? I'll be back in a few minutes."

He needed to conserve the heating oil. Freda had warned

him about that earlier in the week. As he adjusted the settings for the furnace, he tried to think if there was anything else Freda had told him about the house that he needed to take care of before he left. It was only days ago that they'd talked about it. Only days ago she had been alive. He couldn't think of anything else and decided he'd be back for an hour or two before leaving for the airport if he did think of something, so he headed upstairs. Herr Bothmann would also check on the house while he was gone.

Pierre sat on the closed suitcase in the front foyer. "I am sad to leave this house, Monsieur."

"I know."

"Thank you for helping me. I know my papa and maman will also thank you when we find each other again. I know they will want to meet you and talk with you. They will be glad you and Madame took care of me."

Evan stared at Pierre. He sounded so old. The boy accepted Freda's death, Sasha's death, but still could not accept his parents' deaths. He made a mental note to call Paul Cassel the next day from Copenhagen and get a phone number for Pierre's aunt and uncle. He wanted to talk with them without Pierre around, before they came to get him. He wanted to make sure they had a meeting with Dr. Moreau, and that they understood Pierre would need counseling back in France also.

"You're welcome, Pierre. Let's go. Inspector Leiner will be wondering where we are."

The walk to Chimanistrasse took them past the east side of Türkenschanz Park, where they veered right onto Hans-Richter-Gasse. Evan carried the suitcase while Pierre carried a small black satchel full of what he called his essentials. Evan thought of Pierre watching him pack his white tie and tails and other work essentials in his garment bag the night before to carry on the plane. Pierre was imitating him again. Evan smiled, feeling happy and protective at the same time. His relationship with Pierre would probably be as close as he ever came to fatherhood, and he was enjoying it.

As they approached the Leiners' house, walking up the sidewalk flanked by foot-deep snow, Evan remembered the first time he'd seen it the previous summer while on a morning run. Three stories high, the house was painted forest green with ivory trim. Its recessed dark blue front door faced sideways, toward the garage and driveway, and a snow-covered peaked roof protected it. The doorbell chimed. Evan heard dogs barking. The big shaggy dog and the Springer Spaniel he'd seen in the past must be in the backyard.

Leiner opened the door. "Herr Quinn, good morning. Herr Levade, how are you this morning?"

Inside the foyer, they shed their coats and left their boots with other pairs on a thick plastic sheet near the door. The aroma of roasting beef filled the house. Leiner led them into a comfortable, lived-in front room, magazines and newspapers strewn on the sienna-brown couch and walnut coffee table. Pierre grasped Evan's left hand. Evan realized he had not warned Pierre about what he would tell Leiner about him, about his implants, about Harold.

"My wife, Eva," Leiner said, extending his hand to the willowy auburn-haired woman Evan remembered was a runner, as he was. This morning, she wore black wool pants and a blue cardigan over a white blouse. Her smile deepened the laugh lines around her blue eyes.

Evan shook her hand. "Pleased to meet you, Eva. This is Pierre Levade, from Paris."

"Madame," Pierre said, shaking her hand like a proper gentleman.

Eva spoke to him in French, and he grinned. She said to Evan, "Klaus has spoken often of you, Herr Quinn, and I'm happy to finally meet you. And now Pierre, we will have a true Frenchman to tell us if our cassoulet is correct." Her alto voice reminded Evan of Sofia's voice, a viola voice.

Evan chuckled. "He loves to eat."

"Monsieur!" Pierre scowled at him, but his blue eyes were laughing.

The two girls came in from an adjoining room, both dressed in black wool pants and Scandinavian pullover sweaters. The younger poked the older in the side. He remembered that the older, Laura, played the cello. She also resembled her mother. The younger, blond Anna, resembled Leiner, and, Evan remembered, was the fun-loving boy-crazy one, her gregarious, impulsive energy the opposite of her father's thoughtfulness.

"Our daughters, Anna and Laura." Eva pulled Anna forward.

Laura got to Evan first, extending her hand. "I am so honored to meet you, Maestro. I hope someday to play my cello for you."

"I'm happy to meet you, Laura. Your father has told me how much you love Bach. You're giving a recital soon, aren't you?"

She blushed and her sister behind her giggled. "Yes, in May. My first."

"Pierre loves music, too. He plays the piano. He's supposed to practice every day—"

"Monsieur!"

"—and also practice his English. Could I ask you and your sister to help him with those things?"

Pierre squirmed next to him and squeezed his hand hard. The two girls smiled and nodded, looking down at Pierre as if he were a cute baby.

"Inspector, Pierre and I would like a word in private with you before I leave," Evan said.

"You're not staying for lunch, Herr Quinn?" Eva said, disappointment in her lovely voice.

"Sorry, Eva, no. Another time? I still have some things to do before I head out to the airport." He looked down at Pierre, who regarded him as if he'd just said the worst thing possible. The boy might not like what was coming. "Pierre and I need to speak with the inspector on business, actually."

Leiner nodded. Instead of his usual uniform, a regular suit and tie, this morning, the inspector—like Pierre—wore jeans and a light blue sweater.

"My office, Herr Quinn."

They left the women in the front room and followed Leiner downstairs to a large office in the basement. Pierre looked all around the cluttered room, fidgeting with his hands. Evan regretted again not warning him. Leiner sat down at the desk, turning on the computer to the left. Evan thought this office was a clone of Leiner's real office but without a phone. Two tall beige file cabinets and a bookcase stood against one wall.

"Is this about the investigation, Herr Quinn?"

"Yes." Evan pulled from the inner pocket of his sport jacket the notes and drawings that Pierre had made for him the morning after the attack. "I think you'll find these interesting, Inspector. Pierre and I wrote these notes to each other the morning after Freda's death." He handed the notes over, but kept Harold's portrait.

Leiner read the notes. Pierre looked at Evan, shaking his head. The boy's fidgeting was more than nerves. He was frightened.

"Who was listening? What American, Pierre? And how?"

Evan nodded to Pierre. "Please show him what you showed me."

Pierre hesitated.

Evan softened his tone. "I want them to know that the Austrian police know about them. Then we can have the chips removed."

"What chips?" Leiner frowned, his eyes a darker shade of gray.

Pierre grabbed Leiner's hand and brought it up to the chip embedded behind his left ear.

"Mein Gott." Leiner exhaled. He pulled Pierre to him and peered at the tiny bump in the boy's skin. "You said 'chips.' There is more than one?"

"He's got a GPS tracking chip embedded under the skin of his left thigh." Evan reached out and stroked Pierre's hair. The boy looked up at him, his eyes still frightened. "It's OK,

Pierre. You'll be safe here. And once the chips are removed, you'll be free of them."

"I do not care about me, Monsieur Evan. I do not know what he will do. Perhaps he will hurt you."

"Who, Pierre?"

Evan handed Leiner the portrait Pierre had drawn. "He's American. His name is Harold Smith. I knew him when I was a kid."

"American." Leiner was shaking his head. "The Americans said they would leave you alone, nicht? I remember distinctly Herr Morgan from the embassy saying that they would not send anyone after you during your meeting with him and Herr Brown after your defection. They lied?"

"They lied." Evan sighed. "Bernie told me that Morgan had ordered him to kill me. The NEP wanted the money I inherited."

"Ah," Leiner sat back in his chair, smiling at Pierre. "Of course. It is always about money with the Americans. Herr Morgan and Herr Brown mentioned your father's and Joseph Caine's trust funds in London. I remember they were quite interested in them. Is this Harold Smith CIA? Is this connected also to Bernard Brown's defection?"

"You mean, did Morgan send him because Bernie Brown didn't kill me and defected instead? Maybe. Someone killed Bernie in Glasgow. I saw it on the BBC News last weekend. I think the CIA did it. But I don't know about Harold. Morgan's a possibility."

Pierre's blue eyes had deepened in color and widened as he stared at Evan. He couldn't imagine what the boy thought of him. He hoped that Pierre would still want to imitate him.

"Ja, I saw on the news about Herr Brown's death in Glasgow." Leiner smoothed his mustache. "Pierre, you know Harold Smith?" Leiner tapped the portrait.

Pierre nodded. Evan smoothed the boy's hair. He didn't know what else he could do to reassure him.

"You know where he is now? Is he in Vienna?"

"I do not know, Monsieur Inspector."

"You can call me Monsieur Klaus, if you like, Pierre. You and I will talk about your experience with this American. Is he like Herr Quinn?"

Pierre shook his head vigorously, no.

"I think he hurt Pierre, Inspector. Pierre's already talking to a counselor at the French embassy, Dr. Moreau. He has two more appointments with her next week. And his aunt and uncle will be arriving from France, but we don't yet know when."

"Good. We will talk, too, Pierre. If he hurt you, perhaps we can issue a warrant for his arrest, nicht?"

Pierre's shoulders relaxed. He looked up at Evan and smiled. "I want him never to hurt anyone again."

"He's listening right now?" Leiner said, looking from Pierre to Evan.

"Don't know for certain, Inspector. But I think it's important to have the chips removed. They're benign. If he is listening, I want Harold to know the Austrian police are on his case and he'd better leave Pierre alone. I have the name of a doctor that Herr Aschenbeck sent me to last summer. Dr. Maas. He removed the tracking chip I had behind my ear that the ISS had put there."

Pierre started, his eyes wide in surprise. "Why? What is 'ISS'?"

"ISS is the Internal Security Service in America. They put tracking chips behind everyone's ear who's not a member of the NEP elite as a way to control people. I'd had that chip since I was twelve, I think."

The expression on Leiner's face reminded Evan of someone who's finally solved a puzzle. Leiner said, "You have extra security for your travel today and while you are in Copenhagen, Herr Quinn?"

"Yeah. I set it up several weeks ago. What are you thinking, Inspector?"

"I am thinking that you were most definitely Gregori's target the other night. He had come to Vienna to finish the job begun in Buenos Aires. Perhaps Gregori was the assassin in Buenos Aires and this mysterious murdered Chilean woman witnessed it, so he killed her."

"And Gregori was working for Harold Smith. But who does Harold work for?" His eyes met Leiner's steady gray eyes. He knew Pierre would be safe with the Austrian cop. Leiner was on the case now, one hundred percent.

"I will call Copenhagen, Herr Quinn, and brief them. May I keep the notes and drawings?"

"Thanks. Keep them. I think Pierre has given us the best leads we've had."

He expected to see happiness or relief or gratitude in Pierre's expression but saw only concern and fear. When he found Harold Smith, he would make certain that he suffered.

In the front foyer a few minutes later, Evan finished buttoning his cobalt-blue wool coat under Pierre's watchful eyes.

Leiner stood behind the boy. He heard dishes clack in the kitchen, a door close upstairs.

"You will call me every day, Monsieur?" Pierre said. "I want to hear your voice so I will know what is truly going on."

Evan laughed. "OK, OK, Monsieur Pierre. You can expect to hear from me late afternoon or early evening. I think earlier in the day will be pretty busy, OK? Rehearsals, interviews, I don't know what else Neils has set up for me and for the concerts."

Pierre nodded as he stepped forward and threw his arms around Evan's waist. Evan stooped and picked him up. Pierre clung to him. Evan was surprised that he also did not want to let the boy go. But he had to leave.

"Check on the internet, Pierre. Maybe my concerts will be there and you and the Leiners can listen. See you in a week."

He nodded to Leiner and hurried out the door, afraid that the sharp pain he felt in his chest would make him do something ridiculous. He half-jogged, half-walked the eight short blocks straight down Cottagegasse and then up Stern-wartestrasse to his apartment. At the driveway gate, he paused and glanced around before stooping to press his middle right finger on the cold security panel pad and said into the monitor: "Der schattige Affe." As the gate opened, he glanced around again. The street was deserted, cars parked in front of the houses but no one outside. They had not had an air raid for days, and he hoped the Chinese continued to leave them alone. He realized that he hadn't listened to any news in days, either.

Inside his apartment, he cleaned up the kitchen and finished packing. After calling a cab, he called Alicia on his clean cell phone.

"How are you, Evan?" her familiar soprano said in his ear.

"Fine. Ready to travel. Are you at the airport?"

"Yes. As we discussed the other day. So far, it is quiet. I have seen no one who might be waiting for you. Remember our plan?"

She continued to test him on what she had taught, as she had been since Buenos Aires. "Surveillance detection by several cabs to Schwechat airport. Will security be waiting for me when I arrive?"

"Yes."

"See you later."

He heard the car horn honking out on the street. After a quick last-minute check of the apartment and setting his security system, he went out to the cab waiting by the curb. The driver had thick dark hair that tufted out around the edges of his knitted cap. He told Evan he'd emigrated, too, but from Iran five years earlier. Evan instructed him to drive him to the Ninth District and Fürstengasse on the south side of the Palais Liechtenstein's grounds. Robert Waldstein, the Vienna Philharmonic Orchestra's concertmaster, lived nearby, but Evan wouldn't be visiting his friend today.

He walked a block on Liechtensteinstrasse, past stately five-story gray or white nineteenth-century apartment buildings, to a taxi stand where he hired another cab to take him to Wien Mitte. Evan hired yet another cab there to take him to the airport. He had spotted no shadows. The drive out to the airport took about twenty-five minutes, and he arrived ninety minutes before his flight to Copenhagen was scheduled to depart.

Alicia had told him to act as he normally would as a conductor traveling to a gig. He checked one bag and kept his garment bag slung over his shoulder as he headed for security. Alert for any potential attackers, he spotted Alicia waiting near the security checkpoint, with its two conveyor belts and X-ray machines, and X-ray walk-through. She wore jeans and a maroon sweater under her open loden green coat. Their eyes met briefly. Alicia picked up her carry-on and joined the security line ahead of him. He saw no security guards, but trusted that Alicia had worked out a plan with airport security.

What was he expecting? Evan observed the security personnel processing passengers. He saw no one suspicious, no one who took a special interest in him. When it was his turn, the security officer addressed him in German. "Maestro, wohin fahren Sie heute?"

He said in German, "To Copenhagen."

"Gute Fahrt, Maestro."

Sometimes, fame gave him an advantage. He breezed through the security check. On the other side, Alicia walked slowly to the departure gate in front of him. He spotted a uniformed security guard up the corridor on the left. He didn't glance behind him, but he'd bet another security guard followed him.

Arriving passengers walked toward him. An approaching woman smiled at him. Her shoulder-length wavy chestnut-brown hair and long stride reminded him of Sofia. She passed him. He relaxed. They'd made it through the first vulnerable part of the trip.

He wondered who Harold would send after him next. Another American? Or a Russian? *Think like Perceval. What would Perceval do in Harold's place?* The answer came immediately to mind: He would wait. He would let his target relax, and then he would make his move. He felt certain that Harold's next move would be in Copenhagen.

CHAPTER 19

Copenhagen reminded Evan of Amsterdam, another harbor city on islands with a river and canals. Water shimmered in the early morning sunlight outside the car window. The architecture reminded him also of Amsterdam, especially the row houses facing the harbor and canals. From what he'd seen from the car, the Danes favored bright colors for their older buildings, the newer buildings fluid forms in glass and rounded shapes, but their churches and palaces struck Evan as having a Nordic restraint, even the Baroque ones. Because of security concerns, he'd not been able to walk the streets on his own to experience the atmosphere and personality of the city, explore the parks, and smell the air as he usually did when he was guest conducting in a city new to him. He was experiencing Copenhagen through windows.

In the back seat next to him was one bodyguard, Bertel, a hard-muscled man with dark brown hair and blue eyes in a diamond-shaped face who smiled rarely and spoke even less. The second bodyguard, Hans, sat in the front passenger seat, a pillow of a man with blond hair who preferred to wear suits. He was usually the talkative one but this morning exhibited the lethargy and bleary eyes of either lack of sleep or a hangover. The driver, a silent Palestinian named Ahmed, possessed the tense demeanor and shifting eyes of someone expecting trouble around the next corner. Evan didn't know and hadn't asked if Ahmed was part of the security detail assigned to him or a regular driver for the Danish National Symphony. The three of them had met him at the airport on Sunday and had been glued to him ever since. Their presence brought back unpleasant pre-defection memories of his European tour the previous year, when his Arts Council escorts, Dave and Richard, had been in charge of his security; not to keep him safe so much as to ensure he behaved himself to protect the American Arts Council and the New Economic Party.

His other bodyguard, Alicia, stayed in the hotel room adjoining his. He'd introduced her to Bertel and Hans at the airport as his cousin from Madrid and told them he and Alicia had arranged to meet in Copenhagen. She wanted to see him conduct and spend time exploring the city, something that he could not do with the freedom that he preferred. Alicia, of course, was doing far more than explore, but the cover story had worked. She was now the only person not connected to the Danish National Symphony who could come and go in his room and daily life as she pleased. This morning, she had a meeting with a "source" who might be able to help them track down Harold Smith.

His Danish security detail had given him space and privacy only in his hotel room (Bertel and Hans stayed in the room across the hall, while Ahmed went home) and at the concert hall in the Danish Radio complex, called DR Byen, on Amager Island. He understood the Danes' concern and preoccupation with his safety. It wasn't that they'd treated him ill as a result, or that he didn't feel safe, but he felt he'd suffocate.

At his first rehearsal the day before with the Danish National Symphony, they'd worked on the Essay for Orchestra, Op. 12, by Samuel Barber and most of Béla Bartók's Concerto for Orchestra. This morning, they'd work through Barber's Piano Concerto. He'd meet with the pianist, Lars Sven Larson, for an hour before the rehearsal.

Ahmed turned the car into the DR Byen complex and dropped them at the concert hall, a startling midnight-blue box of a building that housed the large auditorium where the Danish National Symphony Orchestra rehearsed and performed, and three smaller concert venues for chamber music, jazz, and vocal music. Inside, Neils Dam waited by the entrance's security station. Evan turned to Bertel and Hans.

"Page us, Evan, when you've finished," Hans said in his pillowy baritone. The two bodyguards left. Evan had no idea where they went while he worked.

"He's waiting for you in one of the warm-up rooms, Evan," Neils said in his tuba-like voice. The Dane gestured toward the hallway.

As they walked, Evan eyed Neils, who stood a good foot shorter than him. He looked more like a passionate adolescent music student than a man in his forties with degrees in political science and law who now worked as the executive artistic assistant for conductors at the Danish National Symphony. His tousled platinum-blond hair contrasted with his dark sea-green eyes. Neils favored tweed, which enhanced his serious demeanor with a scholarly tone. Evan had enjoyed talking with him about American politics. He also admired the man's keen perception of people and his sense of when to talk and when to remain silent.

"What's the plan for the day, Neils?"

"Double rehearsal, of course. Barber Piano Concerto this morning, the Bartók this afternoon. You are having a lunch interview with the music reporter from *Politiken*, one of our newspapers. Her name is Brigitte Arnesen. She is quite knowledgeable, Evan, and wanted me to advise you that she is especially interested in your link with Joseph Caine."

Evan nodded. "Brigitte Arnesen. We're eating close by? Did you warn her about Bertel and Hans?"

Neils smiled, a rueful upturn of his small mouth. "The restaurant in the complex here. I have also made arrangements for Bertel and Hans. Anyone who has contact with you this week outside of the symphony has been vetted by Bertel and Hans."

"The restaurant serves good seafood? Anything after the rehearsal this afternoon?" He needed to call Pierre and then put in some uninterrupted, concentrated score study on Shostakovich's Overture on Russian and Kirghiz Folk Themes for Iceland and Owen's First Symphony, which he'd conduct in Zürich.

"Excellent seafood. I recommend the swordfish. You have free time after the rehearsal this afternoon. I have two phone messages for you." Neils handed him a single sheet of paper on which he'd typed the messages. One was from Pierre's Aunt Dominique Ulliel; he'd called her yesterday but she hadn't been home, so he'd left a voice mail message with Neils' phone number. He needed to call her as soon as possible. The other was from Klaus Leiner. Odd that Leiner hadn't called his cell phone.

"Did Inspector Leiner say what he wanted?"

"No, Evan. Sorry."

Evan pulled out his black cell phone and dialed Dominique's phone number in France. He stopped by the door to the practice room, where he could hear the muffled sound of the piano, the angular lines of the Barber concerto. Neils waited a respectful distance away, looking out the window on the other side of the hallway. Pierre's aunt answered on the second ring.

"Dominique? It's Evan Quinn. How are you and Julien?"

"Monsieur Quinn. I am very happy to speak with you. We are fine. Thank you so much for taking care of Pierre." A honey soprano voice, smooth and full.

"A pleasure. He's a wonderful kid. Listen, I just wanted to make certain that you spoke with Dr. Moreau at the French embassy before you arrived in Vienna. She's been counseling Pierre. He's not yet come to terms with his parents' deaths."

"I know. Monsieur Cassel has warned us of this, but he did not mention Dr. Moreau. Thank you. When will you return to Vienna?"

"On Sunday. Have you finalized your travel arrangements?"

"Oui. We arrive in Vienna Saturday afternoon. We have already spoken with Inspector Leiner, also. I am feeling so much better now. I was so worried about Pierre. We left Paris last September, and he didn't know where we were, but now he is also writing to us. You know, Monsieur, we had believed that he had died with my sister and her husband. When Monsieur Cassel phoned us, I cannot tell you our joy."

"I look forward to meeting you and Julien on Sunday, Dominique. I'm certain Monsieur Cassel can put you in contact with Dr. Moreau. Safe trip to Vienna."

She sounded nice, excited, young. He had somehow gotten it into his head that all the adults in Pierre's family were elderly, that his parents, Georges and Juliette, had been older. Odd the way the mind conjures images from names to support assumptions. He'd not seen photos of any of them. He nodded to Neils.

"I'm set, Neils. This won't take the full hour, I think."

Neils nodded and headed back down the hallway.

Evan knocked on the practice room door and went in. His workday had begun.

Lars Sven Larson shot to his feet from the black grand piano in the middle of the small and spare room. His curly blond shoulder-length hair and immense blue eyes reminded Evan of Vasia. He even dressed like Vasia in an Oxford cotton blue-and-yellow plaid shirt and jeans. His stomach fluttered.

"Maestro Quinn."

Evan shook his hand. "Thanks for jumping in at the last minute, Lars. I'm happy to meet such a courageous pianist."

Lars laughed, and his shoulders relaxed. "A terrible thing, what happened to Helene in Berlin." He shook his head. "This war. It could have been any of us. Have you heard how she is recuperating from the surgery?" His tenor voice reminded Evan of a warm, fleece blanket, and his Swedish accent gave it a slight lilt.

"I called Helene last week. She sounded upbeat and furious at the Chinese for bombing Berlin. She was to have another surgery yesterday. She sounded like a fighter, though."

"She is a determined and very much in-your-face personality. Perfect to play the Barber." Lars chuckled. "Do you have her phone number?"

"Neils has it. Let's get to work."

For the next half an hour, they discussed each movement of the Barber Piano Concerto, Lars's preferred tempos which he demonstrated on the piano, entrances, difficult spots, and the orchestral accompaniment. Evan's impression of the pianist's thinking about the concerto happily agreed with his own. They also chatted amiably for a few minutes after the work, and Evan learned that Lars had been born and grew up in Stockholm, was an avid outdoorsman, and loved American classical music, especially Barber and Caine. He knew and had performed Caine's Piano Concerto. By the time they finished, they had only fifteen minutes before the orchestra rehearsal began.

Evan rushed out, nearly colliding with Neils, who handed him another sheet of paper—his revised schedule for the day, and two more messages, one from Ólafur Alvarson at the Iceland Philharmonic and the other from Leonard Patton at the Scottish BBC Symphony, both regarding the soloists for each program. That didn't sound like good news. He was also waiting to hear, via Nigel, from his two contacts at the Lucerne Symphony and the Tonhalle Orchestra Zürich about security arrangements for his gigs with them in less than a month. He would call Ólafur and Leonard at the rehearsal break and also Nigel. Evan pulled out his regular cell phone and dialed Leiner's phone number as he walked briskly with Neils. Leiner's voice mail answered. Evan left a message, including his number and the best time to call.

To his surprise, Nigel Fox waited for him inside the guest conductor's suite.

"Nigel! I was going to call you at the break. What are you doing here?" Evan shook his British manager's firm, warm hand. "Ólafur in Reykjavik and Leonard in Glasgow have called me here."

"They have my mobile. What did they want?" The lines around Nigel's hawk-like nose deepened into a frown.

"Something about the soloists. Could you find out what's going on?" He handed Nigel the phone messages. "So, is this a social or business visit? I so rarely see you in person anymore." Evan grinned and gave Neils a playful wink.

"I read about the attack in Vienna. Your landlady's death must have been terribly distressing. How are you? How is Pierre?" Nigel's frown softened as he spoke.

"I'm OK. Pierre's staying with Inspector Leiner this week. We both miss Freda. I'm glad to be back to work."

Nigel nodded. "I saw your concerts here as an opportunity to escape London for a few days and the bombing. The Chinese have returned to it, unfortunately. And I wanted to hear Lars Larson." He smiled. "You look far better than you did when I saw you in Buenos Aires."

"Evan, the stage manager will come for you." Neils said before he slipped out.

"He's quite efficient," Nigel said, nodding at the closed door. "How is your security?"

"Superb. You're right about Neils. His only rival, I'd say, would be Juliana Pekelharing in Amsterdam."

"Ah, the lovely Juliana. They've invited you back, by the way."

"When?"

"Next year, in August. We have also discussed another date in November. You haven't been reading your emails, have you?"

Evan shrugged out of his black corduroy sport jacket and hung it up. Today, he wore jeans and a plain long-sleeved black T-shirt. "Guilty. I've had my hands full with other things. You sent me an email with schedule updates, yeah?"

"I did indeed." Nigel sat down in one of the plump chairs. "Amsterdam and Berlin are the only orchestras who seem to be willfully ignoring the difficulties presented by the war. And the Chinese have been bombing Berlin quite a lot." Nigel fixed his piercing green eyes on Evan. "I suppose you also haven't been thinking about where you want to be in five years."

Evan opened his leather briefcase and took out his score and baton. "Five years. I know I want to be alive. Do you think the war will be over by then? I just talked with Pierre's aunt. They're arriving in Vienna on Saturday, but I don't know how long they'll be staying yet."

A knock on the door. The stage manager, a young, skinny guy in jeans and a red T-shirt with black hair pulled back into a ponytail, stepped into the room.

Evan nodded to him. "This is Søren, the brilliant stage manager here who told me yesterday he has a degree in philosophy. Søren, my manager, Nigel Fox."

"The philosophy of wine, women, and music," Søren said, grinning as he shook Nigel's hand. "Good to meet you, sir. Evan, it's time."

"Are you observing rehearsal, Nigel? Come with us."

The musicians of the Danish National Symphony Orchestra had assembled on stage in the concert hall, a meteor-shaped auditorium in subdued earth tones of brown, beige, gold and rose with terraced seats for the audience all around the stage at different levels. Nigel settled in a seat halfway back from the stage. Evan greeted the concertmaster, a Hungarian in his fifties with thick white hair who was taller than him and, as his mother would have said, skinnier than a starving sunfish, in a loose tunic shirt and black jeans. Evan remembered his first name, Istvan, but not his family name. Istvan had a question about the Barber Piano Concerto and the violins' entrance at the beginning. Evan knew there would be more questions as the morning progressed.

Evan stepped up onto the podium and faced the orchestra. It felt great to be back at work. The podium was home. He massaged his right shoulder, then moved his right arm in large circles to relax and stretch the shoulder muscles. He glanced around at the musicians, all in casual clothes, his eyes meeting smiles of greeting, heads bent over music stands, an oboist sliding his reed in and out of his mouth to prime it, the violists talking among themselves. The piano had already been set behind the podium and slightly to Evan's left. Lars entered, his stride brisk and bouncy. He brought his score but dropped it unopened on the floor next to the piano. He shook hands with Istvan and settled on the piano bench.

"Ladies and gentlemen," Evan said, raising his voice to

be heard over the musicians who were still talking. "Ladies and gentlemen, let's get started please. Samuel Barber's Piano Concerto. Let's read through it, please, no stopping."

Evan nodded to Lars. The concerto opened with a piano solo that set the first movement's tone and tempo. The Swedish pianist imbued the opening with a passion and clarity that pleased Evan, the rhythm precise. Three measures before the orchestra entered, Evan picked up the beat with his baton in small movements in front of his chest, then lifted his left hand and broadened his gestures. All eyes were on him. The piano repeated the opening chords, and the strings answered with an exclamation-point chord at the end of the pianist's phrase. This music, a tight fist of angular lines and intervals and industrial rhythms, reminded Evan of New York City, the swagger and spectacle of its streets. He cued the oboe to introduce a lyrical melody picked up by the violins. Barber had been America's neo-romantic composer. Even when the music jumped and danced, skipped and dove through dissonance and abrupt changes in meter or rhythm, Barber gave it a sweet melody at its core, a reflection of the American character as the composer saw it. Barber's dissonance, however, had gotten his music banned by the Arts Council in America. They hadn't understood it at all. As the orchestra played, Evan made mental notes about the hall's acoustics and balancing the sound, problems in the conversation between piano and orchestra, and where the orchestra needed work.

The poignant second movement, the slow canzone, in which Barber seemed to stop time with the stillness between the notes, pulling the listener in and creating a sense of tender intimacy, would require only minor adjustments. This music was more introspective, more introverted, the romantic heart of the concerto. Evan suspected that Joseph Caine had known this music well. He'd heard echoes of it in Caine's First Symphony.

The brass fanfare and cymbal crashes at the beginning of the third movement's unrelenting momentum reminded Evan of riding New York's subway. The quieter passages sparked memories of waiting for a train in a deserted station at night, the gangs of adolescent boys who roamed them, the bums and winos, the eerie mysterious sounds and ethereal celery-green fluorescent light, the pounding rumble of an approaching train. *Lars nailed it*, Evan thought, as he cued the woodwinds and glanced at Lars for the piano's entrance toward the end of the movement. The music built to the spectacular final jarring notes. He cut them off with a flourish of his baton.

"Thank you, Danish National Symphony," Evan said. "Good job! Lars?"

The pianist nodded, grinning.

"The second movement needs only refinement, folks. Beautiful playing there." Evan glanced around at the musicians, some of whom were smiling. "We have some work to do on the first movement." Musicians nodded here and there. "Lars, the tempo in the third movement?" The pianist played his opening for the orchestra. They listened intently, and Evan beat with his baton. "There's a contrast here that we need to make more definite, as far as the tempo in each section of the rondo is concerned," Evan said after Lars finished. "Percussion, please watch me. Let's start with the first movement now, please, page one."

The sound of turning pages filled the air, followed by musicians calling his name to ask their questions. He was surprised at the number of questions about dynamics—had Barber really meant piano here or forte there? As they discussed the composer's intent, he massaged his right shoulder. It wasn't sore and didn't hurt to conduct, but he wanted to keep it as limber as possible. He'd continued his physical therapy exercises, and had brought the last of the hydrocodone with him, though hadn't taken any yet. When he lifted the baton, his shoulder felt normal. He thought fleetingly of Pierre and glanced back at Nigel sitting out in the hall. With all the intense security around him, maybe it would have been OK to bring Pierre with him. The boy would have loved to sit with Nigel out there for the rehearsal.

At the break, Evan remained on the podium to field more questions, before he headed for his empty dressing room. Nigel must have stayed in the concert hall. He splashed cold water on his face in the adjoining bathroom and lay down on the comfortable puce sofa that accommodated his long body. His energy had remained high throughout the day before, and he'd had no problems sleeping last night. But a short rest period now would ensure he'd make it through this day of double rehearsals, his first since before he was shot. He'd ask Søren also for a stool on the podium. He closed his eyes, visualized the orchestra, their sound during the read-through. If only he had an assistant conductor to sit in the auditorium and help him balance the sound. He'd performed that task often in Minneapolis before the music director (Bill something?) had been arrested. Then he'd taken over as co-music director with the second assistant conductor, who'd been terrified of the Arts Council representative in Minneapolis. He couldn't remember the guy's name now, and he realized that he could barely recall the faces of the principal players in the Minneapolis State Symphony Orchestra.

A knock came on the dressing room door. He said, "Coming, Søren." The young Dane used a distinctive knock—two thumps, a second of silence, and one quick rap. Each stage manager he'd met, including Mike in Minneapolis, had possessed unique qualities, but his favorite quality that all possessed had been a no-nonsense approach to their jobs.

He left Søren at the stage door after requesting a stool for the podium. As he walked between the first violin and cello sections, he remembered he'd asked Nigel to call Ólafur and Leonard.

Two gunshots cracked the air. Evan hit the floor on his stomach and covered his head with his arms as the musicians around him gasped and screamed. Chairs tumbled over. Voices shouted in the back of the auditorium, their words indistinguishable. Evan heard another gunshot, this one with the *whoof* of a silencer.

Harold? No, Harold wouldn't choose such a public place with so many witnesses for an attack. Too many people would see him. He'd sent others, however, to try to kill him. Was this another from Harold's gang? Where were Bertel and Hans?

"Evan, it is all right now," Søren said above him.

He opened his eyes, pushed himself to his knees, and looked around. "Is everyone OK? Was anyone hit?" He regained his feet. "Is everyone OK?" An orchestra of fearful eyes met his. "Where's security? What happened?"

Using their chairs, which they'd positioned as shields, musicians pulled themselves off the floor. They began to talk all at once. Søren pointed out into the hall. Evan turned. Nigel walked to the back of the main floor, where two security guards stood speaking into radios attached to their shoulders. Another two guards appeared to be sitting on top of someone.

Evan turned to Søren. "Where's Lars? And what do we do now?"

"We wait for security." He raised his hands to the orchestra, waving for them to stay where they were. "Stay here, everyone. We wait for security."

Evan spotted Lars peeking out the stage door. He was safe. After another quick glance around the stage, the building pressure in his chest like a boulder lowered onto it making it hard to breathe, Evan strode to the stage door and joined a wide-eyed Lars.

He heard over and over the gunshots in his ears, sharp and terrifying. He smelled blood and disinfectant. Spanish voices pushed over the gunshots in his ears. He backed up against the wall backstage and slid down into a squat, his eyes closed.

"Maestro, are you all right?" Lars's soft voice said.

He nodded. "I'm reliving Buenos Aires."

"My God."

He was grateful the Swedish pianist said nothing more as images of the night sky above him on the street, of the hospital emergency room, of faces wearing surgical masks flicked behind his eyes. It had been several weeks since he'd experienced a flashback. This one wasn't as intense. But it came with another memory, the sound of the silencer *whoof* from his CZ, Vasia's terrified blue eyes. The NEP. This was their fault. And Harold. Anger flared in the back of his mind. Harold and his Vigiciv gang had hurt him as a boy, Harold had hurt Pierre, and Harold and his gang of assassins had killed Freda and Sasha and had hurt him again.

"Maestro." Søren's voice.

Evan opened his eyes and looked up at the frowning Dane.

"Mr. Fox and the head of security wish to speak with you now."

Evan got to his feet and followed Søren on stage. Lars stood by the piano. Evan hadn't even noticed that the pianist had left the backstage area. Nigel and a burly uniformed security guard waited by the podium.

"Evan," Nigel said. "The hall is secure. You're safe."

"What was it?" he said, eyeing the security guard who nodded.

"An unfortunate example of the stupidity of certain Islamic terrorists. Only one, Maestro Quinn. Under the influence of a drug—we will determine what drug through tests. He had slipped away from a group touring the radio facilities in the complex. Two of my men chased him, and he shot at them. One of my men shot him in the leg. He will survive. We will increase security during rehearsals when you are present in the complex, Maestro."

Evan let out a long, heavy breath. "I wish you didn't have to increase security for me, but I am glad you will. I wouldn't want anyone else to be hurt because of my presence here. Did this Islamic terrorist specify his target and motive?" He was aware of the listening musicians around them and Lars's grim expression.

"You, Maestro. Because you are American. That is all. And jihad. We have seen this also in the past for many years." The security guard shrugged. "We know what to do. You can return to your work now."

The security guard turned and left the stage, taking side steps down to the main floor of the auditorium. Evan met Nigel's eyes and nodded to his manager who then left by the same route to return to his seat in the hall. Evan patted Søren's shoulder. "Thanks for the stool." Evan nodded at the tall stool on the podium. The stage manager grinned and headed for the stage door.

Evan stepped up onto the podium. He set the stool aside for the moment and faced the orchestra. "Well, at least the guy wasn't upset about the music," he said in a deadpan voice. He heard some titters from the percussion section. "So, let's get back to work." He glanced at the piano. Lars had taken his seat on the bench. The pianist gave him a small smile. "I'm in the mood for the third movement of the Barber concerto. Lars, your tempo, please."

The Swedish pianist played the first page once and then again. Evan raised his baton. The music exploded, and in that moment, it ceased to be a musical portrait of New York City's subway for Evan. It became a running battle between him and an enemy gang intent on overpowering him, killing him. He didn't know why he hadn't seen this in the music before. He stopped the orchestra to work on details—dynamics, articulation—and to answer questions. Lars worked eagerly with them. Evan sensed that the nature of the sound had inspired similar thoughts to his in the musicians' minds, even as they played through the quieter, almost eerie sections of the rondo. Evan heard the enemy sneaking up on them, the piano ambushing the enemy to protect the orchestra. Once he was satisfied that they'd covered all the problems he'd noticed, they played the third movement again straight through, followed by the serenity of the second movement.

The morning rehearsal ended with the subdued final measures of the canzone. Evan cut them off but held his hands in place as if he would give another downbeat. The musicians watched and waited, not moving. Lars waited. Evan felt the power he wielded over them in that moment and knew that the music had cured their fright and distress. He dropped his hands.

"Thank you, folks," he said. He glanced at his watch. One minute remained of the rehearsal. "I don't know about you, but it felt *really* good to play that rondo after being shot at."

Laughter rippled through the people in front of him, and he caught Lars nodding.

"See you all this afternoon for the Bartók. Thank you, Lars." He shook the pianist's hand.

Chairs scraped across the stage as people stood. Lars hovered at the podium.

"Maestro, very productive work, if I may say so. The terrorist never had a chance."

Evan chuckled. "You feel good about the concerto? Satisfied?"

"I feel it solid in my bones. One more rehearsal, I think."

"Tomorrow morning. The orchestra and I are playing the Bartók late afternoon tomorrow for some sort of preview mini-concert. Have you talked to Nigel?" Evan glanced over his shoulder. His manager was still sitting in the hall. "He wanted to hear you play. That's why he's here, you know."

"Really?" The Swede blushed but held Evan's gaze. "Thank you. I'll introduce myself."

The pianist must have a manager already, but Evan knew even so that attention from Nigel Fox could boost a musician's career. He remained on the podium, talked with the principal flutist, the percussionist playing the cymbals, and several brass players before leaving for his dressing room. He couldn't remember if he would be meeting Brigitte Arnesen there or someplace else.

He found Neils in his dressing room watching Alicia pace back and forth and slap a long white envelope against her thigh. She was wearing jeans and a brown turtleneck sweater.

"Neils, where am I meeting the reporter?" Evan said, sinking down on the sofa and smiling at Alicia. She frowned.

"Brigitte Arnesen hasn't arrived yet. She called to say she will be a few minutes late."

"She knows I have a rehearsal this afternoon?"

"Yes. I suggested that you would be at the restaurant already, beginning your lunch."

"Good idea. Alicia?" He started to lift his long body off the sofa.

Alicia said, "I need a minute before you leave."

"I will wait in the hallway." Neils slipped out. Evan thought the guy moved sometimes with the stealth of a cat burglar.

"You don't look happy, cousin," Evan said, his tone teasing. "What's up?"

She handed him the sealed envelope. "Look at the front."

Written on the envelope's front, in large loopy handwriting, was *Maestro Evan Quinn of Minneapolis*. He snorted. He was no longer "of Minneapolis." He opened the envelope. "Alicia, you could have opened it."

"Read it to me," Alicia said.

He shook his head as he read out loud. "Dear Maestro Quinn, I am a friend of Woody Lewis. He told me that you wanted information concerning who has been trying to kill you. I have helped Woody before. I will help you. I have the information you want. Meet me after your concert on Thursday in Christiania, at the corner of Pusher Street and Fabriksområdet. I will carry a copy of your father's novel *The Distance Between Two Points*. Come alone. Bors."

"You will not go alone, Evan." Alicia had begun pacing again. "Who is Woody Lewis?"

Woody. He'd asked Woody to check with his sources to find out who wanted him dead. Apparently, Bors was one of his sources. "Woody Lewis is an old American who owns the Café Chicago in Vienna. I met him not long after I defected last year. He's lived in Europe for years, so I thought he might know people who might be able to tell us who's after me. So, after Buenos Aires I asked Woody if he'd check around."

Alicia nodded her head. "Is he former CIA? Did Bernie know him?"

He settled back on the sofa, staring at the note. "I don't know if he was CIA. I know he taught American Studies at the University of Vienna. Bernie knew him, but I suspect

Woody knows all the Americans in Vienna, whether they work at the embassy or not."

Alicia stopped pacing and faced him. "Interesting that this Bors does not want to meet with you today or tonight. He specifies after your concert on Thursday. I will see about this meeting place today. I am concerned now that it is a trap."

"You heard about the Islamic terrorist at rehearsal? What did your source have to say this morning?"

Alicia sighed, her hands on her hips. "The terrorist was an idiot. Dangerous with a gun, but an idiot. I talked with Bertel. He and Hans will now be with you everywhere, even here in the complex. My source had not heard anything, but he will put his ear to the ground."

Evan stood, picking up his black corduroy sport jacket. His cell phone rang in one of its pockets. "How do we meet with Bors, Alicia, if Bertel and Hans are with us?"

She nodded, her beautiful red lips turned down. Evan answered his cell phone. In his ear, he heard Inspector Leiner's tense voice.

"Herr Quinn, early this morning we picked up electronic surveillance about a specific threat to your life in Copenhagen the evening of Thursday, March twenty-fifth at DR Byen. Do you have a concert that evening?"

CHAPTER 20

Hans stood with his back to the closed dressing room door, a black headset like a monkey's finger curled around his face, an unwelcome guard inside Evan's sanctuary. He'd worn a pressed charcoal-gray wool suit to blend in with the audience at the concert. On the puce sofa, Evan wiped his face again with the white towel Søren had given him as he strode off stage after the Barber Piano Concerto, at the end of the concert's first half. He held a bottle of plain water in the other hand. This evening, Alicia wore a tailored black wool pantsuit with a pastel-blue silk blouse. Her spicy scent filled his nose as she bent forward to adjust his white tie.

"It's fine, Alicia. Please stop fussing." He wanted them all to disappear. He wanted peace and quiet before conducting Béla Bartók's Concerto for Orchestra. The threat against him had upended his usual concert routine and rituals. Too many people clung to him, invaded his musician space. How did they expect him to perform at his best with people pressing in on him and not giving him the quiet he needed? He craved a few minutes of solitude before Søren came for him.

Hans spoke in Danish into the receiver in front of his mouth.

"Søren will be here in a few minutes," Evan said. "I need quiet time to myself. Can you please both wait outside?"

Hans shook his head. Alicia's dark eyes looked up at him. He thought he could read in them a warning as well as understanding. She understood the importance of mental preparation. Conducting an orchestra demanded intense concentration. She had told him after rehearsal yesterday that she loved classical music but rarely had the opportunity to attend concerts, much less observe a rehearsal.

He bent down to whisper in her ear. "What did you tell Bertel about our plans after the concert?"

She turned to Hans. "Hans, has Bertel told you about our plans after the concert? Some musicians are meeting in Nemoland at the corner of Pusher Street and Fabriksområ-det. It is a very popular bar in Christiania."

"I know Nemoland," Hans said in his pillowy baritone.

Evan nodded and excused himself. He slipped into the bathroom, a white-tiled room with a stall shower, sink, toilet, and full-length wall mirror. He stared at his reflection in the mirror: clean-shaven face with long curved jaw, brown eyes, craggy nose, and straight black hair parted on one side and just skimming his collar. His skin looked pale. His white tie and tails hung loose on his body. He'd lost weight during his convalescence. Or was it because of the war? With his strength returning, he could resume his regular routine of daily runs and build up his muscles and stamina. An image of Freda's vegetable garden last summer behind the garage appeared in his mind and then disappeared as if a camera shutter had opened and closed.

He'd brought his new set of work clothes to Copenhagen, the white tie and tails that he'd ordered from a tailor in Vienna last December. Freda had gone with him to the tailor.

He'd wanted Sofia to go, but he'd been afraid to ask her. Sofia's creativity with disguises had helped him and he liked her sense of style in the clothing she wore. He had thought she'd know what looked good on him. But she hadn't been as friendly toward him after Vasia's death. Freda, however, had thought of the vest and picked out the pale sage green satin material embroidered with pastel rose, lilac, and blue swirls for it. He smoothed the front of the vest, the image of Freda picking out the satin so vivid in his mind it could have happened yesterday. What would Freda think? She'd be pleased with the vest and how it looked on him. Freda would want him to be safe. And alive.

Hans and Bertel were convinced someone would try to shoot him during the concert. He'd made it through the first half, the Barber First Essay for Orchestra and the Barber Piano Concerto, without incident. A good house, standing room only, and the audience had been loud and rowdy in appreciation of the music, especially after the concerto. He'd been pleased with the performances, Lars's especially. The Swede had an affinity for American classical music. Nigel was meeting with him now. An image of Vasia Bartyakov playing the piano at his housewarming party last summer flitted through his mind. Nigel had never met Vasia or heard him play.

Bartók. Focus. Concentrate. He needed to think about the Bartók, the meter changes, the dynamic challenges, the tempo challenges. Seeing with his ears to balance the sound in the full hall. Closing his eyes, he visualized the first page of the score, the rising line of the lower strings answered by the violins and flutes.

Søren's distinctive knock on the bathroom door interrupted his thoughts. He opened the door.

Søren's smile was a taut line. "Maestro, it is time." Søren wore a black suit, white shirt, and cobalt-blue tie, his black hair tied back in a neat ponytail at the nape of his neck.

Evan glanced at Hans replacing his black 9mm Ruger in its shoulder holster.

Alicia, her arms crossed over her chest, glowered at Hans.

"Alicia, I hope you enjoy the Bartók." Evan smiled.

"I know I will, Gordo." Her smile reassured him.

In the hallway, Alicia headed for the door to the public lobby and the auditorium. He knew she was sitting in the third row from the stage in the center on the aisle. Bertel was working with a security team from the police and was already in the auditorium. Hans walked to his right, another security guard flanked Søren on his left. This intense security made Evan more nervous than the threat Leiner had reported to him and the Copenhagen police. It intruded into his music work. It bound Perceval, constricted his freedom and ability to defend himself. Although, Perceval knew well that if an assassin wanted to kill him, he would. An assassin would only need to plan and choose his opportunity, as had the Chilean woman in Buenos Aires and the mysterious Chinese-American guy in Vienna. Or Gregori.

Early that morning, Evan had thought again of the night only two weeks ago when someone had set off the security alarms at Freda's house and his apartment but the police had found nothing. After Gregori's attack and Freda's death, he'd told Leiner his suspicions: the false alarm had been Gregori casing the property. Now he couldn't shake the feeling that someone—Harold—was testing his security again at the concert. Nothing would happen this evening, which would lull everyone into a false sense of security. His second concert, on Saturday evening, was probably when Harold or the assassin he'd sent would make his move. He hoped Bors would give them the information they needed to stop him.

He had wanted to invite Hans and Bertel to their meeting with Bors after the concert. Alicia had cautioned him against involving too many people. The note said "come alone." They were meeting an informant, and the guy might be skittish. At the least sign of a threat to his position, Bors might bolt. She was right, as usual. He'd had to agree. He would meet Bors alone. Alicia would monitor his position using his cell phone signal.

At the stage door, Hans took up a position where he could see the back stage approach as well as the stage door itself. Søren pulled on his nose and shook his head.

Evan said in a low voice, "Are they interfering?"

"No, Maestro," Søren said, matching Evan's voice. "We have not seen the metal detectors before. The police set them up at each door to the auditorium even for the interval."

The metal detectors could act as a deterrent and catch metal guns as well as reassure the audience. He knew that guns existed that were not metal. "The musicians?"

"On stage. More concerned for your safety than irritated with the security."

"Yeah, well, *I'm* irritated with the security," Evan whispered.

Søren nodded. "You want a moment? I will dim the lights."

Evan looked up at the monitors above the stage manager's desk. They showed different views of the audience and the stage. The orchestra musicians were doing what orchestra musicians all over the world did the moments before the conductor walked on stage: waiting with instruments ready, some glancing out toward the audience. The backstage lights dimmed.

When he closed his eyes to focus his concentration, the image that came up was not the Bartók score but Pierre, in his favorite jeans and red sweater, sitting at the piano in his apartment the day before he'd taken him to the Leiners' house. Evan had given him a new exercise to strengthen the fourth and fifth fingers, but Pierre had also begun learning a little piece by Mozart. Or had it been a sonatina by Kuhlau? Pierre sometimes drew pictures of the music, the images that came into his mind when he was listening or playing. Evan smiled to himself. What would Pierre draw for Bartók's Concerto for Orchestra?

Leiner had assured him that Pierre was safe. But they didn't know where Harold was, and he'd hurt Pierre before. No, Harold must have heard him talking with Leiner about the listening chip behind Pierre's ear and Leiner's reaction. Harold must know that Leiner was protecting Pierre.

Bartók. Focus on Bartók. He adjusted the gold cufflinks that he always wore for concerts—a gift from Joseph Caine. In his mind, he opened the score to the first page, the lower strings and the ascending intervals, the violins' whispery high answer and the flutes. The lower strings leading into the trumpets' entrance. This music warned that something was coming. Musically, something *was* coming: an outpouring of emotion in sound. The brandy of the damned, as Caine would say.

"Maestro?" Søren said in a low voice next to him.

He took a deep breath and nodded. Søren opened the stage door, and the lights blinded Evan for a second. He bowed his head to allow his eyes to adjust and strode on stage in front of the first violins. Applause rose and fell in waves from the front of the hall to the rear and forward again. He lifted his head at the same time he lifted his arms wide toward the orchestra musicians, who obliged by rising to their feet. He turned slowly 360 degrees, facing the audience surrounding them, and bowed.

Now he was exposed, completely vulnerable. The applause would cover the explosive noise. Where was the gunshot?

He stepped up onto the podium as the musicians sat down. His back faced half the audience. He felt his back had a target painted on it.

All the usual noises—coughing, dropped programs, pages rustling, clothing rustling, voices murmuring—blended in his ear with gurney wheels rumbling across concrete, the pneumatic hiss of the emergency room doors opening, the eruption of Spanish voices. The hospital in Buenos Aires. He waited, holding his hands clasped but relaxed in front of him for the sounds in his ears to subside. The musicians waited, all eyes on him. Normally, this moment of anticipation, the energy from the audience, the control he wielded over all of them exhilarated him. Tonight, he simply stared at the open score on the stand in front of him and waited for the gunshot.

Silence. He picked up the baton from the stand and turned to the lower strings. They watched him, bows ready. In one smooth motion, he lifted the baton and brought it down. The lower strings played the warning tones in rising intervals. As the violins responded to his cue, he met the principal flutist's eyes. Bartók's music seeped through his body and began to take over his mind. He breathed with the beat. If Harold chose to kill him at this moment of calculated surrender to the violins bursting through the dark sounds, there was nothing anyone could do about it. He wrapped himself in the music, breathed, and cued the trumpets.

Evan strode down the hallway, his arms full of bouquets—he loved receiving flowers from the audience because he never received flowers in America. Hans and Bertel flanked him. They were the only people in the hallway. The security guards had made certain that the way would be clear, not allowing the musicians access yet. Alicia waited at the door to the conductor's suite. She applauded softly as he approached.

"I loved it," she said, her voice warm.

He bent down and kissed her. "Thank you. Would you like the flowers?"

She smiled. "You are so thoughtful, Evan. I love them, but I think we could perhaps give them to a hospital or something." She looked from Hans to Bertel. "Or perhaps they would like them for their wives?"

"Not married," Bertel said, his staccato delivery all business.

Hans shrugged. "What is your plan, Evan? Will you change clothes here or return to the hotel before going to Christiania?"

"I'll change here. I need to leave my shirt for Neils to have it cleaned for the concert Saturday night."

The plan to go to Nemoland originated from Evan overhearing two musicians talking about a group of them meeting there after the concert. They hadn't invited Evan; didn't know he'd heard them. But musicians meeting there for a post-concert drink was a plausible cover story for them to tell Hans and Bertel. And the location was perfect.

"Alicia can come in while I change," he said to the two bodyguards. "I would like the two of you to wait here, if you don't mind. I won't be long."

Alicia followed him into the dressing room. "You are not going out to the Green Room, Evan?"

He shrugged out of his suit jacket, revealing the beautiful vest from Freda. "I told Søren and Neils I wouldn't be meeting the public tonight. I talked to a lot of people yesterday after that preview matinee. I'm just relieved there's no public post-concert reception until Saturday night. I'm not fond of receptions."

Alicia sat down on the sofa as he opened the narrow closet. She watched him change out of his white tie and tails and into jeans, a light blue shirt, and a navy-blue crew neck sweater. He noticed her eyes dart to the scars on his right shoulder and his abdomen. He hung all but the formal white shirt in the closet, and slipped the shirt into the dry-cleaning bag Neils had left for him.

"How is your shoulder, Evan? You looked like you were not having any problems with it on stage."

He shrugged into his black corduroy sport jacket. "It's fine. I'm surprised by how fine it is. I did another session of the PT exercises before we left the hotel. I haven't had to take any hydrocodone at all."

"Good. Your stomach wound?"

"No problem. In fact, I'd say I'm ninety-nine-percent. I may be a little sore tomorrow. I was sore after the double rehearsal day. Do you think it's snowed outside?" He slipped his feet into warm cashmere socks and black loafers.

"We shall see." Alicia stood and accepted her loden coat from Evan. "I have heard over and over this week that Copenhagen has had a much colder winter than usual. Spring warmth arrives one week, and the next it snows again. It is the climate change, I think. What a relief to enjoy Danish neutrality in this war."

"No bombings, yeah." He rested his hand on the door's handle. He whispered, "You'll distract Hans and Bertel when I go to the restroom. I'll slip out and meet Bors alone."

"Is your cell phone on?"

He took the black slender cell phone out of his sport jacket pocket and checked it. "Yeah. You're sure you can pick up the signal?" He buttoned his coat.

She stepped to him, slid her arms around him, and hugged. "We tested everything yesterday, Gordo. We have a solid plan."

"And sometimes calling the cops is the best defense." He smiled. "Thanks to Inspector Leiner, the Copenhagen cops are on alert. Promise me?"

"I promise." She released him from her embrace.

He opened the door to Hans and Bertel in the hallway, both men wearing expectant expressions, dark gray wool coats, and the slight bulges of shoulder holsters.

Evan had not been off Amager Island since his arrival. They drove up Amager Fælledvej, the usual route back to his hotel, but instead of turning left onto Amager Boulevard, Bertel drove straight and then left onto Torvegade. They crossed over black water. Although it wasn't frozen, which surprised him, Evan could imagine the water being arctic cold. To the left, he saw lights on old bastions, like this island had once been a fortress in and of itself.

"Hans, this area looks really old."

Hans turned in the front passenger seat to look at Evan. "It is Christianshavn. King Christian the Fourth reclaimed this land in the early sixteen hundreds and made it a fortress to protect the city from attack from the sea."

Bertel turned right onto a picturesque street named Prinsessegade, lined with shops and cafés. On the left they passed a seventeenth-century Dutch Baroque church with a magnificent spire circled by a spiraling stairway. A beautiful iron fence surrounded the church grounds.

"To conserve energy, Copenhagen has joined other cities to become, how do you say?" Hans's eyes darted around as if the word flew like a mosquito in the air. "Yes, 'light on light'. You see, only every second street light is on."

He'd noticed that earlier in the week, studying the city from his hotel room, which overlooked the city facing northwest. The war affected fuel and energy availability everywhere.

"Perhaps the necessity to conserve energy because of the war will have some effect also on the climate?" Alicia said in a quiet voice. "Ironic that war could actually be environmentally friendly."

Hans grinned. "I am certain Muscovites would not agree with you, although we were as surprised and relieved as everyone that the Chinese had used neutron bombs to reduce radiation fallout. Of course, they considered their army, not the Russian people who managed to survive their attack, or the rest of the world."

"The war will only be environmentally friendly if everyone continues to conserve after the war is over," Bertel said in his gruff voice. He had the most unmusical voice Evan had ever heard.

Christiania allowed no cars within its perimeter. Bertel parked the car on Prinsessegade half a block from the entrance, which was framed by what appeared to be two straight denuded trees, the left topped by a *V* like a split trunk, a rough-hewn wood sign attached to them on which *Christiania* was painted in white letters. Fresh snow left a feathery dusting over everything. Bertel walked in front of Evan and Alicia while Hans brought up the rear.

Inside, classic rock music played from open windows in a large renovated warehouse-type brick building to the right of the entrance. People moved in a steady stream in and out at an entrance painted to be part of a picture of a human heart. Another entrance, part of a picture of a giant green pepper, led to an equally busy restaurant. They passed barracks-like buildings on the left housing shops painted with bright-colored murals that reminded Evan of his dreams in the hospital while on morphine. Despite the cold night, tourists with cameras and bags of souvenirs filled the street. On the right, they passed a tourist information kiosk that looked like a renovated tool shed, and, farther along, two newer apartment buildings. A busker played a saxophone in front of a restaurant as they entered a small square lined with rustic stalls selling food and steaming drinks, clothing, music flash drives, jewelry, and souvenirs. From open windows in the upper floor of another old warehouse building came rhythmic hip-hop, loud and driving. Alicia squeezed his arm and nodded to a point up ahead. Nemoland.

A sign on a weathered barracks-like building to their left caught his eye: *Woodstock*. He laughed and pointed.

"My father and Uncle Joe used to talk about Woodstock. It's a town in upstate New York and also the name of a wild rock music festival that occurred outside the town in the summer of 1969. According to Uncle Joe, some of the best rock performers of the time showed up, along with thousands of people who indulged in a lot of sex and illegal drugs. That place looks like it's trying to carry on the festival's spirit."

Bertel glanced back at him, pressed his fingers to the ear nodule of his headset. His eyes returned to scrutinizing the crowd, a human radar.

"I have heard of it, Evan. Have you listened to the music drive?"

"Of the festival? No. There's a music drive?"

Alicia laughed low and throaty. "We must go to a music store tomorrow and buy one for you. I want to be the one to corrupt such a brilliant classical musician with old rock and roll."

"Music is music," he said. Uncle Joe had played old rock music for him when he was a kid. He'd liked the Beatles, Chicago, the Rolling Stones, the Doors, and Blood Sweat &

Tears, among others. Alicia would not be corrupting him. He smiled at her.

They walked through an open area where snow-covered picnic tables clustered to the left and right, and dwarf conifers stood guard among the tables. Inside, jazz fusion filled the air along with the yeasty scent of beer and tobacco smoke tinged with another smoky scent, pungent and harsh. Nemoland's simple white and wood décor reflected a maritime harbor and fishing industry. Yellow and brown fish net and white buoy-shaped lights hung from the ceiling. People lined up at the bar and occupied almost all the rectangular tables. Evan spotted the group of musicians toward the back.

"They're over there. I don't see any room for us. Let's get our own table," Evan said. "I'll go say hello."

He left Alicia to deal with Hans and Bertel. As he approached the musicians' table, he searched his memory for their names. He recognized several violinists, a clarinetist, and two cellists, but then couldn't place the others.

"Maestro! What are you doing here?" one of the cellists said, jumping to his feet. Evan remembered that he was from Greece because he resembled Sofia's Greek father.

"I got tired of being caged," he said, glancing around at the others. His gaze met smiles. "I wanted to celebrate a little. Especially after that Bartók. Wow. I heard this place is good." He glanced around, noting the position of the restrooms and the rear exit sign nearby.

"It is a lot of fun, Maestro," a young blonde said. Her accent sounded Finnish to him, or maybe Hungarian. "The food is all fresh and organic and they have completely renovated in the last year."

"Join us?" the clarinetist said, offering his seat. Evan remembered his name was Gunther something and he was from Leipzig.

"Thanks, but no. I'm with my security detail, of course, and my cousin. I just wanted to say hello and tell you all what a brilliant concert it was tonight. Great job. See you later."

He half waved as he turned. It gave him an opportunity to look around for any familiar faces. The clientele skewed toward grungy, with tourists sticking out among the crowd like pimples. He saw no one else he knew, and no one showed any interest in him.

He took his time finding the table Alicia had claimed for them. The crowded café would give him the cover he needed to slip out, if he needed to, by the front entrance. He could walk on the other side of the room. One problem: he'd need to wear his coat. But it was hot in the bar. The faces around him glistened with sweat. He would not be able to shed his coat and then sit and talk for a while before excusing himself for the restroom. He checked his watch, hoping Bors would wait if he were a few minutes late.

Bertel's clear brown eyes rested on him, steady and cold. Hans had gone to the bar to buy drinks. Alicia grabbed Evan's hand.

"How are the musicians?" she said.

"Yeah, they're fine. Listen, I need to hit the men's room before I get settled here. It's near the musicians' table. Sorry. I'll be back in a minute or two." He squeezed Alicia's hand before releasing it.

"Evan." Bertel rose from his chair.

"It'll be fine, Bertel. Relax." Evan pointed to Bertel's chair. "No one else knew we'd be here tonight, right?"

Bertel stood, his body leaning to walk but his expression uncertain.

"Relax." Evan now waved as if brushing away Bertel's concern. He left for the restroom without looking back. It was Alicia's job to keep the two bodyguards occupied. He ran into Hans carrying a tray with a pitcher of beer and a bottle of mineral water with glasses.

"Where are you going?" Hans said, his voice barely audible above the noisy room.

"Men's room. Save my chair, OK? It's getting crowded in here," Evan said, pausing only a second to pat Hans on the shoulder. "Thanks for the drinks."

Evan pushed on, weaving around the full tables, waving to the musicians as he passed their table. They raised their glasses to him in a toast of smiles. His family, musicians, now more than ever. He owed it to them to be careful.

In the restroom, two men stood at the urinals, but all the stalls were empty. Evan washed his hands as if that was his sole purpose for being in the room. He strode out again, stopping to the right of the door. He could not see Alicia or their table, so they could not see him. The rear exit was only feet away down a short, dark hallway. But when he reached the door, he found it locked and a sign on it in Danish and English: "Fire door. Do not open. Alarm will sound."

Terrific. Going out the front door was no longer a hypothetical. He made his way to the opposite side of the room and found it crowded with people sitting at and standing around tables, singing and talking. He pushed through two groups, excusing himself in German rather than English, and, after almost ten minutes, reached the front door. Glancing back, he saw Bertel standing and looking around but not in his direction. Evan slipped out of Nemoland.

He jogged, weaving around people, to the street and turned right. Up ahead, a huge building dominated the corner of Pusher Street and Fabriksområdet. The sign over the door said *Den Grønne Hal* and the windows displayed a wide array of merchandise from clothes to hardware materials. In front, in the light from this store, Evan found an old man holding a copy of Randall Quinn's novel, *The Distance Between Two Points* as he'd said in his note. Bors. Evan strode up to him.

"Bors? Evan Quinn. Sorry I'm late."

The old man pulled his knitted hat over his forehead and squinted at him. "No Bors," he said, his voice hoarse.

Evan caught a whiff of the guy. Beer. "Where's Bors?" he said.

The old man handed him a folded piece of paper. Evan opened it and read the three words written in black in the center: *Vor Frelsers Kirke*.

"Vor Frelsers Kirke?" he said, grabbing the old man by his wool coat's lapel. He didn't like the sudden change in plans.

"Sankt Annæ Gade," the old man rasped. "Prinsessegade."

"With the spire?" The Dutch Baroque church on Prinsessegade was the only church they'd passed.

The old man nodded, said something in Danish Evan

didn't understand, but pointed back toward the entrance to Christiania.

Suddenly, it made sense to him. Bors was being careful, ensuring his security. This old man was the equivalent of a surveillance-detection run. The old man rubbed his thumb and fingertips together and whispered a word in Danish. Evan didn't need translation. He dug in his jeans pocket for his wallet, gave the old man a five-euro note. The old man nodded, gave him a salute, and shuffled off, still clutching Randall Quinn's book.

Evan headed for Christiania's entrance, unbuttoning his coat and sliding his hand into his sport jacket pocket. The cell phone was still there, still on. Being careful is one thing, but Bors had surprised him and he didn't like surprises. Security, sure, but why change the meeting location when the meeting was only an exchange of information? Maybe Bors's information was more than simply the name of who wanted him dead, who Harold Smith worked for.

He'd soon find out.

CHAPTER 21

Winter-bare trees surrounded Vor Frelsers Kirke and threw pulsing black shadow veins onto the Dutch Baroque façade. The spire pierced the night sky. From a block away, the church appeared closed. Evan passed a middle-aged couple out for a late-night stroll with their Jack Russell terrier. Christianshavn's slushy cobbled streets were empty and quiet, in sharp contrast to the festive activity in Christiania. Some of the city's residents conserved their own human energy as well as conserving electricity and fuel by staying in, going to bed early. His breath clouded the air before his face. His feet felt cold in his loafers, and he wished he'd brought boots to Copenhagen. He glanced behind him, half expecting to see Alicia, Bertel, and Hans running after him, but no one was there.

He checked his watch. He'd been gone from Nemoland for almost twenty-five minutes. He imagined that Alicia had already checked the meeting place and found no one there. She should be tracking his position now. They had not discussed how she would deal with Bertel and Hans if she had to track him. The bodyguards could be a problem. What if Alicia wasn't able to track him? What if he was completely on his own? It wouldn't be the first time.

He slowed his pace as he came to the church's iron fence

on the Prinsessegade side. No lights were on around or inside, and only one streetlight lit the corner. He held his breath and listened. A dog barked. He could smell the sea on the cold night breeze and thought he heard water lapping up against something nearby. No footsteps. No voices.

At the corner, he turned onto Sankt Annæ Gade and strolled through the open gate and up to the main doors as if he planned to attend a service . The doors were locked. Of course. Almost midnight. A moving shadow to his left caught his eye.

"Bors?" he said, his voice low.

The shadow cleared its throat. When it spoke, its voice was a raspy tenor. "Who are you?"

Evan moved out to the sidewalk where the light was better. "Evan Quinn. I expected to meet a man named Bors here. Are you Bors?"

A whistling wheeze of a laugh answered him. The shadow moved out into the light, a man two or three inches shorter than Evan, a froth of salt-and-pepper curls framing intense blue eyes in an old wrinkled face. He was lithe, his movements feline-smooth. His body seemed young to Evan, younger than his face, and this set Evan on edge.

"Are you Bors?"

"I'm to take ya to 'im." The accent sounded like a Scottish brogue.

"Where is he?"

The man gestured to his right, away from Prinsessegade. "He's got a right nice little boat on the canal."

"This seems all very elaborate for passing on some information."

The man bowed, his right arm extended to his right, his left across his chest. "He wishes to share a pint with you."

He wasn't sure why, but he thought the man in front of him was Bors. "Just give me the information now, Bors," he said.

The man laughed, his mouth wide, followed by coughing that bent him double. He pulled a crumpled white handkerchief from his black pea coat pocket and wiped his mouth, peering at Evan, the skin around his eyes crinkled in merriment. He took a deep, wheezing breath. "He'll be amused," he said. "Coming or no?"

Evan followed the man along quiet Sankt Annæ Gade for two blocks and over a bridge to a street of apartment buildings with cafés and shops on the ground floors. The man turned right and walked another block to a street that ran parallel to a canal. The man's gait had a slight bounce to it, as if he were prepared at any second to push off from the balls of his feet into a sprint. Evan wished that Copenhagen wasn't trying to conserve energy and had turned on all its streetlights. The darker sections of the street, places where someone could hide in the shadows, screwed his nerves tight, with the kind of nervousness that warned anything could happen.

He didn't know Bors, and he hadn't called Woody to check on the guy. Why hadn't he called Woody? Common sense to check on a source. He hadn't even thought of it until this moment, and he could easily have checked at any time in the past day and a half since he'd received the message from Bors. Stupid. He blamed it on his less-than-complete Perceval training, on his busy schedule of media interviews and concerts. However, he'd asked Woody a long time ago to ask his sources to find out who was trying to kill him. He'd assumed that anyone who said he knew Woody, whom Woody had asked for help, would be safe. Now he wondered if it was too late to assume no one was safe.

At the canal, the man led him to the right. They walked perhaps half a block before the man veered left to the canal's embankment, a sheer wall of stone that rose about five feet from the water's surface. The nearest streetlight was almost a block away. but one shone from across the canal. The man pointed to a boat moored below. Evan saw that it was a sleek cruiser, medium-sized but longer than other boats moored nearby. No lights burned on it.

"Doesn't look like anyone's home." Evan turned away as if to leave.

"He's here, lad. He's watchin'."

A shiver passed through Evan. "Where?"

With the agility of a cat, the man jumped down into the boat and entered the cabin. The lights came on. He studied the cruiser. He hadn't been on a boat like it since he was a kid. The only thing that struck him as odd was the three five-liter fuel canisters in the back near the engine casing. Were they empty or full?

The man held the cabin door open for him. "Come in, lad, where it's warmer. Give your feet a rest."

He jumped down onto the deck. Mahogany gleamed in the cabin's interior. Evan settled on a plush sofa upholstered in black suede. As he shrugged out of his black pea coat, the man went over to the bar to the right of a closed door. Under the jacket, he wore a blue turtleneck under a garish sweater striped yellow, orange, and red, black jeans, and boots. Evan guessed the closed door led to sleeping quarters. He stared at it, expecting it to open at any moment and for Bors to finally show himself.

"Beer?" the man said.

"Mineral water, if you have it. Where's Bors?"

"Oh, yeah, Woody said you didn't drink alcohol." The man's voice had lost its brogue. He uncapped a bottle of Carlsberg. "That have anything to do with your mother?" His tenor pitch had dropped and the rasp had disappeared. His flat vowels placed his accent firmly in Minnesota.

Evan felt tingling in his face as the blood drained from it. "Who are you?"

"I'm Bors," the man said, removing his salt-and-pepper hair and a wig cap, freeing thick oat blond hair. The face was still wrong, but there was no mistaking that hair color.

"Harold." This moment of revelation was too ordinary, too mundane. Evan had expected something far more volcanic when they finally faced each other. He unbuttoned his coat but resisted the urge to slip his hand in his jacket pocket to touch the cell phone. Harold couldn't know about the cell phone.

The man before him took a swig of Carlsberg from the bottle, and peeled off a wrinkled mask of a face to reveal Harold's chiseled face underneath. "Yeah. Nice to see you again, Quinn." His sarcasm cut through the air. "I told you. I'm your shadow."

Evan's stomach knotted. Had Harold gotten to Bors first and killed him, taking on his identity? Or was Harold one of Woody's sources? Harold and Woody knew each other?

Harold laughed, a whispery wheezing sound from his boyhood that made his hair stand up on the back of his neck. "I'm Bors. And I know who's been trying to kill you." He laughed again, raising his beer bottle to Evan in a salute.

Evan stared, taking slow, deep breaths to stay in the present. Up close, Harold had not changed that much from the teenager who'd terrorized him twenty-six years ago. "Who do you work for? The CIA? Internal Security Services? DIA?"

"Who does everyone work for in America?" Harold uncapped a small mineral water bottle and handed it to Evan.

Everyone in America worked for the New Economic Party in one way or another, whether they were political or not, whether they actually worked for the government or not, whether they wanted to or not. The NEP controlled everything, including the DIA, CIA, and ISS. "Why does the NEP want me dead?" He set the mineral water bottle on the floor. He'd watched Harold uncap it, but he didn't trust that it was pure, that Harold hadn't poisoned it. Woody had told him that Evan didn't drink alcohol. All it would take was a pinprick of a hole in the cap, a syringe full of the poison of his choice.

Woody had known about Harold. Woody had known all along who had been trying to kill him. He understood now why Woody had been out of town on family business. He'd been avoiding him.

"Oh, come on, Quinn." Harold sat down in one of the suede chairs opposite the sofa. He took another swig of beer. "You're Evan Quinn, son of Randall Quinn, persona non grata. The NEP prefers the Quinn family to end here."

"My father's dead. Murdered by the ISS. The NEP was pleased about that, I'm sure."

A slow smile spread across Harold's face, the same cocky smile Evan remembered seeing often as a kid when Harold and his Vigiciv gang had him cornered. He didn't have a gun or knife, only his martial arts training to defend himself. He glanced around the cabin. A small red fire extinguisher hung three feet to the left of the door. A possible weapon.

"Shit, Quinn, you haven't changed at all. It doesn't matter that your father's dead. Actually, sure, they wanted him dead and now he's dead. But like I said, the NEP prefers the Quinn family end here and now."

"Not going to happen."

Harold laughed. "You and Paul Caine. Heretic bastards. We should've burned both of you to a crisp that day in the woods." He laughed again, an ugly sneering sound. Nothing about the sounds this man made was musical. "Besides wanting to wipe you off the face of the earth because you're Randall Quinn's kid, and Randall Quinn stole profit from them, was a leader in the Underground against them, you have something that belongs to them."

Such a mundane reason, he thought. "Even if you're successful, Harold, they won't be able to claim the money from the trust funds. I've made certain of that."

The smile faded a millimeter on Harold's mouth. "That's not my concern."

"You just follow orders."

"Yeah."

"The woman in Buenos Aires, the Chinese-American guy, Gregori, they were all part of your new gang?"

The smile turned into an open-mouthed grin. Harold's teeth shone a brilliant white. One of the NEP elite back in America, undoubtedly, receiving the best in dental care, probably with full insurance coverage. Or maybe Harold didn't even live in America anymore.

"Yeah, they worked for me. I wasn't too pleased with what happened to them, either, Quinn. How did you know about the woman in Buenos Aires? Did you see her?"

He'd slipped. But he knew how to cover it. "Gregori told me in Paris that he'd been tracking her." He gave Harold as confident and knowing a smile as he could muster. "Gregori was a fountain of information."

"You were lucky." Harold swigged his beer. "Really lucky. I'm still trying to figure out how you got the first two. I read about the last in the newspaper."

An image of Alicia standing over the Chinese-American assassin with a knife dripping blood popped into his mind. Harold had no need to know about Alicia. "Answer me this, Harold. Why did Gregori kill Freda Kirsch? Why didn't he just come after me?" Evan looked to Harold's right at the bar. A broken glass bottle could be an effective weapon, but it was too far away. And Harold sat next to the bar. Maybe break the small mineral water bottle by his feet.

Harold nodded. "He was trying to set a scene."

"What scene?" Evan shook his head. He could see that Harold really wanted to brag about his operation against him. Harold hadn't changed.

"You went on a psychotic rampage. Killed Kirsch and the fuckin' boy and then killed yourself. There was enough in the media last year about your mental state when you defected that would have supported your mind finally snapping. I really loved the idea."

The fuckin' boy. That was Pierre he was talking about. A cold, intense anger spread up from his stomach. "Anything to put me in the worst possible light. Prove all the lies to be truths."

"You got it."

"Didn't work out that way, did it?" Evan sneered at him, the cold anger calming him, calming his mind.

Harold's face darkened. "Gregori messed up. He should have killed you first, then set the scene."

"You make me sick." He lunged for the door, surprise on his side. He was out on the boat's deck before Harold had dropped his beer. The boat was still moored to the side of the canal. He could leave, but he didn't. The cold anger brought clarity of purpose. He wanted to end this hunt now. To be prey no longer. He wanted to make certain Pierre would never have to worry about Harold coming after him. Perceval wanted to end Harold so he'd never hurt any more little boys. Or him. He stood near the stern. A banquette of white vinyl cushions lined the port side. He spotted more fuel canisters lined up under the gunwale's six-inch lip on the starboard side. The open deck gave him more room to maneuver but not much more.

Harold slithered out of the cabin, aiming a 9mm Ruger at Evan. "You test my patience, Quinn. Just like when you were a kid."

"Shooting me won't be setting any kind of credible scene, Harold." His voice was calm, cold. He needed to find out what Harold had planned. "Shooting me is murder."

"No one will know." Harold chuckled. "This time I *am* going to burn you to a crisp." The chuckle rose into a cackle. "And I think it's considerate of me to leave the world a really convincing suicide note signed by you in your hotel room."

"Woody Lewis," Evan said. "You said Woody told you I didn't drink. What else did he tell you?"

"He told me you were easy." Harold laughed.

"He's known about your orders all along?"

"Yeah. About you and Bernie Brown."

Brown's name coming out of Harold's mouth shocked him. "What are you talking about? Did you kill Bernie in Glasgow?"

"Not me. Why do you care about Brown?"

Out of the corner of his eye, Evan saw a shadow flit near one of the dark houses facing the canal. He knew how well sound carried over water. "Well, Harold," Evan said, raising his voice. "What do you care that I care?"

"You are such a stupid little shit, Quinn." Harold stepped to the starboard side, reached over, and slipped the mooring rope from its heavy iron ring embedded in the embankment. "I told Woody to expect something spectacular for you. He'll be pleased."

"So Woody Lewis has known all along about you and your assassin gang hunting me?" Again, Evan raised his voice, hoping the shadow would hear him clearly and mark his figure as friendly, as the victim in this situation. Hoping the shadow was Alicia. "All these fuel canisters, Harold. What's the deal with them? Are you going on a long trip?"

In one swift glide forward, Evan brought himself within striking distance and kicked out with his right foot, a hard punch to Harold's stomach, doubling him over. Evan pivoted away at the same time he brought his left hand down in a chopping motion on Harold's back. He reached for the stone embankment before the boat drifted too far away, but Harold kicked him behind his left knee. He crumpled back and down to the deck.

"Nice move for an orchestra conductor, Quinn." The rasp was back in Harold's voice. He lifted his gun to pistol-whip Evan's head. "I'm going to enjoy this."

Evan rolled away toward the stern. He needed more space to fight on the deck. Harold pushed the boat away from the embankment. Evan got to his knees and looked up in time to see Harold's booted foot. The kick caught him under the chin with such force it flung him back against the engine casing.

"You're the one going on the trip, Quinn," Harold said.

The *whoof* of a silenced gunshot came from the dark street above. Harold's right shoulder jerked back, and he crouched, turned toward the embankment. Despite the light coming from the cabin windows, he was difficult to see from the street in that position. He acted as if the bullet through his shoulder hadn't hurt him.

Harold lit a match. In its flare, Evan saw a skinny rope snaking to one of the fuel canisters, its cap off, the fuse disappearing inside. Crude, but effective. Harold lit the fuse. Evan stood up from the engine casing, and kicked at the rope to get it out of the fuel canister but instead hit the Ruger in Harold's hand. The gun tumbled and clacked across the deck. Harold turned and crawled fast for the gun.

He needed to get Harold into the light, exposed. In two

steps Evan was over him. He grabbed Harold by the back of his collar and lifted him off the deck. In a fleeting thought, he realized that Harold hadn't expected a fight from him. He'd expected him to cower as he'd cowered as a young boy, terrified of the big boys. Twenty-six years of living in the NEP's America had changed him a lot. Perceval had changed him. Perceval was not afraid of Harold.

Evan pushed Harold up against the cabin wall and window, punched his kidneys twice. When he swiveled Harold to look into his face, the American sucker punched him in the gut and got his jaw with a left hook. But Harold was standing in full view in the light.

Another *whoof* sounded from farther away.

As Evan fell back, he saw Harold in his peripheral vision. The bullet caught him in the chest on the right side, and he slid down the cabin wall until he sat on the deck, his back to the wall. Evan landed on his butt five feet away. He looked at the burning fuse, the fire climbing toward the open mouth of the fuel canister.

"Who's your shooter?" Harold picked up the Ruger, aimed it at Evan.

"You're the one going on the trip, Harold."

As he scrambled to his feet, Evan heard the Ruger's report and the metallic ping when the bullet hit a fuel canister. He reached the side of the boat in two long strides. Another gunshot. Something hot stung his left arm about five inches from the shoulder. He dove for the water as he heard a crackling *snap* and a loud metallic *pop*.

The shock of icy water enveloping his body forced open his mouth and eyes. Above him, the sky was on fire. His winter clothes weighed him down, and his arms pumped hard to keep him near the surface. He kicked out of his loafers, and swam underwater to get away from the fire, but he didn't know where he was in relation to the embankment. When he surfaced, he found that he'd swum down the canal.

Lit windows revealed the interiors of apartments across the canal. He heard the alternating musical fourth of a police siren approaching, accompanied by another and another. Across the canal a small crowd was gathering. The burning cruiser, a ball of pulsing fire sitting on the water, illuminated the entire area. Had a shadow moved on it? Evan gasped. There was a shadow. Then the fire roared in an explosion of flaming debris. Evan cringed away, feeling the searing heat on his face even as his body shivered in the icy water. No way Harold could survive that. Evan dove to escape the burning debris and swam for the embankment.

This time, he knew where the embankment was, though he felt as if the water pulled him down and his movements were in slow motion. When he surfaced, he spotted a ladder up to the street not far from where the cruiser had been moored and stiffly swam to it. He looked up. Alicia stood at the top, flanked by his scowling Danish bodyguards.

"You are certain, Evan?" Hans said in his pillowy baritone. "This man, Harold Smith, was the one trying to kill you and the source of the threat the Austrian electronic surveillance heard?"

"I am absolutely one hundred percent positive."

He sat in a modern kitchen of pastel-yellow tile and stainless-steel in one of the houses on the street facing the canal. Behind him stood an oak dining table. Two uniformed Copenhagen police officers, with Hans and Bertel, formed a semi-circle in front of him. Alicia sat next to him, one hand rubbing a tiny circle on his upper back. The Copenhagen police had requested the young couple who owned the house to assist in providing him, a crime victim, with something hot to drink and a place to warm himself. The efficient and thorough EMTs had already examined him, bandaged his left arm where Harold's bullet had grazed him, and, satisfied that he was warming up and OK after he'd declined further treatment, left.

The couple, a tall brown-haired man with a scholarly air and a short blond woman who was at least eight months pregnant, both in pajamas and robes, had insisted that he take off all his wet clothes. He sat sipping steaming tea, his naked body wrapped in a fleece blanket. The shivering had stopped. The woman had taken his clothes somewhere after saying something to a police officer.

"She'll bring back my clothes, won't she?"

The police officer nodded. "She dries them, Maestro."

"My coat's probably ruined."

"Evan." Hans put his hand on Evan's shoulder. "Do you know why?"

Bertel moved to stand guard by the door to the front of the house. He looked as if he'd eaten something rotten.

"He was working for the Americans, the New Economic Party. They wanted me dead so they could claim the money I inherited from my father and Joseph Caine." A flood of words, so fast Evan felt he vomited them. "He told me that he'd left a suicide note in my hotel room for the police to find." He felt Alicia's fingers press down hard on his upper spine. "He said he was setting a scene, that he was going to shoot me, then burn me. He had lots of fuel canisters on the boat. He was going to blow it up after shooting me."

Another policeman entered the kitchen, placing one hand on Bertel's arm as Bertel nodded to him. This officer was a plainclothes detective with a diamond-shaped face, dimpled chin, and large nose. He had a distracted demeanor, as if something else preoccupied his mind even when he was talking. Evan had met him earlier but couldn't remember his name.

"Maestro, how are you feeling? Warmer?" the detective said.

"Much better, thanks." Evan took a deep breath. "Have they found him?"

The detective stood with his legs apart and crossed his arms over his dark blue parka as he took a deep breath. "No. The fire fighters have extinguished the fire. No body on what was left of the boat. We will search the canal, of course, but it is possible the body was also blown up in the explosion." The rhythm of his speech and slight British accent reminded Evan of Inspector Leiner.

The detective continued, "We have determined that the boat had been bought by 'Evan Quinn' and paid for in full in cash."

"I didn't buy it. When could I have? Security guarding me constantly—did you show the seller my picture? Did the seller recognize me as the buyer?" Evan frowned. Of course

Harold would masquerade as him to buy the boat in order to complete the suicide scene.

"We continue to interview him, Maestro. But I suspect we will learn that the man who bought the boat was not you. I understand that he was setting up your murder to appear to be a suicide. It would make sense for Harold Smith to say you had bought the boat. We will need for you to provide us with as complete a description of this Harold Smith as you can remember."

"Gladly." He didn't like that they hadn't found Harold's body. He wanted to see him dead. He wanted to know for certain, even if all that was left were pieces. "How could anyone have escaped that inferno?" he said to no one in particular.

The detective smiled. "We do not know he escaped, Maestro. I expect we will find his body in the canal." He glanced at Bertel. "You shot him twice?" Bertel nodded.

Evan stared at Bertel. Alicia hadn't been the shooter defending him. He glanced at her on his right. She nodded. In her dark brown eyes, he thought he could see an eagerness to tell him about it, and relief. He looked back at the bodyguard. "Thanks, Bertel. I was trying to get him in the light."

"I know."

"Maestro, when your clothes are dry, these officers will drive you back to your hotel," the detective said, nodding to the two uniformed policemen.

"Please keep me informed, Detective—I'm sorry, I've forgotten your name. I want to know when you find his body."

"Mortensen." The detective extended his hand and shook Evan's hand. He nodded to Alicia. "I will call you, Maestro."

The detective left, taking the uniformed cops with him. Evan looked from Hans to Bertel to Alicia.

"Thanks for saving my life," he said.

Bertel's face flushed, and he looked away. Hans smiled. "It was a good thing, Evan, that Alicia could track your cell phone. That was smart."

"But it wasn't smart to go off on my own." Evan looked down at his mug of hot tea. He felt no need to say anymore to the two bodyguards.

"I told them, Evan," Alicia said. "About the attack in Vienna, about Freda."

"We are sorry for your loss, Evan," Hans said.

"Yeah, well." He glanced at the two Danes. "I'm glad it's over."

Bertel said something in Danish to Hans, who nodded. "We will wait for you outside." They left the kitchen.

He and Alicia were alone, finally, for the moment. She placed her hand over his on his thigh.

"They will not find his body."

Evan sighed. "I was afraid you'd say that. All he told me was that he worked for the NEP. He didn't say it was CIA or ISS or DIA or something else."

"You had no need to know, even when he expected you would be dead."

"Do you think he's dead, Alicia?" He studied her face. He had a feeling, from her eyes, that she'd be leaving him, returning to her spy work for Spain.

She smiled but shook her head. "I think it is the end. I want to know something. He said in the note he sent that he was a friend of Woody Lewis. I heard him say that this

Woody Lewis knew about his orders to kill you. Perhaps he knows who killed Bernie." Her expression had hardened, the crinkle lines around her eyes smoothed out.

"Yeah." He knew that look on her face. One word from him, and Alicia would save him, save Perceval, the trouble of killing his handler.

She fisted her hands on the table. "This would mean Woody Lewis also works for the NEP, yes? Perhaps the CIA?"

"I don't know, Alicia." He could not bring himself to tell her all he knew about his handler. He could not tell her that he was actually an assassin named Perceval who also had worked for the NEP. He could not tell her that he'd been given the job of killing Bernie Brown but he had decided not to do it. Someone else had killed him.

"Does it matter whether or not he works for the CIA? He works for the NEP, just like Harold Smith. Woody Lewis set me up. Maybe he set up Bernie, too."

"I would like to meet this Woody Lewis."

Perceval smiled.

CHAPTER 22

"You saw his body, Monsieur Evan?"

Pierre climbed higher on the gray metal jungle gym so that Evan had to squint up to see him in the bright sunshine. Two other boys and a girl climbed around Pierre, and the voices of playing children bounced around Türkenschanz Park on this warm afternoon. Rivulets of melted snow streamed into puddles on the park's paths. Spring may have finally arrived in Vienna.

"Be careful, Pierre. Your aunt said you'll be traveling in those clothes today." Evan glanced around at the other adults in the park. The chess tables were full. Mothers chased after snowy toddlers headed for the sand pit. Two fathers with young boys constructed fat men or animal sculptures with the heavy, sticky snow. The park activity reassured him as much as the empty blue sky overhead. The Chinese had not bombed Vienna in weeks. An internet rumor flew around the world that a ceasefire was imminent.

"You saw his body?"

Evan sighed. He hadn't wanted to tell Pierre. He didn't want to give him nightmares. When he'd arrived back in Vienna two days ago, he'd gone first to the Leiners' house to see Pierre. He'd told him that Harold Smith was dead and Pierre was safe. That was enough.

"Pierre, yes, I saw his body." He watched Pierre turn his face to peer at something across the park, his lips pursed.

The Copenhagen police had picked over the remains of the boat for human DNA and had searched the canal for human remains, but found nothing. The official report Detective Mortensen had given him stated that his attacker, Harold Smith, had been atomized in the explosion that Smith had set off on the boat.

The American embassy in Copenhagen had had no official comment, but behind the scenes they had disavowed Harold Smith's existence. They claimed that he had died in a car accident in Virginia ten years ago. They had no reason to believe that the man who had attacked Evan was even an American, and therefore, they saw no reason to release Harold Smith's DNA records to the Danes for identification purposes.

Evan wasn't surprised when Detective Mortensen had called him at his hotel with this news. The Americans would not want any connection to Harold Smith. He'd been an assassin taking orders from the NEP, which would have sullied the government's current clean and collaborative public position in the international community. Their response made him think, however, about Perceval.

He'd known from the beginning that if he were caught or killed while on Perceval business, the NEP would react exactly as they had to Harold Smith. But Harold and his assassin gang had worked hard to set scenes, to set him up for public disgrace, to discredit him even though they were going to kill him. The NEP would have done the same if he'd been caught working as Perceval—disavow him and point out, thanks to Harold's work, that he clearly was a threat to society, and deserved to be imprisoned or executed for his crimes. Everything about Perceval had been a set-up from the beginning and now posed a threat to him and to those closest to him.

He understood that the NEP had never intended to allow him to *live* in freedom to pursue his music career. Perceval had been their idea, not his. They'd forced him, given him no choice, so he'd chosen to live, and become Perceval. He needed to figure out a way to terminate his employment permanently without exposing himself to prosecution or losing his music or his good name or his life.

Pierre swept his light brown bangs from his face. "Good. He deserved to be blown up and sent straight to hell."

"Pierre." The boy's harsh tone disturbed him, but he understood. Harold had hurt him, threatened his life. Would Pierre despise Perceval if he knew? Evan reached up for the boy. His left arm was still sore from the gunshot graze and his back was sore with healing bruises from hitting the cruiser's engine casing, but his right shoulder was fine. He'd enjoyed the irony in that and had no problems conducting the second Copenhagen concert with the help of a hydrocodone pill. "We have to leave now. Your aunt said not to dawdle, remember?"

"Dawdle? What is this word?" Pierre climbed down on his own, frowning.

"It means to be intentionally slow. Drag your feet. Like someone trying to avoid going somewhere. Come on."

The boy jumped down, his boots splashing the brown slush on the ground around the jungle gym. He wore no hat on this mild afternoon, but boots and wool jacket over his favorite jeans and red sweater. He made no move to leave.

"He was CIA, this man?"

"I don't know, Pierre. He worked for the Americans. It really doesn't matter now." It mattered to a certain extent, but Pierre needn't worry about that.

"You are CIA?"

"No. Not even—no. Never. I couldn't work for them or the ISS or any other American government agency." His official denial. A lie. "You haven't said anything about the chips, Pierre. Inspector Leiner took you to Dr. Maas?"

Pierre nodded, his head bowed. "No pain. They are gone."

Evan ruffled his hair. "You'll practice piano every day?"

Pierre craned back his neck to look up at him. The boy still frowned. "You are coming to the airport with us?"

"We talked about that already."

"But you can wait with us. It is not goodbye until we walk on to the plane."

"I know, Pierre." The boy's logic could not be refuted. "My presence at the airport might call unwanted attention to you and your aunt and uncle. I want you to be able to travel without that attention. I do not want the media to find out about you. OK?" The media had hounded him in Copenhagen immediately after the attack. Although it was amazing the media had not pursued him at all since his return to Vienna, he knew that journalists with long noses could sniff things out, things that he wouldn't want the world to know. Like Pierre. He refused to open the opportunity for them. Evan placed his gloved hand on Pierre's shoulder and shook him gently. "Let's walk, Monsieur Pierre."

"You have terrible French." Pierre grinned. "I must teach you." He walked next to Evan, holding his hand. He'd never done that before.

"You'll practice the piano every day?"

"Oui, Monsieur Evan. And I will send you email every day. I will ask Uncle Julien for my own computer for my birthday in May, and then perhaps we can begin your French lessons. Your computer has video, no? You must go a little high tech, no?"

"People are *no* tech, Pierre."

Pierre laughed the infectious giggle of pure boyish amusement. "No tech."

He quizzed Evan on his conducting schedule as they left Türkenschanz Park, and he matched Evan's brisk pace as they walked along Peter-Jordan-Strasse. A red-and-white Number 40 bus passed on the slushy street, followed by two cars. Evan listened to Pierre's flute-like voice tell him about the Levade apartment in Paris and the news Uncle Julien had brought about the legal complications Pierre's reappearance had created. Pierre seemed to enjoy the story up to the point when Julien explained that Pierre would be returning to France to inherit the Paris apartment and his parents' estates. Pierre insisted that they must find his parents and became quite upset that no one had been looking for them. Dominique had cried. Julien had reassured Evan that they would take Pierre to the therapist Dr. Moreau had recommended in Paris.

They walked along Hans-Richter-Gasse to Chimanistrasse. Evan spotted the waiting taxi in front of the Leiners' house before Pierre did. They were late. Dominique Ulliel met them at Leiners' front door. Evan had been startled by her height when he'd first met her two days ago. She was at least six feet, taller than her husband, Julien, and older. Evan imagined that she must look like her sister, Pierre's mother, from whom Pierre had gotten his blue eyes, patrician nose, and fair complexion. In another six or seven years, Pierre might be as tall as his aunt, if not taller.

"Pierre, what had I told you? The taxi waits with the meter running." She smiled at Evan, shaking her head.

"My fault, Dominique," Evan said. "Can I help with the luggage?"

"Pierre, please collect your things," Dominique responded. The boy wiped his boots on the doormat and went inside. To Evan she said, "We have already loaded our luggage into the taxi."

Her husband appeared behind her, his owlish spectacles glinting in the sunlight. "Monsieur Quinn." Julien Ulliel straightened as if addressing a formal meeting. Evan thought he looked like a professor, not a master plumber. "We would like you to know that you are always welcome to visit Pierre and us at any time, in Paris or in Narbonne."

Evan caught sight of Leiner hovering behind Julien. Restlessness took hold of him, thinking of all the people now gathering for a goodbye. The increasing emotion in the air made him want to run home fast without goodbyes.

"Thank you, Julien. I'll let you know when I conduct in Paris again. Will you live in Paris?"

Julien nodded. "Yes, now with the possibility of a cease-fire, Paris will be safe. My family lives in Narbonne, so we will visit there also. Contact us in Paris at the address we gave you."

Pierre pushed past his uncle. He wore a determined expression. He carried Freda's old leather suitcase and his small black satchel out to the taxi, where the driver set them in the trunk. Dominique and Julien put on their coats and joined Evan outside on the sidewalk. Inspector Leiner, Eva, and Laura and Anna followed.

Pierre went first to the Leiners standing on the sidewalk to their house, shaking their hands and accepting kisses on the cheek from the girls, thanking them quite formally in German for their hospitality. Evan smiled at this proper young gentleman. His parents, if they had been alive, would be proud of him. Inspector Leiner gave Pierre a wrapped present. Evan knew that it was a photography book about the architecture of Vienna.

Pierre took Evan's hand and pulled him past the snowbank out to the sidewalk by the taxi while his aunt and uncle said farewell to the Leiners. Evan had one more thing to tell Pierre, and he wasn't sure how to say it. Perhaps the best way would be simply to say what he thought. Evan watched the boy watch his aunt and uncle walk toward them. Dominique smiled at Evan.

"We cannot say it often enough, Monsieur. Thank you for helping Pierre and taking care of him. We have always a guest room for you."

He shook their hands. Pierre looked up at him, shaking his head, his blue eyes glistening with tears. Evan took two steps away from the taxi, waved to Pierre to join him, and squatted, facing Pierre. He needed to say this one thing, and he hoped that he got it right.

"Thank you, Pierre, for saving my life."

Pierre's eyes widened in surprise, a tear escaping and cascading down his cheek. "I tried to protect you, but I failed. Those men attacked you, hurt you. They almost killed you."

Evan squeezed Pierre's upper arms. "I've been thinking about you, those chips Harold embedded under your skin. I realized you made it as hard as possible for Harold, even though you followed his orders. You set off the alarm for me the night Gregori attacked us and ran out to warn me. And then you told me about Harold and the chips, but carefully, so he wouldn't know. You gave me the information I needed to defend myself in Copenhagen. If I hadn't had it, Pierre, I might not be here talking to you right now."

"But Madame Freda and Sasha." Pierre cried now, silently.

"Not your fault. That was the fault of the man who attacked us that night. I found out from Harold what Gregori was trying to do and why he killed them. He wanted it to look like I had done it. You had nothing to do with it. So, I want you always to know that Freda and Sasha love you, and Freda expects you to practice your English, your piano, and to work hard in school and keep drawing, OK?"

Slowly, Pierre put his arms around Evan and hugged him hard. Evan knew he had to let the boy go at some point, but he didn't want to.

"I expect to hear from you, Monsieur Pierre. Email me, call me. I'll call and email, too. I'll send you my conducting schedule as it's finalized."

"Papa and Maman will want to meet you when we find them," Pierre said into his neck. "I told Monsieur Cassel to call you if they are found here."

Evan gently pushed him away so he could see the boy's tear-streaked face. Pierre sniffed. "I want you to remember something. It's very, very important. OK? Whatever happened to your parents, Pierre, it was not your fault. OK? Will you remember that?"

Pierre nodded.

"No goodbyes. Now, you have to get in the cab and go to the airport." Evan straightened, guided Pierre back to the cab. The Ulliels waited by the open passenger door. Evan nodded to them. "Have a safe and uneventful flight to Paris. Call me when you get home."

Dominique put her arm around Pierre as they got into the taxi. Julien shook Evan's hand again before he joined them. The three of them waved out the rear window as the cab drove away down the slushy street. Pierre also stuck out his tongue, which made Evan laugh. He would miss Pierre. And Freda. And Sasha.

"Herr Quinn."

Evan turned to face Inspector Leiner. Eva and the girls had retreated into the house. "Thanks for taking care of Pierre, Inspector. It was important to me that he was protected while I was in Copenhagen."

"Ja, bitte sehr," the Austrian cop said, pushing his hands deep into his black jeans' pockets. He wore a bulky gray wool cardigan over a mauve cotton turtleneck and no coat. "He is a very bright young boy, and it was a pleasure to meet him. I wanted to ask you about Copenhagen, Herr Quinn.

Detective Mortensen called me with a report, but I have one question for you."

Evan studied the cop as he spoke in his smooth tenor voice with its British-inflected English. Leiner looked exactly the same as the first time he'd seen him, in the police interview room last June, the morning after he'd defected. Leiner the interrogator. Intense and focused. One question led to another question. Evan felt his shoulders tense.

"Harold Smith. You mentioned that you knew him from your childhood. How? Had you maintained contact with him at all?"

Evan shook his head. "Harold Smith led the Vigiciv— the Volunteer Civilian Security Service Group—gang in my neighborhood when I was a kid. They were really a vigilante gang. I knew he went to college, but believe me, Inspector, I made no effort to keep in contact with him."

"You believe he was the person behind the attempts on your life?"

"Yeah. He'd assembled a new gang to come after me for the NEP. He said as much."

"The Americans had an interesting response to his death." The cop's gray eyes narrowed. "They disavowed him as if Harold Smith had worked deep cover for the CIA or some other American intelligence agency. Was the money the only reason the Americans came after you?"

Evan pushed his hands deep into his coat pockets. Could Leiner still believe he was an American spy, a deep-cover spy for the CIA? He'd forgotten because Leiner had been helping him, trying to protect him, protecting Pierre. Leiner had been gaining his trust and friendship. But he'd asked a valid question.

"Harold told me they wanted to wipe out my family. I'm the last one. Then I expect they'd hire someone to masquerade as a long-lost son or daughter of Randall Quinn and claim the money after my death. So, I guess no, the money wasn't the only reason. Hatred, revenge, whatever else you want to call it, played a part." And the control and power over a person that determining that person's life or death gave them.

The lines around Leiner's mouth relaxed, but his eyes remained alert, suspicious, studying him for any sign of deception. Leiner's fingers smoothed his dark blond mustache. "What are your plans, Herr Quinn?"

"Return to my life and music. If the rumor is true and we get a ceasefire, my conducting schedule could fill up. I've got a lot of score study to do yet to fill the gaps in my repertoire caused by the American Arts Council policy of banning music they didn't like."

He couldn't say, of course, that his immediate plans involved killing someone. Alicia had insisted on doing it. She'd hadn't needed to persuade him. He had his own reasons. As far as Alicia was concerned, Woody Lewis was CIA and had to pay for Bernie's death. Killing Woody, in her mind, was what Bernie would want her to do. Evan had set up a meeting with Woody for that evening.

Back home, Evan logged on to the internet at the computer in his living room electronics wall, read email and wrote replies. He felt confident about the programs for the concerts in the next six weeks, so he'd decided to spend one or two hours each day dealing with his mail while he was at home. After news of Harold's attempt on his life in Copenhagen hit the global news services and the internet, he'd been astonished by the concern for him in the community of musicians worldwide. He'd received hundreds of notes, half email, half by regular mail that Nigel had forwarded to him, and calls from staff and musicians of orchestras he'd conducted. Musicians were his family; it didn't matter where they lived.

He went through his PT exercises in the living room, watching *BBC World News*. Hope for a ceasefire far exceeded actual reality, but the UN secretary general had persuaded the Chinese to return their delegation to the UN in New York City and had organized meetings among them, the Russians, the European Union, and the Americans. The war was now more than seven months old. As far as Evan was concerned, it should have ended long ago. A ceasefire would be only a beginning to the end of hostilities.

The only other news that interested him concerned the Russian president, Ivan Susanin. He had survived the Chinese nuclear attack on Moscow because he'd been vacationing at his dacha, his summer home, on the Black Sea. He'd had a monumental job assembling the military to defend his country, and now he was organizing elections for a new parliament. He had assigned St. Petersburg as the country's temporary capital months ago and set up his offices in a building behind the General Staff Building across from the Hermitage Museum in Palace Square. Susanin had made it clear to the world that once the war ended, work would begin on rebuilding Moscow.

Nigel had mentioned that the Russians in St. Petersburg wanted to reschedule his canceled conducting gig and had called them "true optimists," considering the effects of the war on Russia, where the Western allies held off the Chinese at the Ural Mountains. The country was experiencing deep deprivations. Evan wanted to conduct there. If Vasia had been any indication, the Russian people needed music, needed the emotional connections music provided. He'd told Nigel to please set it up, maybe something in the autumn, after Helsinki, like the previous autumn.

He didn't feel like cooking. He wasn't particularly hungry. For dinner he zapped a frozen meal in the microwave, and ate sitting in his black leather recliner, watching an old American movie entitled *Tootsie* in which an unemployed actor resorted to dressing as a woman in order to land acting jobs. He thought of Alicia. She'd probably like the movie more than he did. He hadn't seen her since the Copenhagen airport. They had taken different flights to different destinations. She had gone to Nairobi, without explanation, but had promised to be here for the meeting with Woody. She had told him when to schedule it. He finished eating long before the movie had ended, and although it was amusing, he decided he wasn't interested enough that evening to watch it to the end.

Pierre had monopolized his time since his return from Copenhagen. Now he needed to catch up with his post-travel, post-concert chores before leaving for Reykjavik on Sunday. He gathered up his laundry in the baskets Freda had used and trudged over to the house to use Freda's washer and dryer. His washer and dryer. He checked the plumbing and turned up the furnace a bit. He couldn't decide whether or not he wanted to live in the house. Right now, it gave him the creeps. He'd thought of renting it to a family or someone who could serve as his housekeeper. He needed someone there to keep an eye on things while he was traveling. Herr Bothmann had agreed to do it for him while he was gone during the next month or so. He loaded the washer, poured in detergent, and turned it on. He'd need to take his white tie and tails to the dry cleaners on Gersthoferstrasse in the morning.

Outside, the sun had set but it was still dusk. When he'd called Woody to set up the meeting, the old American had suggested late evening and a church away from the café. It was the first time Woody had done that. They'd always met in the café. So, something was up on his side, too. He bent down to speak into the security panel at his outer door: Der schattige Affe. The lock released. He glanced around the quiet, snowy yard and street before going in. He hadn't thought he'd need to do a surveillance-detection run on his way to the meeting, but now he decided it would be prudent to be careful. Harold might be dead (or not?), but the NEP was not. And there were always Islamic terrorists to watch for. They'd tried to kill him twice already.

He called for a cab. In his bedroom, he changed out of his brown corduroy pants, white Oxford shirt and brown sweater, and into black jeans and a black turtleneck sweater. Instead of the cobalt-blue wool coat, he slipped on an olive-green goose-down parka that Freda had said belonged to her husband. It was a perfect fit. His boots were in the foyer. His regular cell phone went into the parka's inner breast pocket.

He heard the two honks of the cab's horn. He patted his pants pockets to check for his wallet and back-up keys as he walked to the security panel by his front door. He activated location monitoring and left.

He instructed the cab driver to take him to the Fischer School of Martial Arts on Löhrgasse north of Westbahnhof. He was glad to see the Chinese had missed the building during their bombing runs targeting the passenger train station and the freight train station in Penzing, two miles or so west. He was looking forward to returning to his lessons and workouts there in the coming weeks.

Only one streetlight per block shone on the dark street, but the school was completely lit up. A group of female students came out, chatting and laughing. They appeared to be in their early twenties and carried identical pink gym bags. Evan followed them at a discreet distance to the Westbahnhof subway station. On the night streets it would be harder to spot someone following him, so he descended into the brightly lit underground and took the U3 subway to Wien Mitte on Landstrasser Hauptstrasse and transferred to the U4 line going north. He hadn't worn a light disguise, so he'd expected people to recognize him and some did; their eyes flashing, but they left him alone. No one showed any unusual interest, and he spotted no familiar faces. When he exited the Schottenring U-Bahn station, no one followed him off the escalator.

Entering the First District, Evan strolled along the Schottenring to Börsegasse, his boots making squishing noises in the thick slush on the sidewalk. The temperature would drop further. The slush and puddles would freeze tonight. Farther on, at the corner with Neutorgasse, he paused and glanced back. The street was empty but full of shifting shadows, its six-story gray nineteenth-century buildings, with cars parked diagonally or half on the sidewalk and half on the street like almost any other old street in the First District. Lighted windows of offices or apartments dotted the buildings' upper floors.

He continued down Neutorgasse to Esslinggasse, where he turned right and walked one block back to Börsegasse, a broader street that took him straight to the steep and shallow steps up to the curved street in front of the church. Maria am Gestade. One of the oldest churches in Vienna, it had been built in the fourteenth century, according to his research online. Over its front entrance, its pale gray tower and filigree Gothic spires pierced the pale golden haze of city lights covering the night sky. Woody had told him to enter by the side door.

The hinges on the metal grillwork gate shrieked in protest when he opened it. He glanced around. The plaza around the church was empty, the narrow street quiet. He had less than an hour before Alicia would arrive, and she'd promised to wait outside so that he could have his conversation with Woody and not arouse Woody's suspicions.

The sudden draft from the open door as he entered flickered a multitude of candle flames terraced on two tables directly ahead on the other side of the church. Evan paused, allowing his eyes to adjust to the dim interior light. The stone-chilled air smelled of dust, sweet incense, and faintly, melted wax. His right hand skimmed the back of the polished wood benches as he moved along the transverse aisle to the center aisle. The section of rear benches on his left was empty. On a bench toward the golden front altar, which was skewed to the right—a crooked nave—sat Woody Lewis.

Evan's boots made a slight scuffing sound on the stone floor as he walked up the center aisle. He looked around at the religious stone figures on the walls and fluted pillars, the alcoves lit by candles. Stained glass windows formed a semi-circle behind the gleaming gold front altar. Wood-paneled cubicles stood along the right side between the recessed alcoves. No other people were in the church.

"Hello, Maestro." Woody had turned on the bench to watch his approach. His white hair floated around his head like downy milkweed gone to seed. His blue eyes seemed to sparkle, reminding Evan suddenly of a recurring nightmare he used to have, the way the Spider Woman's sapphire eyes glittered. Woody wore a dark brown wool coat with a red scarf around his neck.

"I hope the family business that called you away from Vienna recently has been resolved happily." Evan slid onto the same polished wood bench and stopped about three feet from the old American.

Woody handed him a sealed envelope, Evan's name typed on its front in capital letters, and a six-by-eight-inch tablet computer. "I was called away to a meeting. Obviously couldn't tell anyone about it. You know what I mean, Perceval."

Hearing that name made Evan shiver. "What are these?"

"Communication from Washington."

"Harold Smith—Bors—told me that you'd known all along about *his* operation against me."

Woody sighed. "Bors expected to kill you. What happened?"

"He failed." Evan crossed his arms over his chest, puffing out the parka a little. "Bors is dead. So, tell me this, Woody. Are we all working for the same people here? The same bosses in Washington? Harold said he worked for the NEP."

Woody looked straight ahead. "You shared the same boss. You met him during your training. I can't really say anything more. You'd better read the letter."

So, Harold had worked for the same boss as Perceval. But who in the NEP? During his training, besides his instructors, he'd met only the general and a male civilian Evan had understood worked high up in the government, maybe even in the West Wing. Evan looked around the silent church before slitting open the envelope and unfolding the single sheet of white paper inside. Handwritten on it in black ink was one sentence: *Evan, as of March 26, 2049, your employment with us has been terminated.* And it was signed: *General Roger Winton, Army Chief of Staff.*

Evan waved the paper at Woody. "What is this?"

Woody's usually jovial tone changed to a growl. "You made me look bad, Perceval, not following orders. Sure, you surprised everyone with how you handled Jiang Xu, showing creativity and talent. But you were supposed to kill Bernie Brown last fall. You weren't performing according to your employee contract. Watch the video on the tablet." Woody tapped the tablet's screen in Evan's hand, and an image appeared of the office at the northern Minnesota base where he'd trained. The general Evan had met during his training appeared on the screen.

"Evan, we want to thank you for your service to your country," the man said in the bass voice Evan remembered. "You will always be a true son of America. However, since last fall you have not followed orders or performed as expected, as your training and your initial assignment led us to believe you would perform. It saddens me. You showed extraordinary potential. However, as of March 26, 2049, we must terminate your employment with us. Be advised that if you breach the confidentiality agreement you signed, we will release incriminating material about your training that will support the stories about you being a rogue with serious psychological issues. Good luck in your new life. You have ten seconds to remove the video chip before it will self-destruct."

Woody grabbed the tablet from his hands, pressed the eject button, and set the small, square video chip on the stone floor, where it hissed and flared briefly in flame and smoke.

"You're free, Maestro," Woody said.

He couldn't believe it. "The general on the video—was that General Roger Winton?"

"Yes."

"The Americans, the NEP, will leave me alone now?"

Woody nodded wearily. "Yes."

Could he trust Woody? He'd wanted this freedom for as long as he could remember, to be free of the NEP, free of his past. But he needed to know more.

"So General Winton ordered Bors to kill me?"

Woody sighed. "To silence you."

"What if I talk?"

Woody half turned toward him and jabbed the air in front of Evan with his index finger. "Think, Perceval. You're not thinking. What do you suppose would happen if you started talking? If you breached the confidentiality agreement? General Winton told you, but that will be just the beginning, Perceval. Forget them. Go live your life."

"Woody, before the guy Bors sent to jump me near Stadtpark died, I asked him who wanted me dead. He said, 'You need to take your question to the library.' What does that mean?"

Woody shook his head.

Evan leaned in and grabbed the front of his coat in his fist. "What does it mean, old man? Is it code? Was he talking about the Library of Congress? What library, Woody?"

"Just this and no more." Woody wrenched his hand away with surprising strength. "They call themselves The Library. It's a joke, I guess, from their school days. You know, sneaking out to party with friends but telling your mother that you're going to the library."

Evan sat back, nodding. He unzipped his parka and slipped the termination letter into the inner pocket not holding his cell phone. "The Library. Cute. General Roger Winton. He was my boss, Harold's boss. You're not going to tell me anything else, are you?"

"I don't know anything else, Maestro. They're compartmentalized to the extreme. I know only what I have a need to know. Most of it is information concerning the field operatives working for me, who, thanks to you, no longer exist. They didn't like that, you know. They didn't expect you to fight back. I warned them, but they didn't believe me."

"I'm no longer a virgin, right, Woody?" Evan stood to leave.

The old American looked up at him with a wry smile. "Maestro, you are always welcome at the Café Chicago. Our business is concluded." He did not offer his hand to shake.

"See you around." Evan walked back to the side door, glancing over his shoulder once to see Woody still sitting on the bench near the front. As he left the church, he checked his watch. Their conversation had gone faster than he'd expected. Alicia probably hadn't yet arrived.

He was free. He no longer needed to be Perceval, think like him, act like him or kill at all. He was free of the NEP, of America, of that way of life. He was free to live as he wanted, as a musician. Thanks to Bernie Brown's advice to protect the money he inherited from his father and Joseph Caine, the NEP would never be able to get their hands on it. He thought he'd feel elated, like laughing and shouting and dancing out to the snowy plaza around Maria am Gestade. Instead he felt numb. He felt like there was a shoe hanging somewhere, waiting for him to relax too much before it dropped.

Alicia waited across from the side entrance in the shadows thrown by the old buildings. She waved to him. As he approached, he noticed that she wore a knee-length black leather coat and black leather boots. She had tucked her hair up under a black fedora.

"He's the only one in the church, Alicia."

She nodded, reached up with both hands. and grabbed his parka near his throat, bending him to her face. "Evan, you are a much more beautiful human being than you give yourself credit for," she whispered against his ear.

He lifted his face away from hers to look into her dark

eyes. "How are you going to do it?" In Copenhagen, he had told her only that Woody's death must look natural.

She smiled. "The less you know, the better. Now you must leave, go home. Do not look back."

"But I'll see you later, right?" He straightened, looking down at her, his hands on her shoulders.

She looked down, the fedora's brim hiding her face. "No, Evan. I leave Vienna tonight. My employers prefer that I return to my office. You understand?" She looked up at him again, meeting his gaze. "You must live your life, Gordo. It brings such joy to so many people, your music."

"Alicia."

But she had slipped away from his hands and was now walking fast to the side door of the church. He would miss her.

As he headed for the front of the church and the steep stairs that led down to the Tiefer Graben, his cell phone rang in his parka pocket. He unzipped the parka and pulled it out.

"Hello?"

"Evan. It is Sofia."

"Sofia!" He froze at the top of the stairs. "You're back."

"I am back." Her beautiful smoky alto voice sounded amused. "I am at the hospital, Evan. Greta has begun."

"She's in labor?" His heart pounded in his ears. He stumbled over his words. "What does she need? Is she OK? Is the baby OK? Should I come? Which hospital?" Then his mind went blank.

Sofia laughed low and throaty in his ear. "No need now for you to come here, Evan. She is comfortable and the doctor has told us that everything proceeds normally. She will have a long night, I think. I will call you in the morning."

Sofia. He said her name over and over into the phone after she'd broken the connection.

CHAPTER 23

My first baby, he thought as he jogged andante around the grayish-brown puddles on the track in Pötzleinsdorfer Park the next morning. Sure, he'd known musicians in the past who'd become parents, and he'd been happy for them, and enjoyed meeting their babies, but this was different. This was Greta's baby. This was Vasia's baby. This baby terrified him. Because of what he'd done to Vasia, his mortifying secret. He felt a profound responsibility toward this baby and a superstition that Vasia had returned with this new life to haunt him. To punish him for what he'd done.

The eastern sky glowed into dawn's blue, purple, and peach pastels rising from the horizon. He stopped and bent over, massaging his right side and breathing heavily. This was his first run since Buenos Aires ten weeks ago. Not really a run, either, more like a slow, easy jog, and he might have pushed himself too hard and far by choosing this route. He'd walk back to the street.

A bird, an early riser like him, chirped in a nearby tree. The park's deciduous trees stood winter-bare like twigs next to full evergreens, and the fields were covered with snow. It was that blurred, furry darkness that comes just before dawn. The nearest streetlight was perhaps a quarter mile away. He glanced around as he walked, listening, hearing only his own footfalls and an occasional splash as his foot hit a puddle. He passed a bench, and a memory popped into his mind: another run in this park on a bright July day last year, a muscle stitch, stopping by a bench, and seeing Harold and his Vigiciv gang emerge from the trees. An unexplained hallucination. Now Harold was dead. But the park offered many opportunities to hide even in winter, places from which to target someone. He knew it from his own not-well-thought-out shooting practice at night the previous summer. Someone had heard or seen him and called the police. His gaze took in the path ahead, the field on one side of it and the stand of mixed trees on the other. He glanced behind him. All quiet and empty.

The Library, Perceval's ex-bosses in Washington, D.C., who remained hidden and unknown to the world, had let him go, cut him loose, terminated his contract, and he was now free, truly free, to live his life as he wished. Why? He hadn't been a good, productive employee since last September, true enough, and the most important reason in the NEP's corporate guidebook for anyone to lose a job. However, he couldn't shake the nagging pull at the back of his mind that maybe there was something more. The NEP wasn't in the habit of giving him what he wanted without a price. How would they make him pay this time?

He craved the power he'd felt as Perceval, the sense of control, the rush of invincibility and elation he'd felt in Amsterdam when he'd killed Valerie Peters and one of her Islamist terrorist friends in self-defense. He'd never forget it. But he'd not felt the same rush with Vasia or Jiang Xu, or with Gregori.

"You kill someone, you kill your soul, your music," Vasia

had said. Evan heard his voice—the fearful urgency in it—as if the Russian pianist walked next to him in the park. Had he killed his soul? He had not killed his music. What had Vasia meant? He wished he could ask him.

What Evan knew for certain was that Perceval must remain a secret. He could not allow Perceval's existence to threaten his music, Greta and the baby, or Sofia, Owen and Lucia, or Pierre Levade and his family in any way. Or even Klaus Leiner and his family.

Perceval repulsed him. He would never kill again. Perceval must disappear. He didn't know how to do it besides just willfully forgetting it all. But he couldn't. He needed to protect Perceval in order to protect himself. He could use his training to protect others. Perceval's instincts had helped him, given him confidence, strength, focus, power. Even now, walking through this dark park.

But he couldn't shake the feeling that someone might find out. No, he was Evan Quinn, a musician, a conductor. He could not live without his music. This was his undeniable truth. Music was his love, his purpose in life, and now he could focus on it without owing anything to the American New Economic Party. Uncle Joe would expect nothing less than full immersion and dedication to the music.

He increased his pace to a slow jog again and headed for the nearest park exit, which turned out to be on Schafberggasse. He turned left and in less than five minutes arrived at Pötzleinsdorferstrasse, a straight shot to Türkenschanzplatz and home. Tall trees lined the street. Cars in different colors, like a string of square and round beads, parked at the curb. He passed apartment buildings, shops, and the police station, lights shining in its windows. He expected to see the first Number 41 streetcar of the day or had he missed it? Traffic was light at this hour.

A white van drove up the street toward him. He stopped and watched the van approach, feeling lightheaded, his knees weak. He hadn't seen one of these vans in months. He knew it wasn't real. He knew it was a hallucination, like Harold and his Vigiciv gang. He knew Vienna possessed no street cleaner vans that snatched people off the sidewalks and took them away, never to be seen again. They were a unique element of American life, thanks to the NEP and ISS. The van traveled at a snail's pace, as if the driver searched for an open parking place. Evan stood tall, defiant, his eyes fixed on the van and its blackened windows as it passed him. But his stomach heaved. He broke into a run and didn't look back.

"No matter how frightened you feel," Uncle Joe had told him, "never show your fear. Never give them the satisfaction. They get their sense of power from your fear."

By the time he reached Türkenschanzplatz, he'd developed a muscle stitch in his right side. He stopped, bent over, and massaged it while checking the circular plaza, a single car driving around it. His body told him again that he needed to proceed even more slowly than he'd thought in returning to his routine of daily runs. He walked the rest of the way to his apartment.

As he stooped to speak into the security panel by the driveway gate, he noticed a shadow hovering near one of his neighbor's giant oak trees about half a block away. He squinted at it. The shadow remained still. He couldn't tell if it was a human being's shadow behind the tree or the tree's shadow. He spoke his password, and the driveway gate hummed open.

In his apartment, he reset his security system and checked out the front window. Yes, the shadow remained behind the tree; he decided that it was a shadow thrown by the tree's angle away from the streetlight. He checked his voice mail. No messages. He also had not yet heard from Pierre, who should have arrived in Paris the previous evening. The *BBC World News* that morning had not mentioned anything about Paris—no bombings by the Chinese, no plane crashes, no other possible disasters, nothing.

He missed the French boy more than he'd expected. Freda, also. Losing Freda was a trauma that he and Pierre shared. Dr. Moreau had made that clear. She had also talked about the trauma a child experiences when he loses his parents as Pierre had. As Evan had lost his mother and Uncle Joe when he was a boy. He and Pierre also shared the trauma of knowing Harold Smith.

No matter how insistently he told himself it was stupid and ridiculous, his thoughts returned to it as inexorably as dissonance sought to resolve to consonance: Pierre echoed his childhood, a living message that had appeared to show him that *he* had experienced traumatic losses as a boy like Pierre. Uncle Joe's arrest and death. His mother's suicide. He'd not thought of those losses as traumatic before. How could he? His father had never talked with him about them, never defined them. No one had. His father had simply gone on with his life, carried on in the Underground resistance, wrote more books. Evan had been expected to carry on as well.

The difference was that Pierre had people who cared about him, wanted to protect him, wanted him to thrive and be the best he could be, and they had made certain that he'd gotten the help and support he had needed. Evan had seen that Dr. Moreau, a head doctor, had helped Pierre, not hurt him, not tried to brainwash him or control him as would have happened in America. Pierre had liked Dr. Moreau and felt safe with her.

Evan shook his head as he finished toweling off from his shower. He picked up the neon-orange sweatpants and jacket that he'd worn on his run and tossed them into the laundry basket. He felt certain that it was too late for him. No one had cared about him as a boy, and he couldn't imagine anyone truly caring now about him, about Perceval, his shadow. Or was *he* Perceval's shadow? He felt as alone now as he'd felt after Uncle Joe's arrest and death, after his mother's suicide.

The past was the past—nothing he could do about it now.

As he cracked eggs in a bowl to scramble for breakfast, his videophone warbled. In two quick steps he stood in front of it.

"Hello."

Pierre's face, close up on the monitor, popped into view. Sleep had tousled his light brown hair. "Monsieur Evan? Good morning." Pierre grinned.

"Bonjour, Pierre. You arrived safe in Paris?"

"Oui, Monsieur. The plane was very late to leave Vienna, so very late to arrive in Paris. Aunt Dominique and Uncle Julien sleep." Pierre's grin widened. "What are you doing?"

"Making breakfast. I tried to run this morning." Evan

shook his head and grimaced dramatically for the boy. "I am really out of shape. What are you doing?"

Pierre laughed his high-pitched infectious laugh. "What do you think? I am watching a little television, waiting for Aunt Dominique to wake, and calling you. You have done your PT exercises? You will study which score now?"

Evan smiled. "I'll eat breakfast first. Remember my friend Greta? She's having her baby. I'm waiting to hear."

"A boy or a girl?"

"A boy. I'll call you later and tell you about him, OK? Say hello to your aunt and uncle for me. I'm glad you're safe in Paris."

"You promise to call me later?"

"Turn off the TV and practice that Mozart I gave you, Pierre. I'll call you later."

Pierre laughed as his face blinked to black on the monitor. Evan returned to making his scrambled eggs. He ate his breakfast at the kitchen table, listening to a Beethoven string quartet on Radio Österreich Eins.

Sofia called his cell phone an hour later as he read his email and answered notes.

"A boy, of course, Evan," she said, sounding both exhausted and exhilarated. "He's beautiful. Everyone is fine. Greta wants to see you."

"On my way."

He couldn't stop smiling. His stride acquired a happy bounce as he entered the florist shop on Gersthoferstrasse. He bought a huge bouquet of spring flowers and then ran for the Number 41 streetcar. The sun shone in a clear blue sky, and a warm breeze blew from the northwest. The melting snow created streams in the streets. All was well in the world. Thinking about Vasia, Evan noticed little about the landscape outside the streetcar's windows as it rumbled down Währingerstrasse. The pianist would have been ecstatic about the birth of his son.

Owen and Lucia te Kumara were getting out of a cab as Evan arrived at the Allgemeine Krankenhaus's main entrance. Owen carried a wrapped present, Lucia a bouquet of yellow roses.

"Hey, Owen. Lucia. Great to see you," he said as he stopped near them.

"A beautiful morning," Lucia said in her Italian-accented English.

Owen grinned. The Māori composer had gained more weight since Evan had seen him at Greta's music salon, and his bright smile had returned. "I have an image in my mind of Vasia dancing," he said.

"And singing at the top of his voice," Evan said.

They walked together down gleaming hospital corridors, smelling faintly of disinfectant, bustling with nurses, nurse assistants, and the occasional doctor in scrubs and white coat. Crying babies greeted them in the maternity section. They stopped by the nursery window, but Baby Fasching's bassinet was empty.

"Oh, wonderful. He's with her," Lucia said, her voice high with excitement.

Evan's first sight of Greta, her radiant skin dark against the white bed linen, took his breath away. She cradled a bundle wrapped in a pale blue blanket and laughed in delight when they entered her room. She looked tired, especially in the lines around her eyes. Sofia, wearing jeans and a blue cotton tunic, her thick hair pulled back in a ponytail, also looked tired.

"Congratulations! Congratulations!" Owen and Lucia said together.

For the first few minutes, the flurry of hugs and words, laughter and tears, and the arrangement of the flowers in vases along the window sill commanded Evan's attention. He noticed, however, that Greta held the baby close, not letting them see him. Evan's stomach seized. Was something wrong with the baby? But Sofia had said he was beautiful, that everyone was fine. After they'd borrowed chairs from an empty room and were all seated around Greta's bed, she opened the blanket to reveal the sleeping baby.

"I finished feeding him only minutes before you arrived," Greta said. "He fell asleep immediately."

"That's not like Vasia," Owen said.

They laughed. Lucia wiped laugh tears from her face.

Greta took a deep breath after the laughter had subsided and turned to Evan. "Would you like to hold him, Evan?"

He started. "I don't know how." He'd never held a baby. What if he did something wrong?

"It is easy, Evan, see? You support the head this way, cradle his body this way."

He copied Greta's position as she handed him the baby. The child's tiny size in his arms and light weight amazed him. Could this actually be a real human being, the beginning of a life, in his arms?

"You haven't told us his name," Owen said. "I need to know for the dedication."

"What dedication?" Greta's eyes widened.

"I wanted to tell you sooner, Greta, but I thought it better to wait until the baby came. Evan gave me an idea." Owen nodded to him with a wry smile. "When I was being a depressed idiot. He challenged me to write something as big as Vasia's personality. I've sketched out some ideas, and I know it's a symphony, a symphony in memoriam to Vasia. I want to dedicate it to his son."

"You're accepting my dare?" Evan said. Owen nodded.

"Alexander Vassily Bartyakov Fasching," Greta said. "After Vasia, and Vasia's favorite uncle, who made it possible for him to leave the farm and attend the conservatory."

Evan looked down at the baby boy, Alexander. Alex. An innocent, only hours old. Soft blond curls covered his small head. His sleeping eyes kept secret their color for now, but Evan could see that they were large and spaced wide, flanking a pert round nose that resembled Greta's over a wide mouth like Vasia's. Alex's skin was the color of light caramel. Thank God Alex hadn't inherited Vasia's wolf-like nose, but he still resembled his father strongly, giving Evan the eerie feeling that he held a new Vasia in his arms.

"That's beautiful," Sofia said, her tone subdued, her voice a little hoarse. "Is it a commission?"

"I don't know. Evan, is it a commission?" Owen said, jolting Evan's attention away from Alex.

"It was a dare, Owen. I wasn't certain if you'd pick it up."

"You promised to conduct it." Owen's tea-brown eyes flashed.

"And I will. I'll conduct it, if you finish it."

Owen nodded and shrugged at the same time. "Let's talk about it later."

"I think Vasia would be so pleased," Greta said, her voice catching. "Evan, I wanted to ask you something."

He met her gaze, raising his eyebrows in question. She smiled.

"You see, you are holding him fine. I know Vasia would approve when I say that I very much want you to be in Alexander's life. Would you be his godfather?"

"His godfather?" Evan felt the blood drain from his face. He looked down at the innocent baby in his arms. Would Vasia have trusted him with his son? He heard in the back of his mind the toccata to J.S. Bach's Sixth Partita. He knew if he closed his eyes, he'd see Vasia playing it on the grand piano near the front windows in his apartment overlooking Landstrasser Hauptstrasse. "You always have choice!" Vasia's adamant voice said from memory. His stomach fluttered in fear. He'd had no choice about who his parents were, no power to stop his father's brutality or his mother's suicide, Uncle Joe's arrest. Alex stirred, puckering his lips, making sucking noises. This kid deserved a better life than he'd had.

"I think he's hungry even in his sleep," Evan whispered. His eyes welled with tears. Would Vasia, if he were alive, trust him with his son? If Vasia were alive, then they would not have fought in his apartment and Evan would not have had to kill him in order to complete his assignment for the Library. Vasia would not have met Perceval. Alex would never meet Perceval. Alex would know only Evan Quinn, musician and conductor, whose godfather had been Joseph Caine,

American composer, and first music teacher and mentor. He would use Uncle Joe as his model for being a godfather.

"Evan, you are crying," Greta said.

He nodded, not looking up at them. "I was just thinking about Vasia. I was thinking about my godfather, Joseph Caine. Being a godfather, it's daunting."

Greta laughed, her eyes understanding. "You will not be alone, Evan. Sofia has agreed to be his godmother, and Owen and Lucia are his godparents, too. You will have lots of help. And I will know that Alexander will have many fine musicians in his life." Greta smiled at him, nodding, her hands smoothing the long braid of her dark brown hair over her chest.

"It's like being the favorite uncle, mate," Owen said, grinning.

As if to agree, Alex squirmed, his arms twitched, and his tiny hands fisted. A high squeak came from his pursed lips. He opened his eyes wide, and now Evan saw they were blue. Vasia's blue eyes. Alex seemed to be staring at him. Evan shivered. Or was it Vasia staring at him through his son's eyes? Evan looked around at the others. "Any of the other godparents want to hold him?" He handed Alex over to Owen, who cradled the baby easily.

Owen said, "This brings back memories of Chiara." He and Lucia exchanged a tender look.

Evan nodded to Greta. "I'd be honored to be Alex's godfather."

"Vasia, I know, would be so pleased." Greta's smile brightened. "As am I."

Evan nodded, flutters again in his stomach. "You know,

Greta, I'll do whatever I can to help the two of you. You can call me anytime." He thought of his will naming Greta and Vasia's child as his sole heir to protect the money from the NEP. Now he wondered if it had been wise, but he'd told no one, not even Greta. There would be plenty of time for that. Alex would be safe.

They stayed and talked with Greta—at one point listening to Alex exercise his lungs with a long cry that Greta's breast silenced—for another hour or so. Owen and Lucia left first. Greta's eyelids began to droop. She needed sleep. Evan kissed her forehead, stroked Alex's blond curls, and wished them both sweet dreams. Sofia followed him out of the room.

"When is your next job, Evan?" she said. She tucked a strand of wavy, chestnut-brown hair behind her right ear.

He was hyper-aware of her presence next to him as they walked down the corridor, her light floral scent, her hazel-green eyes looking up at him. "I leave on Sunday for Reykjavik for a week, and then I'm back in Vienna. We're having a memorial service for Freda Kirsch that week. Are you in town for a while?" He wanted to take her with him to Iceland, to take her home with him now.

She nodded. "I thought perhaps we might meet before you leave. Perhaps for coffee? I know you have had a difficult time." She stopped with him by the elevator. "Call me?"

Their eyes met. Her face was serious and open. She was giving him an opportunity, perhaps the chance that he'd wanted all along.

"Are you staying here with Greta?"

"Yes, for today. She and Alex will go home tomorrow morning." Sofia sighed. She reached out to his arm and gave it a light squeeze. "I am happy beyond words that you are OK, Evan. When I heard about Copenhagen—"

"That's over now. I don't have to worry about anyone from America coming after me again." He kissed her lightly on the forehead. "I'll call you."

She pressed the elevator call button and walked back up the hall, not looking back. He watched her, missing her already. He'd call her this evening. If she needed someone to talk to, he wanted to listen to her gorgeous smoky viola voice, the gentle lilt her Swiss German accent gave it.

He left the hospital the way he'd entered and headed left up the street for Währinger Strasse and the Number 41 streetcar stop. A compact man dressed in black jeans and a black leather jacket, a fringe of blond hair above his ears circling his bald crown, straightened from leaning against a building across the street. Evan kept him in his peripheral vision. The man didn't look familiar but showed an interest in him, was now walking with him on the opposite side of the street. Two nurses passed the man, but he barely noticed them. The bald guy suddenly pulled a camera from his jacket pocket and began taking pictures of Evan.

Evan sighed. This guy was the first paparazzi he'd seen since he'd left Copenhagen. They usually left him alone in Vienna. He disliked this side of his life as a conductor—the fame, the constant public recognition, the public's intrusion. He preferred anonymity, privacy.

"Maestro."

The male voice came from behind him. Another paparazzi, no doubt, or a reporter. He kept walking.

"Hey, Maestro. There's a café for sale on Czapkagasse in the Third District."

He knew that South Bronx voice. Bernie Brown. But it couldn't be. He was dead. Or?

Evan whirled around, expecting to see Brown's familiar face, his cocky grin, mud-brown hair, and green eyes. The man before him resembled Brown not at all. He was Brown's height, about six feet tall, and Brown's lean build, and he had Brown's green eyes. But his hair was a dark auburn, the shape of his face had changed so his smile broadened in a straight line not sloped, and his nose looked like it'd been broken several times but never set correctly.

"Who are you?"

"The guy who saved your ass in Amsterdam. Remember, Maestro? Those two Islamic terrorists and that woman that lured you to that warehouse area near the harbor?"

No one knew about that. Only Brown knew. "Brown?"

"Yeah. You're the only one who knows except for the doctors who worked on me. I also worked with a vocal coach." Brown extended his hand. When he spoke again, he spoke not with a South Bronx accent but with the gentle lilt of a Canadian. "Heard about Copenhagen."

Evan grasped his hand and held it. "You're alive. Thanks for sending the Spanish package. She saved me more than once, I can tell you. We heard about Glasgow. I guess it wasn't you. She took care of someone for you. Remember Woody Lewis?"

Brown nodded. "So that's how he had a heart attack in Maria am Gestade. She's brilliant with unnatural deaths by natural causes. Saw it on the local news this morning.

I would not have guessed he worked for the CIA. Woody Lewis. Huh." Brown grinned. "Glasgow, yeah. We heard a rumor there'd be an attempt on my life, so I decided to take advantage of it. The Brits set it up. Bernie Brown is now dead. My name is Bernhardt. Stefan Matthias Bernhardt. I'll fill you in on my back story, but for now I'm an unemployed actor looking for an investment partner to buy that café on Czapkagasse. Are you in?"

Evan glanced across the street. Bald Guy was gone. Paparazzi usually stuck around. But maybe Brown—Bernhardt—in the picture hurt the shot. He met Bernhardt's green eyes. "Yeah, Stefan. Count me in."

#########

AUTHOR'S NOTE

Perceval's Shadow, the second novel in the *Perceval* series, is a work of speculative fiction. All characters, locales, and incidents portrayed in the novel are products of my imagination or have been used fictitiously. Any resemblance to any person, living or dead, is entirely coincidental.

The composers Joseph Caine and Owen te Kumara do not exist, but all other composers mentioned in the novel are real, and their music can be heard on MP3, CD or in concert halls. Characters' homes are not real, but the streets on which they are located are.

Other writers in the speculative fiction field have imagined fantastic technology, dire environmental scenarios, or advanced space travel. Often, these future worlds actually become a character in the stories. In the *Perceval* series, I chose to focus on the human aspects rather than technological, scientific, or environmental, i.e. on the geopolitical situation, the arts—specifically classical music—and the effects of childhood trauma on adults who've not been treated for it. My goal was to maintain the focus on Evan Quinn, the human, and the low tech, and not make the future technology a predominant character in the story. I wanted to emphasize freedom of choice in the future.

Artificial Intelligence has progressed to the point that publishers will not accept any books created by AI. This novel is a result of my human imagination and creativity, and AI was not involved at any stage in its creation.

Technological progress has its positives, but I think the Europeans have a crucial point regarding human life, i.e. we need to choose not to forget human intelligence, imagination, and endeavor. As a result, I have chosen to create a future world in which humans freely choose to use objects and systems from the past as well as the present and to *not* be ruled by technology. Classical music and the instruments on which it is played have not changed dramatically for hundreds of years, and I don't expect them to change in the next half century; although I understand that composers can now use computers and software to aid their creative process.

As I write this, the American federal government has been transformed in eight short months into an authoritarian dictatorship by the Republicans and their majority in Congress, Donald Trump, the politically partisan Supreme Court, and Russell Vought and his Project 2025. Whether it endures is an open question. It pains me that actions and ideology that I saw beginning in the 1980's and incorporated into the *Perceval* series future America have come to pass. I would rather American fascism had remained fictional. I'm certain many believed that it could never happen in America; and yet, here we are.

I'm grateful for the invaluable help and support I've received while working on this novel. Thank you to Mariana Paez Escalada for help with the Spanish language. A big thank you to Dr. Nathan Unfeker for meeting with me and answering all my questions about gunshot wounds and basic emergency room protocols for dealing with those patients when he was working as an ER Resident at Hennepin County Medical Center.

Special appreciation for my Beta readers Thora Fisko, John Sokalski, Dianne Hobden, Lou Louis, and Diane Louis.

Thank you to Julie Haight-Curran for being my go-to person for all things orchestral and regarding conductors and composers, especially when she was the Personnel Manager at the Minnesota Orchestral Association, and being so willing to answer my questions. She helped me to connect with the people I needed to talk with and helped arrange for me to attend orchestra rehearsals. The Minnesota Orchestra's Composer Institute gave me the opportunity to watch a professional orchestra working with young composers on their pieces to be premiered by the orchestra. Thank you to Craig Carnahan at the American Composers Forum for his help and guidance. As a result of these connections, I was able to meet two young composers, Garrett Byrnes and Conrad Winslow, talk with them about their work and their lives for creating my composer Owen te Kumara.

I never dreamed that I could be excited going through the editing process, but I was, and I have professional editor Kellie Hultgren at Kellie M. Hultgren Editing to thank for making the process exciting. She caught mistakes I'd made as well as cleaned up the prose, and I appreciate her work in helping me make my writing the best it can be. Thank you to the team at BookNook.Biz for their work converting the manuscript for publication as an e-book and creating the print layout for the paperback, as well as designing the covers for both editions.

If you'd like more information about this novel or the

entire *Perceval* series, please visit *Anatomy of Perceval*, at http://ccyager.wordpress.com. Contact me through the "Contact" page there or through the Perceval Novels Facebook page (the link is at the blog). I love hearing from readers!

Please share the *Perceval* experience with everyone you know! Write a review at Goodreads.com or where you bought your copy, or give the *Perceval* novels as a gift. The first novel in the series, *Perceval's Secret*, is available as an e-book and paperback at Amazon and B&N.com, and IngramSpark.

ABOUT THE AUTHOR

C. C. Yager has worked in advertising and marketing at an advertising agency and for arts organizations. Her advertising copy sold tickets for the Minnesota Orchestra. She has published fiction at FanFiction.net, her novel *Perceval's Secret* (first novel of *Perceval* series), and essays in various publications, including essays about classical music online at Your Classical MPR and the Minnesota Orchestra website. She earned a B.A. in Music from Dickinson College, and studied music in Vienna, Austria, under the auspices of the Institute for European Studies. While she's not conducted an orchestra since her elementary school orchestra, she has performed, first playing the French horn in school orchestras, bands and as a soloist, singing in school choirs, and then as a pianist in college in chamber music groups and as a soloist. Her blog, *Anatomy of Perceval* (http://ccyager.wordpress.com), has covered writing fiction, classical music, the future, and book and movie reviews since September 2007. She launched a Substack in July 2024 called *Creo* ("I create" in Latin) (https://creobyccyager.substack.com). C. C. Yager lives in Minnesota.